IT ALL FALLS DOWN

IT ALL FALLS DOWN

BIRTH OF HEAVY METAL™ BOOK 6

MICHAEL TODD
MICHAEL ANDERLE

DISRUPTIVE IMAGINATION

LMBPN Publishing
PMB 196, 2540 South Maryland Pkwy
Las Vegas, NV 89109

First US edition, July 2019
Version 1.04, December 2025
eBook ISBN: 978-1-64202-392-3
Print ISBN: 978-1-64971-674-3

IT ALL FALLS DOWN TEAM

JIT Readers

Micky Cocker
Dave Hicks
Jeff Eaton
Jeff Goode
John Ashmore
Diane L. Smith
Deb Mader
Nicole Emens
Peter Manis
Kelly O'Donnell
James Caplan

Editor
Skyhunter Editing Team

DEDICATION

*To Family, Friends and
Those Who Love
to Read.
May We All Enjoy Grace
to Live the Life We Are
Called.*

CHAPTER ONE

**A small airfield near Chernobyl**

The world shifted under his feet as the helicopter took off. The shudder that usually accompanied a vehicle heavier than air taking flight registered on his suit as if it were an earthquake. The computer in the gear quickly corrected that and soon, the craft leveled out.

He would never call a helicopter flight anything like smooth, but it was at least tolerable. Besides, his armor was advanced enough that it provided a few creature comforts like shock absorbers that protected him from being knocked around. It wasn't much, but it would have to be enough.

Andy Smythe had a hard time remembering the last time he had been heloed into a drop zone. It had to have been about ten years earlier, back before they used full body armor suits which made it so much simpler to drop people from excessive heights. Special forces in the US had also begun to perform practice runs of literal orbital drops.

That was the rumor anyway, but of course, the Yanks refused to confirm nor deny whether they attempted anything of the kind.

The concept was intriguing, he wouldn't dispute that, but he was in his thirties and already too old for something like that. By the time orbital drops became the norm, he wanted to be behind a desk somewhere, make six or seven figures, and come into work three days a week. He'd spend the rest of his time rebuilding classic American muscle cars.

That was the dream, anyway. Security companies would pay through the nose to have the expertise of a man like him. Even in this day and age of electronic security, there was still a place for bruisers with his training to have their say.

Or he could simply take the money he was paid for this job and retire. He'd heard music like that in his ears before, but this time, he had been paid in full and in advance. That didn't usually bode well for the level of difficulty in a mission like this, but after reading through the details, he thought they'd been through worse.

Of course, the other members of his usual team had passed on the opportunity. Their client had a habit of keeping the facts of the mission to herself. In this instance, all he'd been told was to enter a location where they tested the Zoo goop and retrieve data, but to proceed with care as the facility had gone dark. Simple enough, he reasoned, and he assumed the site wouldn't have had time to become anything like the Zoo he was familiar with. Still, the amount of money involved did raise a few red flags.

Smythe looked at the rest of his team. The ten men

were all geared up in heavily armored and armed suits exactly like he was, and all possessed similar military and combat experience. He'd been told to select his team for the mission, and while they would all be well-compensated for it, he was paid more and in advance since he was the only one among them who was actually qualified to lead them. The reason for this was because he knew—more or less—what they would face.

"What do you think we'll find when they drop us there?" one of the newcomers asked. He was a former SAS operative recently out of the service and in need of the cash. "I've heard conflicting stories about what goes on in the Zoo. The videos I've seen are all the wrong kinds of crazy—you know what I'm talking about?"

"Half of those videos are fakes." A veteran member chuckled. "You do know that, right? It's simply marketing for all these new movies and series they're putting out about the Zoo, only very lightly based on the stuff that actually happens in there. You should read some of the databases they have on creatures that have been documented from inside that fucking jungle. They even have short footage shots of the creatures doing their thing. That's equally as terrifying and far more realistic."

"If I wanted realistic, I wouldn't have been a soldier," another member—who sounded like he was from the French Foreign Legion—grumbled. "I'd have gone into some kind of business that makes money. But no, I had to be the dumb guy who goes out there and runs out of bubblegum and thus must kick ass and work for people who think doing so must very much be its own payment."

"Is that why you're here, then?" Digby, the ex-SAS man

chuckled. "Because you want to be violent regardless of remuneration?"

"Fuck, no." The Frenchman laughed. "Jean is worth the money he'll be paid. Jean got a half-million Euros to spend before coming out here and you have to know that Jean spent every cent of it. Jean—"

"Likes to refer to himself in the third person?" Smythe asked.

"Occasionally." He grinned, apparently unperturbed by the slight sarcasm. "But Jean knows what he's worth. And now that I'm in the private sector, you have to know that I'll get that sweet, sweet cash."

"I don't know if you Frogs know…" Digby laughed before he continued. "But you shouldn't eat your money, no matter how rich the sauce is."

"*Va te faire foutre, connard.*" Jean growled and flipped his British teammate off with his suit's hand.

Smythe smirked. He didn't need the built-in translator software on his suit to know what the intention was behind the man's comment in his native tongue. It was good to see that he had a solid grasp of the heavy suit's mechanics and was able to make such minuscule movements as raising his middle finger so quickly and clearly. The individuals had all been selected for their experience with combat suits for a reason, and it was nice to see that at least one of them hadn't lied on their resumé.

"It's not like any of this shit matters, right?" Digby chuckled and looked at the other team members who were gathered in the helicopter's bay, locked down until the bottom opened and allowed them to jump clear. "Seriously.

We won't even go into the Zoo proper. For all we know, the biggest problem we'll face in Chernobyl is the radiation, which our suits are supposed to be shielded against, right?"

"Right," Andy replied but he didn't feel quite as confident in what the man said. Still, logic told him that Chernobyl—the bogeyman brought up every time someone wanted to build a new nuclear power plant—couldn't be as dangerous as the Zoo was. He'd been in there a grand total of three times, and only one deep into the jungle, and that was fucking enough.

The experiences during that single deep mission were enough to teach him to not underestimate what people spread around the world for whatever weird reason. It was also a good enough reminder to not assume something would be a cakewalk simply because it looked like it on paper.

Human nature being what it was, though, it wasn't enough to keep him from being seduced by the—what was it the Frenchman had called it?—sweet, sweet cash.

The red light came on in the bay, and the team immediately ceased the argument which might have otherwise been protracted since most of them were either British or French. While there were certain interesting and historical rivalries between the two nations, when it came right down to it and that red light came on, it was time to put all that aside.

Whether they believed there was a risk or not, the group would watch each other's backs. When their work took them into a hostile environment, working together was a requirement if they planned to make it home.

He reminded himself that for him, home meant the classic GT40 that waited for him in the garage.

The red light blinked once as he checked his weapons, made sure he had all the ammo he would need, and made one last hasty read-through of the file that had been given to him when he'd finally accepted the cash and signed the Non-Disclosure Agreement.

A lab had been opened in the middle of the irradiated wasteland in Eastern Europe, all to test the infamous goop's ability to soak up radiation. As with all things involving anything Zoo-related, it had gone well until it went dark a few weeks before. The fact that it had taken so long for a team to be sent in indicated that considerable governmental red tape needed to be cut through before a group of heavily armored and armed mercenaries could enter the area.

The government in the Ukraine was still a remnant of the Soviet era, and these were men who had gamed the most corrupt governmental system in the world for decades. There was no getting through them until all the t's were crossed and i's dotted and everyone who mattered walked away with enough untraceable bills to pay for their vacation at the end of the year.

The light turned green, and a small alarm sounded at the front of the bay to focus their attention on the doors that now began to activate. It was intriguing to watch as the floor opened and slid out from under him while he knew the helicopter moved at what felt like an impossible speed and over five thousand meters above the earth. It looked impossible. Of course, it wasn't his first jump, but every time felt like the first time.

To look at the ground from this kind of distance while he hung from magnetic straps attached to his shoulder was something quite...breathtaking.

Even more so was the sensation when the straps suddenly released and he fell away from the craft, which had slowed considerably to allow the men to drop from the bay. There were hundreds of variables that their suits all calculated at the same time as the sky suddenly filled around them. The world rushed up quickly as the two heli-copters grew smaller and smaller. Twenty suits were dropped from the sky into a section of the world that had been abandoned for the better part of fifty years.

From where he plummeted, Smythe wasn't able to discern anything about their actual target location. The Ferris wheel and the reactor four containment dome were obvious, of course, but there was no sign of cars on the network of visible roads and the sun had barely reached its peak in the sky.

They descended rapidly, and the numbers counted down at an impossible speed. A human's terminal velocity was around fifty-three meters per second or one hundred and ninety-five kilometers per hour. In the suits they wore, the team fell instead at two hundred and forty-six meters per second or eight hundred and eighty-five kilometers an hour. He had taken the time to calculate that speed when he had a little trouble sleeping.

It was the kind of speed that would cause a grown man to shit his pants. And, of course, it hadn't helped him to get to sleep.

The fifteen seconds during which they were in free-fall was enough to reach that velocity. Smythe's body bunched inside his suit despite the inertia dampeners, and the parachutes filled the air above him. He swung wildly for a few seconds before he finally corrected his course and looked around to make sure the whole team was positioned close enough that it wouldn't take too long to gather together once they were on the ground—and also far enough away to avoid any midair collisions.

They were a group of mouth-breathers, but they were also pros and all had jump experience. It was another thing he'd looked into to ensure that they at least knew what they were doing in the air.

It took them a few long minutes to reach the drop zone using their suits to guide them into a bunched formation. They were told to expect resistance of an uncertain nature, which was field language for be ready for anything that might want a piece of them. Accordingly, they formed up in groups of five and held their weapons primed and ready.

Smythe hadn't ever been in this section of the world before, of course, but the pictures, movies, and shows about the area had made it live on in infamy across the world. Everyone knew or had at least heard about what happened in Chernobyl in the 1980s. A catastrophe the likes of which had never been seen in the world before or since had left an enormous part of the world uninhabitable for what everyone thought could possibly be millions of years. Worse, enough radiation leaked into the atmosphere to kill off virtually anything in the world.

That wasn't what he saw there. He recalled the pictures that displayed everything as dull gray and captured the way the location looked when it was simply dead. All the trees were lifeless, and the area should have been left a deserted wasteland. Except, of course, that the radiation killed all the bacteria that would normally cause what was left behind to decay. Instead of barren ash-colored desolation, everything remained in an eerie state of preservation in death. He definitely remembered that and had prepared himself for the mental image to become a reality. Now, however, he could only stare at his surroundings in bemusement.

He'd done a little research which had indicated that Mother Nature had stepped in when man had stepped back. Of course, they were working on reactor four as well and the enormous safe containment dome caught and reflected the sunlight a few miles to the north-west. He'd seen that on the way down.

Still, even that information hadn't prepared him for the reality that, against all odds, nature seemed to be winning the battle against man's greatest—albeit inadvertent—destruction. The forest regained life and the underbrush and grasses kept pace, along with smaller shrubs and other scrubby vegetation that pushed resolutely through the scattered snowfalls.

It wasn't completely healed yet—that was the word that came to mind, for some reason—but regeneration was well on its way. He'd heard that animals had moved in again too. Of course, the pictures seared into his brain began to fuzz a little in the face of this new reality, and he had to admit he preferred it this way.

"Okay lads, form up," Smythe ordered over the comms and the group gathered around him. They were all equally as interested and intrigued by what they saw, but they hadn't forgotten their battle-ready instincts and kept their weapons in hand.

"We missed the drop by a couple of klicks, so we have some hiking to do," he explained, and his gaze scanned their surroundings constantly while he held his weapon up and ready. He could see a sliver of the famous Ferris wheel to the south, which meant they now had to move off somewhere to the east. "Let's get moving." He indicated the direction they would go in.

They remained in the teams they'd been assigned to and took up staggered formations. Despite the warning he had issued, they all appeared to be relaxed. They were being paid in excess of six figures for what was basically a retrieval mission, and they alternated between talking about what a dumbass their client was for parting with that much cash and what they would spend it on.

He wished the other members of his familiar team had been up for something like this. It wasn't that he wanted to subject them to the same kind of hell they'd been through in the Zoo—a nightmare that Jacobs had gotten them through with help from his friends. But they would have understood in a way the men he was with couldn't.

For one thing, he hated the fact that he felt paranoid about his suspicion of being watched as they approached the section of the forest where they would locate the lab. He wasn't sure what the point was to put it so far off the beaten track but assumed it had something to do with the fact that it was Zoo-related.

They most likely wanted to avoid too many questions. Well, he'd prefer to avoid them too. It was enough to know that they were researching the goop in a secluded location apparently identified as a hotspot in the exclusion area. The whole point of the exercise, he'd been told, was that they needed to test the goop on all the radiation that had to be soaking into the…well, fucking everything.

The teams fell into relative silence as they covered the few miles to the target coordinates and speech ceased entirely when they finally stopped at the edge of the forest and the location towered above them. It was well-hidden, he had to give them that. The dome was enormous—at least a mile wide, by his estimation, and the length a good deal more. It appeared to be constructed from some kind of steel, which made sense for containment, but whatever the material was, it was entirely non-reflective and seemed to exude a greenish hue. That probably explained why he hadn't noticed it from the air.

He shrugged these details aside and approached cautiously with his team close behind. The large hangar-type door was sealed, but it responded when he keyed in the code the client had given him and it slid open with only a faint hiss. He made sure to seal it behind them before he turned to survey the interior.

An eerie silence enveloped them like they had stepped into a massive cocoon in which the normal sounds of life did not exist. While the metaphor wasn't entirely incorrect, a sense of waiting infused it—a kind of tense anticipation that defied logic. Smythe shook his head impatiently. Now was not the time to indulge nightmare memories of the Zoo.

It took a moment for him to accept that they'd simply stepped from one section of the forest into another. He'd somehow expected to enter a building or at least a compound or something similar. Instead, trees stretched as far as he could see—which explained the size of the containment area. The scientists or whatever they were obviously ran testing on the actual forest, not only in the lab he needed to find.

The woods outside had been a little startling, but what confronted him now was entirely...bizarre.

The lighting had obviously been carefully designed to provide the equivalent of sunlight, and the entire scene might have been one in the outside area and open to the elements—except for the very obvious difference.

Green sprouts pushed through what was once lifeless soil. New leaves budded from what should have been dead branches. Patches of grass burgeoned as far as he could see, and new bushes even boasted flowers as well. The signs of growth made the area seem so much more vital and...well, alive, for lack of a better word. It was nothing at all like the pictures he'd seen before or even the slow recovery of the exclusion area, and he had to admit it was a magical sight. It was, his befuddled brain decided, like the process of rejuvenation had been put on steroids.

The strangest thing of all was that it was in the dead of winter, no less. His suit confirmed that it was a few degrees below freezing and the dome did little to alter that. Yet these plants sprouted and bloomed like it was in the middle of spring. *Fucking weird, that's what it is.*

That said, there other differences he noticed as he led his team into the trees. It was more heavily wooded, for one thing, and the temperature rose dramatically as pushed deeper. He could literally feel the heat and humidity smack into him like a hand to his face. It was difficult to shake off, but it became a little more pleasant when his suit began to adjust to the changes. The temperature spiked to twenty soon after they began the march into the forest itself.

The deeper they got, the easier it was to see the changes that happened around them. Everything bloomed and grew vibrantly, from the trees themselves to the vines and the grass. He couldn't help but feel awestruck by it but then again, he'd been awestruck by his first sight of the Zoo too. And from what he'd heard, this was a similar situation to how the Zoo had begun, so why was he so surprised?

"Some weird fucking shit is happening around here already," he told his team quietly, sensing their shared unease, "but there are no real signs of anything going bad. This is what they were trying to do, apparently." He had seen flora vibrancy like this before and on that occasion, he'd needed every bullet he could get into his gun. The memory of it made him tighten his grip on his weapon.

"If this is a pep talk, you really suck at it." Digby chuckled and shook his head.

"Shut it," he snapped. "We'll move in there, retrieve what we're paid to get, and make it out alive. All of us."

"That's better," the young man admitted.

"You're talking like you expect something bad to happen," Jean said and looked around. Even through his helmet, Smythe could see the same kind of emotions in his expression that he'd felt on his first trip into the Zoo.

It wasn't quite terror but something close. Like he prepared himself to be spooked or something like that but wasn't entirely sure if he wasn't maybe imagining it.

The asinine comments tossed around by the group of

twenty he'd selected suddenly seemed to lack the reverence this place deserved.

"It looks like we'll have our pick of the suites in Vegas, eh, Bracken, mate?" One of the teams that covered their flank continued their chatter. "Bracks? Where's ya now?"

Silence descended on the men at the hint of desperation in the voice. The slightly panicked tone was the kind that made Andy's spine tingle, and his fingers curled instinctively around his weapon to tighten his grasp even more.

"Bracks, where the fuck is ya?" the man asked again, and Smythe checked the groups. One of the teams only had four members in it.

"Shit," he muttered, made sure the safety was off, and upped the sensitivity of his motion sensors. "Not this bullshit again."

The Zoo

He'd been told there weren't many teams that did what they did. No, the actual words they'd used were that they were the first team of their type and they should be equal parts proud and cautious of that fact.

Kozlov decided he would be far more of the latter than the former. There was a reason why people didn't spend more than a week in the Zoo. Those who had sent them in wanted to test tech that would be used in longer missions, of course, but that would never be the focus of the mission. Ultimately, that little truth meant that the effort put into the tech they used for the long-term visit to the Zoo was half-assed—as most government efforts were when it came to the safety and survival of their boots on the ground.

Simply because it was the norm didn't mean Kozlov would lie down and take it. He would bitch and complain about it to basically anyone who would listen, which included a five-page report of how the motion sensors constantly malfunctioned and even the small satellite dish they had set up to maintain steady communication lines with the people running the mission from afar was as spotty as fuck.

It had seemed to work for the first day or so but the newfangled communication had degenerated rapidly from there.

A particular point of frustration was that he had reminded them of how the Zoo reacted to any attempt to communicate beyond its borders. While he personally considered the effort a waste of time, he could understand why they remained determined to pursue a solution.

The problem with effective communication was one of the major reasons why extended missions rarely took place in the jungle. Lengthy operations merely made those involved more vulnerable and prevented any chance that they might be able to alert a rescue team if they needed it, simply because they had no reliable means to reach anyone.

To their credit, the team of scientists whom Kozlov and his men were supposed to protect from the dangers of the jungle seemed to be equally as anxious to get out of there alive as their gunners were, which was something the gunners in question appreciated. The specialists were armed and ready, although slightly lighter than their counterparts, and the two groups remained separate for the most part.

That was fine by him. The animals approached them in waning numbers and backed away at the first sign of resistance like they were merely sniffing around for an easy meal. No casualties after two weeks into the experiment made Kozlov hopeful that they might get out of this shit alive.

Hope was dangerous out there, he reminded himself. It distracted you. He'd chosen a team of veterans, the kind who didn't have family at home or other distractions that might get in the way of them supporting their comrades on a mission. It was a long haul but so far, each man had supported their team honorably.

The scientists returned from a quick inspection of the peripheral experiments they were running. They had brought plants from outside that they exposed to the Zoo's environment, which meant planting them and watching for any changes. From the disappointed looks, Kozlov could tell there still wasn't any conclusive data to collect.

"Chin up, boys," he said in their native Russian. "We still have a week in these conditions. You're bound to find something, right?"

"It's like it is taunting us," one of the lead scientists grumbled and shook his head as he pulled a ration out of his pack and began to prepare his lunch. "It refuses to touch any of the plants we brought like it's waiting for us to turn our backs on it."

"You don't need to anthropomorphize the fucking jungle," Kozlov protested as he sat beside the man. "It's plants and animals, not much more. Sure, there are alien touches to it from what I can tell, but that doesn't change the fact that it's only animals and plants."

"That's where you and I disagree, my friend," the specialist said with a chuckle and dug into his heated potatoes and pork chops. "There is an intelligence here, for lack of a better word. Something that wants us dead or out of here and has worked on building everything bigger, better, stronger, faster, and deadlier with every new development. It's fascinating. Or it would be if everything out here, including the plants, didn't try to bite our faces off."

My friend? Kozlov wondered at that. They'd been out there for the past couple of weeks and he hadn't even bothered to remember the man's name. He had a feeling the specialists had done the same—hardly what one might consider a friend but there was no need to instigate any hostility.

"The plants?" he asked and tilted his head, his expression skeptical. "Seriously? I've never seen anything on the plants trying to kill us."

"I'm serious." The man chuckled. "I've seen some of the footage, although our teams haven't encountered any yet. Perhaps they have yet to move to our sector. Vines drop from the trees when the animals are particularly rowdy and pull people up—and don't always drop them again."

"It sounds like it might be a different kind of animal, right?" he asked as he retrieved a flask of vodka from his suit's pack and opened it. A short silence ensued while he filled two small metallic shot cups with the clear liquid and handed one to the specialist. "Expecting something normal from the Zoo is unrealistic."

"Like expecting plants to not be as dangerous as the animals?" his companion asked with a small smirk as they clinked the cups and downed the vodka quickly.

"Yeah, something like that." Kozlov chuckled, but his mirth was cut short by the sound of a low roar and a harsh clanging that signified a creature fighting to escape a cage positioned at the very center of their little campsite. His good spirits, only slightly helped by the alcohol, vanished rapidly as he scowled at the enclosure they were supposed to protect.

"I don't suppose I could tempt you with a closer look at our subject?" the scientist asked. He toyed with his food and looked more uncomfortable than before.

"How many of them have you lost?" he asked although he already knew the answer. Still, he wanted to hear it from the man responsible for what was done inside those cages.

"We started with five," he admitted, his expression a little haunted as he looked away. "Only one remains, and yet this one proves to be...interesting. The changes coming over its body are more and more impressive. A month or so of this growth and transformation, and I don't think even the cages would be able to hold it."

Kozlov opened his mouth, about to change his mind about taking a closer look. They had injected the test subject at various points of its body with what goop they could find to see the kind of reactions it would trigger. Under any other circumstances, four of the five test subjects dying before the first week of testing had ended would have been considered a dismal failure.

Which, he supposed was one of the reasons why they did it out there in the middle of the fucking nowhere jungle. That and the fact that they needed considerable amounts of that blue stuff, and where better to get it than directly at the source?

This mission had all kinds of parameters that the people in the metaphorical upstairs wanted to test. He ordinarily didn't like being used as a guinea pig, but orders were orders. What mattered was that he had no desire to be recalled and assigned to guard duty at Red Square.

While he was curious, he wasn't curious enough. It was better to leave the specialists to their work. He had enough nightmares to deal with as things stood.

"Something's moving out there," one of the soldiers called over the comms, and Kozlov stood quickly, snapped his helmet into place, and connected his HUD to the defense grid. Sure enough, there was movement on the edges of the limited range they could detect, but in all fairness, there wasn't that much of it.

In the darkness of this fucking jungle, it was difficult to tell anything with his eyes alone, which meant he needed to rely on technology that had been built and provided by the lowest bidder.

Fucking assholes.

"Keep your eyes on it," he ordered and lightly caressed the assault rifle he had attached to his suit's forearm. There had been a time in his life when he would have literally killed to be able to try these suits, but after two weeks in them, all he could think about was getting out of his and into a nice hot shower.

"No movement," one of the gunners said and looked at the leader. "It could be one of the smaller animals attracted by the scent of hot food, right?"

"Right," he responded. "But there's no sense in risking

it. The tiny ones get hungry and make a fuss that draws the bigger bastards in. Keep your weapons trained on it, and don't let them get any closer..."

His voice trailed off as something liquid spattered across his visor. It took him a moment to realize what it was, and the clarity was helped by the crack that came a few seconds after. Sniper rifles weren't that useful in the jungle since the critters tended to be drawn in by the louder noises and it wasn't like you could see that far into the darkness anyway.

Still, the sound was unmistakable, as were the effects. Armor-piercing rounds were used, and while there were two clean holes where the bullet had gone in and emerged on the other side, the inside of the man's helmet was a bloody mess from the shrapnel his helmet had suddenly turned into.

"Fuck!" Kozlov shouted and fell prone as another two cracks were heard. He couldn't see any muzzle flashes, but two more of his men fell with holes in their armor. Their trackers confirmed that they were too dead to care. Another two shots were fired before the remainder of the men pushed past their shock and into their combat mind-sets and returned fire. They weren't sure what they were shooting at or where, but it was better than sitting around and doing nothing.

Below the gunfire, the sounds of the jungle indicated that its denizens had begun to react to the noise from a distance, but that was the least of his worries. Humans hunting humans in the Zoo felt like some kind of bizarre other-world scenario, but that was what they faced at that moment.

He left the actual engagement with their attackers to his men as he pulled back and connected hurriedly to the satellite dish's comm line. He smiled grimly at the futility of the gesture, as the damn thing hadn't functioned for the last thirty-six hours. Still, with the Zoo, one never knew, and he might as well attempt to send a message. Ironically, within another twelve hours or so, the base would send out a retrieval mission anyway if they'd heard nothing. Of course, it would be too late for any of them as it seemed unlikely that his team would survive.

"We're under attack," he advised curtly, the words rushed but spoken clearly to avoid confusion. Instinctively, he pulled the trigger on his assault rifle as a group of their attackers appeared and decimated what was left of his team. The scientists had taken cover, their weapons in hand, but they didn't seem ready to use them. "Under attack and need immediate reinforcements. Oh—fucking shits."

He hissed in frustration as a trio of bullets punched into the dish and severed the connection. While he hadn't held out much hope, if it had worked—however badly—it would have transmitted perhaps snatches of his message from the point where he opened the comm line until it cut out. He wouldn't hold his breath but at least he knew he'd made the attempt.

He doubted anyone would hear it, though.

Kozlov returned fire to protect the scientists in his charge, but it was a futile effort. Whoever these fuckers were, they outnumbered them and were better armed and better equipped than his team were, which gave them better range and protection in these circumstances. A couple nursed wounds but the injuries wouldn't be enough to hinder them.

His knee exploded in a shock of pain and the hydraulic lines cut out and flung him onto his back. He cursed loudly.

One of the attackers came to where he lay on the ground and stared at him for a moment before he drew a sidearm for the coup de grace. Kozlov closed his eyes and waited for the killing shot.

CHAPTER TWO

The Zoo: US Base

People had told him more than once that there was no shame in taking time off for a little well-deserved R and R. It seemed that everyone he knew encouraged him to take a vacation. Heavy Metal could certainly afford a couple of weeks off now that they basically worked with the money they had already made.

A couple of weeks was all they could spare, but as the world started to change around them, he accepted that he might end up needing it. Tough times were coming. People would have told him that relaxation was the way to get back in the saddle.

Salinger Jacobs would have disagreed with those people. Getting back in the saddle meant getting back in the saddle, not sitting on his ass and catching some sunlight.

No, that wasn't true, he thought as Kennedy pulled their Hammerhead up to the security area. He wasn't the kind of guy who was restored by boredom and inactivity.

The way he was wired, the only effective method for him was to tough it out, walk it off, and rush into the fray. Maybe it wasn't the healthiest of approaches according to modern medicine, but he had reason to believe he was beyond that by now.

If the truth be told, he had a couple of constant fears when he thought about stepping away from the Zoo. He hadn't come of his own accord but had learned to love it with the kind of fierce passion he knew the fucking jungle reciprocated. If he walked away, he didn't know if he would be able to bring himself back. He wasn't sure if he was crazy or not, but in the end, the Zoo simply wasn't for everyone, and like it or not, he had never elected to be there. It had been a choice made for him.

Even now, he didn't know himself well enough to make that decision. The best way to make sure he would maintain that annoying, dangerous love affair was to dive right back in.

Oh, there was also the affair with Madigan and Courtney he needed to worry about too. They would both hunt him and drag him back, and they wouldn't even need to do it in person.

Sal couldn't help a small smile. While he hadn't chosen to be there, dragged off in the middle of the night as he had been, they had been the reason he had stayed. Being at the cutting-edge of modern science had something to do with it, but that wasn't the main reason why he had elected to stick it out in the Zoo, risk his life, and put everything on the line every time he went in, willingly or not.

He somehow wanted to prove himself worthy of the two of them. That seemed like the only real reason he was still there, being stupid and making what could only be seen as the same stupid choice over and over again. Thinking with his dick or something like that.

The first time he'd laid eyes on what was now called the US Base to differentiate it from the half a dozen or so other bases that had sprung up all around the Zoo remained a vivid memory. It hadn't been a good day, and the days that had followed had become progressively worse, what with him being dragged into his first trip into the Zoo the very next day. Madigan had led one of the teams inside. It hadn't been all bad, he reminded himself.

The same Madigan who now pulled their Hammerhead to a halt at the inspection point and went through the bureaucratic red tape that was required these days after the kidnapping. All the bases had instituted something similar, so while he blamed his kidnappers for the changes, he did realize that maybe, if this red tape had been in place to begin with, the whole ordeal might not have happened.

Like most things Zoo-related, it wasn't like it had been all bad. Much of the data he'd collected had helped him to finally acquire his PhD. Although, he realized with amusement, people were so used to being corrected over the use of Dr. at the beginning of his name that he wouldn't be surprised if they continued to call him Sal from this point forward. Maybe the new guys would call him Dr. Jacobs, but he would probably end up correcting them anyway simply out of habit.

It might be years before someone knew him as Dr. Salinger Jacobs. That was fine, though. He hadn't gone through everything he had so he could add that silly prefix to his name. Well, not only, anyway.

The vehicle eased through the final gate and beyond the wall and drew to a halt in the Staging Area, from which most teams running from the base pushed out to the Zoo. Sal dropped from his shotgun seat in the Hammerhead as their team started to prepare again.

Those who had been there before them still lived on the base without too much incentive to change their lifestyles. Madigan was there, of course, already getting her Hulk-sized suit ready for use. Courtney had been drawn away from the Zoo and back to Philadelphia, thanks to changes in circumstances that required her to be there. He didn't like it, but she was a successful businesswoman now. It wasn't his place to tell her where she could and couldn't be, and he was very appreciative of the time she took to be with them whenever she could.

Either way, the team would feel a little empty without her.

Matt Davis ran coordination for them and Mick Addams had also joined the team. Both had signed off on their responsibilities to the military on the base and now worked full-time for Heavy Metal after they'd brought Sal back safe and sound after his last trip. It was better for them financially anyway, to the point where Davis had delayed his return home in order to continue to work with them. A special kind of crazy, that guy, he thought with a chuckle and greeted the man with a firm handshake.

A couple of newcomers were making preparations too, and Sal and Madigan took the time to greet them. They were members of what she now called the Heavy Metal Mercenary Company—something she wanted to establish as a kind of legacy to leave behind. Everyone still called them the Heavy Metal Militia, but he honestly didn't really care about that.

"Did you get word on our contact inside?" Davis asked as he began to strap his armor on, starting with the boots. From what Sal could remember, the man was among the gunners who had survived the Zoo the longest, and any team that had him on it had a better chance of getting clear of the jungle.

"He's in and waiting for us," Madigan said before he could answer and hauled the new pieces of her suit out of the crates they were packed in. "Which means we should probably get our rears in gear to be able to catch up with him. I won't have Gregor riding us for being late. Not after what happened the last time."

"Fair enough," Sal said softly and shifted his gaze to a Hammerhead that raced toward them. He looked at the team of eight—himself and Madigan included—and then at his partner. "Were we expecting anyone else to join us?"

The woman did a quick headcount herself and eyed him narrowly. "Not that I can remember. Who the hell is that?"

Their questions were answered in short order as the heavy all-terrain vehicle drew up and only one person stepped out. The man wasn't dressed to head into the Zoo. At all. He looked like he was late for a beach volleyball game in shorts and a t-shirt and not at all like the usually uniformed and stern-looking commandant of the base.

Sal wondered if he had been alerted to the Heavy Metal team's planned Zoo trip while he took R and R and rushed there because he had something he wanted to say to them before they left. It wouldn't have been the first time the

MICHAEL TODD & MICHAEL ANDERLE

powers that be wanted them to do something in the Zoo. Although, if that were the case, it would be the latest last-minute attempt to saddle them with something before they left the base. That was the only thing he could think of that might explain the rush.

"Salinger Jacobs," the commandant said and sounded out of breath as he jogged to where the team was halfway through the process of readying themselves for the trip. "Or should I say, Dr. Salinger Jacobs now, right? Congratulations on that, by the way."

"Appreciate it, sir," Sal said, took the man's proffered hand, and shook it firmly.

"Please, I'm technically off duty here." He chuckled and his gaze swept the team, who stood in silence and stared at him. "Call me Frank."

"Appreciate it...Frank." Sal immediately regretted it. The name simply did not roll easily off the tongue in this situation.

"Anyway, I wanted to catch you before you headed inside," Frank said. He kept his voice low and assumed the mantle of the commander of the whole base once more. "I had something I wanted to talk to you about that could prove profitable for all of us."

"If you don't mind, Fr...sir, you'll have to make it brief," he said quickly. "You caught us with our feet quite literally out the door. We have a business to run." He would never have dreamed of addressing the man like this while he was still employed by the base, of course, but he knew he was in the right. He did have a business to run, and they were on the clock.

"Of course. I'll make it brief." He chuckled and handed a

PDA to Sal, who quickly inspected the contents displayed on the screen. "Ever since that...incident you were involved in, we've tried to find more intel on the people who might or might not enter the Zoo with nefarious purposes. It's obviously complicated as they enter from the various bases that have sprung up like weeds around here, and we've had some...interesting yet inconclusive results.

"I say interesting, but I honestly mean worrying. These are teams that go into the Zoo without any kind of oversight or any effort to report what they are doing in there. We had problems with the unsanctioned bounty hunters when you had only started out, but since their base was destroyed, we'd thought the problem was solved until your...ahem..."

"You can say 'kidnapping,' sir," he said softly and forced a smile.

"Right. Anyway, since then...well, I'll be honest. We're worried, Sal. Worried that the same bounty hunters we thought we'd dealt with a while ago now simply use the other bases—and maybe even this base, who knows?—to run their own privately funded operations into the Zoo. And as we all know, these people don't like to share. They use the other bases to hide themselves and cause trouble out there. We've noticed an up-tick in officially sanctioned teams going dark inside, and while of course they are running operations in one of the most dangerous places on the planet, there is a worrying trend."

There was, Sal noted as he scrutinized the statistics. The Staging Area—and by extension the US base—sent upward of a hundred men and women into the jungle on a weekly basis now that they received far more funding than before. The numbers were rather interesting, all things considered.

His hurried scan of the data revealed that the percentages of the teams going into the Zoo that encountered trouble had steadily increased over the last few weeks. The fact that the start of this trend coincided with the dates when he had been kidnapped had to be a coincidence. He hoped so, anyway. The correlation did not imply causation. Still, it couldn't be ignored.

"Have you considered that it might have something to do with the Zoo simply upping its game?" he asked and began to put his suit on when he realized that most of his team had already geared up. "Let's be honest, there are more than a few...I want to call them updates, but I don't think that would apply here."

"It sounds like it could apply here." Frank chuckled, then shook his head as if to remind himself he was there for a reason. "Anyway, as to why I'm talking to you about this, I would like to make a one-time offer. I wouldn't make this to anyone else heading into the Zoo, so I hope you understand the kind of faith I'm showing in you and the rest of your Heavy Metal team."

Sal looked at the team, then returned his attention to the base commandant. "Sure, I get that. What kind of offer are we talking about?"

The man stepped in a little closer. "Well, I'm willing to pay you and your team an extra percentage if, while in the Zoo, you're willing to do research while you're in there."

"I'll be honest, research is about seventy-five percent of what we plan to do in there," he said. It wasn't a lie—or, if it was, it was one of omission.

"I need to make sure that the teams aren't being killed by other people," Frank said, his voice lower than ever so Sal would be the only one in the group to hear him. "We have enough people terrified of going in there with the knowledge that the flora and the fauna want them dead. When the word gets out that humans present a danger too? We'll have to force them inside at gunpoint."

"They would simply run away," he pointed out and the other man nodded in weary agreement.

"This is a one-time offer, Dr. Jacobs," he continued. "I need information. I don't care if it confirms, substantiates, or denies the rumors that are rife around the base. Something. Anything you can get for me, Jacobs. And there is seventy-five grand in it for you."

Sal raised an eyebrow. "That's a lot of money for information."

"That's a lot of trust in your work, Jacobs," he said. "Do you think you can do that for me?"

"I can't make any promises." He glanced at the rest of the team, who waited with ill-concealed impatience, to make sure they could hear what he said. "If we find something, I'll need you to pay me up-front for it. If you really trust my work, you'll trust that I'll only turn something over to you when I have something you'll want to pay for."

The commandant didn't like that. Sal could tell and simply remained silent until the man nodded. "I appreciate that. Of course, any payment provided will be up-front."

"I appreciate it." He smiled and the two men shook hands. "We'll be in touch when we get back."

As Frank walked away, Madigan approached Sal. He

didn't need to look at her. The heavy impact of her boots on the pavement was undisputable.

"What was that about?" she asked as she attached one of the shoulder-mounted rocket launchers to the suit. "You never insist that we are paid up-front. If I didn't know you better, I'd say you think being paid for scientific discoveries is insulting to those discoveries."

"Frank, as he insisted I call him, said he wanted something," he replied softly as he finished with the lower half of his suit and started on the upper. "What he didn't want to say was that he wanted something specific. I don't know what it was, but if I put my team through the work of finding…whatever puts teams out there in danger, I want them to know that they'll be paid for whatever they find out. That goes for me too, I guess—wait, is that the new X48 launcher shoulder mount?"

Madigan grinned. "I wondered when you would notice. How cool is that? I can mount six more rockets in this baby, and it's light enough that I can put a second one on the other side, although I'd have to juggle positioning with the mini-gun there."

Sal chuckled and added the shoulders on his suit. "Fuck, how did you get your hands on those already? I thought Amanda wouldn't be finished with them for another week."

"Well, Anja and I went to visit her and Bev over the weekend, and we spent time getting the pieces together," she explained as she attached an identical launcher to the other shoulder. "Did you know that you let a bona fide genius walk out of Heavy Metal?"

"I didn't have it in me to tell her to not follow her

heart," he said. "Wait, so you guys get the upgrades because you go and visit? Does that mean that I should visit?"

"Well, yeah, Amanda is still your friend, right?" She chuckled, checked to make sure the launchers were secured, and attached her helmet to the back which would allow it to be pulled on automatically. She turned to help him with his suit. "Besides, she needed to test her improvements on an actual suit, and I…happened to have mine on me."

"You expected to be able to entice her with a quick run into the jungle, didn't you?" He grinned, pulled his helmet on, and activated the HUD to call up their mission parameters. "You sly dog."

"Do you disapprove?" Madigan asked.

"Nope, it's exactly what I would have done," he replied.

"Well, that's not a good sign. No wonder it didn't work." She chuckled, and Sal punched her playfully in the shoulder. Unsurprisingly, she didn't budge an inch.

"Hey, remember that sex we planned to have?" he asked as he attached his assault rifle to his arm. "Ever?"

"Point taken," she grumbled.

"Okay, boys and girls." He cleared his throat and addressed the team over their brand-new comm channel. "Are we ready to roll?"

"Is it true, then?" Davis asked and stepped beside them. "Are we doing an intel run?"

Sal shrugged as the group mounted up in the Hammerhead. "Well, partially anyway. We still have bills to pay."

CHAPTER THREE

<u>Philadelphia: Savage's Apartment</u>

There was something unique about driving across interstate roads. People didn't understand songs that were meant to be listened to while driving, while their head bobbed to the catchy tune and they mumbled the few words they could predict here and there. The appeal lay in letting their minds go to that quiet place where time flew past. It was a kind of meditation, he decided, where you simply let your mind relax and do its thing while the body did what it had done for the past few hours.

Of course, after a long drive, you were back to the normal that defined life. You were sore and aching from having been in the same position for hours and hours, but after a good night's sleep and a quick shower, you would wake up and feel more relaxed than you had in years.

It wasn't a pastime, not by any means. No one wanted to be on a long drive these days, and they only did it if there were no other options and kept themselves occupied for the duration with radio films and shows to make it all go away as quickly as possible. Those people wouldn't be relaxed by a long trip. They wouldn't appreciate the meditative quality of driving around, watching the miles slip past, and nodding their heads to hours on hours of shitty music.

Savage couldn't say he'd felt anything like that for his drive from the prison where Carlson had been incarcerated. He'd looked forward to a cathartic experience but had been diverted en route to run a mission for Monroe. Still, he did feel more relaxed once he'd returned, but there had been a little more to it than simply the driving.

A successful mission with more than its fair share of surprises always brought satisfaction. That said, eliminating Carlson once and for all was a relaxing situation in and of itself. A few days had passed since then without any calls from Anja or Anderson, and he didn't really care. At this point, he was willing to be fired. He had the cash and could move to the West Coast and be close to Abby. Watching her growing up from afar was better than not watching her at all. Maybe at some point in her life, he might step in and tell her he wasn't dead.

Maybe, but probably not. She was still in danger from those who might not want people to know he was still alive. They would lose very profitable careers if the wrong people found out about the wrong things. He'd already put her in enough danger as it was.

Moving closer to her was definitely not an option. *Have another beer, old man, and forget the wishes and imaginings.*

Savage wasn't sure how many times he'd had this conversation with himself. It was upwards of a dozen, he knew that much. The blinds were pulled down and effectively blocked his ability to tell how much time had passed since he'd arrived home. He knew what this feeling was. The inevitable abrupt plunge after a mission's end, going over the details, and convincing himself that it could have been done better.

Post-action depression, the experts called it or something like that. He merely called it a bad mood. The reality was that being in a situation where he needed to be at the peak of his abilities with adrenaline racing through his body to trigger his heightened senses made him feel alive.

When that situation altered, he was left with nothing but the ticking clock until the next mission.

He needed to get out there again and to spend time training to force the ringing out of his ears and the pain... *Fucking pain.* Why was there pain where there'd only been numbness before?

Knocking intruded, loud and insistent. It took a moment for him to return from his thoughts and realize that someone was at the door.

"Fucking hell," Savage grumbled. He heaved himself up from his Barcalounger and staggered somewhat as blood started pumping through his body again.

Anderson waited on the other side of the door when it opened.

"Holy shit, man." The former colonel chuckled as he pushed inside. "You look like shit. And this place smells like a swamp, just saying."

"Nice to see you too, Anderson," he retorted, rubbed his eyes, and winced when his visitor's first act was to stride purposefully to the window and pull the blinds open. Way too much sun for comfort spilled into the room. He didn't like it and wanted to make it go away. "No, sure, come on in."

"You've been locked in your apartment for a week. Sam and Terry wanted to ask you if you would do something for the game tomorrow. For some reason, you still have the better TV of the three of you."

"Why don't we do it at your place?" he asked and rubbed his eyes pointedly. His boss ignored the hint.

"Because I have a kid and a wife who wouldn't want to have four operatives with access to guns potentially getting violent about their favorite sports teams," he said with a grin. "It was one thing when attack was eminent, but things have died down now and I think they're safe enough to have one afternoon's respite from their bodyguards.

"Anyway, that's not why I'm here. Something's come up and we need you to come into Pegasus tomorrow. There've been some complications, and you have to give a statement on your work for the company."

"My actual work?" Savage asked and picked up the beer he'd forgotten earlier. Anderson intercepted it and placed it on the table again.

"No, dumbass," his boss said. "Anja's worked up a presentation for you to deliver to the company. We merely need to justify the amount of money we've paid you. So sober the fuck up, shave, get rid of that hobo beard, and for the love of God, take a shower and clean this place. We'll have the game after the meeting tomorrow—and no offense, dude, but you stink and this place does too."

"There's no need to be hurtful," he protested and glared at his visitor.

"I really feel like there is a need, yes," Anderson said and shook his head. "I really do."

Philadelphia: Pegasus Building

"Don't you worry about a thing, Savage," Anja said into his earpiece. "I've sent you all the details. They should already be on your phone."

"Now, why would I be worried?" he asked caustically and resisted the urge to simply turn and go home. He had done as Anderson told him. He was sobered up—and maybe a little hungover—but he was clean, shaved, and ready for a meeting. His boss had made sure that he had a good suit and tie and looked more or less presentable for something like that.

The operative hadn't really had the opportunity to infiltrate many places where he needed to wear a suit and tie. There simply wasn't much call for someone in his line of work to do that, and never as one of the suit-wearers. It was usually as someone who worked there—the uniformed people like security staff who were more often than not invisible to the people in the suits.

Now, he was one of the dumbasses who weren't able to see any of the people in uniforms.

"So," he grumbled as he scanned the contents of the files she'd sent him, "is any of this true? I know I didn't do any of it, obviously, but how much of this is verifiable?"

"Well, all of it, of course," the hacker said with a soft chuckle. "What, did you think all I did was sit on my ass and get yours out of trouble? I've run security for

MICHAEL TODD & MICHAEL ANDERLE

Courtney and Pegasus ever since we started. I'm simply letting you take the credit for all my hard work."

"Well, not technically," he protested and tilted his head in thought. "I've been the head of operations, which basically means...yeah, I get to take credit for the work of others. Fair enough."

"And you're welcome for that." She laughed. "I've missed you, Savage. I don't get to banter like this with everyone. And the folks around here are always busy running around. It's nice to have someone to talk to, you know?"

"Yeah," he said in a soft voice. "I've missed you too, Anja."

The town car that had been sent to pick him up came to a halt and the driver stepped out to open the door for him. Savage beat him to the punch, though, and had already stepped out to adjust his coat nervously while he eyed the building ahead of him.

"No need for that here, man," he said with a soft pat on the driver's shoulder. He left a crisp hundred-dollar bill in his uniform's coat pocket.

"Much appreciated, sir," the man said with a tip of his cap.

"We all work here, man," he replied. "You have a good day, though."

He stepped into the building and was immediately met by a young female PA who guided him quickly to the elevators. She informed him that the meeting had already started, pinned a nametag to his lapel, and pressed it into his suit a couple too many times. He narrowed his eyes at the possibly flirtatious action as they stepped into the elevator, which took them to the same conference room where Savage had first seen Anderson and Courtney. With a crisp nod at a couple of people who glanced at him, he dropped into one of the few empty chairs in the room.

Those present talked around him. They spoke English but he still didn't understand what they were talking about as they bandied comments about escrows and trusts and a hundred different terms he didn't understand in this kind of context.

These people lived in a world apart from his. He thought he made good money, but as he looked around, he realized they wore suits that would take him about a year to be able to buy, watches that would take even longer, and expensive haircuts and lapel pins. These people lived in a whole other world and they didn't even have a clue.

For a moment, he felt like he had the opportunity to study an alien species.

"And here to give us an overview of the security upgrades we've implemented in our new facilities, please welcome Jeremiah Savage."

He looked up from fiddling with his watch, a hint of surprise on his features as he turned to see Courtney Monroe there in the flesh, unlike how they'd seen her in the previous meetings he'd been a part of. She'd always been in the Zoo and conducted the meetings over a video chat.

The group of CEOs and majority shareholders and God knew what other titles they had for themselves all stared at him, waiting expectantly. Anderson was there too, he realized, seated at the front of the table beside Courtney.

Right. Showtime. All you have to do is think of them as a mob of bloodthirsty goons standing between you and a particularly difficult target and you should be fine. The thought brought an inward smile that helped him unfreeze.

He pulled the files from his binder as the graphs that had been on his phone were transmitted to the TV screen that stretched across the far wall of the room.

"Well, I think you'll be excited about the changes implemented in our new facilities," he began and pitched his voice to carry through the room. "The US government has stringent security standards for the companies they entrust their research grants to, and you'll be pleased to know that as of last week, we've been able to reach and surpass those standards.

"The other positive fact is that most of the cutting-edge technology that has been adapted for this purpose has been provided in-house. This has diminished the expenses of implementing them but in addition, it stands as an example of what we can do for security branches in the future should we see all the facilities running at full capacity within the month..."

He had committed all Anja's data to memory during the car ride, and while he doubted that any of those seated around the table would be impressed with security features they didn't understand at all, that wasn't what he was there for.

This was all a display to up the market share or something like that, Anja had told him. He was merely there to make sure that none of the current shareholders decided to sell before Carlson's stock hit the market, which was scheduled to start in the next week. This wasn't his world, but as a small smattering of claps greeted the end of his ten-minute presentation on exactly how impressive the security that guarded their investment was, he had to assume he had done a passable job.

"Thank you, Savage," Courtney said with a small smile before she leafed through her files. "Next on the agenda, we will go over the overall profits we can expect after the sale of the stocks…"

The operative didn't bother to hide the fact that he fazed all this new information out. He was an underling, there to make his bosses feel better, and that was it. Nothing about his current line of work had anything to do with what was discussed. Besides, he was a fan of Sir Arthur Conan Doyle's theory that the human brain was like an attic. If you constantly crammed it full of useless information, useful information was bound to be pushed into the corners or worse, out of a window.

He doubted there was any science behind it, but it was simple enough for him to understand.

The meeting, despite his boredom, flew by, and before he realized it, everyone adjourned for lunch. With no small measure of relief, he assumed he didn't need to return when they resumed. He stood slowly after the initial crush had exited, stretched discreetly, and followed Courtney's movements as she reached the door with a couple of others in her wake.

"I'll see you all tomorrow," she said and plastered a pleasant smile on her face as she indicated for those lingering around her to take their leave. "Savage, if you wouldn't mind joining me in my office for a moment?"

"Of course," he replied and noted that Anderson joined them too as they made their way to the top of the building where a giant corner office waited for them. He had no idea why she needed this much space to work in, but there was a small conference room in one corner, what looked like a small room where she would be able to spend the night if she wanted to, a wet bar and, of course, an office. It paid to run the business, he thought as she indicated for him to take a seat across her desk. Anderson sat as well, and he looked suspiciously subdued.

Courtney looked like this wouldn't be a pleasant conversation.

"So," she said and pulled a couple of images up on her computer screen. "As you know, Carlson was detained in a minimum-security prison pending trial for his crimes and because he was a federal witness in a handful of cases under investigation by the FBI. When the prison warden reported his death, they weren't precisely sure what had killed him. It looked like he was shot, but there were no bullets found in his body. Bullet holes, but not bullets. You wouldn't know anything about that, would you?"

Savage shook his head. "I'm fairly sure I was at a game that day."

She smirked. "I didn't say what day it was."

"You didn't have to." He growled his irritation and leaned forward in his seat. "Look, am I missing something here? Since when did you guys stop hiring me for all the plausible deniability that having an allegedly dead government operative on the payroll gets you?"

The woman sighed, rubbed her temples, and adjusted herself in her seat so she could lean back. "This sale is going to happen. No one questions that. We worked on our side to be ready for it and prepared what we needed to have in place. Then you jumped the gun, quite literally, on Carlson and that accelerated our plans beyond what was convenient, for lack of a better word. That's why I need to know when you intend to pull this kind of shit. Some warning, at least."

"I wasn't made aware of any plans," he said and kept his voice calm. "All that preparation and getting ready for sales is above my pay grade. Eliminating Banks revealed there was another player on the field. Some…client who coordinated the actions of the people we've butted heads with all this time. I thought it would be prudent not to sit on that, since they do have a way to access our personal information.

"There was someone who was vulnerable and in a position to give us information on this mysterious client, and I thought it was the wisest move to make sure that we weren't sitting on our asses should this key player decide to target us again."

"Right." Courtney chuckled although her expression said she didn't quite like his tone. "And this had nothing to do with revenge?"

"That depends," Savage replied.

"On?" she asked.

"Whether you want me to lie or not," he snapped smoothly. "I had a score to settle with Carlson, sure, but if you think for a second that I would have gone after him for purely personal reasons, you clearly don't think you have the right man here."

She opened her mouth to say something but shut it again quickly. That told him she knew he had a point—or it looked like that, anyway.

"Fine." She sighed finally and rubbed her eyes gently so as to not ruin her makeup. "I don't like this, but we have bigger concerns right now anyway. We need your help, Savage, to put out the fires that have flared up around the sale of the stocks. We need boots on the ground to make sure that nothing interferes with that. And we need to dig into this mysterious client…what was her name?"

"Elena," he said softly. "Elena Molina."

CHAPTER FOUR

The Zoo

The critical things that needed to be done before they headed into the Zoo came naturally to every member of the Heavy Metal team by now. They had all gone through the procedures of checking their weapons and suits as they scrambled out of the Hammerhead at least a hundred times before and knew it was one of the primary reasons why they'd made it this far. Hopefully, they would live to do it a hundred times more. Or live to not have to do it anymore. Sal wasn't sure which one he would actually prefer.

Either way, they were through the checks and ready to roll almost as soon as boots hit the sand. There wasn't much in the way of banter. That would come later. They would make sure there was something to banter about first. The group of eight was ready to roll into the jungle beyond where the Hammerheads would be able to take them a few minutes after they arrived.

Sal indicated their ingress point, a small, pleasant glade he assumed would contain the famous Pita plants in the near future. It still seemed almost unbelievable that something so seemingly inconsequential had made them so much money in the past. He marked the coordinates for a possible later venture when he'd be able to confirm his hypothesis with the software that helped them to find clusters of the plant. That was one of the things he loved about the jungle—its ability to keep his mind rolling in the effort to discover and understand new things.

"Do you have any contact from our Russian friends?" Madigan asked once they began their march with her taking point. He walked mostly beside her although he also took time to collect as many samples as he could. There was a time when he would have been selective of exactly what he took home, but at this point and at the rate the Zoo grew and changed, it made more sense to simply collect as much as he could lay his hands on and sift the known from the unknown later.

"They left us the coordinates to find them," he replied, noticed a new vine that grew on some trees, and barely even paused his stride as he took a sample and tucked it into his bag. "Given the numbers they usually bring in here, I wouldn't be surprised if we hear them long before we see them."

"You have a point." Madigan chuckled. "That said, though, we'll probably have to step in to save them from a massive attack and they can consider our debt to them paid."

"That's not the point of this," Sal said. "There are... tensions between the Russians and Americans, with all kinds of hints about the history of the two. The fact that they brought a whole platoon to help me when I needed them was an unprecedented olive branch extension. We want to stay on their good side. They are the best suppliers of vodka in these parts if you recall."

"I do recall." She grinned. "Vividly. I merely don't like having to dance around the commandant like that. It feels...slimy, for lack of a better word."

"If he finds out that we've helped the Russians with a recovery job, I'd guess the trust he has in us will go the way of the dodo." When she narrowed her eyes at him, he explained casually, "The bird. A bird that went extinct. His trust would go away is my point."

"I know what a fucking dodo bird is, Sal," she retorted.

"Right." He grinned and knew full well that she considered the temptation to wipe him out of existence at this point. "He probably already knows we've had jobs from the other bases by now, but there's knowing and then there's knowing. Outright telling him might mean he sends less jobs our way. You know how he is. We have a business to run."

"Do you really think he can afford to not give us more work these days?" Madigan asked as they picked their pace up, knowing they would be late at the rendezvous if they didn't.

"He's not a soldier," Sal reminded her. "Have you seen his record? All his time in the military has been spent in administrative roles with no stints in the field. What he's looking for might not necessarily be what he can afford. It'll always be what impacts his reputation back in the States with his family grooming him for a career in politics. But that's neither here nor there."

"It seems like it might be here, between you and me,"

she retorted. He knew for a fact that she didn't like bad-mouthing soldiers behind their backs and preferred to pull that kind of shit right in their faces. It was more respectful that way.

That sentiment clashed with her disdain for playing politics, so he could understand why she was uncomfortable with the topic of conversation even though she didn't step in and put a stop to it. He decided he didn't want to put her in that kind of bind and changed the subject—not a difficult thing to do when he looked at the jungle they trudged through.

"Is it only me or are things a little...peaceful around here?" he asked and scrutinized their surroundings a little more carefully. He didn't merely pull the topic out of thin air, either, although it was meant to change the subject. There was normally a sensation of tension very openly displayed by the Zoo in its entirety. It was difficult to put a finger on it, but you knew it when you felt it. The general sense was like the trees themselves were pissed by your presence, and all you could do was try not to piss them off further.

Sal didn't get that vibe this time, though. Well, not as much as usual, anyway. There was almost no animal movement around them. From what he could detect, there were animals on the periphery at the limit of the team's range of sight, but those that could be seen did what regular animals did when they heard or saw a group of humans trooping through their habitat—run like hell in the opposite direction. It wasn't to say the beasties weren't being smart, but being smart wasn't exactly what he had come to expect from them during his time in the Zoo. Or, at least, not to the point of self-preservation.

He wasn't complaining because it was a hell of a lot easier not having to fight through. Still, there was something about the jungle that made his nerves work overtime whenever it diverged from what he had come to expect from it.

"You feel it too, huh?" Davis asked. He jogged closer to them and left someone else to bring up the rear of their squad. "Like the calm before a storm?"

Sal looked around and realized the man was talking to him and not Madigan. "That's...not really what I felt, but there's something definitely off about what's going on. Like it's trying to lull us into a false sense of security."

"That is what you call the calm before the storm, isn't it?" Madigan asked and pulled up some data from the sensors in her suit.

"I mean...sure, but..." He shook his head because he really didn't know how to explain it. There was a calm before the storm and a lulling into false sense of security. They were two different things when you thought about it, and what he felt was definitely the latter. Less tension and more something waiting for them to drop their guard.

"Anyway," she said when he didn't finish his thought. "I get what you mean about running a business. Making sure our clients are collectively happy is important, even if it means leaving them in the dark as to the entirety of our operation."

"Unless we want to start importing booze full time," he responded. "It would be less money—at first, anyway—but it has to be a safer way to make a living. I know the main reason why we do it is to keep our relationships and contacts on the other bases from souring or getting cold, but we could always simply keep upgrading it, right?"

"Have you seen how people protect their market shares around these parts?" Davis asked with a chuckle. "You folks might want to keep pushing vodka to the various bars in the bases around the Zoo as a part-time job, at least until you can force some of the other importers out of business."

"You never know what could happen out here," Sal said with a feral grin. "Sometimes, these supply drops simply… disappear."

"You've become a little more ruthless since you were kidnapped," the other man grumbled and looked away.

"I like it," Madigan commented and punched Sal gently on the arm. He didn't think it would be wise to tell her she had almost knocked his arm out of joint, so he rolled it and worked it off with a nervous chuckle as the team pressed forward through the underbrush.

He wasn't sure how he knew, but the prickle in the back of his mind told him they wouldn't encounter much trouble from the beasties that tended to cause it around these parts. He liked to call it instinct coupled with an innate knowledge of the place after…hell, he wasn't sure how many trips into the Zoo by now. Dozens, at least, and possibly even scores. Coming up on hundreds.

He didn't let himself relax, though. Feelings were all well and good until a panther pounced from the branches and pumped you full of neurotoxin. And he was still working on helping them to develop software that would let the suits carry anti-toxins with the first aid they could administer.

His thought was to maybe take a blood test to determine the kind of poison that had been injected and so be
able to treat it immediately, but Anja told him the software
would need to be a little more complex than that. Either
way, she helped Pegasus to develop new and improved
suits thanks to the experiences of the Heavy Metal Militia,
as they were called lately.

Sal raised his hand quickly. He still felt iffy about their
situation in the Zoo, but unless they were suddenly
attacked by at least twenty two-and-a-half ton creatures,
they were rapidly approaching the location where they
expected to meet their Russian friends.

"Salinger Jacobs, is that you coming at us?" A man
spoke over an open comm line. The voice and accent were
easily recognizable by now.

"It's Dr. Salinger Jacobs now, Gregor," he said with a
chuckle as a group wearing armor headed in their direction. The Russians knew how to make their suits hardy and
tough. Like their APVs, they were reliable under the
toughest of circumstances, even if they left much to be
desired when it came to function and versatility. Sal took
inspiration from many of their designs to improve the
armor functions of the newer suits he helped to develop,
both for Pegasus and for himself in Amanda's work.

She still told him that his aspirations were way, way
too lofty, but they were in this business to dream big.
Well, she wasn't anymore, not directly anyway. He still
thought of her as a part of Heavy Metal, but part-
time now.

"What?" Gregor asked and jogged to where the Heavy
Metal team stood. "When we met first, it was all 'I'm not a

doctor' and now I have to change that? You ask too much of me, Salinger Jacobs."

"You're a friend, Gregor," Madigan said with a grin and greeted the man with a hug, awkward though it was with their bulky suits. "You can call him Sal."

"I don't suppose I get a say in all this?" Sal asked, foregoing the hug and simply bumping armored fists with the Russian.

"Nope," she replied and turned to Gregor. "How the hell are you?"

"I can complain, but I shouldn't," the man said with a chuckle and left his team of twenty to greet and interact with the Heavy Metal team. "Things have been good but busy for me. People think I am worthy of greater responsibility, and while that means more money for me, it also means more work, which is why we are out here. Where… where is Dr. Monroe? Did you leave her behind again?"

"Yes and no," Sal replied. "She's the head of a large company in the States and they needed her there to run the company instead."

"Hah!" he exclaimed. "If I've heard right, dealing with the corporate jackals in civilization can be equally as dangerous and life-threatening as coming out here in the Zoo."

"Yeah, only because you can't walk around the city wearing a full suit of battle armor," Madigan snarked and it sounded like it was something she would change if she ever took over the world.

Gregor looked at their troop. "Are these all the people you brought, my friends? After I called in a small army to help you when you were in trouble?"

"It was all who could be assembled in the short time frame you gave us," Sal explained. "The fact that you wanted us to keep it under wraps that we were coming out to help you didn't help things either."

"Not that it matters anyway," Madigan said and stepped in firmly. "These people are all hardened Zoo vets, more than capable of holding their own, someone else's, and five other people's on top of that. You couldn't ask for a better team to support your mission. Which was...what again? You didn't exactly brim with details in your message."

"Well, unfortunately, I could not be too forthcoming with the specifics," he said, suddenly defensive.

"No shit," Sal commented. "But we'll be out here in the jungle with you guys, so we'd prefer it if you had the common courtesy to let us know what we'll risk our lives for."

"In all honesty, I don't know all the details either," he admitted and shrugged.

"I love how you think that's comforting," Madigan said. "Why the hell did you take a job you didn't know all the details for? I thought you were smarter than that, Gregor."

"I am...usually." He looked around shiftily. "It's a mission sent directly from the FSB. Government involvement means they'll be a little iffy about sharing all their secrets, and honestly, I had no desire to ask. They told us to jump, and we asked how high. It's why I thought we might need your help."

Sal exchanged a look with Madigan. Having the FSB snooping around Heavy Metal was never a good idea, especially in light of the fact that they harbored someone in their compound the Russians wanted to get their hands on. He knew Anja would be able to keep herself safe if the situation called for it, especially with Connie running... interference on anyone who might try to break in. Either way, though, it wasn't a good idea to hang around those folks for too long.

"You thought it was a good idea to involve us with your government's shenanigans?" Madigan asked.

"If it was an easy job, I wouldn't need your help, now would I?" the Russian asked and his tone implied a raised eyebrow.

Sal nodded and placed a hand on Madigan's shoulder. "That's a good point and we do owe you, Gregor. So, lay it out for us. What's the mission?"

Gregor connected to the Heavy Metal comm line and transferred a selection of files that Sal took the precaution of checking for any hidden worms or trojans with software Anja had connected to the suits before he accessed the files themselves.

"There was a team running important research inside the Zoo," the other man said as the team looked through the files, which was new information to the Russian team as well by the looks of it. "We weren't told what kind of research they were running and honestly, I didn't bother to ask. All that was shared is that they went dark about forty-eight hours ago, although we are required to wait for twenty-four hours before we send a team out.

"While communications were never good—as we know is the case in the Zoo—there has apparently always been an indication that a connection was active, even though it didn't transmit or receive any messages during the blackout period. This link completely inactive very suddenly and there is a suspicion of foul play involved."

Sal narrowed his eyes. They had experimented with getting comms to work through the radiation emitted by what he believed was the trees' high content of the alien goop, and while he had made a few breakthroughs, success was haphazard at best. If a team was working in the Zoo and had exchanged comms in and out as their friend suggested, he wasn't sure he liked the idea of the Russians making advances ahead of him.

If nothing else, it meant they had connection to an ongoing network. While it evidently didn't function as required, it's existence was able to warn someone of the possibility of foul play. Call it ego, but it might mean he had started to lose his edge. He had been a little distracted of late, but that felt like making excuses.

"We were given the coordinates where the research team was last known to be," Gregor continued and noted Sal's lack of focus with narrowed eyes. "We should be able to find them and from there, determine what caused them to go dark the way they did. Hopefully, we can track them and get them out of the Zoo."

"You do know that the likelihood of anyone still being alive is astronomically low, right?" he asked as he looked at the group, and Gregor nodded.

"Then we recover what we can of their research data and return it to base as intact as we can manage," the man continued. "Make no mistake. The priority is to recover the research data. Those who conducted the research will be a secondary concern."

Madigan connected with Sal over a private comm

channel as the teams merged and forged ahead in the direction of the coordinates Gregor had provided.

"Well, it's not usual that the mission parameters are 'get info first, rescue people alive second,'" she commented.

He nodded. "Honestly, those are almost always the parameters when it comes to research in the Zoo. They merely don't usually state it as explicitly. It's a little blunt but at least it's honest."

"Do you think this could have something to do with what the commandant had to say about teams heading into the Zoo and killing other teams?" she asked.

Sal shrugged. "It could be. I suppose there's only one way to find out. Track the fuckers, shoot first, shoot second, third, and shoot some more, and if anyone's left alive, try to get in a question or two."

"Davis is right," Madigan pointed out. "You have become more ruthless since your kidnapping."

"I'll take that as a compliment." He smirked.

CHAPTER FIVE

Philadelphia: Pegasus Building

Anderson stepped out of Courtney's office behind Savage and both men strode toward the elevator. There were a number of things the two of them needed to discuss, but as the members of the board now began to trickle in from their lunch adjournment, there wasn't much they could discuss openly with this many people around. Savage wondered exactly what these executives thought he was doing there since it was obvious he was there at Courtney and Anderson's behest.

They probably didn't think there was any kind of personal relationship except for perhaps the kind that was forged between Marines and Special Forces men, with Courtney tolerating Savage due to his friendship with Anderson. He didn't really care what they thought as long as the truth never occurred to them. There wouldn't be much stock bought if the truth of what he did for Pegasus became public knowledge.

Then again, what he did was mostly retaliation against

the man who had run the company before, so maybe the people who were in the know of how Pegasus was run—be it under the old guard or the new—would take advantage of what would be cheap stocks to buy into a Fortune Five-Hundred company. It wasn't like the way Carlson used to run things was any kind of secret. He had called hits on Anderson quite openly while still on the board, so it was unlikely that people wouldn't be in the know.

They would merely pretend to be offended and clutch their proverbial pearls or some shit like that.

Anderson and Savage were the only ones going down, which meant they had the elevator to themselves as the doors closed.

"You have to cut her some slack," the ex-colonel said softly a few seconds after the doors ensured they had privacy. "There was some shit going on in the Zoo before she had to come back here to deal with the sale of the stocks. She's good at running a business, don't get me wrong, but I know her well enough to know that she would rather be out there in the middle of it instead of here dealing with bureaucrats and red tape. It's weird, I know."

"Not that weird," he said and folded his arms in front of his chest. "Out there, you know what you're getting into. It's dangerous, sure, but you already have that in the back of your mind and you're ready for it. You know who your friends and your enemies are, and you know what your priorities are.

"I assume it's much like being out in the field. You do what you must to survive and make sure the people who count on you do the same. Everything else is of secondary importance. In this situation, all the people who might wish her harm are the ones who smile to her face, shake her hand, and talk about how much they believe she can make the company a success. It can play tricks with your mind if you're not careful and make you paranoid."

"Are you really paranoid if they are out to get you?" Anderson asked and frowned.

"The fact that someone might be coming for you does not change the state of your paranoia. That means yes, you are paranoid no matter who might or might not be coming for you," he responded with a small smirk, which disappeared quickly. "That said, I do respect Dr. Monroe and given that she's one of the two people who cut me my paychecks, I wouldn't want to piss her off as much as I wouldn't want to piss you off. It makes me feel a little shitty for heading off to deal with Carlson on my own."

"Right. Why did you go after Carlson like that? Like Courtney said, we planned to eliminate him eventually. Believe me, the man sent people with guns to assassinate me while my family was in the house, so you can bet your ass I don't mind knowing he's in the dirt permanently. But did you go after him for some kind of revenge?"

Savage shrugged and hesitated before he answered because the elevator doors opened to provide them with a clear view of the lobby, still clogged with people returning to the meeting. None looked like they paid attention to the two men, but that wasn't enough for them to trust that nothing they said wouldn't be overheard and remembered. It was safer for them to maintain their silence until they were outside and waiting for the town car that would drive the operative to his apartment. It was cold enough outside that anyone who didn't need to be there wouldn't be, which gave them the privacy they needed.

It would be the only time he was thankful for cold weather, Savage thought ruefully.

"I wanted to get back in the saddle after getting clear of the hospital," he said and kept his voice low despite the fact that no one was around them. "Carlson seemed like as good a target as any. I told him I would be back to finish the job if he tried anything after I put one through his kneecap, and the way I saw it, I was entitled to head in there to keep that promise. And I wanted more information on this client of Banks' so couldn't let Carlson walk away."

"But he did give you the information, right?" Anderson asked and fixed him with a firm look. "He gave you a name, which you claimed was all he knew about this...Elena Molina character, if that's even her real name."

"That's the weird part, to be honest," he responded and rubbed to restore the feeling into his arms as the cold had started to seep through his coat. "He said he would give me all the information he had, but only if I promised to kill him. I know that sounds weird, but he said something to the effect that he didn't expect to survive if he told me anything, and this way, he would go out with a little dignity and as little pain as possible. Well, as near to that as he could get. I did pop him a couple of times with a golf club. I had some stuff to work out."

"Huh." Anderson grunted. "There goes my plausible deniability about that."

"How much did you really have in the first place?" he asked, and the man shrugged with a chuckle. "If it makes you feel better, I do feel like trash for putting all Monroe's work at risk because I felt impulsive and antsy one day, as much as I hate to admit it. You could have told me what you two had planned, and that would have meant I'd have put it off, despite having very good reasons for our little meeting. But...yeah, I guess what I'm trying to say is that I'm sorry for being an impulsive ass."

The former colonel nodded. "Don't worry about it. I can handle Courtney. It's not like there was any real damage done and to be fair, knowing who is targeting us will be worth the trouble. She might not feel that way right now, but she knows you've been more than worth your salt, as they say."

"Worth your salt...where the fuck does that come from?" he asked.

"I think it had something to do with the Roman soldiers back in the day. They used to get paid in salt instead of money."

"Because salt was worth more than money back then?" He sounded as disbelieving as he felt.

"How the fuck should I know?" His companion shrugged as the town car stopped at the front. "Remember, we're all coming at five for the game. We'll bring drinks and food, but you might want to stock up on some of that on your own. You know how Sam gets when her boys start losing."

"She wouldn't need to get like that if she knew how to pick a winning team." Savage chuckled and stepped into the car. "All she really knows is based on her Football League, and that's nothing like the NFL."

"You're telling me," Anderson concurred. "Have a nice drive home. I'll see you at five."

"Yeah," he murmured, closed the door, and leaned back as the driver pulled away from the Pegasus building. He liked having a team to come over to watch a game with him. They would make a mess of his apartment, of course, and Sam would probably start to get drunk when the team that she chose—usually against Savage, Terry, and Anderson—started to lose. It was still better than getting drunk on his own to watch the game.

Besides, the place had been a mess yesterday anyway.

It was a short ride to his apartment when they didn't have to negotiate the morning traffic. He had a few hours to kill before the crew arrived, which allowed him to step out and collect supplies for his contribution as well as make sure everything was as ready as it could be. That wasn't really saying much. He had the big TV and there were enough couches to make sure the four of them would be seated comfortably. Aside from that and the kitchen, there wasn't much else to prepare. He still had enough booze left from his latest binge so he was able to sit with a beer as he turned the TV on and waited for them to arrive.

"Hey, Savage," Anja said. He startled when she came alive in the earbud he still wore, for some reason. "How did the presentation go?"

He shrugged. "About as well as it could have, given that it was merely a show of trust for the rest of the board. But then you already knew that, didn't you?"

"Of course I knew, but I wanted to know if you would tell me the truth," she replied as he took a sip of his beer.

"Truth about what?" he asked, his eyes narrowed.

"Well, I did see that you went into Monroe's office with Anderson, but I made sure nobody would be able to listen in on what happens in that office while Monroe is in there, not even me," the hacker explained. The familiar squeak told him she had leaned back in her still loud chair. "So, tell me the truth. Did you or did you not engage in a three-some with her and Anderson?"

Savage blinked. "What the actual fuck, dude?"

"I'm...mostly kidding." She chuckled. "She has some interesting bedfellows, if you know what I mean. Call me crazy, but I'm curious about what she does when she's away from the Zoo."

"You're weird," Savage protested. "She laid into me for going after Carlson when I did since it meant she needed to come back to Philly to deal with the stock sale or what-ever. She didn't like it as it interfered with a master plan she had for the company or something. Which begs the question, of course, of why the fuck you didn't tell me there was a plan when we plotted our way into Carlson's prison?"

"If there was any plotting and planning, she didn't fill me in," the Russian said. "There are some things that even I'm not aware of, sadly. Thanks, by the way, for not selling me out in there."

"Hey, I ain't no snitch." He chuckled and took another sip of his beer. "They do want us to start tracking this Elena Molina chick as soon as possible, though, since she is the one who actively wants to remove us from the picture."

"Right, and I've worked on that since we got the name. There's a small problem, though. This woman is as good at covering her tracks as I am at covering yours. Seriously, I don't doubt that she has someone like me on her payroll. I found a couple of birth certificates in the US and Monaco, but aside from that, she's a fucking ghost."

"Well, if you have a location and you have the names of at least two of her known associates, may they rest in peace, wouldn't that be enough for you to triangulate some kind of location for her?" Savage asked. It wasn't like he knew anything about that but he had heard her talking enough to be able to predict where her mind would go.

"Well, true, I could do that," she mused aloud. "It'll still be difficult, though. There's no real confirmation that she even met with Banks or Carlson, but it is something to work with, anyway."

"You're the best, Anja." He chuckled. "I believe in you."

"Well, yes, I am, but your faith is appreciated." She sounded like she was smiling broadly. "Anyway, I won't keep you since it would appear that your visitors have begun to arrive. I'll let you know if I find something."

"Appreciate it." Savage leaned back in his lounger as the pre-game program started.

Sam was the first to arrive and stepped inside without so much as a greeting and looked around the apartment. She toted a six-pack from a local brewery as well as a bag with what looked like chips, salsa mix, and a bottle of scotch.

"Well, don't you clean up nice?" she said, and her tone clearly suggested that she'd arrived early to make sure he was ready to entertain.

"I thought you didn't like people talking to you like that."

"Well, it's not anyone talking to me but rather someone

talking to you," she replied and punched him gently on the shoulder. "You never told me you minded someone talking to you like that. Do you? Because I'll respect the hell out of it since you did the same for me."

"I don't mind, no." He chuckled, shook his head, and offered her a cold beer before he took the supplies she had brought from her hands. "I was poking a little fun at you, is all."

"Good to know." She grinned at him, accepted the beer, and took a long swig from it.

"Who are you cheering for today, then?" he asked as he put her beers in the fridge and started mixing the salsa.

"Well, you're a Seahawks man, right?" Sam asked with a sly glance at him.

Savage shrugged. "I don't really have a team but yeah, I tend to lean toward the Seattle teams."

"Ah, good. Since you always choose badly, I'll cheer for the Patriots today." She grinned when he rolled his eyes.

"You're only saying that to piss me off," he grumbled.

"What is she saying to piss you off?" Anderson asked as he stepped inside. He'd arrived with Terry and brought wings and more beer, as well as gin.

"She's cheering for the Pats today," Savage explained, and their boss laughed.

"Well, at least she won't be all depressed when her team loses," Terry said. He seemed in an uncharacteristically good mood, complete with his version of trash-talking.

Savage grimaced. "You're only trying to get on my nerves. I know it."

"Nope, I did my research," Sam said, took her phone

out, and showed that most of the pundits talking about the game believed the Patriots would win it.

"What, do you honestly listen to the experts?" He shook his head. "They're wrong, like…seventy-five percent of the time. You'd be better off simply closing your eyes and pointing at one of the two teams to pick."

"Well, I did that too." She took another long swig from her beer.

He laughed and she grinned in response as Anderson came to the kitchen to help him to prepare the food. Terry caught the beer Savage tossed him and moved to take a seat with Sam. The sniper had loosened up somewhat on his stern lifestyle since he'd joined their little team. Whether that had something to do with his time with Sam or with Anderson's family, Savage didn't really care. He looked like he was having a good time, anyway, while Sam celebrated the fact that they were both on the same side of something for once.

"Do you really think Sam is doing this simply to piss you off?" Anderson asked with a chuckle, and he shook his head. He carried the dip and chips out to the coffee table and dropped onto his favorite seat. The former colonel left the wings to stay warm in the oven until the game started and joined them with a scotch and soda instead of a beer in his hand.

"What do you think, Savage? Do you want to put money on this?" Sam asked. She'd apparently decided to continue with her ribbing.

"Say…fifty bucks?" he proposed. "That the Seahawks take the game."

"I could do with more drinking money," she said and leaned back in her seat.

"We can all agree that you have more than enough drinking money, Sam," Anderson pointed out.

"Are you trying to say something about me, James?" she asked and raised an eyebrow.

"I'm not *trying* to say anything," he responded smartly.

It was way too cold to do this shit. There had to be enough people in their line of work who smoked, even in this day and age. They were in a business in which many would consider dying of lung cancer a win—although of course, with the medical advances being made, death by smoking wasn't really a problem anymore.

But no. They had stuck him with a group that didn't smoke, which meant that if he needed to indulge in his particular vice, he would have to do it outside and freeze his ass off while he sucked on the little white cylinder.

It wasn't that he thought everyone should smoke. Marvin Frost merely wished he didn't need to be out of the toasty-warm SUV to enjoy a nice drag and maybe some company. Nicotine hits were always better done in company.

But there he was, standing on his own in the sub-freezing temperatures while he kept an eye on the Pegasus building and waited for one of the high-rollers inside to leave.

He finished the cigarette, dropped it, and ground it under his heel as he cursed softly and popped chewing gum into his mouth before he entered the vehicle again. The other four men in the SUV looked at him in disapproval. They could obviously still pick up the inevitable stench that followed his habit.

Fuck them. He ignored the silent criticism and continued to chew his gum.

"Are there any updates from the building?" he asked, accustomed to their scowls by now.

"People are leaving," the man in the driver's seat grumbled. He toyed with his cell phone and left the surveillance of the location to his teammates. "Our target is still in the building, though."

Frost sighed and shook his head. With modern technology being what it was, there really was no reason to have to wait out there. The days of old-school spying should have ended by now. They had tried to access the building's security to at least obtain an idea of their target's schedule, but whoever had set the system up in Pegasus was the kind of good that was paid seven figures a year.

Of course, they could have hacked it if they'd had a couple of months to prepare, but all their IT specialist had managed to achieve with the two-day notice they'd had for the job was to locate a blind spot for the SUV from where they'd be able to keep an eye on the entrance without raising suspicions.

The marginal advantage wasn't much benefit at all. If their target decided to simply use another exit, take a town car instead of her usual vehicle, or leave with someone else, they would be forced to wait yet again. She had to be in a position where she could be approached without hundreds of police officers descending on them from all around the city. Despite the fact that it worked to their advantage that she once again scorned to make use of any bodyguards, they still needed her to be in a situation where she was both alone and vulnerable.

Frost checked his phone to refresh the details of their target in his mind. She looked a little young to be a de facto head of a Fortune Five-Hundred company like Pegasus. The word was that a former colonel worked as her second in command, who in turn had a spook—special forces or CIA—working as an enforcer for them.

All that probably meant she got the job because she had the right connections. The bio they had been sent didn't include any personal details. All it contained were Dr. Courtney Monroe's habits and a picture of her, clear enough that she could be recognized even from this distance. It was a difficult mission, but he assumed the team had been through worse.

Then again, he really would have preferred to have had more time to plot and plan for this kind of operation. Unfortunately, the word from the client was that Monroe was only in Philly for a limited window, after which she would leave the country for parts unknown. This would be their one and only chance.

He shook his head. The timetable still didn't work. The client should have hired a long-range specialist, someone with a rifle who could position themselves safely a mile away, ready to knock her head off and disappear once the deed was done.

Vaguely, he recalled the client mentioning something about a show of force, but he had admittedly been entranced by the seven-million-dollar bounty on the woman's head—per operative. For that much money, he would have been willing to kill her with his bare hands if that was what the client wanted. He would still have bitched and complained about it, but that was neither here nor there.

"Heads up. We have another group on their way out." The man in the shotgun seat of the SUV alerted them, and Frost trained a pair of digital binoculars on the entrance. He enhanced the image until he could focus on the group that slowly exited the building.

Sure enough, their target was there. She looked tired and annoyed while she answered questions from the folks in expensive suits around her. A valet pulled her car up to the entrance and she pointed at it and shook her head, perhaps telling these people that she would answer more questions later.

Frost doubted it. She had the look of someone who had no intention to indulge anyone.

"Get ready to move out," he commanded as he retrieved the duffel bag that carried their small arsenal of firearms. He alerted their support that the team was on the move and the operation now officially in progress.

CHAPTER SIX

The Zoo

"Well, Gregor," Sal said and looked at the glass in his hand still half full of clear liquid, "I have to say I'm a little disappointed that you've held out on the good stuff. Why haven't we moved this to bars around the Zoo? You would make a killing."

"I wish I could, my friend," the Russian said with a chuckle and leaned over to refill Sal's, Madigan's, and his glass with a few more fingers of the vodka before he took another sip and sighed with satisfaction. "But this is my personal stash, passed on to me by my grandfather for special occasions. They don't make vodka like this anymore. I don't know the science behind it, but the truth is, this vodka is limited edition. I only share it because the two of you are good friends who come to my aid when I ask."

Davis looked up from his glass. "Well, Gregor, I wouldn't say we know each other well enough to be called friends, but if you connect your friends with alcohol of this quality, I wouldn't mind."

Gregor chuckled. "Well, you came to my aid in time of need as well. If that isn't what friends are, I don't know what is."

Sal smiled and leaned back in the seat he had improvised from pieces of his suit as well as his pack, which he'd hardened to help with that idea in mind. It had been a long day of trudging through the Zoo, but as the night began to fall, it appeared they wouldn't reach the coordinates anyway. The group of twenty-eight decided to set up camp and resume their trek in the morning. It didn't need to be said that everyone hoped the researchers they were tracking merely had a bad case of technical difficulties.

The odds of that, though, were even more astronomical than those of them still being alive. Sal didn't want to bring that up with Gregor, of course, since the man's reputation —and possibly even his life—relied on them finding something, however miniscule, from the researchers to bring back to his FSB overlords. He knew he needed to talk to the man about not mentioning to them that Heavy Metal had been involved in the mission. They didn't need Russian intelligence breathing down their neck for any reason, especially with Anja still at the base.

That was something to focus his mind on, of course, something to worry about that would distract him from the fact that the Zoo was still a little too quiet for his comfort.

"So," Gregor said and turned to face him. "What have you been up to since we got you out of the Zoo?"

IT ALL FALLS DOWN

He noted that Madigan's immediate reaction was to look away and avoid the topic of conversation. She didn't like the fact that he'd been scientist-napped on her watch, even though she had been the one to lead the team in there to get him out again. He didn't like seeing her like this, so he decided to keep his answer on the topic short and to the point.

"I actually finished my PhD thesis using the data I collected on that little adventure," he said. "Hence the whole doctor thing. Plus, the mercs who took me left me with a top-of-the-line suit that I actually helped to develop. Of course, I still have a couple of improvements I need done, but that will have to wait until I can get my hands on Amanda back on the French base."

"Right, so would you say it was a profitable experience for you, then?" the other man asked.

"There was a profit involved, sure." He shrugged. Madigan had stood and moved to another corner of the camp. "But it doesn't mean I would be happy for it to happen to me again. There are easier ways to make money and collect dissertation-worthy data than being dragged out into the Zoo by a group of green mercs. If you guys will excuse me?" He pointed to where Madigan had headed off to, and the men nodded as he pushed to his feet and followed her.

"What does this American expression 'green' mean?" Sal heard Gregor ask and Davis began to explain. He tuned the conversation out as he crossed to where she had found another seat, still nursing her glass of vodka.

"Is everything okay?" he asked and settled beside her.

There was no seat for him, but thanks to his lighter, more agile suit, he was able to sit cross-legged on the ground. "I know you don't like talking about what happened when I was taken. Maybe I shouldn't have encouraged it."

She chuckled and shook her head, leaned down to kiss his lips gently, and stroked his hair. "No, nothing like that, dumbass. Well, maybe a little about that, but that's not what's been on my mind."

He smiled like an idiot over the kiss and shook his head to bring himself firmly back to the here and now. "Well, do tell. What's been on your mind? Maybe I can help you? Unfortunately, I don't think a quickie is an option for us, given that we're in close proximity with twenty-six others. Although I'm willing to try a little hand adventure if you are."

"Get your mind out of the gutter, Jacobs," she retorted. He knew her well enough to know she wanted to be serious when she addressed him by his surname.

"Mind…is removed from the gutter," he said apologetically. "What's up, Madigan?"

She shrugged. "It's only…I remember what you were like when you first arrived. Sharp as a tack, I guess, but lacking the kind of physicality that would allow you to last in this kind of life. I recall thinking how you wouldn't last very long around here, even if you survived that first trip. And you proved me wrong on that."

"I…uh, thanks?" he responded questioningly. "You have a weird way to compliment me, you know that?"

"That's not what I mean," she replied, her voice low. "At first, I thought your improvements might be a result of you applying yourself to the work, and I'm sure that plays a role in it too. But I've wondered lately if your suddenly growing and flourishing abilities come from your...to put this delicately, tasting Madie now more than before. And I don't mean you going down on me."

Sal shrugged. "I haven't taken any more of the stuff lately than I have before. I'm careful to keep my doses light and make sure to keep detailed notes on what's changed in my body since I started taking it. Sure, there are physical changes that might have something to do with it, but nothing definitive yet. I still need to do more tests."

"Are you sure that's wise?" Madigan tilted her head and regarded him with a slight frown. "I mean...sure, I'm glad it's helped you to get better at this since it has kept your ass alive longer than it would have been otherwise. But have you considered that there might be some side effects you haven't noticed—things you might not notice until it's already too late? Not only in your body but in your mind too?"

He narrowed his eyes and rocked gently as he let his gaze wander across the darkness that extended beyond their little campsite. The warning sensors had already been planted in the ground and the groups had divided themselves into three teams that would keep watch during the night. There seemed to be some argument in broken Russian and English between them over who would take the middle of the three shifts. It was the worst one, of course, since it allowed the fewest hours of uninterrupted sleep and the argument was one he'd heard a hundred times before.

Focus, damn it, this is important. To her, which makes it

important to you. He shook his head to force his thoughts back to the conversation.

"I...really don't think that's the case," Sal said softly, although even as he said it, he didn't really believe it, at least not fully. There had been small alterations in his thought processes. His initial thought was that it was only about him being more confident in his abilities, which allowed him to step in and do things he would never have thought himself capable of.

At least to himself, he had to acknowledge that it had extended beyond that, though. It was like Davis and Madigan had both mentioned. He was a little more ruthless, a little colder to the people around him, and possessed a massively increased sex drive, although he wasn't sure if that was a physical or psychological change.

The Heavy Metal group hadn't been subjected to the brunt of his changes, obviously, but everyone else had. He'd never addressed it, mainly because he didn't want to think there was anything wrong with these changes in himself.

Maybe it wasn't the best idea he'd ever had and he was annoyed that he'd opted to cover up and ignore something as his go-to response rather than study and address it openly. He was supposed to be a scientist, after all. His newly acquired PhD in biology shouldn't change that. On the contrary, it was supposed to make him hungrier for knowledge.

He looked at Madigan, and despite the fact that she seemed willing to accept his assurances, he could tell she had the same doubts he did. But she had been through enough at his expense already and he didn't want her to worry about it. She was his gunner, so her responsibility was with his physical safety while out in the Zoo. He didn't need to burden her with his mental issues, especially when they were of his own making.

And there he was, doing it again. She was more than his gunner. They were closer than that. His instinct should be to share and be honest with her but unfortunately, he wasn't quite ready for that yet.

"I'll be fine," Sal said finally with a nod that he used to convince himself as well as Madigan, who nodded and patted him gently on the shoulder.

"I'm here for you, Sal," she whispered and sipped her vodka. "Whatever you need from me, let me know, and I'll do my best to help you. But I can't do that if you shut me out."

He nodded. "I'm not...shutting you out. I simply don't understand the changes myself or if there even are changes to talk about at all. I...need time to think it through before I can address it with someone else, if that makes sense."

She nodded and leaned closer to place another kiss on his lips before she wandered to the little tent she shared with him. He drew in a deep breath, shook his head, and tried to get rid of the annoying chill that ran down his spine as he pushed from his seat and drained the last of the vodka.

Of course, it would have no effect on him. It had been a while since any alcohol had any effect on him, but that didn't keep him from making the attempt anyway. He sauntered to where it looked like Davis and Gregor were already in the process of sleeping it off and left his glass where the Russian would find it before he went to the tent where Madigan had already fallen asleep.

Before he drifted off, however, he pulled his private pad out and called up the file in which he recorded his ongoing changes. He drew a deep breath and nodded before he created a new sub folder titled *Psychological Changes.* That done, he settled beside her and allowed sleep to claim him.

CHAPTER SEVEN

<u>*Philadelphia*</u>

It had been a long day. Not stressful since she did—even if it was only barely—have all her ducks in a row in time for the marathon of meetings she was dragged into. The real problem was the sheer volume of them where she had to listen to people say the same thing over and over again.

She'd lost count of how many times she'd heard the same issues repeated like variations of the same theme. Yes, the stocks would be sold. Yes, it was because of the death of the former CEO, who had been in jail for fraud as well as a hundred other smaller infractions. Pegasus had already disavowed the man who had made more than enough of the kinds of enemies who would rather he was shot in the head a couple of times than risk him talking to the feds.

The fact that she had to deliver a story she knew was bullshit simply made it all a little more exhausting. She missed Sal and she missed Madigan and Anja. She would never admit it, but she missed Connie too, and Amanda. All her Heavy Metal folks, if truth be told.

Damn it, she even missed the Zoo. This was a bad case of reverse homesickness and she didn't like it.

No, wait, it wasn't bullshit, Courtney thought as she packed her shit in her office before her trip to the apartment Pegasus kept ready for her in case she visited. Carlson had made an enemy of Savage as well as the people who employed the operative, which happened to be her and Anderson. Yeah, sure, the fact that it was technically true made everything better for some fucking reason.

She didn't want to return to the apartment. It was pleasant and it had a decent view and was close access to all the places she might want to order from if she didn't feel like cooking. Someone had told her she should hire someone to make her meals for her, but she doubted she would stick around long enough to make that a viable investment of her time and money.

A similar location existed in LA for when she decided to visit what had been her father's company, given that she'd sold the house. Knowing someone had killed him in those walls had ruined what once was home for her, and it hadn't taken much soul-searching before she decided to simply put it on the market. It had sold quickly, thanks to the reduced price and elevated security, which left her with a comfortable little nest egg in a savings account should she ever decide to find a home in the country where she could live permanently.

That was her looking ahead, assuming she would be around long enough to need a place for herself. There were other issues to consider—like would Sal live with her?

Maybe she would live with him? Would Madigan live there with them or would they all have separate living arrangements?

She, Sal, and Madigan needed to define and refine the kind of situation they were in. It was mostly based on the fact that they didn't assume they would survive for much longer, and the whole "love the one you're with" was a lifestyle they could live by. But now that they had accumulated responsibilities outside the Zoo, it raised the question of what came next, rather than who.

Her phone rang as she reached the elevator. The caller ID told her that it was Amanda's new number—the one Anja had set the woman up with after she moved away from the facility. It had become an emptier place without the armorer's constant arguing with Connie the AI.

"Hey, girl," she answered, unable to keep a small smile from her lips as the elevator doors closed behind her. "How's life on the French Base? How's Bev?"

"Bev's great, and the French Base is okay, if a little boring," Amanda said and sounded bored too. "I had Madigan and Anja here on the weekend. They said Sal is up and about and they're planning another trip into the Zoo."

"What?" she snapped and scowled at her reflection in the mirrored wall. "He's not ready for that."

"Oh." The other woman grunted softly. "So they didn't tell you?"

Courtney somehow already knew what Madigan and Sal hadn't told her, but she had to get it out there. "What didn't they tell me?"

"Your Russian friend Gregor called for help. He said Sal

owed him for bringing a team in to help him out of the trouble he was in," the armorer explained and sounded uncomfortable that she was the one to share this news with her. "Anyway, Sal and Madigan headed into the Zoo with a smallish team earlier today to meet the Russians inside. Madigan filled me in on the details yesterday. I assumed they'd told you about it too."

She wondered if it was a bad thing that this was already the second time this month she thought she would kill Sal. While she hadn't meant it then and definitely didn't now, the man was impossible to deal with, damn it. And with his PhD in hand, she knew he would become even more impossible as time went by. She really needed to talk to him about this—and maybe, hopefully, get him to take care of himself.

"Are you still there, Courtney love?" Amanda asked. That sounded like something Madigan would come up with, she thought with a quirk of her bottom lip.

"Yep, still here," she grumbled, shook her head, and rubbed her temple. "I'm simply wondering what the most creative way would be to kill Sal that would also show my annoyance with him."

"I'm reasonably sure the Zoo will do your work for you," her friend pointed out.

Courtney shook her head. "Nope. Have you seen him in the Zoo? The guy's a monster. I'm not even kidding about that."

"Ah...well, what makes you think you'd be able to kill him in person if the Zoo can't do it?"

"Well, I'd be able to move in close and get him to turn his back," she replied matter of factly.

"I'm, like…seventy-five percent sure you're joking right now." Amanda chuckled nervously.

"Good call," she grumbled. "I'm totally joking. Totally not even a little serious."

"Okay, it dropped to sixty percent."

"I'd better hang up before it drops below fifty percent and you go ahead and warn Sal about my totally joking intentions." She laughed. "Thanks for the update, Amanda. If you could, drop me a line when they get back."

"I have your back, girl," the armorer said but still sounded worried. "You be careful there in Philly."

"I'm never careful," Courtney quipped as the elevator doors opened again and she stepped into the lobby. "I have people for that. Take care, Amanda."

The line cut out as she hesitated and surveyed the number of board members who were still in the building, supposedly waiting for their vehicles to be brought up from the parking lot. They apparently kept themselves occupied with various calls in the meantime but watched her as she moved to the front desk.

"Hey, Mark, right?" she asked and noticed that the volume of the voices had dropped substantially. From what she had been able to see with a quick glance, they were all secretly buying up what few shares they could through shell corporations which would, when the sales were complete, quietly transfer those same shares to their own names. There were a few ways to do that legally and all the rest were illegal, so she did take the time to ask Anja to keep an eye on them to make sure none of them tried to gain an advantage the illegal way.

Pegasus didn't need any more bad press at this point.

"Yes, ma'am," the tall, bulky security guard at the front desk said with a nod. "Will you need your car?"

"If it's not too much trouble," Courtney replied with a small smile and handed her keys to the man, who took them and passed them in turn to one of the young valets who hovered in the background. He moved quickly to the service elevator in the back. She couldn't see it but her paranoia had prompted her to examine the building's schematics and, with Anja's help a few months before, keep track of the people who worked there. It would take the valet a maximum of five minutes to get her car up. Any longer, and she would suspect something.

There were times when she wondered if she was too suspicious of her surroundings. Then she would remind herself that she had survived more attempts on her life than most people did in three or four lifetimes and told herself that paranoia kept her alive.

It was also one of the reasons why she refused an armed escort. Anderson had tried to dissuade her—as he always did—but she'd proven how capable she was of defending herself. Besides, they were in a lull. It would take time for their enemy, whoever they were, to regroup after their recent losses and by the time they did, she would be far away and back in the Zoo.

The car was outside in three minutes and established once and for all that if anyone wanted to try anything with her vehicle, they would have to be really fast about it. She didn't know if that was for the better or for the worse, but she couldn't do anything about it now, so she took her keys from the valet and stepped into the vehicle. Of course, she could have had someone drive her around like an invalid, but what kind of message would that send? Carlson could be driven around however he liked, but for her and for now, people needed to see that she handled herself with confidence.

Besides that, she really didn't like being driven anywhere. It was something that came from the time before she was all paranoid about shit. She merely liked to drive herself when she could. Madigan was always better at driving the Hammerheads on the base so she let the woman do that when the opportunity arose for them to leave the Heavy Metal facility together. When it was only her, though, she was more than capable of driving those big bastards.

Courtney pulled away from the Pegasus building and enjoyed the Jaguar's deft handling. The lightest touch to the gas pedal hurtled her down the road at a higher speed than she'd intended, and she'd fortunately spent a few hours over the past few days getting used to it. Driving was a good way to unwind, she realized, and after today, she really needed it.

She pulled out into the road toward the interstate and turned the radio on. It wasn't set to any channel in particular, but it had to be music and play almost constantly. It wasn't that long a drive to her apartment, but she had decided on the scenic route to enjoy the highway all the way home.

"Life is a highway," she sang quietly as she turned onto the access lane. "I'm gonna ride it all night looong…if you're going my—son of a bitch!"

Her exclamation came at the point when she was about to ease onto the interstate and a large, heavy SUV pulled in front of her and cut her off. The driver braked hard in his attempt to avoid the water barrels that were supposed to protect him from the concrete cinderblocks that separated the road from the accessway to the interstate.

Courtney was forced to brake sharply as well and the tires screeched to an almost complete halt, but she narrowly avoided a collision with the massive vehicle. The driver didn't even pause to make sure everything was okay and simply accelerated again as it continued to the interstate.

"Asshole," she muttered and leaned a few times on the horn of her overpriced vehicle. Her car stalled and she cursed as she restarted and resumed her journey a little shakily. She'd almost slid into the groove of her favorite driving song when the Chevy in front of her braked abruptly again and blocked the entire width of the accessway.

Alarm bells triggered noisily in her head and she twisted to look over her shoulder. Another car—a silver sedan this time—swung in to stop at an angle and blocked the entrance behind her. She unbuckled her belt in response as a line of cars began to pull up beyond the sedan and a cacophony of horns erupted from people who were in a hurry to reach their destinations.

Their haste vanished when a group of five men exited the car. All toted pistols and sub-machine guns and fired a few rounds in the air to emphasize their point. The alarm bells were confirmed at this point, but it was already too late. The trap was closed, she was caught, and she simply waited for the hunters to close in.

But be damned if she would let them take or kill her

without one hell of a fight, Courtney decided. She ducked behind the wheel as another group of gunmen spilled from the SUV. They were in an elevated position, which didn't bode well for her, even if the dashboard on the Jag was raised compared to other vehicles. It gave her some semblance of cover, anyway, although it would only last for a few minutes, if that.

It would have to do. She shielded her head as the glass shattered and covered her in shards. Prone as she was, it was easy to reach over to the glove compartment on the other side. She yanked it open and retrieved a pistol from inside—a Walther PPS Anderson had put into it when she'd arrived. It was smaller, fitted her hand easier without the comfort of a suit, and was reportedly able to withstand anything up to and possibly even a nuclear blast and still be able to fire.

The only downside was that it had a comparatively small mag, with seven rounds plus one in the chamber. There were a couple of extra mags stashed inside, so she snatched those as well and placed them on the passenger seat of the car.

The next item on the list was one of Anja's earbuds, placed there by Anderson too. Stupidly, she hadn't thought to put it in before she left the Pegasus building—so much for her capabilities. It was sheer arrogance to ignore what was simple common sense. Courtney knew having someone of the Russian's particular set of skills would always be handy in a fight like this. She shoved it into her ear and peered through the gun's witness opening to make sure there was a round in the chamber.

"Anja?" she yelled to be heard over the gunfire that peppered her insanely expensive car. "Are you there?"

"What?" the Russian asked. "New phone, who is this?"

"This is not the time, Anja!" she almost roared and flattened herself even further in the car seat to protect herself from the glass that erupted from the other windows.

"Right, what seems to be the problem?" the hacker asked and sounded far too upbeat. She supposed the woman was tracking to find her based on her phone's location. It didn't take very long, and a wide selection of traffic cams gave her a very clear view of what was going on.

Thank you, Big Brother.

"Do I need to spell it out for you or would you like a wooden box?" she demanded and immediately wondered where that had come from. Lord of the Rings? How the hell had it come to this, anyway? Had she hung around Sal too much and some of his nerdiness had rubbed off on her, along with a couple of other things? That was as likely a possibility as her watching those films, much less reading the books.

"Nope, I have the full picture," Anja said softly. "Are you armed? Ready for a fight? Anything like that?"

"I have a Walther PPS with eight rounds and two more seven-round mags," she said quickly and checked again. She wasn't sure if it would be enough. These guys were causing one hell of a ruckus, which would have to draw the police sooner rather than later. Of course, she would have to still be alive for that to be relevant.

"Okay, I'll map an escape route for you, but first things first. You'll have to deal with that hunky hunk of a man coming up on the driver side window," Anja said. Courtney twisted hastily to adjust her aim and narrowed her eyes. She could barely see him from her awkward angle with her vision half-obscured by the hood—which she supposed she should call a "bonnet" since the car's makers were based in Britain.

Weird thought to have at this point. Get with the program. She raised her weapon to train its sights on the man who moved beside her vehicle and into clear view. He'd apparently forgotten to check the windshield as he came closer, his eyes probably trained on the side window. She would make him pay for the mistake, she decided as she pulled the trigger.

The confines of the car made the noise from the comparatively small weapon worse than it would have been otherwise, and her ears rang uncomfortably as she pulled the trigger twice. The man dropped, although she couldn't confirm the kill yet. She avoided the temptation to peek out the window since that would get her shot as well. A small hint of red spray on the windshield frame was enough to tell her that she had scored a hit, though.

She had no time to gloat since she needed to take advantage of the fact that her attackers suddenly scrambled for cover. A quick glance out of the now missing rear window confirmed that the men behind her hid behind their vehicle.

"Operator!" Courtney yelled as she shoved the Jag into reverse and pounded her foot into the accelerator. "Get me the hell out of here."

"Matrix reference, nice," the hacker grunted. "First off, get out from being boxed in there."

She pulled her belt around her and held onto it as she

MICHAEL TODD & MICHAEL ANDERLE

twisted the car to hammer rear-first into the tail of the sedan. A couple of rounds pinged off the side of the Jag but none made it through the aluminum exterior. This indicated that softer rounds were used, and she took the chance and sat hunched over while she maintained her pressure on the accelerator until she was clear of the vehicle and back on the road she had tried to get off of. Thankfully, the motorists behind them had, for once, opted to rubberneck from a much safer distance and had eased back from the gunfight. This allowed her enough space to careen to freedom, although there were a few close calls and instinctive horn-blowing from alarmed drivers.

Now free from the trap, she straightened fully behind the dash, took aim, and pulled the trigger of the little PPS until the slider came back and stayed there. It didn't look like she had hit any of them, although a few sprawled on the asphalt, possibly the victims of the impact from their car when she'd forced it aside on her way to freedom. She ignored the chorus of car horns that erupted indignantly before her attackers regrouped with determined intent. The commuters would be too busy ducking behind their dashboards to make much more of a fuss.

"Get on the opposite side of the road and head into Philly," Anja said and sounded more serious now. "From what I can hear, there's noise on the police channels on the topic of shots fired in your area, so you should have backup from the boys in blue before too long."

Courtney didn't have the time to respond as she spun the nimble car into a one-eighty turn by pulling the handbrake and releasing it almost instantly when her vehicle came about to face the way from which she had come. She was already too far away to allow the men in the other cars to shoot with any degree of accuracy. They stopped altogether and scrambled into their vehicles.

"Where am I going?" she asked as she glanced back to see the Sedan and then the SUV pull out on the road after her. These guys didn't appear to care that police were on their way, which meant they were either very motivated or very stupid. Or maybe both, for all she knew.

"Anderson, Terry, Sam, and Savage are all at Savage's place watching a game," the hacker explained. "They should be able to hold the attackers off for you until the cops show up."

"Good plan." They'd all let their guard down, obviously, but it definitely helped that the operatives would be at the same location when she needed them. Grimly, she pressed the accelerator on the Jag to the floor. She wasn't sure if it was only the adrenaline pumping through her body like jet fuel or if one of the rounds fired at her had damaged the motor somehow, but the sports car didn't accelerate in the way she thought it would in a combat situation.

The speedometer showed that she had pushed past sixty miles per hour and knocked on the door of seventy, so it might only be her. Either way, she could see she hadn't shaken her two pursuers. They hadn't gained on her, but they hadn't fallen back either. Worse, she had no indication as to whether these were the only people involved in the attack.

Either way, she needed reinforcements and soon.

CHAPTER EIGHT

Philadelphia: Savage's Apartment

It was a tough game. The damn Patriots gave the Seahawks a hard time in Seattle and led to considerable ribbing from Sam, which made Savage and Anderson miserable. The defense played appallingly, although both teams exchanged touchdowns to be elated and disheartened in turn as time went by.

Savage was a Seahawks fan, of course, with Anderson more for the Eagles. Terry appeared to not have any preference, but he cheered against the Patriots anyway. Everyone hated the team these days. Except for Patriots fans, he supposed. And Sam. She was annoying enough to be a fan, he thought with a nod as he headed to the fridge for more beers for the group during a commercial break at the beginning of the third quarter.

"So, why do all of you hate the Pats if none of you cheer for the same team?" Sam asked when he returned.

"You know how everyone seems to hate Manchester United in the UK?" Anderson asked.

"Ah, so you hate them because they win all the time?" She looked a little smug.

"Not really," Savage interjected quickly. "They used to win all the time but not so much anymore. They hate the reminder."

"It seems like they're winning now, though." She grinned cheekily and took a sip of her beer. "You might need to see the ICU because you just got burned, laddie."

"Yeah, yeah, we'll see," he grumbled and settled into his seat. "We still have twenty-five minutes left in the game. We'll see who laughs last."

"A quick preview—I'll be laughing, that's who." Sam chuckled. He didn't think she understood enough of the game to comment on it like this, but trash-talking was as old as sports and he liked to think he was as good at handing it out as he was at taking it. There was no need to be a poor sport about it, after all.

"Ping for the US Heavy Metal team," Anja said into his earpiece. "US Heavy Metal team, please respond."

"I thought we were Team Savage," Sam commented as she looked up curiously. From the way everyone in the room suddenly came to attention at the same time and their gazes swung away from the TV screen and lost focus, he could tell they all wore their earpieces and listened to what Anja said on the line.

"What the hell is Heavy Metal?" he asked, his eyes narrowed.

"The name of the company Courtney helped to found," Anderson explained and set his glass down on the side table. "Out in the Zoo. The team Anja is still a part of."

"You're all Heavy Metal. That's the point," the Russian

interrupted quickly. "Will you ask me why the hell I've interrupted game time? 'Please, do tell us, Anja, because what we're talking about totally doesn't matter by comparison.'"

"That was a terrible Sam impression," Savage protested.

"Excuse you, it was clearly supposed to be Anderson," Sam replied quickly.

"I don't have a high pitch like that," Anderson said defensively.

"Well, Anja clearly can't meet the low pitch necessary." Terry chuckled. "Other than that, clearly an Anderson impression."

"You guys are doing it again," Anja snapped. "We have a developing situation I need your help with."

"Sorry, Anja," the former colonel responded and audibly altered his pitch and tone. "Go ahead."

"Courtney was involved in a gunfight while she was on her way home from the Pegasus building." She spoke quickly and in a serious tone. "She's managed to escape the trap, but she still has people on her tail. The cops are on their way, but she might need backup, so I'm sending her to you."

The light mood in the room evaporated instantly when the news was delivered. Savage was the first to react. He shoved from his seat and left his beer, still full and cold out of the fridge, and strode into his bedroom. Less than a minute later, he returned with a large duffel bag in his hands.

"Dammit," he muttered darkly. "We fucked up. Someone should have been with her."

"I tried," Anderson reminded him. "You know Courtney. She was convinced she had it all under control."

"Yeah, and we all stupidly assumed that Molina woman would hold off for a while and lay low." The operative scowled and unzipped the bag. "That's what we get for being too complacent and full of ourselves. Winning one battle doesn't fucking mean the war is over."

"We'll be ready for them, Anja," Anderson said.

"Not to be the infamous Captain Obvious or anything," Terry said. "But if someone's gunning for Courtney, the chances are they'll have you in their sights too, Anderson."

"A good point," the ex-colonel admitted and glanced at the other team members.

"Yes, it is." Savage retrieved an under-shoulder holster from inside the bag first and strapped it on. "What about your family?"

"I dropped them with a friend on my way here. The husband's ex-military. I'll message him and if need be, he can call in a few of his buddies to watch over them."

The operative nodded. "How far out is Courtney from our position, Anja?"

"About five minutes, maybe less," she replied quickly.

"Well, we need to have someone on Anderson, just in case," he said, thinking quickly as he hauled the weapons out from inside the bag and laid them on the coffee table in the center of the room. "Sam, that's you. We have to assume that if they do attack, they know we're all here.

"My guess is they'll rely on us being relaxed and maybe a little too drunk to respond effectively. Still, it means they'll send a larger team to be able to take care of all of us. I'll go down to the street to give Courtney ground cover.

Terry, do you mind giving both teams long-distance assistance?"

"It's what I do, even if it is with a pea-shooter," the sniper grouched as he selected the smaller rifle with a scope mounted on it. The rounds were spread on the table as well, and Sam and Anderson had a choice between a shotgun, a Glock handgun, and a couple of 1911 .45s. Sam, unsurprisingly, already had a weapon, but she picked the shotgun up, loaded it quickly, and packed the ammo in her pocket for quick access. Anderson did not have anything on him, and he started with the Glock. Terry stuck with the rifle and loaded it rapidly and smoothly as he got to know the unfamiliar weapon.

"Are we all good with the plan?" Savage asked as he checked his needle-gun and primed it for the first shot.

"It's as good as we'll get," Anderson replied. "Good luck, everyone."

The operative nodded, ready for the fight, and kept his gun in hand as he pulled the front door open and indicated to the others that it was clear. No one waited in the hallway as yet, although if Terry was right and someone had targeted Anderson as well, he doubted that would be true for long. If he ran a two-pronged attack like this, he would make sure they were coordinated down to the second so one didn't have the opportunity to warn the other, as had happened in missions before.

Then again, with as many variables involved in striking two well-placed members of a Fortune Five-Hundred company, he supposed they would be lucky to succeed with two hits on the same day. Hopefully, they would be

MICHAEL TODD & MICHAEL ANDERLE

unaware that the team had forewarning and would be ready and waiting.

Satisfied that his team was happy with their weapons, he shoved everything else into the bag, moved out into the hallway, and waited for someone to close and lock it behind him before he strode toward the elevator. After a second thought, he realized the stairs were probably a better choice. Anyone heading up to his floor would most likely use the elevator. He could move to intercept them, but he thought better of it. There were too many problems with fighting in or around an elevator, and his job was to protect Courtney, after all.

Then again, the enemy could have two teams—one heading up the stairs, and another on the elevators—to ensure their target didn't slip by them. Given the numbers he anticipated, it would make sense.

Either way, it would be better to engage them on a stairwell than in an open hallway or isolated elevator, especially on his own. Besides, he still had about...three minutes to reach the street, maybe less. He could do with the extra exercise.

Savage descended quickly and took the steps two at a time. Speed could be dangerous, but the days of him getting yelled at for running down the stairs were long gone.

He moved rapidly, but when he was about three floors down, doors were flung open below him and heavy boots pounded up the stairwell. There wasn't much banter between the group of about four, maybe five. With the distortion in the narrow space, it was hard to tell. He couldn't see them from where he was, but he slowed his steps and tried to gauge where the best position for a defensive stand would be.

The top of the steps, he decided after a moment and stepped into the slight cover provided by the turn at the landing. He waited with his weapon ready as the thump of boots grew closer.

Patiently, he allowed the first man to step fully into view and another to move in behind before he pulled the trigger. The suppressed sound of the weapon made sure they didn't notice they were under attack until the man at the front doubled over when three needles rocketed into his midsection, through his body armor, and ventilated the soft flesh beneath.

Savage pivoted slightly and tried to catch the second man as he pulled back into cover on their half-landing. He thought he'd caught one of the men on the shoulder before they disappeared, but he couldn't be sure. A second later, one of them pushed a sub-machine gun around the corner and fired blindly.

With a weapon shooting that rapidly in these tight conditions, it was only a matter of time before one of the rounds found him. He had no desire to wait around for that to happen and he ducked behind cover again as the wall behind him suddenly became a Jackson Pollock painting of spats on white paint.

No, that was a terrible analogy, he thought and shook his head at the stupidity of it. A break in the firefight spurred him to follow the example of the previous shooter and his blind barrage persisted until they retaliated again.

Anderson checked the Glock Savage had loaned him for the duration of this emergency. He'd been in firefights fairly recently but rarely had the time to prepare for them beforehand. They had all been desperate, kill-or-be-killed scenarios. He wasn't sure if the wait would make the situation easier or more difficult. It meant they had time to plot and prepare, but the anticipation of someone coming to kill them made him exceedingly jittery.

He decided knowing about an impending attack and having time to prepare was definitely better. Terry, with the rifle in hand, stepped out the window onto the steel fire escape that hung off the side of the building. It gave him a decent view of the road Anja said Courtney would arrive on, a clear view of the apartment door, and cover in case anyone attacked through there. He was fucked if anyone wanted to try to shoot him from below, though, at least where cover was concerned. Hopefully, for anything that wasn't a rifle, the range would be too great for accurate targeting.

The sniper fiddled with the dials on the scope as Sam positioned herself behind the front door, her shotgun loaded and ready, and indicated for Anderson to make his way behind the small bar that separated the living room from the kitchen.

"I have eyes on SUVs and cars parked illegally outside the building, so it appears someone's already here to kill you, Anderson," Terry shouted through the open window.

"Fan-fucking-tastic." The ex-colonel growled his irritation and shivered with the chill that always rippled through his system when the adrenaline surged. "Anja, shouldn't you have called the police by now?"

"Already done, Anderson," she replied. "But you guys might want to think about getting your weapons out of sight before they get there. None of those are licensed and I'm sure they have their serial numbers shaved off."

"We'll cross that bridge when we get there," Sam retorted and rolled her shoulders.

"Hey, guys, I found a small group in the stairwell," Savage warned them over the comms. "I'll hold them up for the moment, but you might want to prepare for another team from the elevator, just in case—no, what the fuck? Get back inside—now!"

"What?" Sam asked and narrowed her eyes.

"I'm reasonably sure he wasn't talking to us," Anderson replied.

"No shit." She sounded annoyed. "I merely wondered who the fuck he was talking to and if they actually listened to him. I assume it's not his attackers."

"My attackers, technically," the former colonel corrected with a smirk. "And yeah, that's a safe assumption. As is that of another team coming up in the elevator. They would want to make sure there's no way for their prey to slip their net and would cover all points of egress. And they're might also already be aware that we know about the attack if they have comms like we do."

"No offense, but no one in the world has comms like we do." Anja sounded deeply offended by the comparison. "I'll have you know that the earbuds you wear are independently linked to a satellite connection, the code of which I created from scratch to allow for all members of the team who wear them to be able to connect across the planet in a matter of microseconds. Who are the people with that kind of technology? The FSB, the NSA, and me. Who was able to get all the tech pieces together to make a top-of-the-line comms system that works all around the world? Me. That's it."

"Okay, fair enough," Anderson grumbled. "You're the absolute best."

"Technically, the Patriots are the absolute best," Sam pointed out and directed his attention to the TV, where the named team had scored another touchdown. They had left it on to create the impression that they weren't expecting an attack.

"Shut the fuck up, Sam," he retorted and shook his head. She sliced her hand quickly across her throat to prompt him to silence and gestured toward the slit under the door. Shadows suddenly broke the light outside, and he nodded and trained his weapon toward it. He assumed he could simply fire at them through the barrier, but he had no idea if and what kind of reinforcement the operative had installed and he didn't want to use their element of surprise until he had a clear shot.

Sam dropped to a crouch near the door and tilted her head in an effort to determine what the invaders had planned. She didn't need to get that close, he realized, as even he could hear the metallic click on the other side. They were placing shaped charges on the barrier and intended to blow their way in. Her cover would be short-lived, along with her if she didn't move.

She spun away from her position, sprinted to the bar where Anderson currently hid, and indicated in passing for Terry to cover the entrance for her. Thinking fast, she snatched the duffel bag as she slid into her new position.

The couch wouldn't provide adequate cover, and the bar was the only place in the room that would enable her to still be a part of the fight.

These were the kinds of thoughts that went through the minds of professionals every second, Anderson realized with a small smile and ducked behind their tenuous shield as she settled quickly beside him. He didn't like combat from a theoretical standpoint, and he'd had the time to decide he was actually something of a pacifist that way. But there weren't many highs in the world that compared with the sudden need to defend yourself and everything that was yours and being adequately trained and equipped to do so.

He had missed this, he acknowledged and covered his ears a split second before the shaped charges on the door detonated.

The whole room flashed brightly, and his ears rang even with the protection his hands had provided. Smoke and dust filled the air.

Terry already had his rifle trained on the entrance, looked through the scope despite the shorter distance than what he was used to, and pulled the trigger. The small rifle cracked and the distinctive thump of a body on the floor confirmed that his shot had struck home.

Anderson had positioned himself to fire around the edge of the bar and left Sam to take the top for the moment. The door itself still seemed intact, warped and bent though it was, which confirmed that he was right and Savage had put work into his home fortifications. There was no real surprise there, of course. Paranoia should have been the middle of his intentionally chosen name. The explosives had done a number on it, though, and effectively separated it from the wall. It clattered heavily when it fell.

Terry's target lay prone, dead and with half the back of his head missing. The man wore body armor—it looked like a chest piece of Kevlar or maybe ceramic plates, but they hadn't thought to equip their people with helmets. Or maybe they couldn't, given that they assaulted a civilian residence.

Either way, it was something they would be able to take advantage of. Sam had already launched into action, hauled herself up from where she crouched behind the bar, her shotgun in hand, and pulled the trigger in the same moment that she stood. The range was in her favor, of course. The man who entered next was barely five feet away from her when he was battered by the swarm of pellets. His head snapped to the side and he collapsed without a sound.

The other attackers hesitated as if suddenly rethinking their original strategy to try to take their target and all his friends by surprise. Anderson wondered what kind of intel they had been given and if they had been told that three or four highly trained operatives would be waiting for them, knowing they were coming, and they decided to attack anyway. It was a good question. Who would be stupid enough to try that? Of course, as Savage had suggested, they might have assumed they'd catch them under the influence and unable to mount a good defense.

Maybe their intel was shit? Whatever quality it might or might not have been, he knew they would quickly determine that they needed a plan B. He aimed and fired, and his bullet caught one of them in the chest. The others backed hastily away from the door. His target's body armor absorbed the strike, but it would still hurt like hell. He knew from both experience as well as from the shouted expletive from the hallway.

"That's right bitches, you'd better run!" Sam yelled after them and ducked when they directed a volley of return fire into the room. Terry found cover under the window, and Anderson hid behind the bar until the burst had stopped. She took another shot at the fuckers and peppered the walls and what was left of the door frame before she hunkered behind the bar again to avoid the frenzied barrage that followed.

Fun times. Anderson chuckled softly despite the gravity of the situation.

"What are you laughing at?" Sam shouted over the clatter of gunfire.

"I thought about how crazy our lives are," he replied, still chuckling. "And how much crazier they'll probably get."

"Talk about crazy..." She grinned manically at him before she bolted upright for her next attempt but scrambled back before she could get another shot off. Another attacker now launched a determined assault from behind the barrier of the ruined door. "That's kind of my middle name."

CHAPTER NINE

<u>*Philadelphia: Savage's Apartment*</u>

Savage growled in frustration as his warning to his team was cut off. Someone from one of the surrounding apartments had come out to see what all the commotion was about—a character with a man-bun and a very long beard—but when he saw the guns and the battle that raged in the stairwell, he wisely decided to retreat. Hopefully, he locked his door for good measure.

"Fucking hipster," he muttered and resisted the urge to check the ammo in his revolver. "You hear gunfire and shouting, and you decide now is the time to take out the trash?"

It wasn't likely that the man had tried to take the trash out, but the idea was the same. People tended to make the worst decisions in times like these, but so far, no one had decided to be a hero and try to put things right with the weapon they took to the range three or four times a month. He wondered if it was too much to ask that they would continue to not do stupid things and call the police instead. It wasn't often that he wanted the cops to come and help, but at this point, he preferred to deal with them rather than whoever these attackers were.

They were well-trained enough to be a significant problem. Savage was pinned on the landing of the second floor of his building and they overlapped their firing patterns to ensure that he wouldn't have any opportunity to fire with any real accuracy. Then again, they were caught in a similar situation and unable to move any higher on the staircase without abandoning the only protection they had. He wondered if they knew he didn't have to stop to reload his weapon. Probably not, but could he use that against them?

He'd have to see, wouldn't he?

Explosions upstairs were rapidly followed by a violent exchange of gunfire, and he could only assume he held up the people who were supposed to reinforce the team that was already upstairs. It was his job, after all—to run inter-ference—but things had got a little too close to him lately, and he wasn't sure he liked it.

"If you guys wreck my house too much, I will hunt you all to clean the mess up," he warned through the comms, knowing they wouldn't answer given that they had their attention focused on the fight for their lives. It wouldn't be an easy one. Savage knew that much. The fact that they'd had some prior warning had been enough to give them a chance, but they were still outnumbered, outgunned, and now fought on the defensive. They needed to go on the attack.

He needed to go on the attack. Savage rolled his shoulders and dragged in a deep breath as he heard tentative footsteps start up the stairs. He curled his arm around the edge of the wall and fired a couple of shots until he heard the group below him scramble for cover again. Despite the small measure of satisfaction that brought, he was fairly certain he didn't hit any of them. He was only playing for time, of course, and would need to devise something solid in order to get the men out of his path. Courtney was only minutes away, and while Terry could provide some cover from above, if they still had a hold on the room up there, it was always best to have another gun on the ground too.

First things first, he needed to get past the group half a flight of stairs below him. He was almost certain there were only three of them but there might as well be a hundred if he couldn't fire cleanly around the corner without getting shot. Their concerted assault came too close for comfort and chipped away at the corners of the wall he hid behind.

The gun battle continued upstairs, although he was too far away to identify what might be happening with any certainty. Besides, he needed to focus on his troubles. Savage cursed loudly and banged around as if searching for more ammo. As weak as the bait was, the men were as desperate to get upstairs as he was to get down, and it wasn't long before one of them made another effort to ascend.

He flattened himself against the wall and took another deep breath as the footsteps inched closer toward the top. A pro would hug the wall to minimize the opportunity for anyone on the other side of the cover to reach them. Another would follow close behind at a crouch and use his comrade as a shield in case they were caught off guard.

He'd have his hand on the first man's shoulder to keep them aware of the other's presence, and the last man would hold his position at the bottom of the steps, ready to provide blanket fire should they need to beat a hasty retreat.

They would need to retreat if they lived long enough. Either way, he would make sure they didn't get far.

He thrust his weapon forward and aimed blindly at where he would have been had he been the man on the staircase, pulled the trigger three times, and spun into the open, hugging tightly to the wall.

The man in front fell back with three visible holes in his body armor. Savage moved quickly and used the first man as his own kind of human shield as he pulled the trigger again and attempted to eliminate the man behind. He missed but tackled the dead man down the steps and toppled his comrade too. They tumbled ten steps down, but it was enough to make the impact hard to absorb, even with the two men he brought down with him to provide cushioning for the fall.

Pain shafted through his shoulder and into his ribs as he twisted toward the last invader. The third man at the bottom of the stairs was already pulling the trigger on his sub-machine gun as he lowered it to aim at him.

The operative was quicker, though, and delivered a needle through the man's kneecap. His attacker fell and screamed in pain and he kicked the weapon out of his hands, rolled off the two men he had tackled down the stairs, and pulled the trigger twice. It wasn't a difficult shot, even though he was still on his side, which made the angle a little awkward.

He reminded himself that the fight wasn't over, though. The attacker caught below his dead teammate was still alive, as evidenced by his ability to reach out and grab his gun hand by the wrist. The man pushed it up and away from him at the very moment that it fired and two of the deadly needles pierced the ceiling. For an odd moment, Savage wondered if the needles would keep going and possibly hit someone on the other side, but he was brought back to reality when a gloved fist hammered into his jaw and bowled him back. He took hold of his attacker's hand as the man tried to turn to grasp his neck.

Both opponents growled with frustration as they struggled for control, hindered by the body trapped between them.

"Fuck!" Savage roared, pivoted, and used the leverage of the wall behind him to heave them both clear of the corpse. The combatants rolled together to the other side of the half-landing.

They reached their feet at almost the same time and instinctively, each clutched the hand of the other that held a firearm. The adversaries were evenly matched, both in physical power and technical mastery, but Savage had a very clear advantage. Two, if he really thought about it. Firstly, his weapon was far lighter and smaller and required less maneuvering into a firing position.

The second was that he had his back to a wall. The other man had his back to a flight of stairs.

He abandoned his hold on the man's weapon and let it swing wildly as he raised his foot and brought it down hard on his opponent's knee. A soft crack was followed by a piercing scream. He twisted in place, locked his arm

113

around the merc's gun hand, and snapped his head forward to crunch into his nose before he yanked the weapon clear hard enough to pound his elbow into the suddenly panicked gunman's jaw.

With his opponent off balance and held in place only by the strap of his sub-machine gun, Savage shoved him hard enough that while his strap didn't break, he whiplashed to where it wasn't over his shoulder anymore, and he fell head-first into the top step behind him. He was out immediately, unconscious and possibly dead judging by the blood that trailed behind him as he rolled to the last landing.

His adversaries eliminated, he took a moment to make sure he wasn't too badly injured. A bruise on his cheek and some aches around his shoulder and ribs, both still sensitive from his lifetime of hard work, seemed to be the only issues. *Mostly all right*, he mused and jogged down the steps to where the man lay face down.

"Let the team up in the apartment know the stairway is clear if they have the opportunity to escort Anderson out," he instructed into his comms as he checked the sub-machine gun he'd pulled off the man. He punched two needles into his head, just in case, and tucked the pistol into the holster when he decided that any shooting he would have to take care of on the ground level would need more firepower.

"Will do," Anja said. She sounded distracted, possibly because she was coordinating a rescue op for Monroe. "Courtney should arrive at your location in less than a minute, and I don't see you on the ground, Savage."

"I was temporarily held up," he muttered and picked up the pace to get down to the ground floor.

"Excuses, excuses." She chuckled, and he shook his head.

Sam understood what Anderson was going through. Well, she'd never been in those particular circumstances herself, but she could empathize, at least. The man was in a difficult position. He was trained and armed for a fight like this, but the reality of the situation was that these men had targeted him for a reason that had to be fairly obvious at this point.

They either wanted control of Pegasus or they wanted Courtney and Anderson out of the driver's seat of the company. Since getting them out legally could be tied up in litigation for years and years, the quickest and simplest way was to simply erase them from the picture. They'd tried to do it subtly before, but it seemed like there was now some desperation in the enemy camp and that a hint of a time element had come into play.

Either way, it didn't matter what Anderson wanted and he could help to protect the apartment and fight their attackers off. He was their ultimate target and they would focus their fire on him once they realized where he was in the room. The circumstances relegated him to the position every operative in the world hated the most—the package.

She glanced at him and identified the frustration etched clearly on his face. While she could empathize, there wouldn't ever be a time when she would wish to change places with him. The choices were clear, and he had to stay safe so Ivy and Damon could see him again, no matter how helpless and frustrated he felt. He would have to suck it up and wait this one out, which was the most difficult thing for people of action to do.

"Savage cleared the stairs and he's headed down," Anja announced in their earpieces. "He said if you guys want to get Anderson out of there—"

Sam didn't respond and simply let the burst one of their attackers fired through the door say what needed to be said.

"Right." The hacker grunted. "Well, anyway, I have an eye on Courtney, and she should arrive there in thirty seconds if traffic holds as is. That woman can drive, but I wouldn't recommend any of you get in the car with her when she's in that kind of mood."

Sam shook her head and while she waited for Anja to get back on topic, propped her shotgun over the top of the bar and released a couple of shots at the door to keep their attackers at bay.

"Anyway," the other woman grumbled, "I think she'd like to have some help from on high until Savage can get his lazy ass down there. Terry, do you think you can cover that?"

"I'm on it," the sniper said softly and displayed the cool collectedness Sam had come to expect from the man when he was under fire. He also implicitly trusted his two team-mates inside to watch his back while he watched Monroe's.

Well, she wouldn't let him down. She would never live it down if she did.

"In other news, it looks like someone actively worked

to keep the cops away from our little fun in the sun here," the Russian informed them, and the clatter of her keyboard provided a busy soundtrack in the background. "I finally have a couple of cars heading your way. They should be a couple more minutes, though, so hang in there."

Yeah, right. Sam wasn't the kind to wait around and let someone else—much less the fuzz—come in and rescue her. Besides, Terry was counting on her to keep the enemy off his back and away from Anderson. That was her responsibility, not some badge's.

She muttered a few choice curses as she reloaded the shotgun with what few shells she still had on hand. Six left, plus one still in the chamber, gave her a total of seven. It would have to be enough, she decided as she fumbled in Savage's duffel bag and ferreted around until she found what she was looking for.

Stun grenades—also called flashbangs by the kind of people who would call guns "boomsticks"—were first used by the SAS in the 1970s and were interesting ordnance. Their flash was intended to activate all the eye's photoreceptors and leave the victims temporarily blinded and with an inhibiting afterimage that affected their aiming capabilities. The other half was a bang louder than a hundred and seventy decibels, enough to deafen anyone in range and, if you were close enough to disturb the fluid in the inner ear, make them lose their balance.

As non-lethal weapons went, they were one of her favorites, right up there with bean-bag shotgun rounds.

She pulled the pin and lobbed the stun grenade over her shoulder, then waited and listened for it to clatter on the floor before she covered her ears quickly and closed her eyes.

Even through her hands, the noise was deafening, and the flash was still bright through her closed eyes. It was enough protection to leave her somewhat untouched by the effects and she hefted her shotgun and vaulted over the top of the bar. Two of their attackers had been unlucky enough to try to breach the room at the same moment she'd thrown it, which made them easy pickings. She pulled the trigger three times and they collapsed quickly before they could see who had opened fire on them.

The remaining three appeared to realize they were under attack and tried to return fire. All three missed with their first bursts, which either pounded into the wall or through the window to rain glass on Terry. Hopefully, he'd escaped injury as all she heard from him was a muttered something that sounded like "fudging idiots."

She grinned and eliminated a third man with another shot before she was forced into cover behind the wall. A quick count put her down to three shells left. It was probably enough to deal with the two of them, but maybe not. The odds were close to even and she wasn't there to play games of chance with her life and those of the people around her. She dropped the weapon and immediately reached down to draw the HK45, which she'd holstered on her hip.

One of the two remaining men had obviously heard the clatter of the shotgun and barreled in before she had the weapon ready. It was a smart move on his part, or it would have been had he not still been recovering from the flash-bang. He looked into the room, missed her completely, and pushed past her as she drew her pistol. Sam extended a foot and tripped him but another pair of hands from outside caught her gun hand and her shoulder and hauled her clear of the room.

Anderson would have to take care of the poor dumbass she'd left behind for him.

Sam had a more pressing engagement. She was thrown clear of the room and her back impacted with the wall on the other side of the hallway. Her instinctual response was to grasp the barrel of the sub-machine gun the man still had in his hands. She wondered why he hadn't simply shot her with it, but there were times when you didn't look metaphorical gift horses in their metaphorical mouths.

Her assailant looked powerfully built, a little too large to be one of the special forces guys—those teams usually went for lean and mean. Engineers and drill sergeants were the ones who liked to have that much bulk on them, which begged the question of what exactly he was doing there.

Well, there'd be time for that later. She ducked below the fist he powered at her. He was definitely not a well-trained individual, so was probably the kind who knew he had power over most of the people he fought and didn't see much use for training beyond that. To punch someone with their back to the wall was a rookie move, though, and when she simply evaded the blow, his fist collided with the concrete wall hard enough that she heard a couple of cracks from his bones. He uttered a scream of pain, retreated a few steps, and cradled his hand.

Sam acted before he thought to swing his weapon to bear on her. She followed his small retreat, raised her foot quickly, and stamped as powerfully as she could on the gunner's instep. He lost his balance and barely managed to catch it using the wall of Savage's apartment for support.

Her adversary grunted softly and looked around, obviously still disoriented although he tried to fight. She knew that if he recovered sufficiently and she gave him the opportunity, his sheer size and weight put her at a disadvantage, and he would overpower her. In a rapid motion, she punched the barrel of her pistol into the man's throat and as he choked for a second, she used a backhand strike to hit him in the temple with the grip of the gun. His eyes rolled back, and he sank slowly into a heap. A small trickle of blood oozed from where she'd struck him.

She paused for a second, still breathing heavily at the short yet strenuous exertion of the fight, and glanced around the hallway to make sure he didn't have any friends coming to help him anytime soon. Savage had done his part and eliminated his half of the group on his own, but there was no need to get too arrogant at this point of the mission. In her line of work, it was almost inevitable that she'd take a bullet at some point, but she would damn well do her best to make sure it never came down to a shot in the back because she'd been in too much of a hurry to clear a room or something totally dumb like that.

When she stepped into Savage's living room again, her gun in hand, and swept the room, the man she had tripped still lay face-down, two holes in the back of his head from which blood seeped into the carpet.

"Savage will definitely not like this," Anderson grumbled and checked the Glock in his hands a couple of times.

"Yeah," Sam responded. "I'm sure Pegasus will be able to pay to refurbish this place."

"Hell, at this point, it will be cheaper to get him a new apartment," he replied.

"If you guys aren't too busy," Terry called in that chillingly calm voice of his, "I have Courtney in my sights and would appreciate a little peace and quiet out here."

"Sorry." She gave the room one last casual scrutiny and headed into the hallway where she'd left the thug she'd pistol-whipped. He was still unconscious but alive, judging by the way his chest rose and fell slowly. Hell, if it weren't for the bruising on his throat and the swelling starting to show on his temple, she might have been able to say he was taking a quick nap.

Then again, people napping didn't usually sleep heavily enough for them to not wake when they were dragged into the apartment.

"Savage, where are you?" Terry asked over the comms as Sam placed the unconscious man against the couch. "We're about to have some action out here and I think you should be a part of it."

"I'm already out here," he confirmed.

The sniper didn't respond, but as she moved to the broken window, it was obvious that his mind was already elsewhere. The longest shot he could anticipate here couldn't be more than five hundred yards, which child's play for a man of Terry's caliber. At the same time, though, he was shooting with a smaller, unfamiliar hunting rifle. While he was good, there were still many variables for someone in his position to plan for. Too many, Sam would have thought.

"I have eyes on bogeys heading in behind Courtney," he said, his voice still in the low, distant tone as he stared down the scope and with a pause in his breath, squeezed the trigger.

The rifle boomed and kicked hard against his shoulder, but he kept it propped on the railing of the fire escape. He had crouched and hunched over in order to keep the shot steady, which looked like a very uncomfortable position to be in.

He cursed softly, which indicated, even though she couldn't see where he had aimed, that his first shot had gone awry. While he whispered the changes he needed to make to himself, he drew the bolt action back and thrust it forward again, loaded another round into the chamber mechanically, and pulled the trigger again. No curse followed this time, merely another quick and practiced reloading action and a shot in rapid succession.

CHAPTER TEN

Anja did her best to keep her boss updated on what was happening around Anderson but also tried not to distract the woman from what she had to do. Talking on the phone while driving was never a good idea under any circumstances. The hacker had to assume that the thought extended to when you drove aggressively to escape people with guns who pursued you with every intention to use those guns, even if it was using the earbud comms. A distraction remained exactly that and could be as deadly.

It was a challenging endeavor for Courtney to wind her way through the city as the traffic gradually intensified with the onset of the rush hour. She had originally hoped to get home before there was a horde of cars all headed onto the streets with the same intention. So much for that idea, and now, she was forced even deeper into the city to where Savage lived in the hopes that the team would be in a position to help her when she arrived.

For a little while, it had been touch and go. The route

Anja led her on traversed streets of the city she was unfamiliar with. All the while, she heard and—in some instances, felt—gunshots as her pursuers seemed to almost sense where she would turn next. On top of all this, she tried to keep up with what was happening in the building.

Apparently, these people had thought to deliver a solid double-whammy against Pegasus and planned to eliminate her and Anderson in one two-pronged assault. She had to assume it was the mysterious client Savage had been tasked to track. In all fairness, he probably hadn't had the time to even start on it yet. There was the possibility that someone else was behind this, of course. They had made their fair share of enemies during the process of taking control of Pegasus and even simply from working in the Zoo as both she and Anderson had done.

But no. It had to be this Elena Molina chick, right? Having to trace someone else who tried to kill them was too exhausting a thought to even contemplate. All Courtney had to do was escape this situation alive, and she could delegate all the work of hunting and punishing the guilty parties involved in this mess. She couldn't be blamed, either, for heading out to the Zoo where she had a fully functional fortress between her and anyone who might want her dead.

Someone had painted a very large target on her back, after all, and unless the board members wanted their stock prices to fall further this close to the sale of Carlson's stocks, they would want to make sure the company CEO didn't suddenly drop dead from a suspicious case of lead poisoning.

A lane opened and allowed her to slip through the jam that held most of the city at a slow crawl. She pushed forward quickly but had to stop again soon after. The only real bright side she could think of right now was the fact that her attackers were caught in the same traffic. The police would be heavily stalled in their attempt to intercede as well, though, which was a dark side on a bright side.

She instinctively uttered a low scream at the sound of gunfire again. More bullets peppered her Jag and glass from the last remaining backseat window sprayed across the vehicle. Something stung and blood dripped on her arm and she grimaced as she looked to see what it was. The injury wasn't bad and could have been from glass or a grazing bullet. Next time, she vowed, she would invest in a car with bullet-proof glass and reinforced sides so she wouldn't have to deal with these problems.

The reason for the Jag had simply been that she'd always liked the car. When Pegasus offered her a choice of vehicles to be rented for her stay in Philly, Courtney had selected a car she had wanted to drive since she was a little girl. And it had been everything she dreamed it would be right up to the point when people decided to use it for target practice.

"Fucking assholes!" She scowled out her window. A couple of her attackers had taken advantage of the stalled traffic to move forward on foot. It was a smart move, or it would have been if they had managed to hit her. As it was, they were left stranded on the sidewalk with no cover and no way to find any in a hurry.

She aimed her pistol and fired through the window opening, the glass long since removed by the first barrage on the access ramp. One of the men stumbled back and clutched his chest where she had delivered a bullet into his body armor. The second dove to the ground and crawled toward the cars. People screamed and yelled in reaction to the gunfire exchanged between the two parties. Most tried to get out of the way and to be cautious as well. In their confusion, they could as easily run into the shooting while trying to avoid it.

With that said, the dumb bastards who had missed her did give her a good idea. The Jag was a fairly small car with a decent suspension—the kind that would be able to take the punishment of driving up onto the sidewalk. She could only hope there was enough space between the traffic and the buildings to allow her to get ahead of her attackers. There would be the small problem of the lights and poles that were placed on the sidewalk too, but she could cross that bridge when she got to it.

Courtney immediately eased the vehicle up the curb and pressed the accelerator as the powerful engine roared to bring her fully onto the sidewalk. It jostled and bounced, then settled, and she increased speed. While she still moved at under twenty miles an hour, it was faster than the five miles an hour the rest of the traffic was stuck at. People honked at her for cheating, and she flipped them off. *Yell at me when you're getting your ass shot at, fucker.*

In their defense, the fuckers did shut the hell up when the sound of gunfire resumed again. The SUV was too large to fit on the sidewalk and she couldn't see it in the traffic anymore, but the sedan was small enough to allow it to come after her. They paused to pick up their man who was still on the ground.

He rubbed furiously at his body armor, most likely to coax feeling back into his chest after her shot, but he scrambled in and they remained determined in their pursuit. It was impossible to move quickly on the sidewalk, but it was better than simply waiting around for her assailants to devise newer and better ways to get close to her and complete their mission. She was well aware that she wouldn't get the deposit on the car back, that much was certain.

Courtney praised the traffic gods when she saw it had begun to ease farther ahead. She continued in the direction Anja had told her to go although she didn't know Philly that well and relied mostly on mapping apps to help her navigate through the city. Of course, her first engagement had destroyed the screen that had guided her over the past few days, which meant she was essentially driving blind without Anja's help. The hacker had fallen silent for the past few minutes and likely had to help the team in Savage's building to keep Anderson alive. Not knowing about what was happening there was another issue that played on her last damn nerve.

She yanked the vehicle onto the road, floored the accelerator, and put as much distance between herself and the sedan as she could.

"Courtney, how are you doing out there?" Anja asked as she finally returned to the earbud.

"Oh, yeah, I'm doing just dandy," she snarked, sarcasm getting the better of her for the moment, but she suddenly lacked the energy to follow through with it. She had been exhausted and done with her day before the attack and it had gone on for what felt like forever. She didn't have to look at her watch to know it was far less than that, but who gave a damn?

In other words, she was too tired to be sarcastic. She'd never thought the day would ever come, but there she was. In all honesty, she was as surprised as Anja probably was, waiting for the punchline to her starter.

She sighed, glanced into her rearview mirror—which somehow remained miraculously intact—and cursed when the SUV pulled into the almost empty street behind her. They'd been stuck in traffic, but perhaps they'd found a handy side street that enabled them to catch up to her. The tires screeched loudly and yet another fusillade of bullets was unleashed. None of them hit the Jag, though, for which she was eternally grateful.

"My car's fucked up," Courtney said and scowled as she looked around the vehicle. "I don't have windows anymore, and the body is doing its best swiss cheese impression. The engine's holding so I don't think it sustained major damage, but it seems sluggish, and I don't think it'll go much faster than this. Please give me some good news from Anderson's team."

"Savage cleared a team on their way up through the stairwell. Sam, Anderson, and Terry dealt with a second team from the elevator that attacked the apartment," the hacker explained. "Terry has a view of the outside, so once you pull onto the road in front of Savage's building, you'll have someone watching over you from above."

Courtney nodded and tried to coax a little more speed from the vehicle, but she had already slowed a little and she'd pressed the accelerator as far as it could go. Something was definitely wrong, although she had no clue what it might be. All she knew was that it was not what she needed at that moment.

"You need to take the next left, by the way," Anja said suddenly. Her gaze snapped to the turn that was less than a hundred feet away.

"That left?" she asked.

"I can't see what you're pointing at, but I assume yes since I did say the next fucking left," the Russian snapped. It sounded like she was a little stressed by all this trouble as well.

Just let her be the one who has bullets flying around. She honestly didn't feel particularly charitable toward the woman as she had to release the accelerator and apply the brakes enough for her to yank the wheel without flipping the car. Tire smoke rose behind her, but she managed to turn hard left and slipped into the skinny two-lane road in front of Savage's apartment building.

"I have eyes on Courtney." She felt somewhat reassured to hear the chilling voice of Terry, the sniper. She couldn't see him and had no idea where he was supposed to be, but if he had eyes on her that quickly, she could only hope he would direct lead downrange to the people in pursuit.

The Jag coughed and backfired in quick succession, which cost her acceleration. It had slowed to a top speed of about thirty miles an hour, and that figure lowered rapidly.

"Shit, shit, shit," Courtney cursed with a wild glance behind her. The SUV entered the street first. It had handling issues when it turned into the narrow street, but the man behind the wheel looked like he knew what he was doing.

The loud crack of a rifle from above brought a surge of hope, but it had no effect on the vehicle careening toward her. Terry obviously had difficulty aiming, and this seriously wasn't the best time for that. She muttered another few choice curses, raised her pistol, and pulled the trigger three times. Only two bullets were fired, though, and the last trigger pull clicked empty.

Behind her, the SUV continued at the same relentless pace.

"Fuck!" She hissed her frustration and fumbled for her last mag. It was almost impossible to retrieve it without taking her foot off the accelerator or moving her gaze from her attackers.

Only seconds later—although it felt like years—a second shot rang out, followed closely by another. A large hole appeared in the SUV's windshield exactly where the driver would be, and the vehicle jerked and shuddered. She assumed others had managed to grab the wheel to maintain some kind of control, and the massive car drew slowly to a halt in front of a light post.

None of the men inside showed any intention to exit their vehicle. They obviously knew the tables had turned, and they were the hunted now. There was no point in being picked off by someone who clearly had the height and distance advantage on them. Courtney liked to think they were simply hiding inside their car, huddled together while they prayed that Terry didn't take any more shots at them.

He didn't, which made her wonder why until she saw

the sedan turn into the street as well. The message of a sniper in the area was passed on seconds too late, apparently. The car stopped with a squeal of tires and began to reverse when another snapped shot from Terry opened a hole through the windshield of that vehicle too and brought it to an abrupt halt. No one wanted to make a move, it seemed, or to risk having their asses shot by a man with a rifle from however far away he was.

The sonsofbitches were actually hiding, she thought as she finally stopped the Jag outside the building Anja had directed her to. Of course, from what she heard over the comms, it sounded like Pegasus would have to find somewhere for Savage to live after this—somewhere a little less accessible to the riffraff and wannabe assassins.

The guy had earned it, she decided.

She turned carefully to see what was happening with her attackers. Terry didn't appear to have any clear line of sight on anyone inside and had decided against shooting the people who were in there. Instead, he chose to put a couple of rounds into the engine blocks of both vehicles. If the men wanted to get out of the situation, they would have to do so with him perfectly positioned to eliminated them one by one from above.

Courtney wondered what she should do in this case. There was the option of simply staying in the car until everything was resolved and the cops arrived. She could play the damsel in distress and hopefully get their sympathy on her side. Somehow, she doubted anyone would believe that once the footage of what she'd done was reviewed. *Fuck that.*

She could also head into the building to check on her

people. There were still gunners inside the cars, but they weren't going anywhere and seemed to have the fight knocked out of them for now. Let Terry keep them in place until the cops arrived and arrested them. No...she didn't like that.

Honestly, what she really wanted was to get in there and pump the last seven rounds of her Walther PPS into the assholes who had made her day far more exhausting and stressful than it needed to be.

Someone stepped out of the building. He was little more than a shadow at first and made his way carefully over the ice and snow that had started to collect on the sidewalk. Courtney aimed her weapon at him, half-expecting one of the men who had attacked the building, but as he stooped to peek into the mostly ruined car, Savage's familiar face prompted her to lower her weapon.

"Are you okay?" he asked. He didn't look at her but kept his gaze on the cars full of killers. "Did they injure you at all?"

"Only a scratch on my arm. I'm fine," she said quickly. "How's Anderson?"

"He and the others are fine." She realized with some surprise that he held a sub-machinegun similar to those she'd seen her attackers carrying. The expensive H&K MP5s could have been a part of his arsenal, although the more likely scenario was that he had filched it from one of the men he'd killed. "Do you have any idea how many attackers are in there?"

"Ummm..." Courtney took a minute to quickly run through those who were probably dead at this point. "I tagged a couple of them during my escape and caught another one in the chest, but they're wearing body armor. Terry took two more, and my guess would be five men per car, so…six? Maybe seven."

Savage nodded and checked the weapon in his hands and how full the magazine was. It was apparently an acceptable number of bullets as he snapped the mag in again and made sure there was a round in the chamber.

"You stay there," he commanded. "When the coast is clear, get up to the apartment. Anja said you should meet with the folks there and go over your cover story for when the cops get here."

"And what will you do?" she asked, her eyes narrowed.

"Get rid of these motherfuckers," he said with an almost crazed grin. "That's my job, isn't it?"

It was, but she suddenly didn't feel comfortable unleashing him on the men who had, until a minute ago, tried to kill her. The man looked downright possessed in a way that made her— no stranger to violence of all types— feel a little uncomfortable. He strode to the cars and started with the SUV since it was the closest. The operative raised the sub-machine gun and opened fire. It was set to three-round bursts, and he brought it up to what looked like full auto after a couple of volleys. Courtney lost count of the rounds, but the extended mag she could see on the weapon told her that it probably had around thirty or forty rounds, maybe less if he'd taken it from one of his victims.

He continued to fire until the mag was empty, and he dropped the weapon carelessly. Apparently, he hadn't thought to collect extras from his downed opponents. He wasn't left completely weaponless, though, she realized when he drew what looked like a revolver with an extended barrel. He pulled the new weapon's trigger a few times with none of the signs of conventional bullets and no loud gunshot either. It looked different too.

"It must be one of ours," she muttered and hauled herself clear of the ruined Jag. Logic told her to go upstairs but she was unable to tear herself away as Savage proceeded to peer cautiously into the SUV. He moved carefully and remained low to keep from being shot by anyone inside. He peered over the top, saw someone who was still alive, and crouched again as he pulled the trigger five or six times without needing to reload. Holes drilled into the body of the SUV. When he checked the back seat again, he looked more relaxed but still delivered a couple of the rounds—or whatever the weapon fired—into the car for good measure.

One of the men in the sedan realized what was happening to their comrades and opened the door. He looked like he would rather put up a fight instead of simply sitting around, waiting to be killed. Savage raised his weapon to deal with him, but a solid crack from above beat him to it. The man's head exploded out the back and he fell as blood and brains painted the white snow around him in gory red.

Another seemed to have the same idea, but when he saw what happened to his teammate, he tried to duck quickly into the car. Savage turned his weapon toward him and fired three shots with calm precision. Courtney knew they had at least wounded the man since he fell on the sidewalk without bothering to close the door.

Rude, she thought with a small smirk and turned away as a combination of shots from above and the operative's silenced revolver eliminated the last man inside. With that, an eerie silence descended before the sounds of sirens gradually seeped in and drew ever closer. She didn't look forward to having to deal with the cops, but it was a necessary evil since the entire shootout had happened in the open. Why their attackers had thought that was a good idea was beyond her.

Not that it hadn't almost worked. She was sure almost any other business executive in the world would have had a much harder time of it if they'd been caught alone and without security backup. It made her wonder if these mercs simply weren't told that they would attack someone who had her and Anderson's kind of experience and muscle. Of course, it was equally possible that they did know and merely had no clue how to handle them.

Either way, it was something to think about. For later.

Courtney jogged to the elevator and brushed off the glass that had collected on her clothes, careful not to cut herself. There were a few bruises and cuts that she didn't remember getting. The adrenaline now started to fade, and she became more acutely aware of the pain and stress her body had been under, but this was far from over.

The aftermath and mopping up would be as stressful in a different way. She stepped into the elevator and tried not to look like she needed a week-long nap and instead, focused on Anja's hasty explanation of the story they'd concocted for the authorities. The elevator dinged when she reached the floor where Savage's apartment was located.

There was no mistaking the place. Bullet holes scarred the walls and the acrid smell of cordite filled the air as she hurried toward the one apartment on the floor that had a hole where the doorway was supposed to be.

When she stepped inside, Sam knelt beside one of the attackers. He looked more than a little the worse for wear, bruised and beaten up, but he was conscious and alive for the moment as the woman searched him quickly.

A hint of movement made Courtney spin and aim her weapon toward the corner of the room where Anderson, still covering the entrance with a small grin, raised his hands in mock surrender.

"Nice to see you alive, Anderson," she said with a chuckle, lowered her weapon hastily, and eased her finger off the trigger.

"Right back at you," he said and moved from the bar area. The apartment was completely trashed. The bullet holes on almost every wall made it difficult to determine where the damage caused by the attackers ended and where Savage's own destructive attitude began. She had heard from Anderson that the man had suffered a depressed streak after he'd dealt with Carlson, which made her feel a little bad for laying into him in the meeting earlier in the day.

He had rebounded rather admirably, as she recalled, and had laid into the men in the cars like it was a cathartic experience. And maybe it was, for him.

In the meantime, Sam fiddled with a phone she had snagged from the single survivor of the attackers and plugged a small device into it—probably on Anja's orders. Which reminded her of what they needed to do.

"Right, then," Courtney said briskly and looked at the group, including Terry, who climbed in through what was left of the window. "Is everyone clear on the story we'll sell to the cops?"

They all nodded. She made a note to give Terry a raise for his work today in saving her ass. Hell, they all deserved raises, and so did she. The sirens were close, though, so all thoughts of remuneration were yet another something they would have to deal with later.

CHAPTER ELEVEN

The Zoo

Finally, this felt more like the Zoo he knew and had a love-hate relationship with. More monsters now raced around and roared their hatred for the fact that humans intruded into their territory. That definitely felt more like what the animals should have done rather than simply watching the team make their way through without putting up even a token resistance. It begged the question of why they had taken it easy on the humans until this point and if they finally intended to make up for that lazy attitude.

That said, Sal instantly started to miss not having to deal with monsters that charged at him through the dense jungle every ten seconds. There would have been a time when attacks of this magnitude would have been enough to make people have second thoughts about delving too deeply into the damned jungle. Even the pros would have told them to take their time, form up, and keep moving. These days, any attacks that weren't launched in such awe-inspiring, crap-inducing waves of sheer numbers that you actually couldn't miss—even if you sprayed and prayed with your eyes closed—was a survivable attack.

Walk it off, soldier. Wait until the real attacks hit you.

His earlier unease and irritation at the sense that the Zoo was behaving out of character notwithstanding, he had to admit it had been useful. These attacks, although more in keeping with the true nature of the alien jungle, seriously slowed their progress, and they were on a clock. With the Russians making up most of the numbers of their group, Sal and Kennedy elected to be a part of the spearhead formation at the front to hold the line against the creatures that attacked them from all sides.

His skills with a gun could not be denied. However, he was still no match for the calm, steady precision she claimed. There wasn't much flash in her style, but he chalked that up to her military discipline or something like that. For him, he had to make sure there was pizazz to what he did. Even among the Russians, people had come to expect that from him. They'd seen the videos, filmed both by himself and his teammates, that showed him performing death-defying stunts in the name of getting rid of the bigger and badder monsters in the area.

He was well aware that it wouldn't last and that eventually, he would run into a monster that wised up to his antics. But until then, he would keep at it and have fun while he did so.

Kennedy ducked to let her assault rifle reload. The sheer size of the weapon and the number of bullets contained in the massive magazines meant it took a hot second. While she had the rocket launchers and minigun mounted on her shoulders, Sal still had to step in and cover where she was shooting. The group that attacked them looked like they were all but finished and knowing that, decided they would push in harder and faster. It meant this was their last push—a final stand, as it were.

He maintained fire and noticed a couple of panthers barrel in through the hole he had left when he stepped forward. Still firing, he drew the sword he carried on his back with his free hand. He'd persuaded Amanda to add improvements to the weapon to make it what she called a vibro-sword—she said that it was a *Star Wars* reference, and it made him a little pissed-off that he'd missed it—that was far more effective than your regular piece of sharp metal. It was plugged into the pack that powered his suit and vibrated the blade between three micrometers of space and several thousand times per minute when he took hold of it.

Sal had gone over the basics of the technology use, even though he didn't know much about engineering or the kind of tech that would have to go into something like this to make it work, but the point remained. With the blade moving like that, he was able to cut through virtually anything like the world was made of butter and he held a hot knife.

The fact that he tested this new weapon out in the field where it could end up not working was worrisome, but even without the vibrations, it would still function as an effective melee weapon. He pushed the thought aside and stepped forward to stop the panthers in their tracks. His suit's software took control of firing at the other monsters, while he swung the blade up and down in quick succession

MICHAEL TODD & MICHAEL ANDERLE

and aimed at the creature's neck. After the first moment of doubt, he was glad to have it.

Aside from a hint of red spray, the blade worked like a dream. He barely felt any resistance from the monster's muscles and bones as the head fell away and the body writhed in its death throes.

The second seemed almost as surprised as he was by the new weapon, but it snarled, peeled its lips back to show its fangs gleaming with venom as it leapt up to one of the nearby trees, and immediately pounced on him. He raised his weapon again and swiped it to cut into the animal's midsection before it could try to sink its fangs through his suit. Again, almost no resistance hindered the strike, and a hint of red sprayed as he cut the creature in half.

Madigan, loaded and ready to fight again, looked surprised too.

"Amanda's work?" she asked, and he nodded in response.

"Oh yeah." He chuckled and turned the blade off before he slid it into the sheath on his back. "I'm starting to have serious second thoughts about letting her walk away from Heavy Metal the way she did."

"You didn't let her do anything," she reminded him as they regrouped and performed a quick headcount to make sure they hadn't lost anyone during the attack. "She made the decision to follow her heart to be with a woman who might be the one for her. I don't think there's anything you could have done to change her mind."

Sal shrugged. "I could have at least made a token effort to persuade her to stay. Maybe pushed her with a small guilt trip or offered her more money. Or both. Something. Honestly, the woman has serious skills."

"On that we can agree." She smirked but their conversation was cut short when the earth vibrated ominously. Gone was the time when he might have thought it was an earthquake. Now, he knew full well the vibrations were caused by one of the larger creatures thundering toward them. Maybe the humans were a little too close to its home and they wouldn't allow them any farther.

Or maybe the Zoo itself told the creature to do it. He still didn't know what really motivated any of the mutants, least of all the enormous monsters. What he did know was that it was on its way and they needed to be ready for it.

He checked on the motion sensors for a moment, long enough to be able to identify what approached. They had begun to be used more and more in the Zoo, and he couldn't understand why. Of course, they were fucking huge and the horns at the front of their heads and the opposable thumbs made their attacks more powerful and allowed them to move faster, although they were still too large to be able to climb trees.

The huge gorilla-like creatures with rhino horns protruding from their heads still had no real name. There was a scientific name, of course—*Gorillini Rhinocerotidae* since the people who named these critters had absolutely no imagination. At the same time, it was better than anything he had been able to come up with. Rhinorilla was the best he'd managed thus far. Unless he wanted to try something directed more toward King Kong? That might have potential.

Sal took his cue from the panther he'd split in two and

powered the jumpers in his suit to enable him to leap into one of the nearby trees. He made it out of the way easily as the creature lumbered into view and shoved a few of the nearby trunks aside to make a path for itself.

It uttered an ear-splitting roar when it saw the humans, who immediately fired at it. Madigan launched a couple of rockets from her shoulder mounts and guided the creature to the tree he currently perched in and from which he peered down as it moved closer.

When it was directly below him, he used the jumpers again to thrust out of the tree and plummeted with his blade extended. The monster, its attention wholly focused on Madigan, was oblivious to his attack. The vibro-blade connected first and sliced smoothly through the thick fur, skin, and even the skull to find the brain beneath. He alighted abruptly on its shoulders, dwarfed by the sheer size of it, and balanced himself as it began its slow, ponderous fall.

The jarring impact caused a responsive tremor in the earth. He vaulted clear, rolled over his shoulder, and finished lightly on his feet. When he jogged to the team, he knew they were watching and nonchalantly deactivated his sword and slid it into its sheath.

Madigan was the only one who didn't seem transfixed by the entire action and instead of awe, offered her fist for him to bump. He did so with a cheeky grin.

"Showoff," she grumbled as he turned to collect the sacs of goop he knew could be found at the base of the creature's skull and which he had carefully avoided in his assault. Before they started moving again, Gregor felt the need to congratulate him on his efforts, which earned another eye-roll from Madigan.

"Seriously, there's no one else I know in the Zoo who is willing to do the crazy shit you do, Dr. Jacobs," the Russian said as Madigan jogged to catch up with them. "I mean it. If you weren't so serious about being a scientist and shit, I know—know, mind you—there would be huge potential for you in Russia making movies. You would be a star in weeks. Well, maybe months. You would need to learn Russian first."

"Come on, man," she complained and punched the man on the shoulder. "Why the hell are you making his head any bigger than it needs to be? It takes all the time I have to spare to make it smaller as is. I don't need you guys starting a fan club around here."

"If there were fan club, I would join," he responded with a laugh and eased his weapon into a more comfortable position. "Well, maybe not join, but I would attend meetings. Many people know about the legendary Heavy Metal team that is growing, by the looks of it, so you have a fan club too. That is something to keep in mind, I think."

"In all seriousness, though…" Sal chuckled. "Everything I learned about the Zoo and how to survive it and kill everything that gets in my way was taught to me by this woman here. If there's any fan club anywhere, she's the one who deserves it."

"Are you fucking kidding me?" She snorted. "I don't have time to have a club of any kind, and if I did, it wouldn't be about what I do in the Zoo."

He shrugged. "Well, you can consider me the founding member of that fan club. You won't even need to do any of the work. Well, you might have to sign autographs, but that's nothing for someone like you, right? Fifteen seconds out of the day here and there. And you get all the merch money."

"Well, if there's money in it for me, maybe I could spare more than fifteen seconds every other day," she acquiesced with a nod, which drew a loud laugh from Gregor as they continued their push toward the coordinates passed on to them by the FSB. Sal tried to forget the fact that those motherfuckers were involved in all this and to simply keep himself calm. This was about helping a friend, nothing more and nothing less.

Well, maybe about testing new toys too, but that was secondary. They could do both without compromising the main objective.

Once they reached the target area, though, there were innumerable signs to confirm that they had arrived in the correct location. A few trees had been cleared and defensive positions put in place which were already partly overgrown by the jungle. From what Sal knew the Zoo was capable of, the fact that the entire camp wasn't already overgrown by plants and trees said that whatever had happened there had been very recent.

"There—you see they were testing new comm systems for the Zoo," the Russian said and pointed out what appeared to have once been something like a satellite dish, although it too was almost reclaimed by the Zoo.

"We have bodies," Madigan said and called Sal to one of the corners of the camp.

"Bodies are right," he said softly and studied the group. He wasn't sure how many of them there were originally, but they had all been piled into this corner. Unless they wanted to dig through the vines that dragged the bodies—still in their combat suits—under the ground, they would have to limit their investigation to the few who were still on the surface.

He crouched beside the top one, narrowed his eyes, and traced his fingers over the suit. The metal had already begun to corrode in the way that only the armor could. Every time they came out, small repairs needed to be done where pieces had simply fallen off or oxidation had occurred at a speed that would have been unthinkable anywhere else in the world. The jungle itself had a horrifying effect on anything that entered it.

But the Zoo wasn't what had killed these men.

"Bullet holes," he said softly and indicated the grouping on the man's chest. He turned the body over and pointed out a larger wound corresponding with the holes on the front. "Armor-piercing rounds. Who the hell brings armor piercing rounds into the Zoo?"

"I've seen some specialists use them," Madigan said as she knelt beside him. "They interchange between shredders, hollow points, and armor-piercing to deal with the larger numbers and the bigger but softer targets or those with carapaces or some other kind of armor. But still... yeah, it's not that common around here, especially for teams who don't enter through the US base. Someone came out here specifically with the intention to use bullets designed to punch through hard armor."

"So...I guess this indisputably establishes the narrative of foul play, right?" he asked and raised an eyebrow as Gregor began to stride toward them.

"More to the point," she said, her head tilted in thought, "I would even say someone came in here specifically to target this group and take whatever they were testing."

"What makes you say that?" Gregor asked as he stepped close.

"The fact that the bodies all seem to be gunners," she pointed out. "As far as I can see, none of the specialists were killed in the shooting, and it's very likely they were taken captive and forced to go with the people who attacked them."

"And it looks like they have what they came here for and are making their way out already," the Russian said. "But they will move slow and will be easy to track."

"What makes you say tha—oh, right." Sal's question cut off when he realized that something huge—possibly a cube about ten feet squared and very heavy—had been dragged clear of the location.

"I don't suppose you'd know exactly what the research they worked on is, would you, Gregor?" Madigan asked and glanced at the team as they searched quickly through the campsite.

"I honestly don't know," he replied and shook his head. "But it was something that was apparently very interesting to the Russian government since they were willing to send a group out so quickly to make sure nothing was lost or went missing out here. Almost before we even knew there was a Russian team doing research. They didn't tell us what we were retrieving, only to retrieve it and not ask any questions."

"And here I thought we were all friends out here." Sal grunted, the protest tinged with derision.

"We are all friends in the Zoo, Dr. Jacobs," the other man said. He sounded less enthusiastic about their mission and the irrefutable evidence that they had something concrete to substantiate the rumor of foul play. "Which is why I hoped you would come. We need more friends like Heavy Metal around us if we plan to survive here for much longer."

"Agreed." Madigan growled with restrained anger and turned to the team. "Well, if we want to recover whatever the fuck we were sent for, we might as well get going. I don't think our quarry will have made it very far, given what they're transporting, but there's no telling what kind of head start they might have on us. Let's close that gap as quickly as possible."

The men and women in both the American and Russian groups galvanized into action and followed her orders quickly and without question.

CHAPTER TWELVE

The Zoo

They weren't being paid enough for this shit.

This was Pirlo's constant internal complaint, despite the fact that the remuneration was undeniably significant. For a week's work, they would receive what most of his team saw in their bank accounts over a whole year, all tax-free and ready to access the moment they set foot in their home countries.

For him, the number was more realistically placed at three or four times what he had made during his entire stint with the Italian military, simply to lead this group of idiots through one of the toughest terrains in the world. The purpose of the mission was to collect what had to be one of the most annoying packages of all time and bring it out of the Zoo and to the French base for delivery.

That said, he still wasn't being paid enough for this shit. He'd received most of his military assignments through his connections with *La Cosa Nostra*. The mafia organization had become so deeply entrenched in Italy, people had long since forgotten what it was like to live in the area without their backs watched by some of the most violent and well-connected criminals of all time. He had been born into a family full of those connections who had ensured that his father was elected as mayor of a small town in the south of the country, while his mother helped to run most of the illegal imports through the city's port.

They had sent him to the military to accumulate enough prestige to raise him into higher positions in the political hierarchy—with all the various honors associated with the status in store for him in what seemed to be a bright future. As it turned out, he was damn good at it all. People essentially forgot that living a life in which secrecy and violence were day-to-day occurrences turned young men like he had once been into the kind of cold-blooded killers needed in the military. He didn't complain. Once his terms were up, he elected to take another couple of tours, the last of which had been to make a few runs into the Zoo.

It had been a while before, but as he waited for his position to be selected based on where it would be the most beneficial to the families, an offer had come in. He could head into the Zoo with a highly trained team, retrieve a package and deliver it, and walk away with enough money for him to be able to go into business for himself.

Quite simply, it was a no-brainer. The families liked for their *capos* to be motivated and work creatively to acquire more money and influence without being told to do so. Having these kinds of connections outside the family couldn't hurt either. You never knew when you might need to suddenly and mysteriously disappear from the world for a few years.

He'd been in the area some six months before when the Italians considered opening a base of their own. Between then and now, the Zoo had become darker, heavier, and more violent. The monsters were more and more creative, and he assumed one had to be in and out of the jungle regularly to be able to keep up with the changes that took place on almost a daily basis.

What he liked least of all was that the changes went beyond simply the physical. Pirlo had entered the jungle with a group of thirty men. There were eighteen now, and a handful struggled to keep up due to serious injuries.

The monsters hadn't even attacked them that often. It was merely difficult to really predict what they would do next. The creatures seemed a little too intelligent for animals. Of course, they had been that way on his first couple of trips, but this was different. It went beyond intelligence like it was cold and calculating—even sinister.

Before he entered the Zoo almost a week before, he would have said it was impossible. But there they were, their ranks decimated by an enemy that slyly defied the conventions of what was possible. He wasn't too worried about the casualties, though. The client had told him that the fewer men who made it out of the Zoo alive, the bigger his bonus would be—to the tune of ten percent of what they would have paid the men who were dead.

He wasn't a monster and definitely wouldn't kill his own men merely for a bigger paycheck. But the fact remained that he worked with a group of professional assholes and therefore wouldn't lose much sleep over whether they made it home or not. Knowing he would be paid more simply to not care made it that much easier on his conscience. He knew none of these men would lose much sleep over him dying either.

They would all simply have to come to terms with it. As many people as they could get out would go home. He'd also made sure to hide the fact that he would be paid significantly more than they would, lest jealousy raise its nasty little green head. He wouldn't reject the notion that some might try to leave him behind with a couple of bullets in the back.

Part of his frustration stemmed from his ignorance. He didn't know who this client of theirs was or what they wanted with the big fucking cube they'd dragged through the Zoo for the past few days. If there was one thing he had learned from his time with *La Cosa Nostra*, though, it was to not ask questions. Not even about whatever banged continuously on the inside in an attempt to escape with enough strength to jolt and shift the cube itself.

Their intelligence had been good. They'd found the Russians at the coordinates they had been told to locate. It had made sense to kill them immediately as well as disarm those scientists whom they had managed to take alive. Thankfully, it had been all of them. It wasn't a matter of curiosity but rather prudency. They didn't want to know what their client was willing to pay upwards of three million euros to acquire, but if whatever they now transported somehow escaped or caused trouble, it only made sense to have someone on hand who at least knew what the hell it was.

Of course, they were also useful to help to move the cube. Back in his time inside the Zoo, the specialists whom they sent inside wore little more than glorified hazmat suits. These days, with the Zoo a much more dangerous place than ever before, they didn't mind giving even the geekiest in the geek squad enough power armor and weapons to allow them to defend themselves.

It hadn't helped when it came down to actually using said weapons, but it did allow them to move the cage on their own. That left Pirlo's team—or what was left of them anyway—to watch their surroundings and drive the Zoo creatures off while they inched closer and closer to where they had parked their Hammerheads.

He had wondered now and then whether he should have simply had his team do the heavy work since their stronger and more powerful suits would have brought them out of the jungle faster. Then again, trained soldiers would always complain if forced into manual labor when there were others who could do the work for them.

Besides, he could already see the light ahead had become a little brighter. That told him they were close to the final push beyond the confines of this fucking place, which meant it wouldn't be long before they all sat on one of the largest paydays of their collective careers.

With the end so close, he decided that it was perhaps easy money after all. Or as easy as money could be in the Zoo, he thought with a soft chuckle.

"*Che?*" one of the others asked, presumably about why he had laughed.

"It's nothing," he responded in English and shook his head. "We're close to the end of our little trek out here."

"And it can't be finished too soon," said one of the others, who sounded and looked like he was from Japan. The man still limped, having been bitten by one of the panther monsters. They had administered the antidote to the poison, but the animal had taken a chunk of his leg away with it before they managed to gun it down. It was the most expensive meal that son of a bitch would ever eat, Pirlo had thought at the time. And it was still funny, even now, although he decided not to share the humor.

He had originally asked the client why they would pay so much for this trip, and they had told him it was because they might run into trouble that didn't originate from the Zoo. It had seemed like an idiotic distinction. They were going into the Zoo so any of the dangers they might face would be from the Zoo, right? That was how it worked. Unless they had suggested that the group might run into trouble with someone at the bases. Either way, the French base was nowhere near organized enough to create any difficulties for the men they had brought, even with their depleted numbers and as wounded and tired as they were. Yes, indeed, easy money.

The thought of the end of the mission spurred the men into a final effort. They both dragged and pushed now, and the mercs began to help the scientists to get the cage out of the jungle quicker. Minutes ticked past and Pirlo decided the group could manage the cargo without him. He jogged ahead with a group of five others who obviously had the same idea. They didn't want to simply hang around and wait for their teammates to do what they had to do at a much slower pace.

The men stepped out into the sun after almost a week of being stuck under the cover of the trees. It felt like the first excursion outside after being indoors all winter when one could simply suck in that deep breath of fresh spring air. There were all kinds of negatives that came with it like hay fever and insects galore, but at least in this situation, he had left the jungle behind for good.

His analogy seemed a little disappointing after the reminder of reality, but he was honestly past caring. The sky overhead, bright blue and without a trace of cloud cover, was the most beautiful sight he'd seen that didn't involve the dimples above a woman's ass.

The sheer pleasure of the moment had distracted him to the point where it took him longer than he liked to admit to realize something was wrong. They had plotted their path carefully through the Zoo to make sure they didn't have to drag their prize out in the open. Having made it all the way to the perimeter, they didn't want to risk someone seeing it and trying to take it for themselves.

It meant they had spent a few more days out in the jungle, of course, but the end result was more than worth it. Their Hammerheads were there waiting for them, as expected, but not in the haphazard formation the mercs had left them in. They were all neatly arranged to form a half circle.

"*Cazzo.*" Pirlo growled and hefted his weapon as a group appeared over the top of the ATVs. Most of them apparently wore the same kind of armor as the Russians they had killed. They even carried mostly the same weapons—the kind that would take a few shots to break through the hardened armor the mercs had been supplied with. There were almost thirty of them, though, and they had better cover and the advantage of numbers over his team as well as the element of surprise.

The battle began before he could call for them to simply

surrender. He didn't care if the other mercs he was with lived or died, but he was at the front and dead center of the group now fired on from above, which meant he was squarely in the crossfire.

His survival instinct clicked in and he flung himself aside as the rest of his team emerged from the Zoo, ready for a fight. They immediately released a defensive barrage at their attackers but wasted most of their shots on the Hammerheads the group used for cover.

It wouldn't be enough, he noted, distracted by two figures who emerged from the jungle. Their armor was different than what the Russians used. One wore what looked like a tank that only lacked the tracks. A massive assault rifle was held in one hand, and the other appeared to be mainly used for melee attacks. Rocket launchers were mounted on both shoulders along with a mini-gun. They held back on using the rockets, something he could only feel grateful for.

The second figure was different, though. He wore a suit similar in weight and power as the scientists they had pulling the cage, but he moved much faster and with considerably more agility than he'd seen in the specialists. Either the Russians had held out on him or this suit was something of a hybrid between a combat suit and a specialist suit.

It didn't matter, though. The man held a powerful assault rifle in one hand and a fucking sword in the other. And not an ordinary sword either, Pirlo realized during his effort to scramble away as quickly as possible. The newcomer stepped into the fray, swung the blade easily, and decapitated one of the mercs before he snatched the weapon from his victim's hand.

"Okay, okay, fucking stop!" Pirlo shouted and used his suit's speakers to yell over the gunfire and screams of pain. "Just stop! We surrender. Drop your fucking weapons, you *bastardo idiotas!*"

The mercs did as they were told when they realized they were outnumbered, outgunned, and would be massacred if they continued to fight. Thankfully, the Russians and non-Russians understood the concept of surrender and ceased firing, although they kept their weapons trained on Pirlo and his men even though they had already dropped their weapons.

It was a good call, he thought as he tossed his weapon aside as well as his sidearm and the knife he had tucked into the back of his suit. Even without weapons, these were called combat suits for a reason. They could crush a man's skull with a single strike.

"Fucking hell," he said and shook his head as he pulled his helmet back and gazed at the scene. Five more of his men had been killed and a few more wounded. He doubted he would be paid since the Russians were probably there to reclaim their property, but he didn't really care about that. Another thing you learned when you worked with *La Cosa Nostra* was that there was no point in making money if you were too dead to spend it.

CHAPTER THIRTEEN

The Zoo

He wasn't really sure what he had expected to find, which meant Sal couldn't tell if he felt disappointed or not.

The group that had come out of the Zoo had been about on par with what he had anticipated with maybe a few differences. He had presumed they'd be a larger group, given the losses the Russian research team had taken. Although, from the look of the remaining mercs, they had started out with larger numbers and the Zoo had steadily chipped away at them until they were left with those he could see in front of him.

Only a few of them had the telltale bullet marks on their suits from where the Russians had defended themselves. There were fewer than one might have thought, although he supposed it could be chalked up to a surprise attack. Either way, these characters had given up fairly easily, which meant they were probably out there for the reason most other folks were willing to head into the Zoo —money.

They looked fairly competent and were very well-equipped to handle all the surprises the jungle could throw at them. What they weren't prepared for was a surprise attack orchestrated by humans who outnumbered and—in Sal, Madigan, and the rest of the Heavy Metal Team's case —outgunned them.

They were mercs, in this for the money, and there was no point in being loyal if it meant you wouldn't have a chance to spend the money. It was better to have a rep of giving up on impossible missions and stay alive than to have the rep of someone who took those impossible missions and died. People never remembered anyone in the second category anyway.

Sal could see it in their eyes. They wouldn't lose much sleep over being beaten like this. They were frustrated and none too happy that someone had the drop on them, but it was a cost of doing business out there. Quite simply, they were relieved to be given the option to walk away. Not everyone had that.

There wasn't a benefit in killing the fuckers once they had already surrendered. Madigan and Davis had both said he had begun to be a little ruthless. Maybe it was true, but not that ruthless.

He approached a member of the group that had been captured and squatted beside him. The man wasn't that tall and fell barely short of six feet with the lean, dry look about him that told of someone who was used to living on the edge. His skin was darker, almost like Sal's, but he couldn't tell if it was a natural tan or if he had simply spent that much time in the sun.

A little of both, he decided.

IT ALL FALLS DOWN

"So," he said grimly and fixed the man with a firm look. "It looks like you and your merry band have branched out into a bright new life of criminal intent. I hate to say it, but you guys seriously suck at it. I'd say it's your first job out in the Zoo—together, anyway—and you lost many people with more wounded, all to get...this big fucking box out of the jungle. Being slowed like that is not good. You asked to be attacked by one of the bigger monsters, and you would have been fucked in the ass with no lube."

The merc smirked at the choice of words, which was why he had used them. Shock value was the best way to break the ice with characters like this. "We were lucky," the captive said after a moment's pause.

"Not lucky enough to get out of the Zoo before the Russians decided to take back what was theirs," he pointed out. "But yeah, lucky that you're still alive. Now we've established that you speak English, do you want to tell me why you guys attacked this Russian research camp? And don't say you simply tripped over it."

"Do you mind if I ask you something first?" the man asked after a pause like he had debated with himself and allowed his personal curiosity to win. His accent was Mediterranean—Italian, unless Sal missed his guess. "Who are you? You're not with the Russians and are clearly American. You and your team are experts, use high-tech modified suits, and are armed to the teeth, from the looks of that...uh, sword of yours."

Sal wondered if it was wise to give the man any information. Control was a tricky thing and could be handed over in a moment that turned the tables. He had it now, but if his prisoner escaped with revenge on his mind, giving him a name to work with would be all the start he needed.

"I'll tell you what," he replied and nodded. "I'll answer your question if you answer mine. As an olive branch, I'll tell you my name is Salinger Jacobs."

The merc narrowed his eyes immediately as if the name rang a bell. In a moment, he smirked. "Ah…the Salinger Jacobs? Of Heavy Metal? No fucking wonder the client was willing to put up so much money for 'threats not originating from the Zoo.' The fucking bitch knew we would run into your team out here. I'm Andres Pirlo, by the way."

"Interesting, Andres Pirlo, given that we didn't know we would be out here," he said. "We owed the Russians a favor. Honestly, if we hadn't come, they would have found you, as we did, and simply gunned you down on the spot. Who is this client of yours?"

"I met her once," he said. "Back home. She had connections in the families that were willing to hire muscle for her if she was willing to pay. And, oh boy, was she willing to pay. She told us there was something in the Zoo she wanted, gave us coordinates and everything, and said I would lead a team she'd put together. All Zoo veterans, or so she said. None as much as me, though, which is why I was leading. It wasn't that great a recommendation if you know I was only in here three times before, and all of them six or so months ago."

"The place had changed considerably since then." Sal grunted as his mind worked through the ramifications of this information. Courtney had updated him, more or less, on the problems she and Anderson were attempting to resolve. There had been mention made of a client—a female client—who was behind most if not all their troubles. His gut told him what had happened there tied into what they were trying to get under control in Philly.

More importantly, this kind of activity was more familiar to him out there and closer to home. It was weird how he thought of the Zoo as his home these days. Then he remembered there had been another team sent into the Zoo in search of something. In that case, though, the Zoo had been in an uproar and they had been forced to retreat and survived only with his help. They'd been told to never come back. Madigan had personally delivered the threat, which would ensure that they knew she would personally fuck them up in ways they would have never dreamed were possible if they tried to return.

Even Sal had felt a little intimidated by the way she carried her threats out. She was known to follow through on them. And he was supposed to be the ruthless one?

"Did this client of yours tell you what you were supposed to retrieve?" he asked and watched the man's expression carefully. He was no expert in reading body language or anything like that, but there was a certain facial response when people lied. The features usually shifted, and their face seemed to freeze and go blank as their eyes moved away from his. This man showed none of those things.

"She didn't say and I didn't ask," Pirlo said and shook his head decisively. "When people like that want something in a cage trapped in the middle of the fucking Zoo, you don't ask questions." He paused and his gaze snapped to the side when a metallic thud resounded from the cage and dragged Sal's attention away as well. "You know how sometimes, you have a strange feeling of curiosity that almost makes you break the promise you made to never look and never want to look?"

"Yeah?" he replied waited for the response.

"I don't feel it at all here," the merc whispered and shook his head again. "I appreciate you sparing our lives and everything and I'd appreciate it even more if you could keep us out of the hands of the Russians since they are known to be sadistic bastards when it comes to avenging their own. But between you and me, I want to get as far away from this fucking jungle as I can."

He nodded. "Well, not killing you is one thing and w'll leave here soon enough. I can't make any promises about keeping you out of the Russians' hands, though."

"That's fair, I suppose." Pirlo chuckled and leaned against one of their vehicles. Sal had a few more questions he wanted to bring up with the man, but they would have to wait. He had an itch to scratch, and it wouldn't happen while talking to a professional like this fellow. The man would share some information—enough to keep himself and maybe his team alive—but if he wanted to get to the proverbial meat of the matter, he would have to dig deeper.

Gregor and Madigan were already huddled together a short distance away and stared at the cage while they spoke in hushed whispers.

"So, should we put any money on what's in there?" he asked and caught their attention.

"Gregor here says they captured one of the beasties from inside," she said and nudged her elbow into the man's ribs. "I don't think so. I would have thought there would be far more trouble involved for anyone who tried to drag one of their own out, right? That's how the whole thing about getting animals out of there alive works, which is why we were the first to do it."

"I remember that," the Russian said. "What happened with Shuri, anyway? Dr. Monroe told me you named her."

"She stuck around the base for a while until she was old enough to travel," Sal replied and looked away. "She's on a world tour right now, visiting various labs and being looked at by Zoology experts. I don't like it, but hey, we were paid for our ability to get an animal out, and she's something of a celebrity now. You know they opened an Instagram account for her?"

"It's good to know they're keeping her safe, at least," Gregor said with a nod. "Anyway, you don't think it's an animal in there?"

He shrugged. "I don't think it's safe for us to rule anything out at this point. Whatever's in there wants to get out. Do we really want to know what it is?"

"I confess, I'm maybe too curious to see what it is in there," Madigan said.

"You know what they say about what curiosity did to the cat, right?" he asked.

"Yeah, curiosity killed the cat," she admitted. "But satisfaction brought it back. Not many people know how the full saying, or that they're misquoting a proverb that means the opposite of the point they want to make."

"What, seriously?" he asked and narrowed his eyes. "Satisfaction brought it back? How can that be the second half of the proverb?"

"I'll bet you anything." She grinned. "Look it up."

"I won't bet on a proverb," he grumbled, half-sure she

was right anyway. "I'll bet on what's inside there, though. What kind of odds are we thinking?"

"Come on, what do I look like, a bookie?" Gregor laughed. "The three of us take a guess and put the same amount of money down, and the person who makes the right guess takes the pot. If nobody gets it right, we each take our money."

"Sounds fair," Madigan agreed.

"Do you mind?" one of the nearby scientists snarled. "Our friends and team members were killed and we were kidnapped and enslaved to drag this fucking cage out of the Zoo. Could you have a little respect?"

"That depends," she replied and fixed him with a hard look. "Are you willing to tell us about what you've been doing in the Zoo and what exactly is in that cage?"

The man retreated quickly, his gaze averted. Sal wasn't surprised. Discussions with Anja had given him insight into what the likes of the FSB were willing to do to protect their secrets and the lengths to which they would go to make sure no one got their hands on them. They were scary, that much was certain.

His colleagues showed no inclination to continue the protest. They didn't look happy about the fact that Sal, Madigan, and Gregor were digging into their object of research, but they would neither interfere nor help, by all appearances. They had the haunted look of people who were done with the Zoo and everything it had to offer. Sal could relate, even if the need to head in captured him once in a while.

"I say...beastie found inside." Gregor grunted decisively and tapped his helmet.

"My guess is an animal they brought in from the outside," Sal said easily. "I saw evidence that they had brought plants in from the outside and transplanted them into the ground next to some trees. It could be they wanted to study the Zoo's effects on living creatures."

"Both good guesses," Madigan conceded, but she shook her head, apparently unconvinced. "I have no idea why you would need to trap either of those in a cage with a door and a couple of holes on the top. That's a containment device they brought in, knowing they would need it. They wouldn't need that kind of protection for regular animals, and if they planned to study something inside it, they would want glass panels so they could actually see it to study it. Nah, my guess is the Russians caught someone—either one of their own gone rogue or someone from the outside—and this is their way to punish them. It has nothing to do with the research."

"Huh." Sal grunted, his expression thoughtful. "I didn't even think about that."

The Russian shrugged. "Knowing the people I work for, it's entirely possible. I stand by my guess, though, to the tune of…shall we say a case of vodka?"

"That sounds fair," he agreed, and Madigan nodded. "What say I crack this baby open and see who'll get two cases of vodka for Christmas this year?"

"We both know that if Jacobs wins, Kennedy still gets most of the booze anyway." Their companion laughed at his own joke and she simply nodded again in agreement.

Sal shrugged. "I'll have to settle for the bragging rights of being the best guesser between the three of us."

It took him a while to determine how to open the cage.

Various mechanisms were built into the door, but most of them seemed to be designed to keep whatever was incarcerated in, while it gave easier access to anyone who tried to get in from the outside. It reinforced his idea that they used whatever was in there for a scientific purpose and weakened Madigan's theory, but he wouldn't say that aloud now, not while she could still back out and change her mind.

The only way to open it from the outside was through a simple padlock that held all the bolts in place. He tested it a couple of times and tried to tug it open, and when it resisted, he drew his sword. Amanda had adapted it to the high speeds to which it would be subjected thanks to the vibrations, which resulted in a titanium alloy that was more than capable of holding up against the pressure of the lock as he slipped the blade through the arch and pulled.

Even with the full weight and strength of his suit, it took him a few long tugs to finally feel any give. To the blade's credit, while it bent when it was used as a lever, it immediately resumed its normal shape and size when he released it. Finally, a crack signified that the inner mechanisms of the lock had given way under the pressure. After a few more tugs, it popped open.

Madigan stepped closer to help him draw the bolts.

"Are you ready?" she asked with a grin. He shrugged—not wanting to say he was born ready but it was the only thing that came to mind—and they worked in tandem to haul the gate open. It was reinforced, and it showed in the weight of it. The thought that the scientists had dragged the cage through the harsh environment of the jungle said something about their resolve to get out of there alive.

The first sign of what was imprisoned showed in the dents he could see on the inside of the door as it opened. They hadn't been visible on the outside, which clearly indicated the amount of work that had gone into designing and building the enclosure. The fact that whatever was incarcerated needed this to contain it put him even more on guard than he already was. Any normal kind of animal —even those the Zoo habitually churned out from its nightmare handbook—would have been left with crushed bones if they attempted to fight their way out.

Any other cage would have been destroyed too, judging by the damage inflicted.

The light that spilled into the front half of the box had an immediate effect on the creature inside. It scrambled quickly to the other side and huddled in the shadows, breathing heavily. Bright eyes gleamed in the darkness as they caught the light from the three holes at the top of the cage and reflected it back to the people standing outside.

"Hello, there," Sal said, but Madigan placed a hand on his shoulder and drew him back.

"Don't get too close," she warned.

He indicated the chains at the base of the cage. "Our friend won't go anywhere anytime soon. Those look like they would need considerable power to break free from them."

"Enough power to put dents in a reinforced steel door?" she reminded him.

"Good point," he admitted and took a step back from the cage. Whatever was inside must have noted their retreat since it no longer cowered in the back of the enclosure. The eyes, which had blinked rapidly, suddenly remained open and fixed on the humans. After a few moments of consideration, it moved forward slowly into the light.

"What the fuck?" Madigan gasped. Sal would have said the same, but she beat him to the punch.

As it stepped into the view of the group, one thing became apparent. All their bets were wrong. Well, Sal's and Gregor's definitely were and Kennedy's skated on thin ice. Bipedal was the first conclusion they could establish. Everything about it looked human—in profile, anyway. It stood on two feet, had two arms and a head with hair much like any person, but the same could not be said of most of the rest of the body. This wasn't a humanoid simian. It was human.

Emphasis on was, Sal decided. It appeared to have been in captivity for a while and was as naked as the day it had been born. A foul smell spilled out of the container, even though there wasn't any sign of the wastes that usually came from a human body. They could have cleaned the cage from the outside, he reasoned.

But that wasn't the most notable detail about the creature.

The fact that it was blue was what held his attention. Not all blue, he realized after a more detailed study. Its skin was still normal skin, but the veins beneath were a bright, very familiar shade of blue. There was enough of it to make it seem, at first glance, that it was all blue, even the eyes.

"It looks like you all owe me some booze," Madigan said with a somewhat smug glance at her two companions.

"We…don't know that it was someone they brought in," Gregor protested.

"I'm sure we'll find out." She chuckled and took a step forward. "Hey, do you speak English?"

It tilted its head and stared curiously at the group but seemed to become a little bolder and dropped to its haunches. Sal noted that it slowly gathered up the links of the chains.

"I think you need to get back now," he warned her, and she turned to face him as if to question his warning while her weapon remained trained at its head.

It was all the opening the creature needed. Sal wasn't at all sure why he felt a sudden need to launch into action at that moment, but he was glad he listened to his gut. The aberration stood suddenly and bellowed with the effort required to rip its chains free. Without so much as a pause, it attacked Madigan. She managed a hasty shot, which missed and rebounded around the cage behind it before Sal reached her, shoved her clear of the attacker's path, and flung himself out of the way after her.

It was fast but didn't know how to control either its strength or speed and it stumbled and fell when its target evaded the attack.

Sal was already on his feet, but he'd lost his rifle in his effort to shove her out of the way of the creature. It seemed foolish to do that, in retrospect, since her suit could probably have withstood its power.

Still, he had his sword. He drew it swiftly from its sheath

173

on his back, connected it to the power socket in the hand of his suit, and activated it while the beast collected itself and looked around. Escape was on its mind, but the sands of the Sahara held no appeal. Neither did the group of Russians who had seen what happened and had begun to retrieve their weapons to prepare to fire. Some self-preservation instinct remained in it, whatever it was. It wouldn't simply attack the way most Zoo animals did, even when outnumbered.

Sal held his breath as its gaze settled on the Hammerhead they had been hitching to the back of the cage to transport it to one of the bases and then to Sal and Madigan, who still struggled to her feet.

"Well...shit." He lowered his stance as his adversary bared its teeth and without further warning, it launched itself toward him, snarling like a beast. While he wanted to think there was some intelligence in its eyes when it had stared at him, there wasn't much time to contemplate that. He raised the blade and held it between himself and the creature, surprised to see that it simply continued its assault. The rapidly vibrating sword sliced smoothly through its skin, and still, it barely slowed.

Fuck, it was bleeding blue too.

The sheer power of it, even while it was impaled, hurled him off his feet. With his blade effectively trapped, he was forced to watch helplessly as it tried to bite his neck. It encountered the steel-titanium alloy instead, roared with annoyance, and pulled back to make another attempt. He honestly didn't want to kill it. A human so deeply influenced by the Zoo was something to be studied, learned from, and hopefully, helped.

But it wouldn't stop until he was out of the way, and

Madigan was too far away to be able to help. Besides, how could he be sure she would fare any better?

He made a split-second decision, one he knew he would regret but it had to be done. His teeth gritted, he twisted the blade where it remained stuck in the monster's chest. There was a hint of resistance when the vibro-blade caught in its ribcage, but it was brief. He forced the blade around to carve through its insides, then plunged it in deeper until he found the spine. While he knew he'd already inflicted a mortal wound, he continued to cut until the beast finally collapsed on top of him, twitching here and there.

Sal took a moment to make sure it wouldn't recover again before he struggled out from under it and tried to brush the obscenely blue blood from his armor. His weapon, when it came clear, cleaned itself through the rapid vibrations. He let it run for a second before he turned it off.

"Are you okay?" Madigan asked and looked like she was ready to make sure the aberration was dead once and for all. He understood the instinct but given the gaping hole he had left in its torso, he assumed it wouldn't be necessary. Besides, they had bigger problems to deal with.

His eyes were drawn to the group of scientists, who had watched the entire battle. Some of them clearly knew what the reaction to what they were doing would be and hung their heads in shame. They seemed determined to avoid the accusatory glares from the people who had come to their aid.

Others, though, looked aghast and horrified.

"What have you done?" the man who had spoken before yelled when he suddenly found his voice again. "Why did you kill him? Months of work simply swept away because you couldn't keep your little pointy stick to yourself."

"Keep talking, Professor, and you'll have a taste of my pointy stick too," he snapped in response. "What the fuck was that?"

The man remained visibly indignant, but his gaze settled on the sword in the other man's hands and, having been present for not one but two demonstrations on how effective it was, he decided not to press the point. He stepped back among his own people, shook his head, and mumbled what could only be a string of less than flattering remarks. That was fine, though, since Sal didn't want to talk to them anyway. He felt he would throw punches if he even looked at them for too long.

"Is that what the Russians are doing out here, Gregor?" Madigan asked the man, who looked as horrified as they felt. "Are you guys running human testing out here where they think no one will find them and judge them for it?"

The Russian shook his head in disgust. "Not to my knowledge. These...*mudak* who don't deserve to be called scientists will be taken to Moscow where they will be put on trial for what they have done here."

In the light of the fact that the FSB was there and likely very well aware of what tests were conducted, it was doubtful there would be any serious repercussions aside from a whole slew of cover-ups.

"This was necessary," the scientist shouted, obviously under the impression that he was safe while among his own. "This is the next stage of human evolution. All we are doing here is...controlling it."

"I'm reasonably sure that if that piece of shit talks to me

again, I'll shoot him," Sal whispered to Madigan, who shrugged.

"You'd have my blessing." She grunted her disgust. "Shoot away."

Gregor shook his head. "I'd rather you didn't. I still need to turn these scientists over to the FSB. They'll tell if the team I brought along was responsible for gunning one of them down, and it won't do for me."

"I think they might mention something about us killing their experiment," she pointed out.

"Well, there's nothing we can do about that," he grumbled. "But we can make sure they aren't able to talk about how you killed them."

"Either way, it seems Heavy Metal will be put on the FSB's map." Sal shook his head in annoyance. "I need to make a few calls. Are you guys good with cleaning this whole mess?"

Madigan knew what he was talking about and nodded. He strode in the other direction and connected to the Heavy Metal commlink to warn Anja about what had happened.

"Hey, Anja, are you there?" he asked. Knowing her, he could expect her to be anywhere between a meal, a nap, or working on something at any given hour of the day. She had told him she wouldn't let something so trivial as the earth spinning on its axis tell her how to spend her time. And for someone in her particular profession, that was an option.

Either way, it might take her a while to get back to him. Which meant he might as well leave a message if she didn't answer him anytime soon.

"Anja, if you're not there, I'll simply—" The words cut off when he saw her line connect to the commlink.

"Sal, is that you?" she asked and sounded like she was awake and had been for a while.

"Yes, we just made it out of the Zoo and there's a situation I thought you should be aware of."

"That's great, because I have a situation for you too," she said quickly. "It's Courtney. Someone tried to kill her in Philly."

CHAPTER FOURTEEN

Philadelphia: Police Interrogation Room

"So, Mr. Savage—am I pronouncing that right?" one of the officers asked as he looked at a file on the metal table across from where the operative sat, chained to a steel chair. "Jeremiah Savage?"

He shook his head. "It's not some French bullshit. Just Savage."

"Savage?" the other detective asked.

"Like you pronounce it in the good old US of A," he replied with a chuckle. "Do you want me to use it in a sentence? Okay, then. The way I fucked your wife last night was really quite savage."

The detective, who had introduced himself as Jennings, smirked as he fiddled with his wedding band. "You're cute, you know that? Real cute. What I want to know is who the fuck names their kid Jeremiah Savage. Did your parents hate you or did they simply run out of names to give to the rest of their litter?"

"What?" he asked and frowned. "Nah, man, I changed it to Jeremiah Savage."

"So you had the opportunity to change your name," the other detective asked and took a sip of coffee from a plastic cup. "And you changed it...to Jeremiah Savage."

"Oh, yeah." He nodded.

"What was the name originally?" the first detective asked.

He shrugged. "Biggus Dickus."

The detective with the coffee snorted some of it out. The one who stood closer to Savage wasn't quite so amused.

They obviously tried to play the good cop, bad cop routine, but the operative had decided he wouldn't join the game with them. He'd told them that nothing would be said until his attorney was present, and he decided that was how he would continue to manage the situation. As it turned out, they weren't really great at eliciting information from suspects and so far, he rather enjoyed giving them the runaround.

Courtney had laid the rules of engagement out when they were all in the apartment waiting for the police to arrive. They had a story to follow, of course. They were all called in, still on duty, to protect their employer. As Savage, Sam, and Terry were employed as security consultants, they were entitled to act in defense of their client. Anderson would be treated according to a similar law, although it might end up a little more complicated for him. That was how she knew the law, though, and Anja had provided a hint of support but there were literal volumes she needed to look into before she was able to support the call with absolute certainty.

Which lead to their boss' second order—until there was a lawyer in the room, shut the fuck up.

It seemed like the right call, Savage thought, and tried not to show any emotion on his face. He had made sure to keep all his answers to the police calm and short and to never volunteer any information that might be twisted and used against them in a court of law.

Which left them sitting in a police station, waiting for a lawyer to show up and not saying a damn thing. Any excuse they tried to make or story they tried to tell would be used and twisted in court, which meant it was always better to simply let legal counsel do the talking until they got to a court of law where they could present a single front with all of them telling the same story.

It might not get to that, of course. If there was one thing he looked forward to, it was finding out how police treated people in the upper strata of society. He wanted to find out what was true in person.

The people in the upper levels of financial security were Monroe and Anderson, but they would get Savage, Sam, and Terry out of trouble as well, given that the three of them had saved their lives not that long before. They also had to know the team would come after them with a vengeance if they were left to eat the charges. He didn't think Anderson and Monroe were the kind to do that, but it was still better to be prepared if the occasion arose.

"Well, you're a funny guy, Savage, I have to say," the less than amused detective snarked and dropped into the seat opposite him, leaned forward, and tried to look intimidating. "Do you want to hear something really funny, though? Here's what I think is fucking hysterical—the fact that these people had supposedly targeted your boss, a Mr. James Anderson—"

"It's Colonel James Anderson, if you don't mind," he interjected. "The guy served the country. He deserves to be recognized for it."

"Right, of course, Colonel James Anderson." The man chuckled. "Anyway, they attacked your boss, but did so in an apartment that was in your name. Doesn't that strike you as odd as well as hilarious?"

"Do you want to know what's hilarious?" Savage asked, leaned forward to match his adversary's movements, and lowered his voice to speak confidentially to the man. "It's odd too, how I said I wouldn't talk without a lawyer present, and you guys still try to trick me into doing so."

The other detective shook his head, pushed his chair back, and stood slowly. He looked like he had once been a fitness freak, but that time was behind him by about a year. Muscles were still evident in his arms and shoulders, but a trace of a gut had begun to present and press at the lower buttons of his shirt. He would need to be fitted for new clothes soon. That or work out again. He put the odds of either happening at around even.

"What are you hiding?" the supposed good cop asked, although his frustration now showed at the lack of anything offered by their detainee. Nothing that they could use, anyway.

"Hiding?" Savage asked and tilted his head innocently.

"Now what on earth could a security consultant be hiding from the likes of you honorable officers?"

"The fact that we can't find anything on your name until a few months ago?" The bad cop growled his annoyance and thumped his hands down on the table.

He looked at the man, unimpressed. "You should try looking up my original name. Do you need me to spell it for you?"

"Come on, Baker," the other detective said and placed his hand on his colleague's shoulder. He'd obviously remembered his role in this whole charade and he fixed Savage with a firm look. "You need to think about what'll happen to you if you don't cooperate. Your pals in the other cells have already spilled their guts about this whole situation and pointed you out as the mastermind behind it all."

He couldn't help a smirk at that. "You must be desperate if you're trying to sell me on that particular brand of bullshit. Do either of you have any idea when my lawyer will get here? Or maybe I could have coffee? I'll need one or the other."

Both were about to say something and looked like they were about to do something stupid that would get him released without any need for his lawyer when the door opened and a woman stepped in. She was tall and dressed in an elegant and expensive pantsuit, her brown hair in a severe and professional ponytail, and wore four-inch heels and walked like someone who was used to that height.

Lawyer, he thought to himself.

"Detectives Jennings and Baker, is that right?" she asked

and adjusted her glasses, which were difficult to see to the point where he had missed them at first. "I'll need you to release my client."

"There's been no bail hearing." One of them—Baker, he reminded himself—scowled.

"And there won't be," she said with a small, professional smile as she placed a hand on Savage's shoulders. "I don't need to remind you there's a self-defense statute in this state that allows men and women working in the field my client, Mr. Savage, is working in to act in the way that he did.

"Now, I know you might want to press charges on my client, but you'll have to understand that I've already spoken to the Attorney General. He is very aware of the fact that Pennsylvania is a stand-your-ground state with many guns-rights activists who would object to any precedent being applied to criminal charges on self-defense.

"He has therefore said in this statement"—she paused to place a written copy of the statement on the metal table in front of Savage— "that he has no intention of pursuing charges against any of the people working under the employ of Pegasus Incorporated who were arrested this evening. So, unless you two would like to charge my client against the wishes of the Attorney General, I would ask you to release him, please."

Savage raised his eyebrows. The woman had gone through what sounded like a very well-rehearsed speech with barely a pause to take a breath and didn't look like she was breathless from the effort. It had been delivered very well too, and made both detectives scowl in frustration.

One of them—Jennings, the good cop—removed a set

of keys from his pocket and undid the manacles that held the detainee's wrists locked onto the table. Savage took a moment to rub the feeling back before he pushed from his seat and nodded to the detectives. They were decent enough at their jobs, he conceded, but he doubted they had ever encountered someone quite like him before.

That said, they would probably want to ask to keep him and the others under surveillance as the investigation progressed and that was completely unacceptable. He had every intention of breaking the law once he got out of there, and he didn't need a group of law enforcement babysitters following him around.

They stepped out of the interrogation room and he turned his attention to the lawyer who had apparently worked overtime to secure their release.

"Jeremiah Savage," he said with a small smile and offered her his hand.

"Allison Marie, Esq," she replied and shook firmly.

"That was impressive work," he said as they turned toward the building's exit. "I can't imagine it's easy to get the attention of the Attorney General after hours."

"Under normal circumstances, you would be correct," Marie replied and kept pace with him easily. "But when the man heard that two high-ranking Pegasus employees were taken into custody after an attempt on their lives was thwarted, I think he waited at the phone for my call. With elections coming, I doubt he would want to get himself into this kind of sticky mess. He thought it best to resolve it quickly and let everyone go before the mess got deeper and practically faxed me the statement before I even called."

"Interesting," Savage said. "Will we wait for the others?"

"The others are already released and waiting for you in Dr. Monroe's personal apartment," the attorney replied and smiled as he beat her to the door and held it open for her. "The police around here were all too happy to let them go, but given the footage the police found on you, Mr. Savage, I think they really didn't feel comfortable to release you into the general populace."

"Between you and me, I think the general populace would agree," he said with a small, grim smirk as they strode to the parking lot. He still had no idea where he was going but he assumed the woman wanted him to follow her.

"Well, it's not for me to judge," she replied with a chuckle. "Dr. Monroe asked me to give you a ride to her apartment, which is where the rest of them are gathered, as I said. Apparently, there is big news that needs to be shared. She didn't include me on the list of people who needed to know this news, though."

Savage nodded as they approached a silver Hyundai sedan, which she unlocked with a press of a button on the key to allow them to step inside. "I wouldn't feel too bad about it."

"I'm a lawyer," she replied and started the car once he had buckled himself in. "I don't feel bad about things."

He grinned. "Are you really the kind of unfeeling robot people expect lawyers to be these days, or do you merely play the part? And play it well, I should point out."

"Wouldn't you like to know?" she countered, turned out of the parking lot, and pushed the car to full speed rather quickly as she maneuvered it through the streets, which were empty at this late hour.

"I would, yeah," he replied. "Exactly like I'm sure that, under your cold, unfeeling exterior, you wonder if I'm actually the killer the cops didn't want to release based on the footage they had of me."

"Are you?" she asked but didn't turn to look at him. "And remember that anything you say to me is bound by attorney-client privilege."

"I can be," Savage admitted and relaxed into the comfortable leather seat. "When Monroe and Anderson hired me, they asked me the same question and I think I gave them a similar answer. Paraphrased, anyway. How about you?"

She smirked. "I can be."

He nodded, unsure if he wanted the conversation to continue. Instead, he fell silent as they headed deeper into the city until they arrived at one of the skyscrapers at the center and drove into the underground parking lot. From there, they took the elevator to the thirty-fifth floor, all without a word exchanged between them. It didn't feel like an awkward silence, at least not to him, merely like there wasn't much else to be said between them. They were both professionals who did what they did for their own reasons and didn't need validation from anyone else.

The elevator doors opened directly into the living room of Monroe's apartment and revealed a lavish if somewhat assembly-line living room. A fireplace was built into the center of the room with leather couches around it and a large TV on the other side of the room. The walls boasted expensive-looking and yet instantly forgettable art. These were the kinds of places set up for visiting CEOs and VIPs whom Pegasus wanted to accommodate in a luxurious and secure yet hidden location. Which applied to Courtney, he supposed.

The couches around the fireplace were filled by the team. Anderson and Monroe were both seated on loungers and Sam and Terry attacked Chinese food that had been ordered in.

"Savage, I'm glad you could make it," Anderson called but Monroe stood and moved to greet them. She shook Marie's hand before she turned to the operative and patted him on the shoulder.

"How are you doing?" she asked and examined him carefully. "The cops didn't work you over too hard."

"When you say it like that, it sounds dirty," Sam called from where she paused between mouthfuls of stir-fried rice and chicken.

"True," Savage agreed. "And either way, no. They wanted me to roll over on you guys, but when Mi...ss?" He turned to her and she nodded. "Miss Marie told them to eat a whole bag of soggy dicks, they let me go reasonably quickly. I'm paraphrasing, of course."

"She's good, isn't she?" his boss asked, chuckled, and patted the lawyer on the shoulder. "I brought her into the fold after she proved her worth with my home-defense problem way back when and I assumed we might face similar issues down the line."

"And you're lucky you did, Dr. Monroe," Marie replied with a smile. "Is that Chinese? I'm starving."

"Help yourself," Monroe said with a chuckle and gestured for him to join them as well, although he didn't feel peckish yet. He would be in a while, though, if he knew himself. Probably once everyone else had finished.

"So why did Savage have to be dragged into the station again?" Sam asked. "I thought the whole idea of having him on the team was so you could have someone working outside the law and not on his ass being talked down to by cops."

"That was the idea, yes," Anja said over the speakers in the room. "But there were people who saw him there, and footage, so I couldn't simply have him disappear. Besides, the cops had their hands on the footage of what he was doing before I could erase it. If he vanished, there would be a manhunt for him, and that definitely wouldn't do."

"Shit." Savage growled irritably as he settled himself in an available seat. "Exactly how much exposure am I looking at here? Will I be any use to you guys here in Philly?"

"That remains to be seen," Monroe said. "The cops have your face, so they might be waiting for you to trip up to put out an arrest warrant for you. There are also a few questions around that special pistol of yours which leaves no bullets—and which links you to a previous incident and has definitely stirred their suspicions. I know you and Anja have been careful about keeping your tracks covered, so I'm not that worried about it. Still, you might want to think about laying low for the moment."

"Well, we'll have to decide how I'll manage to both lay low and track the people who have tried to kill us," he grumbled and folded his arms. He didn't like the idea of having to hide or remain housebound. Being left alone with his thoughts wasn't a very enticing situation, and neither was the concept—which he was sure they were considering—of him having a desk job for a few months.

"Actually, we do have updates on that," Anja said. "I think we should have a quick talk with our Heavy Metal team. They just got back from the Zoo, and they have some news."

CHAPTER FIFTEEN

<u>*Philadelphia: Courtney Monroe's Apartment*</u>

"Should I be here for this?" Marie asked bluntly as the group gathered in front of the rather massive TV screen on the other side of the room. She looked vaguely uncomfortable but also very reluctant to leave the box of chicken chow mein she'd barely started on unfinished. Savage could relate to the discomfort, although he hadn't had the allure of Chinese to tempt him during the tedious board meetings.

Anja, it appeared, had begun to connect them to the team in the Zoo and had obviously coordinated things to make sure they were all around at the same time. He already knew Salinger Jacobs and Madigan Kennedy, but there was someone called Connie who would be included as well. Mention was also made of Amanda Gutierrez, but they all seemed to think that she would probably be too busy to be involved.

That left Anja, whom he knew well. He wondered exactly how many others were a part of this Heavy Metal team of which he had heard mention but hadn't interacted with much. Well, apart from Monroe, who was a part of the team as well but was also his employer.

Anderson, it appeared, was a part of his team—or he was a part of Anderson's team—as were Sam and Terry, and while the groups had worked in tandem with each other, they'd never gathered like this before, at least to his knowledge. Then again, things had never been quite this bad before.

"Do you want to be here for this?" Monroe asked her and tilted her head in what might have been a challenge. "You're a part of my legal team, so you might want to be aware of what our plans are."

"I don't want to, no," Marie replied and scrambled out of the overstuffed leather chair she had chosen. "As much as I appreciate the business you send my way, Dr. Monroe, I'd like to have as much plausible deniability of your actions as possible, which would allow me to continue to plead your cases with as much legal fervor as I can muster. I think it would be better if I left in case what you discuss here might have illegal elements to it."

"The chances are high that some measure of illegality will be a part of this conversation, yes," Savage said, and Monroe agreed.

"Then I hope you have a safe trip home, Marie." She gave the woman a quick hug. "I've already wired you your fee, so it should arrive in your bank account by tomorrow."

"I appreciate it." Marie returned the hug with less awkwardness than Savage would have anticipated. "I'll make sure to stay in contact with all of you if there are any updates on the case. I don't think there will be since it will take the police literal years to sift through all the available data, and they usually want to avoid cases like these. They tend to blow up in everyone's faces when too much digging is done."

She started to make her way to the elevator but paused, turned, and strode to where Savage leaned with his back against one of the pillars in the room.

"Here's my card," she said, slid it into his hand, and continued in a confidential tone. "It has my personal number on it in case you need any...representation."

"Do you think I will?" he asked.

She pursed her lips and tilted her head. "Well, if the police try to harass you in any way. Or if you have any doubts about the case and would like to discuss them over a cup of coffee, maybe?"

He nodded and pocketed the card she'd handed him quickly without looking at the number. "Understood. I'll be in touch."

"You won't regret it," she replied with a small smile before she hurried to the elevator and pressed the button. The team waited until she had gone before they resumed the process to connect with their other half in the Sahara Desert. Sam watched him carefully as he made his way to one of the couches.

"How the fuck do you do that?" she asked, and it took him a moment to realize she had spoken to him.

He narrowed his eyes at her. "Do what?"

"You know what, ya sly bastard." She chuckled. "I don't believe for a minute that you think she gave you her card so you could learn the minutiae of self-defense law in Pennsylvania. You'll go out for coffee with her, and she'll come to you for a little extra cream, if you know what I'm saying."

"Come on, Sam, a little discretion, please," Courtney snapped at her.

"What? I'm only saying what all of us are thinking," she replied defensively.

"I can assure you that I wasn't thinking anything of the sort," Terry said with a shake of his head.

"Same," Anderson called and raised his hand. "I am now, though. I've seen the kind of effect Savage has on women, and it's...uh, interesting."

"Changing the subject—like, right now," Savage protested.

"Aw, I think we're making Jer here uncomfortable." Anja chuckled over the speakers. "Anyway, the team in the Heavy Metal compound is ready for a conversation if you guys are done talking about Savage's love life."

He shook his head and rolled his eyes as the rest of them gathered closer to the TV, which apparently had an embedded camera. They could see their faces reflected at them as the screen came alive with images of the Heavy Metal team. Anja was there with Jacobs and Kennedy, and another man Savage didn't recognize was seated at the back.

"Hey, guys, how's everyone doing?" Monroe asked and suddenly looked much softer when her gaze fell on Kennedy and Jacobs than she usually did. Anja had mentioned something about the three of them being involved in a ménage of sorts, which raised a whole series of questions in his mind, but he put them aside for the moment.

"We just got back from the Zoo so are a little tired, but otherwise not too bad," Jacobs replied. He scowled when he saw the bandage on Monroe's arm. "What happened to you?"

"Some dumbasses decided to test me on the highway," she replied with a chuckle. "I went full road-rage on them and let Savage handle what was left. They tried to kill Anderson too, but the team was there to save his ass."

Savage smirked.

"How about you guys?" Anderson asked. The hacker frowned but didn't correct Monroe's version of events. "Anja tells us there were some developments we should be made aware of."

"Correct," Kennedy cut in. "Our friend Gregor from the Russian Base was called in by the FSB, who wanted him to lead an expedition to find a research team that had gone dark while they were testing some kind of comm system that they hoped would work even while deep in the jungle. Anyway, we tracked them and the people who had made them go dark—as in killed the gunners and kidnapped the scientists. We also saw exactly what the Russians were testing in there."

"They were running human testing with the goop they were getting directly from the Zoo, FYI," Jacobs interjected, and his expression settled into an angry glare at the mention of it. Savage looked at the group when they all went silent for a few moments. Human testing would always be a dark and forbidden subject for scientists, which meant those in the conversation would be properly horrified by it.

"Anyway," Kennedy continued. "A merc team was hired

to target the people running these tests and tasked with dragging them out, together with the subject of their experiments. The plan, I believe, was to export them out of the Zoo via the French base to a mysterious client."

Savage narrowed his eyes when something clicked, and he suddenly saw where this was going.

"I tracked the money that paid these guys—which, incidentally, was the same money used to hire the team that kidnapped Sal and took him into the Zoo. It took me a while and a whole host of favors called in to track it through a series of wire transfers that bounced me all around the world. The trail finally came to an end at a very private and very high-end bank in Monaco, a branch of a banking company from Switzerland. I put in considerable work, and all I got from my inquiries was a name."

"Let me guess," he interjected. "Someone by the name of Elena Molina?"

"Cookie for the smart attack dog," Kennedy grumbled. He narrowed his eyes. Being talked down to like that was annoying, but given that Kennedy was supposed to be one of his employers—or at least close enough to his employers to be seen as the same—he resisted the instinctive urge to tell her off.

That wouldn't happen again, though, if she kept that shit up.

"Can we find her?" Jacobs asked and looked at Anja, who shrugged.

"I tried to locate her after Carlson gave Savage her name," the hacker said and worked on a laptop on the coffee table in front of her. "I didn't know where exactly to find her before, and all I had was a name and a birth certificate, so I literally tried to find a needle in a haystack of needles. But now I have a bead on her finances, I know where she is and where she might have visited in person, and I've been able to narrow it down."

"It sounds like I'll take a field trip to Monaco," Savage stated coldly. As the team looked at him, he shrugged and explained, "The people who have their eyes on me here won't be able to see what I do while I'm abroad unless they somehow get the CIA involved. This is the perfect way to make sure I lay low while still hunting the bitch who is trying to have us all killed."

"Actually," Sal said and glanced at his Heavy Metal team before he addressed the group on the other side of the screen, "I think it might be best if we have our full team in on the mission. This woman clearly has serious resources behind her and having only one person target her might not be the best move since we might have only the one opportunity."

"I am the...attack dog, as Kennedy put it," he countered and eyed the woman with a scowl. "I'm the one who's replaceable and here to be the enforcer of whatever shit the rest of you pull, right? And all the while, provide you guys with your precious plausible deniability. Getting my hands dirty is kind of my thing."

"Oy, our thing," Sam snapped.

"Yep, our thing," Terry chimed in. "Team Savage's thing."

"Huh, I didn't know you guys had a name like that." Jacobs chuckled and studied the operatives. "I mean...sure, we have a name, but we didn't get to choose it."

"You were the one who called our company Heavy Metal," Kennedy reminded him and raised an eyebrow.

"Oh…right, of course. Yes, we are team Heavy Metal." He nodded and folded his arms. "Wait, no, we're the Heavy Metal Militia. That sounds better, don't you think?"

"Very snappy, yeah," Monroe said. "Could we bring ourselves back to the topic at hand, guys?"

"Right," he grumbled. "Anyway, I still feel like we should all go together. Again, we only have one shot at this, and if you fail—"

"She's already targeted us. What exactly can she do that she hasn't already done?" Sam asked.

"Well, we've worked in defensive mode up until this point," Anderson said. "If we go after her, she'll take that shit personally. I don't know about the rest of you, but I do remember the difference between…shall we say, Savage, when he simply did his job and when he starting to take shit personally."

"Yep, that's a good point," Savage admitted.

"Okay, so we go after this bitch all together, shall we?" Monroe said and looked at both her teams. "Does anyone else think this might be a little too neat? That someone as careful and…let's call it as paranoid as this Elena chick would simply leave traces that would lead us directly not only to the country she lives in but to the banking firms that represent her? The last time a trail was left this clearly, it led into a witch's stewpot."

"That's not how the story goes," Jacobs pointed out and she shrugged.

"Anyway," she grumbled. "How carefully this might be

crafted to lead us to her concerns me. It smells like a trap to me."

"Agreed," Kennedy said, and other members of the group nodded, apparently all thinking the same thing. Even if they weren't before, they would be now.

She had a point, Savage thought. Elena, so careful to make sure all her actions were delegated to the likes of Banks and Carlson, suddenly exposing herself like this didn't feel right. She was playing them, and until he knew what kind of game she was trying to pull, it would have been safer to keep the likes of Anderson, Monroe, Jacobs, and Kennedy out of it.

But he wasn't the one who made the decisions. Exactly as it was in the field, it was the people on top who called the shots and the likes of Savage, Terry, and Sam who put in the hours on the ground to make their expectations come true. At least in this case, the decision made by the people calling the shots was that they would go into the field with the grunts.

Jacobs did seem like the kind of man who preferred to be in the thick of it and ditto Anderson, Monroe, and Kennedy. That still didn't make their call any smarter, though.

They would have a little while to think about it while they all coordinated their plans.

"Well, you know what the best thing is to do when someone lays a carefully planned trap in front of you," Jacobs was saying when Savage brought himself back from his thoughts. "You spring the trap."

"Who else will come?" Monroe asked. "I think I should

be in on this, and Savage, Terry, and Sam should come with me."

"I can stick it out here at home," Anderson said. "With these kinds of threats looming over us, I don't think I should be that far away from my family."

"Agreed." She turned to the Heavy Metal half of the group.

Jacobs replied with a gentle shrug. "Madigan and I are obviously in this with you, Courtney," he said with a chuckle. "And with the FSB sniffing this close to us, I don't feel comfortable leaving Anja behind, even with Connie to take care of her."

"I don't think we should leave the base with only Connie to take care of it, though," Kennedy pointed out.

"I'm sorry, am I missing something?" Sam asked and voiced the questions in the minds of the entire US group. "Who the fuck is Connie?"

"The AI running the defenses on the base," Jacobs explained and grinned. "We got her secondhand and apparently, her previous owner liked his AIs to have an attitude."

"Huh." Savage grunted and recalled the AIs that used to run point on the defenses of the various military bases he'd been a part of. The memories were mostly mentions made of them by the various technicians who had been called in to work them. They were known for being developed with sassy personalities to make interaction with them more agreeable.

Recent studies had shown that AIs without developed personalities coded into their programming were less likely to be trusted by the humans who ran them. It was an idiotic point, but thanks to a veritable shit-ton of movies on the topic, humans simply didn't trust their own creations.

People smarter than him had said that humans mistrusted AIs because they didn't trust them to not treat them in the way they were treated. It was a fair point and a good reason to be afraid too. The AIs were designed by humans, after all, and it made sense that they would mirror the personalities of their creators.

Of course, he knew nothing about how AIs were developed and if the people who made them disagreed, maybe they were the authorities to be listened to. Then again, you wanted people to trust the AIs you were developing enough to buy them in bulk to run homes, buildings, complexes, and bases, which meant you had to go with what sold best. Which meant giving your AIs a personality that had nothing to do with their core functions, and that would only make them less versatile.

Humans were fucking stupid, he concluded.

"I can keep an eye on the base while you guys are out," said the man in the back who had been introduced as Davis. "Connie will be sure to report what I do when you get back."

"You're damn right about that, pervert," came the disembodied female voice Savage assumed was the AI in question.

"Well, it looks like we have a plan in place," Jacobs said and hastily took charge of the situation before Davis started an argument with the AI. "I guess I'll see you all on the other side."

.

CHAPTER SIXTEEN

Monaco: A Small Café

"Miss Molina?"

She startled and looked up from her arm to see who had addressed her. It was annoying to have her mind drift off in the middle of a conversation. It had been a condition they addressed early on in her life. Attention Deficit Hyperactivity Disorder had been her problem, which made it difficult to learn basically anything while she was seated and told to focus on what was said by teachers.

Simple relaxation, a conscious choice, came more easily because there was no pressure involved. But for her to absorb information, she needed to fully engage and be able to move to keep her focus on track.

Thankfully, her father was more than capable and willing to find teachers who were specialists in teaching children like her, and he'd provided a full and educative time for her formative years. It was a little more complex in the Ivy League schools she had been sent to, but that had been solved with medication and therapy. It had been a thorn in her side for her whole life, and she had learned to cope with it.

It didn't mean she didn't annoy herself when conversations slipped past as her mind wandered thanks to its inability to tolerate stagnation.

Elena sighed, took a moment to stir her already lukewarm espresso, and wondered if she should ask the people working in the little café she had come to favor during her time in Monaco to reheat it or to simply order another one.

Order another one, she decided. Reheat an espresso too many times and you started to taste the pot instead of the ridiculously overpriced coffee beans.

"Miss Molina, please focus," the man seated in front of her pleaded in English. He looked like he tried to contain his annoyance at the fact that she seemed to not even bother to pay attention to what he was saying. It was true. She didn't want to have to deal with him right now.

"We have been over this before, Ricardo," she said, raised her hand to call one of the baristas to her table, and adjusted her summer dress before she crossed her tanned legs. She scowled at the tall, lean man in a pale, caramel-colored suit in front of her. "Everything that happened has been carefully thought out and planned, with the various formalities handled and variables accounted for."

"Have you thought about the fact that the Russians have the group of men you hired for the job in the Zoo—one of whom, need I remind you, has seen your face?" he stated with exasperation. "Do you really want to find out the headache it is to have the FSB put a crosshair on your back?"

"The FSB won't bother to interrogate them in the less than secure Russian base," she replied and sighed softly as she indicated for the barista to get her another espresso. "They'll need to fly them to Moscow for a proper interrogation, and arrangements have already been made to ensure they do not survive the trip. I thought you were the one who handled those arrangements for me, which has my mind spinning as to why exactly you are acting out like this."

"I'm not acting out," he snapped in response and tried to keep his voice down while another espresso was put on the table and Elena took a sip from it. "All I see are threats building against you and your…dare I say it, apathy toward these threats that could claim your life if you are not careful."

She put the tiny cup down after a tantalizing sip from the bitter-yet-sweet coffee, exhaled a slow sigh of contentment, and focused her gaze directly on the man in front of her.

"And now we have this Heavy Metal group involved, and in numbers enough to prove a threat should they decide to target you personally," he continued. He completely missed the dangerous glare she had focused on him until the last syllable escaped his lips. His eyes widened as he tried to utter an apology, but she raised her hand to prevent any further words.

"Regarding Salinger Jacobs and his Heavy Metal team, I have actually tried to deal with them over the past few months," she said, her voice calm before she took another sip from her cup. "The lack of success on that front has been nothing if not a thorn in my side, and I have decided that the effort needed to deal with them would be too much compared to the possible rewards to be reaped from their demise. As such, I've decided to employ the age-old tactic of 'if you can't beat them, join them.' Temporarily, at least."

"How do you know..." Ricardo started to ask but his voice trailed off when she glared at him again.

"How do I know they'll join me?" She completed his question. "I don't. But I believe an attempt to bring them onto our side has to be worth the effort. Besides, I have a job that only they will be able to fulfill for me, and if what I know about this Jacobs character is correct, he won't be able to help his curiosity over it. The others listen to him."

He nodded in response and didn't dare to interrupt her again.

"As for my apparent—what was the word you used?— ah, yes, apathy," she said, her voice level as she finished her espresso and placed the cup gently onto the saucer. "If you think I have come this far in life by being apathetic regarding threats, I have to say I'm disappointed. If you think the fact that I do not panic like an untamed stallion over threats that have been assessed and thought out clearly constitutes apathy, I have to say I am disappointed. How does it feel to have disappointed me doubly, Ricardo?"

He didn't answer.

Elena had always wondered what people looked like when their lives flashed before their eyes. She knew now. It was disappointing to know that he was a terrified little shit. She'd had higher hopes for him and wanted to bring him into the upper echelons of her operation and show him everything she had planned. The fact that he had no control over himself when challenges arose was saddening, but it was better revealed now than later when he was in deeper.

A shame, really. He was incredible in bed.

The man took to his feet and nodded gently to her, and she noted that his hands trembled almost imperceptibly as he closed the top button on his coat and turned to make his way out. His mind was already on getting a plane ticket out of the country—somewhere like Southeast Asia, or maybe Australia. Somewhere he hoped she wouldn't find him.

He wouldn't survive his trip to the airport, Elena mused, entered a text into her phone, and pressed the send button. She didn't know how they would deal with poor Ricardo and honestly didn't care. Make it look like an accident, she'd told them. A car crash on the way, maybe.

"Tout va bien?" One of the waitresses in the café smiled politely as she cleaned the table.

"Tout est excellent, merci," Elena replied with a smile, leaned back in her seat, and adjusted her glasses before she gazed out at the beach and wondered if she had the time to squeeze in a sunbathing session in her villa before Jacobs and his crew arrived.

Probably, she mused. Besides, they were coming to her, so it wasn't like she needed to alter her schedule to fit theirs.

Italy: A Small Airfield Near Turin

Sal watched the private plane that had dropped him, Madigan, and Anja off at the airstrip disappear into the clouds. It had taken them a couple of hops to get clear of the Sahara Desert, and from Casablanca, Courtney had managed to arrange a private jet to take them across the Mediterranean.

He wasn't sure how she'd managed that on such short notice, but he wouldn't complain. Getting their weapons and suits out of the Zoo would have been a headache without her help, so there was no looking this particular gift horse in the mouth.

The small airstrip was located outside of Turin, where they would wait for Courtney, Savage, and the others to arrive.

It was a bright, sunny day, he noted, and only a few tufts of clouds drifted through the atmosphere to complete the vista of an idyllic paradise. The airstrip had been created on a plateau above a small village nestled in a valley between two mountains. The very center of the valley had a snow-fed lake with a small river leading out of it. The settlement was built beside the lake, of course, although whether it had been established before the resorts he could see dotted along the waterside or after was something he would like to take time to discover.

This was as close as they'd come to civilization in a while. Since they'd gone with Courtney for her father's funeral, in fact, which felt like decades but was less than a year. It was totally weird how seeing a little town in the north of Italy was enough to make him nostalgic. This location could not look less like the places in which he had spent his time. Those had been mostly dry and arid when he was growing up. From there, he'd moved to California for his studies and then landed in the Zoo.

This was different and almost quaint. There were even forests growing in the distance, pushing up to the Alps so it looked like something straight out of a Disney movie.

Weird shit, he thought with a shake of his head.

"They should touch down in a few minutes," Madigan said as she gave him a quick glance and squeezed his shoulder. "Are you sure about this, Sal? There is a reason why we have Savage on the team, remember, and it's literally about pulling shit like this so we don't have to."

"Come on, didn't you want to get out of the Zoo for a little while?" Sal grinned and slid his hand over hers. "Come out to Monte Carlo, stay in an actual hotel with actual chefs making actual food, maybe gamble a little while we try to find out who is trying to kill us and why, and perhaps even kill her."

"Having an meal might be nice." She grunted and shrugged. "And maybe a soak in a hot tub?"

"Oh, yes, the hot tub." He chuckled. "I think I might join you for that."

"Now that sounds like a plan." She leaned in lazily to place a soft kiss on his lips. "After we've dealt with this Molina bitch."

A moment later, the sound of airplane engines whining in the distance distracted them from each other and they turned quickly. Another private plane circled and made its landing on one of the other airstrips beside the one their plane had used. The facility wasn't abandoned since there were more than a few people who wanted to come to the location for a vacation, but none of them wanted to use it in the dead of winter.

That was precisely why Courtney had chosen it as a

rendezvous point. Her assumption had been that Molina would be paranoid enough to have eyes and ears everywhere on her own turf—and maybe in the whole of Monaco—which meant they definitely wouldn't be able to land in the sole heliport of the principality without being identified and caught. Landing only a few miles from the border and driving in, though, made it a little more difficult for her to locate them, and the sheer number of people entering Monaco from Italy along the Grand Tour road would make sure they had enough safety in numbers.

Not enough safety for them to feel safe, of course. They would all come in armed to the teeth—and, in Sal, Madigan, and Courtney's case, with their combat suits only a few minutes away—should the woman decide she wanted to try to intercept them on the road like she'd attempted with Courtney a few days before.

They didn't expect any resistance or action en route, but Sal really did pity the fool who tried to stop them from reaching Molina.

The plane taxied to where the Heavy Metal team stood beside a couple of rented SUVs and waited for the team from the US to disembark. Courtney had put considerable time and effort into making sure they would spend as little time out in the open as possible. The planes had been brought in on Pegasus' dime, so if someone tracked the movements by the company, they would know someone high up on the company's roster would attend a meeting in Northern Italy and the right kind of person would be able to peek in on what was happening.

Anja was one of those people, and she was inside one of the vehicles, taking advantage of the Wi-Fi provided to run as much interference as she could. Even she had said, though, that her abilities were limited and she wouldn't be able to stop all the eyes that could be turned on them from seeing through her defenses.

It was probably the first time she had ever admitted to having any limitations regarding her skills on a computer. It was a sign of how nervous she was. The Russian had a healthy fear of her former employers and wanted to put as much distance between her and them as possible, which was why it hadn't been a difficult choice to pull her out of the Zoo while the FSB's eyes were on the location and possibly directed at Heavy Metal.

Gregor had told them he would let them know about how the meeting with those he'd sarcastically called his overlords went, and since then, they hadn't heard a peep from him. They were probably keeping the whole mission quiet until they were finished with the investigation, and he wouldn't risk any communication while the FSB still hung around the Russian base.

Hopefully, he hadn't run into any problems. Sal didn't want Gregor to be in any kind of trouble. There was also the issue of their vodka supply being threatened, but compared to the lives of friends and comrades—someone whose skin he'd saved and who had saved his skin in return while in the Zoo—it wasn't that relevant.

But he couldn't think about that for the moment. Their focus needed to be on Molina and the necessary action they had all geared themselves to take.

The plane came to a halt, and after a few minutes, the door opened and the steps descended gently. Once they lowered fully, another door was opened by what looked like a flight attendant, who immediately drew back to allow the passengers to disembark.

Courtney emerged first and looked like she was dressed for business in a pale-gray suit and heels. It made an odd sight, to be sure—at least regarding the heels—but still a sight for sore eyes.

She strode across the tarmac, smiling broadly as she approached them, and all but tackled Sal in a hug. He managed to keep her from knocking him flat on his back by taking a few steps back and laughed in surprise when she caught each side of his face and held him in place so she could kiss him.

"Hey, you," she whispered with a grin. "Did you miss me?"

"Like you wouldn't believe," he replied. He swung her off her feet for a moment and eased her down again. She ran her fingers slowly over his shoulder, enjoying the thin white shirt he wore beneath his jacket, then down his chest before she turned to Madigan.

"Hey, Ceecee." Madigan smirked and wrapped her in a warm embrace.

"Hey, Madie," she replied and leaned into the hug. "How about you?"

"Of course I missed you." She grinned and ruffled the woman's perfect hairdo. "Do you think Sal is easy to keep in line on my own?"

"Ah, well, I think I can help with that now that I'm here." Courtney chuckled and glanced over her shoulder to where he pretended not to listen to them. He walked to where the rest of the team had already disembarked.

Sal had seen considerable footage on Savage and even

talked to him on the video chat a couple of times, but he still wasn't fully prepared to meet him in person. There was something about him that sent chills down his spine, and for the life of him, he couldn't identify what it was exactly. There was literally nothing about him that stood out—average height, lean build, brown hair, and green eyes. Maybe something about the gauntness of his face made his skin prickle. He honestly couldn't tell, and it left him feeling a little wary.

If the man noticed he was staring, he didn't say anything about it as he came to where he stood and extended his hand, which he shook firmly.

Savage took his hand back with a small smirk and rubbed absently at his fingers. "Nice to finally meet you in person, Dr. Jacobs. I've heard a lot of stuff about you."

"All of it good, I hope?" he asked, and the man shrugged.

"Most of it, anyway." He chuckled.

"Well, I've heard a lot about you too, and I think you'll be pleased to hear that all of it is bad," he replied with a grin.

"You know, that is pleasant to hear." Savage patted him on the shoulder. "I'd like to introduce you—in person, anyway—to Samantha Davis, who goes by Sam, and this is Terrence Mixon, who goes by Terry."

Sal shook their hands as well. Both had the dangerous look of retired special forces although very distinctive, he thought. Terry looked far calmer and more collected, the kind of man who could break every bone in your body while he named each one. Sam was different—hyper and destructive. She too could probably break every bone in his body while commenting on which was her favorite to break, and why.

"It's nice to meet you, Dr. Jacobs," Terry said with a smile. Sam merely shook his hand, nodded, and made no comment as her eyes drifted to where Courtney and Madigan walked closer to join them.

"You guys can call me Sal," he said. He watched as Madigan stopped in front of Savage and extended her hand to him.

He took it with a smile although she didn't offer a similar gesture but simply shook firmly.

"Sergeant Kennedy, right?" he said and tried to get a read on her.

"It's nice to meet you in person, Mr. Savage," she replied. "Just Madigan Kennedy these days, though. I wanted to make sure we are on the same page here. Anderson might run a fairly loose ship in Philly and let you have autonomy while you do your thing. But I want to make sure you will follow our lead on this, understood? That you won't go off and kill people simply because you think it's the right call."

Savage nodded. "Understood. You guys are running the show. Sam, Terry, and I are here in a support role only."

She offered him a smile that didn't reach her eyes. "As long as we're clear."

"You're paying the bills and you make the rules," he agreed again before she relinquished his hand. Sal hadn't seen her like this before. She wasn't so childish that she would feel threatened by him, although she had been the one to voice doubts as to them bringing someone like him in. She had abided by Sal's decision, but maybe now that they would actually work in a closer proximity, she wanted to lay down some ground rules.

It made him recall a certain conversation he'd had with her on his first trip into the Zoo. Somehow, they'd raised the subject of dick-measuring and she'd stated how the rest of the men she served with would regret it if she had to whip her inches out. He knew her well enough to know she hadn't spoken literally, obviously, but she wasn't the type to take shit from anyone. He also knew she would make sure Savage fought at their side by her rules. She was their gunner, and she would keep them from danger that originated anywhere, even from their own team.

One thing he did notice was the fact that, as Savage approached the vehicles, Anja scrambled out of the far one and called his name—or Jer, rather. Short for Jeremiah, he assumed. He'd only ever heard anyone call the man Savage.

Sal couldn't help a soft chuckle. Jer was such a personal appropriation of the man's first name that it seemed out of place, but she used it openly with no fear of rebuttal. He knew she had helped him and Anderson run their operations from a distance, which meant they were far from strangers, although this was the first time they'd met in person.

It wasn't entirely surprising. If he worked as the man's eye in the sky in tight and life-threatening situations, he might be able to call him whatever he pleased too.

She flung herself at Savage, hugged him tightly, and squealed.

"It's…uh, nice to finally meet you in person too, Anja." He chuckled and wrapped her in a tight hug for a few minutes before he set her on her feet. "You're taller than I expected."

"And you're shorter, but who's counting here?" she joked and poked him laughingly in the shoulder.

"Will you join us in the field for this one?" he asked as the teams began to load and enter the SUVs.

"You wish." The hacker snorted. "Nah, I had to get clear of the Zoo while my countrymen are in a position where they might discover where I am. In which case, I guess I'll be as close to the field as I've ever been, but I'll always work from the comfort and safety of a…I guess a hotel room or something like that."

"That's right," Sal said as he climbed into the shotgun seat of one of the vehicles. "We need Anja alive and well in order to keep us all alive for missions to come, right?"

"No argument here, boss," Savage said and climbed into the same vehicle in the driver's seat. Sal narrowed his eyes at the man. He'd automatically assumed Kennedy would drive but saw her getting into the other car. Anja scrambled into the back seat behind Sal, while Courtney rode shotgun with Madigan and Sam and Terry took the seats in the back.

"Don't worry, Jacobs." Savage grinned as he started the car. "Kennedy made it perfectly clear that I wasn't supposed to kill anyone without the express say-so of one of the three of you. Well, four, if you count Anderson, but since he's not here, three of you. Shall we?"

Sal nodded and gestured for him to start after the other team. "You can call me Sal, you know."

The operative nodded. "Sure thing, Sal."

Anja leaned forward and patted them on their shoulders. "It's so nice to see both my boys getting along so well."

"Are...we your boys?" Sal asked and twisted a little to look at her. She nodded emphatically.

"Otherwise, whose boys would you two be?" she asked.

"Well, I'm technically Courtney and Madigan's boy," he pointed out.

Savage shrugged. "I'm unclaimed for the moment, so I'll be one of your boys, Anja."

"Yes!" she celebrated, patted him on the shoulder again, and turned to Sal. "I'll win you over yet, Sal."

"I...look forward to it?" he said, not sure what she meant by that. For now, he was content to simply leave the conversation at that since he was well aware that the rest of the team was connected via earbud. It was honestly best not to incur the wrath of both Madigan and Courtney. He was still working off their annoyance at having to rescue him from the Zoo only once.

CHAPTER SEVENTEEN

Monte Carlo: The Street Outside La Vigie Restaurant

Savage decided that even though it never needed to be said, Monte Carlo wasn't his kind of place.

He was one of those people for whom sunlight and bright colors would always feel garish and uncomfortable. It was less populated than Philly, yet it seemed far busier. More people were out on the street, even in the winter, to enjoy the mild weather the small European country experienced. People were on the beaches, sunning themselves and playing in the water. This was a vacation town, and he wasn't there on vacation, which made him feel out of place.

That said, Courtney had insisted they look as much like tourists as possible and decreeed a shopping spree inside the casino and hotel she had booked for them. She had instructed them to dress to look like tourists while they ran the recon on their target.

Anja, on top of offering to help them walk away with a killing on the casino floors, had been able to track Molina to a higher-end section of the city, which in turn meant they needed to fit in there too. Savage was dressed in a light-colored, lightweight set of tan shirt and slacks. Courtney had made sure all his colors matched, not only with each other but with the sunglasses she'd included for him as well as the loafers.

He looked like a fucking playboy, he had grumbled at the time. Seriously, he was a diamond-studded Rolex away from being a spoiled brat whose father had never paid him enough attention. It was embarrassing.

Sam would never let him live this down if not for the fact that she wore a sundress with a wide-brimmed straw hat, Armani sunglasses, and flat pumps to make her look equally as tourist-y as her "husband." Anja had even procured fake IDs that would pass them off as an American and British couple with no intention of letting anything come between them and a vacation that was supposed to rekindle their marriage or some shit like that.

The Russian hacker had guilted them into memorizing every detail of their legends by saying she had put so much work into them that if they needed to answer any questions and fumbled, it would be their fault.

By now, he had begun to doubt that she'd put that much work into the matter. She probably had them stashed away somewhere on the off-chance that the team might need them.

"Don't fucking look at me," Sam complained. She played her part well and held herself close to him, her hand tucked in his arm, and kept pace with his leisurely stroll with all the elegance of someone who had done this for real at some point. "I look like a fucking housewife who drives a minivan to get her son to and from football and then drinks a whole bottle of chardonnay to get her through a day of lounging around the house."

"Are you kidding me?" he grumbled. "I'm the poster boy for the 'my dad's a lawyer so you'd better not touch me or this baggie that is obviously cocaine' look."

She pulled back and gave him an objective scrutiny and even lowered her sunglasses to improve her vision. "Yep, that's one hundred percent accurate. At least in your case, the rich young ones will flock with the right mix of daddy issues and gold digging."

"The rich ones are always psychotic," he said and shook his head. "It's not helpful, of course, that you'd attract the psychotic kind of lazy man who wants a sugar momma. They'll think they are God's gift to womenkind and that someone like you should be lucky simply to 'score' with guys like them."

Sam made a gagging noise and dragged a chuckle from him as they continued their stroll.

"Lucky for you, then, that you're 'married' to me," he said and studied their surroundings casually. "I'll beat the dumbasses back, and if they prove a little too insistent, I'll simply shoot them."

"Much obliged, I'm sure, although I'm perfectly capable of breaking and or shooting them on my own." She grinned. "Still, I can't say I would do the same for you. Watching you stumble into bad decision after bad decision is too hilarious to not sit back and watch."

"How disappointing." He adopted an expression of mock woundedness. "Here I was thinking we were friends."

"We are friends, Savage," she replied and nudged his

ribs with her elbow. "Which is why I'd only sit, watch, and laugh and certainly not encourage."

"You're actually married, in case the two of you have forgotten," Terry said through their earpieces. The man had eyes on them from a nearby nest he'd set up on an abandoned construction site Anja had found for him, ever diligent as overwatch, even for a simple recon mission. "Do you guys mind remembering that you're supposed to fit in?"

"No matter what kind of outfit I have on, I'll always look like a tomboy," Sam pointed out. "I have too much power and muscle to look like anything else that would fit in around here."

"She makes a good point." Savage chuckled. "So...what do you guys think about the Heavy Metal gang?"

"What do we think about them?" she asked. "Like personal opinions based on the two and a half-hour drive across the border?"

"Something like that," he replied. "I only want to get impressions on them from an outside source, in case mine are...you know, faulty."

"They're essentially what we expected them to be," Terry replied, clearly sufficiently bored in his current position to let himself be entangled in a conversation this easily. "We already knew Monroe. She's a little...intense, to say the least, but she means well, for the most part. The whole ends justify the means kind of person."

"Kennedy's different, though," Sam pointed out. "Intense too, well-meaning too, but less the kind of person who would do shitty stuff for good reasons. Fresh out of the military, a true believer who will do anything to make sure the members of her team get out alive. Nothing like us, right, Savage?"

He shrugged. "I don't know. I'd do some messed up shit to get the two of you out of trouble if you needed me to."

"That's the difference, though, isn't it, Savage?" Terry mused aloud. "We're all competent individuals who don't need anyone to get us out of the tough situations. In fact, I'd say we've been the ones to bail you out more than you have us."

"Which is why I would do the messed-up stuff to get you out of trouble," he pointed out. "That and the fact that I know you guys will never actually need me to bail you two out."

"That's a sound policy," she said with a nod. "What about Jacobs? What kind of impression did you get from him while you gave him the 'Driving Miss Daisy' treatment?"

"You've never watched that movie, have you?" Savage asked.

She shook her head. "Nope. I watched a trailer and was bored to tears. And I'm usually a Morgan Freeman fan too."

"Yeah, I can see that," Savage said. "During the drive, though… He's a hard man to pin down. He's as sharp as anyone I've ever seen, and he's competent with a gun if his record is anything to go by. He's on edge most of the time, though—a little too jumpy to be an effective black-ops operative."

"That's what going into the Zoo regularly does to you, I guess," Terry surmised. "All the rules are changed in there. I've seen the footage of what teams had to do to stay alive in the jungle, and it's not always pretty. But it has to be effective, otherwise, you'll find yourself shat out of a monster a few hours later."

"My word, Terrence!" Sam gasped and raised a hand to her mouth in mock-shock. "Watch your gosh-darned language. My stars...or some shit like that."

"Yeah, yeah, I know." The sniper laughed. "I guess you're rubbing off on me. You are such a bad influence, Samantha."

"Oh, God." Savage rolled his eyes.

"Well, if you two aren't too shocked by my gosh-darned language, you should know that the target has entered a nearby café," Terry mentioned casually.

Neither of his teammates showed any sign that they had heard what he said. Sam let her gaze drift casually to the nearby beachfront restaurant with a terrace that extended onto the beach. They needed to get closer, so the two of them took another leisurely walk.

When they were close enough, Savage turned his back on the establishment and she naturally stepped in closer to him. They managed to look like they were a couple in the midst of a romantic moment—the kind that would encourage most people to avert their eyes—while he scanned the location for threats and she took a detailed look at their target.

"She's moving out onto the terrace," she said and kept her voice low so it would look like she whispered something in his ear and smiled when he placed his hands on her hips. "A place called La Vigie. It doesn't look like there's any kind of security there at all, but our gal isn't rolling alone. I see two muscle-bound bodyguards at the table next to her. She's sitting alone...someone brought her coffee and a menu, and it doesn't look like she's expecting any company."

"Send the word to the rest of our team," Savage stated quietly. It took a few seconds before another commlink keyed into their line.

"Are you guys in position?" Anja asked and sounded a little stressed.

"Oh yes," Savage replied, still up close and personal with Sam. "And it looks like our target is ready for our approach, so whenever Team One is ready to move—"

"They're good to go when you are," Anja said. "When-ever you and Sam are finished with your moment, that is."

"Don't judge. Savage is a good hugger," Sam replied with a grin but nudged him a step back and indicated that they should give the location a walk-around before the rest of their team arrived.

"What do you mean, what's my impression of Savage?" Sal asked and fiddled with the minibar in their limo.

Madigan shrugged impatiently. "You were around him during your drive and have therefore spent the most time with him out of all of us. I don't think even Courtney's had the pleasure of exchanging more than a few sentences with the man, so you are in a prime position to provide an actual inside view of our hired attack dog."

"You need to stop calling him that," Courtney pointed out, her eyes narrowed. "He's not merely a…hitman. He's fully engaged in what we're doing with Pegasus, and he saved my and Anderson's lives not that long ago."

The other woman stared in response, her expression hard. "I know a cold killer when I see one, and he's a cold killer. The kind of guy who will walk away from a tough situation simply because he doesn't like the look of it and screw the consequences. In my experience, those are the guys who will shoot you in the back because they get a better offer."

"He seemed more complicated than that," Sal protested. "I don't know. The way he looks at people simply gets your hackles up, but he does seem to have some kind of...honor to him. Or at least a sense of morals. He'll make split-second, life-or-death decisions when he's under pressure to do so, but he does have a set of rules he won't break. And call me crazy, but it seemed like one of those rules was 'thou shalt not shoot thy employer in the back when you get a better offer.'"

"You're right," she grumbled. "You are crazy."

"Hey, you asked for my impression of the man," he replied defensively. "That was my impression. If you don't like it, don't ask for it."

"I don't want to make you feel outnumbered, but I actually agree with Sal," Courtney interjected and grinned when he narrowed his eyes at her. "I know, crazy, right? I've worked with him, though. He's as tough as nails and he makes some iffy moral choices sometimes, but he has our back."

Madigan still looked disgruntled. "I won't suddenly change my mind and trust him, but I can't pretend your impressions don't matter to me. I'll...tone down my distrust of the man."

"What about the other two?" Sal asked. The two women

had been in the car with Sam and Terry. "You had the opportunity to get an impression of them while you were driving, right?"

"Yeah, they didn't actually say that much while on the trip," Courtney said and seemed to think about it. "I think they still see me as their boss, so they're not that comfortable with shooting the breeze, as it were, while I'm around. They feel more comfortable around Anderson, though."

"They're soldiers, through and through." Madigan seemed pensive. "Sam looked like she was the most... outwardly violent of the two, but from what I've seen of Terry's record, he's not the kind of man to necessarily reveal exactly how dangerous he can be. Both looked like professionals."

"Neither of them rubbed you the wrong way like Savage did," Sal commented dryly.

"Yeah, you could say that," she replied. "They looked like pros. Soldiers who would kill when told to, but they leave the hard decisions to others and make sure to cover each other's backs as a priority."

Courtney nodded agreement. "It takes a soldier to know a soldier, I guess. I suppose I would be able to read a researcher or a scientist the way Madigan read those guys."

"It's a superpower." The other woman grinned. "One I can't promise to only use for good."

"I'm not sure there are any ways that you could use that power in a naughty fashion," Sal interjected and winked at her.

"You need to pay attention." She smirked. "It's kind of the reason why you and I got together in the first place."

"Ahem," Anja's voice said through their earbuds. "Am I interrupting something?"

"That depends." Courtney laughed.

"You guys will pull up at a restaurant called 'La Vigie' momentarily, which is where our target is currently situated. I wanted to make sure you were ready for the encounter or if you needed a few more seconds." She'd barely finished speaking when the limo eased to a halt alongside the curb.

"We're good to go, Anja," Madigan said as she stood and opened the limo door. She waited for her teammates to alight before she shut it behind her and nodded to the driver, who looked shocked that his services hadn't been required to help them out. "What's the sitrep?"

"She's out on the terrace having coffee," Anja advised them. "She does have muscle in there with her, so you'll need to be careful and time your arrival perfectly."

"How's our greeting party?" Sal asked. He looked around casually and adjusted his suit jacket to fit a little better over his shoulders.

"They're taking care of her greeting party," Anja said. "Whenever you're ready."

CHAPTER EIGHTEEN

<u>Monte Carlo: La Vigie Restaurant</u>

It was an exceedingly pleasant afternoon, Elena decided. The sun gleamed, still high in the sky, and brightened everything around her with a pleasant golden glow. The sky was blue with a handful of clouds on the horizon, which indicated that there might be a drizzle a little later in the day. That was what her weather app predicted, anyway, and it had been a while since anyone had thought to doubt the weather predictions.

The technology that went into it was insane. She would know, given that it was one of her companies' specialties. Still, weather in the Mediterranean would always continue to be a little wonky, so maybe instead of a drizzle in the afternoon it would arrive in the evening.

Such minor vagaries in the weather were inconsequential and she really liked the winters in Monte Carlo. It sprawled in that sweet spot under the French Alps that made sure it was never oppressively warm during the summers like it was in Ibiza. The fact that it was on the

Mediterranean meant it would always mingle warm air from the Sahara and the icy winds from the mountains in the north, with the result that it was mild all year around. It was the best place to vacation for winter if you weren't the ski resort kind of person.

She detested skiing, even if she was passable at it, and simply couldn't stand the cold. Her body always needed to be someplace warm for as long as possible. Still, she had vaguely considered heading up there for a while, maybe once all these issues were dealt with. While she didn't like the skiing, she did enjoy the resort part where there were warm Jacuzzis and supple Olympians training and in need of the kind of relaxation she was more than willing to provide. After Ricardo's unfortunate demise in a car accident, she needed someone new to distract her from the problems that constantly raised their ugly little heads to complicate her existence.

Still, those were problems for another time, and she was taking the time to relax. Being out in the open wasn't a luxury she could afford to indulge in too often, so when she could sit out on a terrace and enjoy a pleasant cup of coffee and maybe a light salad for lunch, she would make the most of it.

Her gaze drifted to her security team, two men who were ill-disguised as yet another couple of tourists in the city. Something about them simply screamed that they were hired muscle. Maybe it was the muscle, she mused and tilted her head in thought as she scrutinized them. And the sunglasses and the big, thick, bushy beards that were more than helpful in intimidating people who didn't know any better. They were armed but it had been artfully concealed under their clothes. Fitting in had been the idea, so sport coats were used to cover their underarm holsters.

They were more for show than anything else. Anyone who might be surveilling her would think it was too much of an invitation if she was seen wandering around without any evidence of an escort. Elena had made more than enough enemies to warrant having people with guns and a bad attitude follow her around and take their foul mood out on anyone who might want to do her harm.

But her attention was drawn to them for another reason. They were hired from a firm and she therefore hadn't had the time to actually vet them—which explained, she assumed, why they put their hands to their ears and talked into earbuds people weren't supposed to know they had. Something clearly had them concerned, which meant something was wrong.

They were obviously trying to contact the people they had patrolling the outside of the restaurant. The fact that they were all supposed to be within two hundred meters of their location—and therefore could not have technical difficulties in communicating with the rest of their team—was definitely something to worry about.

If these men weren't able to start acting like professionals, she would have to look into simply hiring her own. Perhaps it was time to hand-pick from the best like Anderson and Monroe had done. Maybe if she had played things that way instead of outsourcing those decisions to people she paid to do work for her, she might have more success in nailing these assholes to the wall.

A couple stepped onto the terrace. They were foreigners and spoke English as they pointed at the admittedly gorgeous view beyond the railings. Most people didn't come outside despite the mild weather that currently prevailed and preferred the nicer, more intimate booths closer to the kitchens where they could avoid the potentially icy gusts outside. These two didn't seem to mind. They stared at the waves that curled in to lap gently at pristine beaches and talked and laughed as they moved closer and looked for somewhere to sit.

Elena narrowed her eyes as they chose the table her bodyguards had selected for themselves. In fairness, there were two open seats and they were nice enough to ask. They weren't nice enough to listen when the two burly men denied their request and sat anyway, still talking.

"Come on, you two look like you could use some company," the man said in a voice she somehow found vaguely familiar.

"Right?" the woman replied. "Two guys, sitting around and not doing much, not even having anything to drink or eat and no conversation between you. Merely sitting there with your...what do you think they are, Desert Eagles?"

"Mark XIX, I'd say," the man replied, and both her men suddenly stiffened and looked at one another as if to determine exactly how fucked they were.

She knew they were more than a little fucked even before she saw that the couple had weapons in their hands as well—pistols aimed at the two bodyguards to keep them pinned in place. First the man, then the woman, reached over and subtly removed the large weapons from inside the men's jackets and tucked them away where no one would be able to see them.

Elena sighed, dropped her head into her hands, and

rubbed her temples as three newcomers moved onto the terrace. These, she recognized. Well, she recognized one of them enough to be able to deduce who the other two were.

Dr. Salinger Jacobs and former Sergeant Madigan Kennedy were the known associates and possible lovers of the head of Pegasus Inc, Dr. Courtney Monroe. Or as Elena liked to say, her personal thorn in her side.

Which meant the man who had disarmed her body-guards both figuratively and very, very literally, was the one and only Jeremiah Savage, formerly known as Sergeant Jeremiah Johnson, supposedly killed in action.

It looked like they'd brought the entire team in for this, she thought and felt a little flattered as the Heavy Metal trio settled into the free seats at her table—Salinger across from her, Kennedy to her left, and Courtney to her right. Their confidence to simply sit in the open with her told her that they probably had a couple of eyes in the sky. She couldn't recall the name of the woman Savage had walked in with, but she was clearly a professional judging by the way she held her weapon, and she had known that the man worked with a team. The only question that remained was whether or not the two of them were actually a couple or not. They played the part well enough.

"Elena Molina," Jacobs said, leaned back in his seat, and tilted his sunglasses to rest them on the crown of his head. "Have I pronounced that right?"

"You have," she replied with a smile and sipped her coffee.

"Well, you're a hard woman to find, Miss Molina," he said with a small chuckle. "Understatement of the century, though, right?"

They paused in their conversation as a waitress came out. Weapons were smoothly concealed by Savage and his comrade, but the woman clearly understood that the four at the table were working and immediately moved to Elena's table.

"Will there be any orders from the table?" she asked softly with a smile and a heavy French accent and looked at each of them. Jacobs, Kennedy, and Monroe raised their hands and shook their heads quickly to indicate that they would not place an order.

"Are you sure?" Elena asked magnanimously. "I will pay, of course. The coffee here is absolutely sublime."

"We wouldn't dream of imposing ourselves like that," Monroe said quickly with a small smirk.

"I'm insulted that you are afraid I might somehow tamper with the food or drink like that, Dr. Monroe," she replied, her eyes narrowed. "Not only would it be utterly ill-mannered, but I would also never dream of doing anything so heinous in such a public place."

The waitress raised an eyebrow at the exchange but showed no other sign that the mention of poison was in any way untoward.

"All right, then," Jacobs said quickly. "We'll have a coffee if it comes so highly recommended."

"*Convenez-vous*," Elena replied with a shrug and turned to face the waitress. "*Une salade César et trois cafés, s'il vous plait.*"

"*Bien sûr, à venir*," she replied with a smile and a nod before she beat a hasty retreat into the restaurant.

"You don't know what you're missing," she insisted, finished her coffee, and pushed the cup and saucer to the center of the table. "The chef here makes superb grilled dishes. You should at least try it once we are done discussing business."

"I don't think we'll stay that long," Monroe replied and raised an eyebrow. "Or are we still pretending you haven't tried to kill almost everyone at this table—as well as a few others—at least once."

"Please." She chuckled and shook her head. "You are the only one at this table I ever showed any real intention to kill. Jacobs and Kennedy were mere...victims of their approximation to you."

"So, it's their fault they were caught in your murderous crossfire, then?" Courtney asked and leaned forward. Elena noted that the woman had a weapon hidden in her purse and something of a murderous glint in her eyes. It seemed to suggest she might not care that they were in the open like this and decide to kill her there and then.

Well, it was best not to test her, then.

"What is the American term..." she said. "If the shoe fits? Either way, I do not mean to offend. You have to know this is all about business to me. I honestly admire all of you and what you're doing. I even admire why, no matter how misguided it might be."

"Yeah, I'm sure we don't give a shit about what you do or don't admire, Miss Molina," Kennedy retorted acidly.

"Well, then, why don't you explain to us why it seemed you wanted us to find you?" Courtney asked. "You know, before we tell Savage over there to break your neck and let us all walk away from this with some form of dignity intact."

The operative looked at her from the table where he kept her bodyguards company and waved cheerfully.

"Perhaps I have a few snipers overlooking our position?" Elena asked and immediately regretted it. She had planned what she would say to them beforehand, but sometimes, the ideas didn't carry over into what happened.

It didn't matter, of course, she told herself. Even if they did take her seriously on that issue, it would only make them underestimate her and feel a little more comfortable and therefore more open to what she had to say.

"Well, we considered that." Courtney regarded her with a bland expression. "But then we also have a sniper overlooking our position who already eliminated the man you had in overwatch, so I think we're in the clear for the moment."

She narrowed her eyes. For a moment, she wasn't sure how to respond. She hadn't put anyone with a sniper rifle in position. While she had considered an option that was extremely tempting, it had seemed like overkill when she wanted to have a conversation with these people. The idea was for them to feel as safe as possible. They would suspect something was awry if she arrived without any security, but there was no need to go overboard on it.

Which made her wonder. Either Courtney was lying or there was a sniper out there who had nothing to do with either of the parties present. It was a problem for another time, but a problem it most definitely was.

They paused their conversation when the waitress returned with a tray of four coffees and a plate of the salad she had ordered. The young woman didn't seem to notice that the conversation had suddenly stopped on her arrival and was probably accustomed to dealing with business meetings held on the terrace. By now, she would have a good idea of what to do while they were in progress.

She placed the coffees around the table and the salad in front of Elena. Once again, she didn't bother to try to take an order from the other table where the muscle was currently seated and merely walked into the restaurant.

Jacobs looked like the more reasonable of the three as he was the first one to take a sip from his coffee. He raised his eyebrows and looked at her.

"Oh...wow, this really is good," he said with a chuckle. The other two decided to try it as well—begrudgingly—although both seemed to be similarly surprised by the quality.

"I come here rather regularly, and they never fail to impress," Elena lied smoothly. She took a sip of hers and left her salad for later.

"Well," Jacobs started and placed his cup on its saucer, "you're the one who brought us here, Miss Molina. Why don't you go ahead and say your piece?"

CHAPTER NINETEEN

<u>*Monte Carlo: La Vigie Restaurant*</u>

Sal waited calmly and simply watched Elena as she sighed and took another sip of her coffee. In her defense, the brew was absolutely fantastic, although his taste was prejudiced by the fact that he had used instant coffee since he'd arrived at the Zoo. Before that, it had been the shitty coffee they made in the Caltech research labs.

The latter had been effective, though, since the people who worked there needed to have their energy and wits about them while they pushed the boundaries of scientific discovery. But merely because it was effective didn't mean it didn't taste like it had been plumbed from the oil pan of a car that had used the same oil for the past thirty years or so.

This was bitter but aromatic in a way that made sure the bitter was an aspect of the full taste and not an over-powering sensation that punched you in the face until you were awake. The kind he was used to was a necessary evil that came with the need to stay awake for hours on end while watching nothing happen over long periods of time.

The woman took her time in getting to the point, but a prompt from Courtney concerning Savage's enthusiasm at the prospect of being able to deliver a well-placed and very final bullet did the trick and Elena reached for her purse. The operative's hand had already swiveled in case any kind of threat presented itself, but a weapon wasn't what she took out. It was a tablet, although Sal's attention was directed to her arm when it came out of her sleeve, rather than at the device. The sunlight on her skin showed some of the veins beneath, which were a very distinctive and familiar shade of blue.

It wasn't a comforting sight, given that the last time he'd seen it, the creature he'd seen it in had literally attacked him and impaled itself on his combat suit's sword. His eyebrows raised instinctively when he realized what he was looking at, but he didn't mention it out loud, even though it brought a few alarming details to light.

When he recalled the strength of the man he had encountered coming out of the Zoo, it made him wonder if their assumption that Savage would be able to handle and potentially kill this woman was in doubt. Based on his studies of what she was undoubtedly taking on a regular basis—and in much larger quantities than he was—the more likely possibility was that she could pick the operative up and toss him off the deck while still calmly sipping her coffee.

Then again, he had exposed himself to the goop for months and had seen the changes that had come over his body. He had higher energy and better stamina. While he hadn't run any medical tests so couldn't be sure, his muscular structure had started to feel a little denser, and he had put on considerably more weight while losing mass. He would like to talk to an doctor about it at some point.

Well, he was an doctor, but not the kind he needed. Maybe a rheumatology diagnostician. Someone with an open mind who didn't much mind talking about a specialist performing tests on him or herself. Well, himself, in his case, obviously.

He might want to talk to Courtney and Madigan about it first, although Madigan wouldn't be the one to consult about the details of the possible implications of denser muscles and the likely increase in density of his bones to accommodate them.

There were certain things you simply didn't bring up with your girlfriend unless she had a professional interest. Honestly, if she had any idea of the variety of changes his body was undergoing, she would probably try to persuade him to stop. That was all well and good—and even logical, perhaps—but if there was one thing he didn't want to discover, it was what would happen to his body if he stopped taking the blue stuff. Licking Madie, as they had started to call it so affectionately.

"What do you think about this, Sal?" Courtney asked, and the question brought him back rather abruptly from the line of thought he'd inadvertently been sucked into. All for the better, he decided, given that he did have a propensity to overthink things. Yes, he would probably be fine. He would most likely not develop the same symptoms Molina appeared to demonstrate, which she had in common with a man who had gone feral as a result of experiments run on him by the Russian scientists in the Zoo.

His caution and systematic approach meant he would be absolutely fine. After all, he took great care to control his dose. His fears were groundless and based on nothing more than his own trepidation about using himself as a test subject.

Probably.

Sal's gaze dropped to the tablet, and he tilted his head while he concentrated on the information. He needed to make a note on his own tablet about the fact that it had become difficult to focus on one thing at a time. It could simply be a sign of something else—a natural side-effect of the fact that his body was far more active than it used to be and his brain still had to catch up. It could also mean that the blue stuff had increased his synaptic transmission speed. He didn't know if that was even possible, but then again, he probably needed a neurologist to help to establish anything as a fact. All he could really do was keep recording all the details about everything he experienced.

"Sal?" Madigan asked, and he frowned again and shook his head.

"Sorry, I'm a little distracted," he said with a sigh.

"You take your time. I'm in no hurry," Elena replied with a soft chuckle. She leaned back and regarded him with almost an amused expression.

"And as you probably already know, the rest of us are hourly," Savage pointed out with a firm nod.

"Not all of us." Courtney scowled at him and the man shrugged, his weapon once again trained on the two bodyguards.

Sal paid no attention to any of them, scanned the tablet again, and frowned when he began to read it in detail.

"Well, don't keep us all in suspense. What does it say?" Sam asked. She leaned over to try to sneak a peek at what had his attention.

He glanced at her. She still had her weapon trained on the second bodyguard, although she now looked away. To her credit, her aim never wavered from where her weapon was directed squarely between the man's eyes.

"Well, apparently, a variety of European Union governments had the approval of the Ukrainian government to set up a top-secret laboratory in Chernobyl about six months after the whole Zoo shit hit the proverbial fan," he said and absorbed the details as quickly as he could.

He explained how they'd managed to set a lab up when the whole area was an irradiated wasteland. It made very interesting reading that he would like to look at more closely when they had more time. The collective minds involved in the project were a veritable who's who of the non-American winners of a variety of Nobel prizes, as well as other major names and prize winners across the various branches of science. The fact that no Americans were included was a clear indication of how the Zoo debacle had affected the worldview of the American scientific research communities.

Focus, dammit.

"Right... It looks like there was considerable funding from the local governments, most of it coming from Moscow in the hopes of making the region livable sometime in the foreseeable future," he continued after a pause that was longer than necessary. "The latest estimates of when the area will be considered livable again are at around three thousand years or so, and the goop has been noted to cause an absorption of radiation from the atmosphere, as impossible as that might sound."

"Yeah, because all of us are keeping up to date with that shit," Savage quipped.

"Shut up, Savage," Madigan growled, and the man responded with a nod.

"Anyway, from the looks of these studies, the work they've conducted has seen some fantastic and—if all of this is true—ground-breaking results, with the levels of radioactivity dropping by more than half since the lab was founded," Sal added and ignored them all. "Ukraine has seen drops of kilobecquerels per square meter to under fifteen thousand."

"Holy shit, is that true?" Courtney asked.

"It's hard to say. To be honest, I have a hard time believing any of this," Sal replied. "No offense, but we simply don't trust anything you give us."

"Hey, I deserve that after trying to kill most of those present," Elena responded with every indication that she hadn't taken offense at his bluntness.

"Anyway, they did this by siphoning what little of the original goop remained after the Zoo fiasco." He rolled his eyes and turned his attention to the tablet. "Once that ran out, they harvested the blue stuff from the flowers in the Zoo—the little they didn't sell as youth creams around the world—which is something quite interesting. And it's annoying that they didn't share the concept of similarities between the original goop and what they've harvested from the flowers."

"Wait, so there's a group of people who smear something structurally similar to the original alien goop on their faces because it helps them look younger?" Savage asked, his expression both disbelieving and disapproving. "Isn't that...what's the word I'm looking for? Oh, right, alarming?"

"The attack dog has a good point," Madigan said and seemed to genuinely have a hard time believing she had found common ground with the man. "Shouldn't we raise this point with everyone who will listen?"

"It's been tried," Sal recalled. "Most of the attempts to disseminate the information have been challenged due to the fact that people make a phenomenal amount of money from it. And there's also the fact that none of the structural details of the original goop have been shared with the public and are still considered highly classified. Long story short, anyone who's brought it up has been dismissed as a conspiracy theorist."

"Been there, done that." Savage chuckled darkly.

"Oh, for fuck's sake." Elena hissed her annoyance. "Would you please get to the point and stop with this squabbling?"

"All right." Sal sighed and flashed her a quick frown. "Anyway, while the effects of the lab's work can be seen in the country, everything had looked promising until a few weeks ago, when the lab suddenly went dark without explanation. Who could have guessed that would happen?"

She smiled. "As it turns out, I have a great deal of my own money invested in the project, and I would like the best team available to be sent in to investigate what happened in the lab. In the interest of keeping everything above-board, you won't be the first team I have sent in. In fact, the last team reported some very...interesting details about what they found. But they disappeared almost immediately. I thought we might need to know more about what's happening in there before I sent another, so I hoped to gather what the Russians had discovered on the topic of human exposure to the goop before bringing you into the mix. Thanks to Team Heavy Metal, that was royally fucked up, so you'll have to go into that blind."

"I thought we'd decided on Heavy Metal Militia," Madigan reminded the others. "It rolls off the tongue a little better, don't you think?"

"I honestly don't care." The woman scowled.

"Well, given that you appear to want to hire the Heavy Metal Militia, I'd suggest you start caring," Courtney snapped in response.

"Either way, what makes you think we'll take the job?" Sal asked, his expression one of confusion. "You did try to kill Courtney, and... Well, let's be honest, with the sheer number of people you lost in that attempt, I can understand why you would need to hire from the outside."

"Good burn, Sal." Madigan chuckled.

"Be that as it may, you can call that my way of getting people's attention," Elena said with a smile. "Besides, I needed to audition the part of your team that hasn't been in the Zoo. I've seen the efficacy of that team from the police reports rather than simply heard about it from the absurdly incompetent people I've hired. Or had other people hire, anyway. I assume that was my downfall—not doing things myself."

Savage tipped an imaginary hat at her attempt at a compliment.

"Anyway, I'm well aware that you run a business and that you will all engage in life-threatening situations in order to bring the operation to a successful conclusion. So, of course, you can name whatever price you think is fair," she continued. "And I will pay your price up front. Call it a sign of good faith on my part. You can use the data you find yourselves, obviously. All I'm paying you for is to share what you find with me as well."

Madigan and Courtney shared a confused look, but Sal nodded, cleared his throat, and finished his coffee. "We'll do it."

"I beg your pardon?" Courtney asked, her eyebrows raised in response.

"I think what Courtney is a little too polite to say is 'why the fuck are you taking a job from the spoiled princess-slash-heiress bitch who tried to kill us, you dumbass?'" Madigan explained.

"Yeah, I'm with that line of reasoning," Sam called from the other table.

"Because we are running a business here," he said and fixed each member of the team with a stubborn look in turn. "And honestly, the opportunity to dig into the effects of the alien goop on parts of the world that aren't sand is too good to pass up on. With us being paid...shall we say, ten million US dollars for each member engaged in the operation, it seems like an even better opportunity."

"You know what they say about opportunities that are too good to be true, right?" Madigan asked.

He nodded and shrugged dismissively. "Ten million US

dollars each, paid up front, to each member of the team heading in should be the kind of opportunity that is too good to pass up, even if it is too good to be true," he said.

"Done," Elena said. "I'll have the money in accounts in your individual names before the end of the day. I already have a plane waiting to fly us to the Ukraine and made the arrangements to have you and your collective team suited to your individual preferences. For those who have never been in the Zoo and have no experience with combat suits…well, I had some specialists to consult, but it was mostly guesswork from our end. I have to apologize in advance for any preferences that might have been overlooked in the absence of actual data. I hear the location you'll go into is dangerous, and you'll need all the help you can get."

"We're good to go when you are," he confirmed, pushed out of his seat, and smoothed his jacket with a distracted motion.

CHAPTER TWENTY

A Private Jet En route To Kiev

"Are you still single, Savage?"

Sal's eyes opened at the question and he twisted in his seat to look behind him at the other seats on the plane. The man didn't show any inclination to answer the question, which had been proposed to him by Elena. They were all on board and currently en route to the Ukraine via a private plane they had to board in France. A helicopter had waited at the heliport in the city, which brought them out to the private airstrip in the Côte d'Azur.

From there, it was a three-and-a-half-hour flight to Kiev, which would enable them to reach the infamous area of Chernobyl, their ultimate destination. Of course, even with the changes that had allegedly taken place, it was still supposed to be a heavily irradiated area, which meant they would have to be suited up at all times.

It definitely wouldn't be the most pleasant of trips, but they knew that before they took the job. Ten million already sitting pretty in their accounts was enough of an incentive—for Sal, anyway. There were other reasons why he had taken this job, though, reasons that might be considered selfish.

He would need to talk to Madigan and Courtney about it when they touched down again to make sure they knew what they were getting into. They wouldn't like that he'd made the decision without discussing it with them first, but it wasn't like he could do so while Elena sat with them or simply trust Savage, Sam, and Terry to hold the fort indefinitely. There would be various long and involved stages of what he knew would be a very drawn-out conversation.

This way, he would simply try the commonly used expression of it being easier to ask for forgiveness than permission.

That said, hearing Elena ask Savage if he was still single was enough to distract him from the problems he currently faced in his relationships.

It was a decent enough distraction. Of all the people to wonder about Savage's marital status, she didn't seem like the kind of person who really cared about what kind of relationship issues the mercenaries she'd paid a considerable amount of money might face. In this case, though, it looked like she might have ulterior motives in her line of questioning.

"Oh, yes," the operative replied. He made no effort to look up from the tablet he used to get a feel for the terrain they would enter when they arrived. "Why do you ask? Are you looking for more people to kill, by any chance?"

"Quite the contrary," she said and pushed some of the long, silky black strands of hair from her face. "I ask because I need a partner for stress relief, and you meet all the markers I need in my partners. In...you know, sexual stress relief."

Sal bit back a chuckle and for a moment, thought she might be joking, but she stared at Savage, unblinking, and looked entirely serious. A somewhat awkward silence followed and finally, her brows drew together in a frown when he delayed even an attempt to answer.

"Is there any confusion as to what I've asked?" She looked annoyed and Sal now had to fight back a full-bellied laugh.

"Not about what you've asked, no, but there is some confusion," the operative replied, his attention still fixed on the device. "I'm merely wondering if you recall the fact that you were directly involved in the attempted murder of my family. And, if that fact escaped your memory, whether the recollection of it might encourage you to rethink your proposition."

"Of course I remember. I wasn't asking you to enter into an emotional relationship," she retorted and sipped her glass of champagne. "Sex can be used as a simple stress relief and a primal release of endorphins in the brain that would allow us both to function much better in our respective jobs."

"While that's true, I do think I can do better than the bitch who tried to kill my daughter and ex-wife," he replied with a small smirk.

"I'll skip the foreplay," she offered.

"Tempting, but I'll still have to pass," Savage replied coldly. "I don't think it'll come down to it, but I hope you're not offended when I tell you that I'd rather pay for sex."

Elena shrugged his curt dismissal off like it had made no impression at all. "I merely thought I'd ask." She finished the glass of bubbly and handed it to the flight attendant who swooped in quickly and seemingly out of nowhere to help them before she disappeared into the back of the plane once again.

Sal chuckled softly and now made no effort to hide his amusement at how the man had coldly and effectively rejected the woman's blatant attempts to seduce him. She was clearly looking for some kind of leverage over the group. Or maybe she simply needed someone to bump uglies with. Either way, it had been handled as bluntly as it needed to be.

It wasn't a long flight, and they spent most of the time familiarizing themselves with the details of their proposed mission. The group was one of the best when it came to devising a plan of attack and there were a few important considerations they would need to take into account.

The data they were looking for would most probably be found in the lab that had gone dark. Given the nature of what they had tested there and what they were likely to find, it was a good idea to bring Sal, Madigan, and Courtney in to deal with it. That said, it wasn't a terrible idea to have Savage, Sam, and Terry in the mix to back them up. Anja would be their support as well, although she obviously wouldn't join them inside.

She and Amanda had looked into creating suits to work from a remote location. There were some situations in which it would work, which was to say anywhere in the world where a satellite could connect. It meant anywhere in the world but the Zoo, which was the one place they needed her to be able to actually do it. Honestly, if they could find a way to control suits that went into the Zoo without needing to send experienced gunners to do so, they would be able to make a fucking mint. Oh, and they would keep countless lives safe from the dangers of the alien jungle as well.

That was the priority, of course. Unfortunately, they still had issues with connecting simple comm units from inside the jungle, which meant it was impossible to transmit the data needed to be able to run a full combat suit. There were issues that could be resolved in software updates but not everything, and there were innumerable other problems to deal with as well.

Sal had already sent some of the updates to various people to test, and they'd actually had a couple of interesting runs on the simulators with suits that were allowed to handle any close-quarters combat situations with extreme prejudice. The only problem that arose was that one had to put the suit into combat mode in order to stop it from attacking the various members of one's own team, and even then, there were potentially deadly bugs that popped up here and there.

Anja had suggested they include tracking devices in the suits that were deployed to allow the software to recognize a basic friend or foe system in the chips that would keep them from attacking their own comrades. The possibility of deadly bugs still arose, but she said she was secretly helping them update the code on the operations to keep them from happening and was being well-paid for her efforts.

Everything she did online was based on her own work

without Heavy Metal being involved, so he declined to ask her any questions about it. He was curious to see her work in action, but given that she essentially worked non-stop to keep the rest of the team alive in the field and hold anyone who might want to cause them harm at bay, he really didn't want to push his luck where the Russian hacker was concerned. They did provide her with a service as well, but it was one that could be found basically anywhere else in the world, so it wasn't like they had something unique to offer.

Besides that, he had become attached to and protective of the woman. Not in the same way he felt about Madigan and Courtney, of course, but as a friend.

His ears began to pop uncomfortably as they descended from the clouds toward the airstrip that had been designated as their landing point.

It didn't take them long to realize that something was wrong. As the aircraft taxied around the strip, even their limited view displayed the capital of the country in the distance with sufficient sunlight at the end of the day to illuminate it in a gorgeous skyline that spread boldly across the whole of the horizon.

Their attention, however, was drawn instead to the group of black cars where the private jet was supposed to park and so forced them to a premature stop.

"Who are those guys?" Elena wondered aloud.

"So, I guess that they aren't your local greeting party?" Savage thrust his hand into his coat and drew a pistol from it. It looked like a revolver, but the barrel was half a length longer than most others and a few wires visible on the barrel itself revealed that it was a technologically advanced weapon.

The other team members were armed as well and all focused intently on the group that had assembled on the airstrip. They appeared ready for a fight. All were dressed in gray suits and some wore sunglasses, although ten of the twenty-five or so carried assault rifles hung from straps around their necks.

"I assume they're waiting for something in particular— something other than the death of everyone inside the plane," Savage stated and looked pointedly at Elena as he lowered the shades over the windows. "Otherwise, they would have filled this plane with holes by now. There are a hundred different reasons why they would wait for us here, but I'll go out on a limb and assume that about seventy-five percent of those reasons have something to do with you, Miss Molina."

"Well, you would be right, but given that the only people who know about my involvement in anything that might call for a reaction like this are in the plane with me, I doubt they are here for me, my love," she replied and appeared to be far more calm than she had a right to be. "If I were to make a guess as to their origins, though, I would say they look like Russians. And, from the look of their cheap suits, I am forced to assume they are in the employ of their government."

Sal's gaze snapped to look at Anja, whose face paled a little more with every word the woman spoke. His first instinct was to refute that—after all, Russia and the Ukraine were not on the best of terms—but it really was the only situation that made sense when he thought about it.

The Ukrainians had no reason to ambush them, especially not with Molina on board, who had no doubt greased the right palms and was a significant shareholder in the research project. While the last thing he'd expected was for the FSB to show up so close to the Ukrainian capital, the isolated landing strip was perfect for a quick clandestine operation. And, of course, there were no doubt a few greedy individuals who would be willing to turn a blind eye or even lend a helping hand.

It was significant that the Russians had chosen to follow them since their encounter in the Zoo, but whether they searched for Anja herself or merely had a bone to pick with Heavy Metal as a whole was the question.

The result would essentially be the same, though, Sal thought as he drew his pistol from the underarm holster he wore. The hacker needed to stay away from the fight and out of sight of the men who would probably at least threaten them with violence, if not implement it.

"What do we do, boss?" Savage asked, although his focus was squarely on Madigan rather than him. He felt a moment of annoyance at that instinct before he remembered she had told the man, upon their first meeting, that he had to work with the idea that she would shoot him if he did something she didn't like. It made sense that he would look to her to call the shots in order to avoid being ventilated five or six times.

Besides, they were in a situation where she was the one who would, in fact, call the shots and it made sense that the operative and his team would wait for her to devise their strategy and issue orders.

"They have us pinned down, no doubt about it," she pointed out and tapped the walls of the plane lightly. They wouldn't provide much cover, especially if their Russian friends carried armor-piercing rounds. She grimaced and considered their options hastily.

They would need to leave the aircraft, that much was clear.

"Terry, get to the back of the plane," Savage instructed. The sniper nodded, hauled his carry-on from the overhead compartment, and began to assemble the rifle stored inside. It was a collapsible .22—a peashooter, basically, but the range of this firefight would probably not exceed fifty yards. As a result, size of the bullets honestly wouldn't matter much, especially considering the skill of the man who pulled the trigger. He eased himself snugly against the window but kept the blinds down for the moment.

"Are we good to go?" Madigan asked with a glance at the team. The others in the group had spread out around the plane except for Molina, who still sat calmly in her seat.

"Good to go." Sam nodded.

"Savage, you're with me," Madigan snapped, and the operative was quick to join her as they made their way to the door. It was fairly simple to operate and opened after only a few seconds of tinkering. The steps descended immediately. Sal moved behind them, ready to provide covering fire if they needed it. There only enough room for two people on the steps anyway, but if he positioned himself at the door, he would at least be above them if he needed to fire.

She stepped out first and shielded her eyes against the setting sun. Savage followed her and used the fact that she was in front to hide the weapon he held in his hands. Sam eased past Sal and followed them a few paces back.

The group of armed men exchanged glances before a couple of them moved forward. Sal descended from the plane as well, surprised to see Anja beside him, her face white but resolved.

"What are you doing?" he asked in a hushed whisper. There was no way to hide her now that she had exposed herself, so all he could really hope for was that she had a plan.

"They're here for me," she said with a small gesture toward the men who shouted commands at Savage and Madigan, neither of whom appeared to understand what was said. The intensity with which it was said, however, could not be mistaken, and neither could the sudden and—to Sal's mind, anyway—uncalled for threatening brandishing of weapons. They wanted what they wanted, and they clearly wouldn't take 'I don't know what the fuck you're saying' for an answer.

A few of them saw Anja descend from the plane, and it looked like she was who they were there for since they started to move in to intercept her, but Savage stepped in their path.

"I don't care what they're here for," the man said with a small smile. He held his gaze very firmly on the man in front of him and looked calmer than even Molina had in the plane. "They won't get you, and that's final."

The men had spoken only Russian to this point, but they appeared to understand English, at any rate. The man scowled, backed away a few steps, and aimed his weapon at the operative's head.

"Well, that escalated quickly," Savage commented but made no effort to move away from where he stood between Anja and the men who appeared to want to apprehend her.

The hacker, for her part, looked terrified and like she had begun to regret her choice to step off the plane. Despite this, she remained where she was, her body stiff and expression focused. She stood less than a step behind Savage as Sal moved in beside Madigan and Sam.

Whatever now played out, there appeared to be a plan in the way the three of them inched away from where their teammate made his stand. They could have been moving out of the way of where the other man would undoubtedly take the brunt of the Russians' fire. It was also as likely that they tried to draw some of the focus away from where he stood much like a meat shield for Anja.

The young woman, to her credit, didn't move a muscle and appeared to implicitly trust his ability to keep her safe. Either that or she would rather go down in a firefight than be dragged into a torture chamber if they captured her.

Despite the sudden silence, it was clear that things had escalated, especially as the Russians could now see that Savage was armed. He didn't do anything, though, and simply stood his ground and waited for something to happen.

"Now, Terry," Madigan snapped.

Her command generated a chain reaction that began with a sharp report. It confirmed that Terry had waited for her order. Sal reacted instinctively and flung himself down and out of any possible line of fire. Madigan had timed it perfectly for the moment when the Russian's weapon was not aimed at either of their teammates. The sniper proved his worth and easily felled the man who had waved his weapon at them. A split second was all that was needed as the operative was already in motion almost before the target's head exploded like an overripe watermelon.

The return fire seemed to be directed primarily at the two at the steps, although the distance between the men with the assault rifle and him was great enough that most of the bullets whistled harmlessly wide and didn't even strike the plane behind him. The few that did hit the target, however, impacted the dead man Terry had shot, who wore body armor.

Savage used him as a shield now and kept himself and Anja behind the body he all but carried as he thrust his futuristic weapon through under the dead man's armpit and pulled the trigger.

A soft whine and a whomp was all Sal heard before he opened fire on their adversaries, who scrambled hastily into cover behind their cars. They must have hoped that a show of force and numbers would help to avoid any bloodshed and looked woefully unprepared for the fight they currently faced. Their miscalculations were a welcome oversight as it meant that for a while, at least, they weren't shooting at the group.

Another snap from behind confirmed that their sniper continued to calmly select his targets, and while Madigan laid cover fire down, Sam retrieved two grenades from inside her jacket and pulled the pins from both.

"You had those on you while we were on the plane?"

Madigan shouted over the barrage as the woman lobbed the knobbly spheres to where the men had begun retaliatory fire.

"You never know when you'll need a couple of grenades, love." Sam grinned and covered her ears. Her two very decent right-handed throws arced the grenades over the cars the Russians used for cover.

"*Blyat!*" The yelled expletive voiced the confusion as a group of them dove frantically away from the ordnance before they detonated. Some managed to avoid the ensuing explosions, although many did so only to be methodically and precisely terminated by Terry with his little rifle.

It made Sal realize that while he constantly upped his game when it came to combat in the Zoo, when it came to combat outside the jungle where he had to deal with humans who shot back, he still needed work.

That said, the group he had with him was more than up to the challenge. Even though they were outgunned and outnumbered, their steady stream of aggressive fire kept their enemies on their toes and the dead now almost outnumbered the living. The Heavy Metal Militia hadn't sustained any losses or even injuries thus far.

Savage was more than willing to press their advantage. He made sure Anja took cover with Sal, Madigan, and Sam before he sprinted toward the Russians while he maintained a steady stream of the needles fired from his weird yet effective weapon. While their adversaries appeared to wear some kind of body armor, his ammunition simply drilled through and men fell quickly, bleeding and dying.

Sal watched, almost fascinated, as the operative vaulted smoothly over the hood of one of the cars and hammered the butt of his pistol into the nearest man's throat to knock him back. His target choked and coughed for a few moments before he sagged when two holes appeared in his forehead.

Most of the Russians were down by this point, and those who remained looked shocked at the way their plans and purposes had so dramatically unraveled. They realized that while they were supposed to outnumber and outgun the people in the plane, they were severely outmatched. The survivors dropped their weapons hastily and raised their hands.

"What are they saying?" Sal asked Anja. She hadn't taken any fire herself but she looked pale and her hands trembled slightly.

"Th...they're surrendering," she replied thickly and cleared her throat of a hint of obstruction. "They ask not to be shot...that kind of thing."

Madigan raised an eyebrow as she focused on the men as they fell to their knees in front of Savage, who collected their discarded weapons. "No shit. I think I could have deduced that from the context."

"What do you think, boss?" Sam asked and again directed the question to Madigan instead of Sal. "Drop them or leave them be?"

She paused and studied the group she was supposed to be leading. Savage clearly waited for orders too. He held his weapon trained on the Russians with one hand, and the other toted one of the weapons they'd dropped.

"What do you think, Sal?" she asked and turned to face him but kept her weapons aimed at the survivors.

"We still need to work with these people," he said and

narrowed his eyes. "Let them go with the kind of warning that says if they try this kind of bullshit again, we'll target the motherfuckers who ordered it next. I know this is the FSB but dammit, they can't get away with shit like this. They need to leave us the fuck alone."

Anja nodded and seemed to agree with the sentiment. These people were still her compatriots, whether she liked it or not, and he wondered if there wasn't some lingering sentiment of loyalty to her homeland despite the fact that the FSB had driven her out.

"Savage, we'll let them go," Madigan snapped and inched her weapon toward him as if she expected the man to ignore his orders and ventilate the entire group.

But Sal had come to expect better of the people Anderson had recruited, and with only a hint of hesitation, he relaxed his stance, gathered the remaining weapons, and carried them to where Sal, Sam, and Madigan still shielded Anja.

"We can take their vehicles—the ones that are still working, anyway—and leave them here to give us a head start," the operative suggested. Madigan nodded and before she took the weapons, she gestured for those still waiting inside the plane to get the hell out.

Elena was the last to disembark and looked supremely bored as she descended the stairs. "Are we done yet?" she asked dryly. "I think it's time we get to work, don't you?"

Savage flipped her off, which elicited a soft laugh from her as they chose the few vehicles that were still in working order, disabled the rest, and drove away from the airstrip.

CHAPTER TWENTY-ONE

Kiev: Elena Molina's Warehouse

It was a short journey to the outskirts of Kiev before Elena guided them to what looked like a warehouse district connected to a long-defunct train line. A few of the structures seemed to still be used for vehicle storage, but the remainder appeared to have been abandoned for decades.

"There once was a time when Kiev was the heart of all the trade between the various European states of the Second Soviet Union," she explained. "It became a center for all the oil barons to export their product to the European Union afterward.

"Once they went out of business, the politicians around here decided they would rather their city rely more on the legal commerce from the south of the country connected to the Black Sea. They chose not to deal with the criminals who remained from the brutal dictatorships that had held their country hostage for so long. Either way, most of the train lines lost their business here and took it elsewhere, which left considerable vacant space for anyone who wants to store large quantities of product they don't want anyone else to find."

"Let me guess," Sal said. "You're one of those lucky few."

"Cookie for the brilliant scientist." She chuckled and leaned against the seat. While she seemed calm and relaxed, there was a tension about her, evidenced by the way she fidgeted incessantly and tapped her nails on the door. He couldn't help but recognize it. Too much about the woman's behavior felt familiar to him—enough to make him worried about what he might face in the future himself.

They arrived at one of the few occupied warehouses, which was also surrounded by a troop of armed guards. Sophisticated security systems protected the gates, which Elena knew all the codes for. One of the mercs hired to guard the building jogged forward to greet them as they disembarked.

"Apologies, ma'am," he said in English with a hint of a British accent, although he looked Indian. "The people who were sent to greet you returned and stated that what looked like government cars were waiting for them and told them to get lost or get shot."

"It would have been better if they had been shot, but I have no time for that now," she quipped but sounded like she was only slightly joking. "I'm here to outfit the team hired to head to the lab."

"Another one?" the man asked and frowned. "I would think you would have…cut your losses, as the term goes."

"Are you really questioning my motives here, George?" Elena asked and her expression turned cold. She looked a few moments away from shooting the man with his own sidearm. Sal felt bad for him and did not judge him in the slightest for taking a small step away from the dangerous woman as he raised a hand in apology.

"Not at all, ma'am," he replied quickly and guided them toward the massive warehouse building. "I merely wondered if we might have better results if we were to rethink our strategy, is all."

"That's why I brought in a small team of specialists," she replied and gestured to the group that moved closer to them. "Experts in Zoo combat in ways the rest of the teams that failed me definitely lacked. Which is why we will arm them with only the best that money can buy in terms of armor and weapons."

"This I'd like to see," Madigan stated with an edge of derision to her tone. None of the group looked particularly happy to be there, Anja least of all, who still looked like she needed a drink after her unexpected exposure to the fire-fight at the airstrip.

They entered the warehouse and stepped into a massive room where a number of suits were set up, Sal assumed, for their viewing. There was a variety, although they were essentially on par with what they had seen displayed else-where. The better specs of each individual suit were inter-esting, though, and as he examined one of the hybrids, Elena glided beside him.

"It's a prototype, thoroughly tested and already cleared for human trials," she explained and motioned for one of the specialists to approach and prepare it for use. "I think you'll find some of the upgrades quite revolutionary."

"How so?" he asked and fiddled with the pieces as he started to pull it on.

"Well, there were enough suggestions to make them more compatible to what would be encountered in the Zoo, which demanded some interesting software and hardware upgrades," the technician explained as he stepped in to assist. Most of the hardware looked virtually the same, but when Sal activated the software, he saw additions to the HUD.

Within seconds, the display showed him exactly what they had meant by revolutionary upgrades.

"The first change, you'll notice, is the lack of rocket propulsion in the back and boots," the man continued. "Instead, we've used magnetic propulsion. It's a little like those bouncy stilt boots that are all the rage online these days but increased by a factor of a hundred. Not only would they provide you with similar propulsion from the ground as the rocket packs, they also function as viable weapons. In addition, they assist you to traverse rough terrain, all with a negligible effect on the battery packs of the suit. There is no longer the need to carry the hyper compressed and frankly, rather dangerous rocket fuel inside the suit at all."

Sal tested the mobility and moved around the warehouse as the team tested their selections. It looked like all their suits had been outfitted with the magnetic upgrades instead of rocket packs, and they did appear to move far more easily and smoothly. Even Madigan's tank of a suit seemed light on its feet.

"What's this?" he asked and activated what he guessed was the combat mode. The bounciness of the boots quickly diminished, and while it still allowed him to move faster, it kept him more or less steady and his aim was automatically adjusted to compensate for the slight buoyancy added to his movements. It was a useful and very practical addition, as was the sudden detection of all the other armor around him, evidence of a very advanced friend or foe system implemented. He would have put money down on Anja being responsible for that.

Of course, the change that dramatically demanded his attention was the additional two sets of arms that connected beside his to create a total of six. They drew weapons from the back of his suit—four in total—and held them out in an open formation to cover all possible points of attack, be it from above, below, or the sides.

Better still, they responded intuitively to commands and followed his eye movements as tracked by the HUD, accessed his motion sensors and all the other sensors to create a virtual map of his surroundings, and pinpointed all those who weren't identified as friendlies.

'Engage?' the suit asked him, and he used his chin to nudge the decline option and deactivate the suddenly very hostile extra arms.

They lowered obediently but retained the weapons and simply assumed a passive stance, still ready for combat at a second's notice.

"Impressive, right?" The techie chuckled and patted the back of the hybrid suit. "That's the only suit with eight limbs, unfortunately. It's very much a prototype, although you do seem like exactly the right person to take her out for a maiden voyage. You'll find it useful for far more than only combat if you look through the options."

Sal needed no further encouragement. It included climbing options, all-terrain movement that would allow him to skitter across the ground like an insect, and more. Not only that, but it also had the possibility to combine different programs and mix and match as each arm appeared to have an independent CPU.

"I think I'm in love," he said, awestruck by the technological marvel he currently wore.

"Careful, Sal, you don't want to make us all jealous," Courtney warned him jokingly.

He noted that Elena's interest had drifted to where Savage was currently being fitted into his suit. From the man's record, it didn't look like he'd put in much time in combat suits, so this would be unusual for him. Still, folks like him were quick learners, and after a few trial runs to adjust to having to move a little more deliberately to get a combat suit to move as well, he settled into an efficient rhythm.

In size terms, the suit he wore looked like a hybrid—lean and agile—and lacked the bulk and power the others had. Interestingly enough, though, it looked like it had been specially designed for the man without the fine-tuned small-movement dexterity of the fingers that allowed scientific interaction with the Zoo without having to get out of the protective confines of the suit.

Still, there were changes Sal needed a moment to inspect. Something of an endoskeleton followed the form of it and provided a little more structure, but there was a connection to it from the gloves into two weapons that were held in holsters at his hips. Honestly, it looked like Iron Man watched three weeks' worth of cowboy movies and decided to make something new and exciting based on them. It wasn't completely unlikely, of course.

The way comic books were desperate to increase sales these days, he wondered why they hadn't come up with the idea already. Either way, a pistol-sized weapon fitted snugly in both holsters with the same elongated barrels the man's current pistol had.

"We watched you in action and one of our specialists was able to recreate the kind of weapon you used," Elena explained and ran her hand down the suit. "Then, they turned it up to eleven. The magnetic strip in the barrel is powered by the fusion reactor that drives the suit, which makes it capable of launching those deadly little needles accurately up to five hundred yards. More importantly, you can adapt the barrel to launch more than only the needles. Proper bullets of all sizes, for one thing, and you can even attach a longer barrel and work those babies like rifles. Or you can use them to launch grenades and all kinds of fun things you might need. It's the last word in versatility."

Sal narrowed his eyes. Elena had struck him as the cold, rational, and frankly psychopathic type who needed little or no encouragement to break away from attachments as soon as they weren't convenient to her anymore. And there she was, fawning all over Savage like a prom queen over the popular high school quarterback.

He couldn't tell if the woman was playing some kind of game or if she was actually attracted to the operative for some reason, although he couldn't see the appeal of the man personally. He wasn't terrible-looking, but at the same time, there wasn't anything physically outstanding about him at all.

Then again, what the hell did he know about any of

this? He'd essentially stumbled into the relationships he had right now. No, that wasn't true. Both women had come to him, and there were people who would wonder how he managed that.

Still, her apparent interest seemed decidedly odd, whichever way he looked at it.

"I do approve of the added firepower," Savage admitted, drew the pistols clear of their holsters, and connected them to the HUD in his helmet. There were problems that would come from him having to track two weapons at the same time. He apparently came to the same conclusion, shoved one of them into its holster, and aimed the remaining one around the warehouse.

"Ask me nicely and I'll let you keep it," Elena replied and drew another surprised and confused look from both Sal and Savage in turn, but there wasn't any kind of reaction that would be the right one. The operative looked like he wanted to keep the suit and the weapons it had, but he didn't want to owe the woman who had been responsible for the attempt on his daughter's and ex-wife's life.

They worked together right now so needed to at least be somewhat civil to each other, but what she tried to do was make sure there was something to pursue by way of a relationship, whether professional or—maybe in Savage's case—physical. It would allow her to keep clear of the Heavy Metal team's bad side once this entire crazy mission was over and done with.

Sal didn't like that idea. Not at all.

"So, will we drive to the Chernobyl area in Hammerheads, the way we do in the Zoo?" Courtney asked the group in an attempt to break the tense silence that had fallen over them but also to test the comm systems in the new suits. Anja had already started to work on them.

"As of right now, the only vehicles that would be able to get you close enough to the site are military helicopters," Elena explained. "There are apparently many reasons for that, mostly political and boorishly presented the last time I tried to get a team in there. Anyway, the point remains that we need to fly there."

"Can we drop directly onto the site of the lab?" Savage asked. "If we don't intend to waste time with the scenic route and don't need to stroll through the place, that would reduce the need for heavy artillery. Not that I'm complaining about the heaviness of our artillery. I'm always a fan of a 'shoot first, shoot second, shoot some more and then once nothing's moving, ask a question or two' approach to…alien dangers."

Sal opened his mouth to talk about how he wanted to take time to inspect the area they would traverse. It was the researcher in him who wanted to see what changes had been effected in the almost fictional land of Chernobyl. Technically, he had wanted to visit the area for a long time, mostly because of the fame of the disaster that had happened there. Yet now that he knew it was the site for more Zoo-related goop testing, it was almost terrifyingly magnetic to him and people like him. Courtney was probably equally as excited as he was.

What had his attention at the moment was the fact that Savage, despite being in a suit of armor that would have the famed Master Chief panting, looked genuinely nervous. It was unnerving to see someone as icy as him that way.

"We'll prepare to leave tomorrow morning," Elena said and turned reluctantly away from the operative to address the group as a whole. "Until then, you should have almost free range of the fantastic city of Kiev. Except maybe Miss Anja, who…well, you should probably stay out of sight, given that there are still some elements of our greeting party in the area."

"Good point," the hacker agreed and looked like the reality of having to agree with someone like Elena might make her physically sick.

"Very well, then," the woman said and clapped decisively. "You all have reservations at the local Radisson, and there will be a town car available tomorrow morning to bring you all out to the location from where we will head into the Zoo—oh, I mean Chernobyl."

Savage looked visibly uncomfortable again at the mention of the jungle in question as they started to disassemble the suits they wore.

Sal made a note to talk to him once they were out of earshot of their employer and her minions.

CHAPTER TWENTY-TWO

__Kiev: The Radisson Hotel__

He really had no idea what this woman's problem was. She very clearly wasn't used to hearing the word no, given her current position as what he could only assume was a supervillain waiting for her Superman or Batman to sprout from somewhere. It had been gratifying to turn her request down at first, but she had followed it up with a call to his hotel room to ask him to meet her for drinks in a swanky cigar bar near the center of the city. This invitation had stirred less gratification and more...what was the word?

Oh yeah, annoyance. He needed a drink, but damned if he would head out to someplace where a glass of neat scotch would cost him what most people spent on used cars, all while being pestered by someone whom he hated to his core.

That said, there was a hotel bar and he had every intention to put it to good use. Not only that, but he had been informed on checking in that anything he ate or drank in the bar or restaurant could be charged to his room. It might be petty revenge but since the woman probably made enough money every five minutes or so to cover however much it cost to put the whole team up in a five-star hotel, it was still some measure of revenge. He would have a drink and she would pay for it, but it probably wasn't what she envisioned when she made the proposal.

The small pleasures of life were the ones that made it worth living, he thought smugly as he stepped into the small yet elegant and cozy lounge the bar masqueraded as.

It was small enough that it didn't take him long to realize that Jacobs, Kennedy, and Monroe were already there, getting their drink on and celebrating...something. Or maybe merely enjoying the fact that they could do this without any kind of dent in their wallets. When he recalled the amount of money Monroe and Anderson paid to keep him on retainer, he assumed they could absorb the expenses without too much concern but that wasn't the point either.

He paused at the bar to ask for a beer—the nearest thing to a lager they had on tap. The bartender acknowledged that it would go on his room tab and told him to find a seat, and he made his way to the booth the trio had claimed for their own.

"Hey, guys," he said with what he hoped was a pleasant, friendly smile. "Do you mind if I join you?"

"Sure," Jacobs said quickly, but the operator could tell that Kennedy was about to deny his request. She paused, considered simply overriding Sal's invitation to join them, and quickly decided against it. To cover her response, she took a slow sip of her drink, which looked like a Long Island Iced Tea.

"I still need to buy you a drink, don't I, Savage?" Monroe asked as he slid into the booth next to her and across from Jacobs and Kennedy. "You know, for coming out of your apartment building in Philly and gunning down the assholes Terry and I had already handled."

"Well, if you intended to buy anyone drinks, now is definitely the time," he pointed out as a waitress arrived with his frosty and frothy mug of beer. "You can bill it all back to Molina. I've emptied the hotel room of the minibar and anything that isn't bolted down—which isn't much in a swanky place like this—and decided she should pay for it."

"It sounds like something that I should have thought of first," Jacobs said and looked a little disappointed.

"Oh, and the point of having people like Terry and myself on the payroll is to kill assholes who try to kill you regardless of how well handled the situation is," the operative continued and took a long sip of his beer. "So, no need to thank me, but know I'll probably be there the next time too. You and Anderson get in too much trouble for people who are supposedly straight-shooters."

Jacobs and Monroe laughed at that, but Kennedy seemed less than amused. Ever since they'd joined forces, the woman appeared to have little time or patience for him or his antics. He didn't know why, and all he did know was that he didn't want to aggravate it. She was a very competent operative in her own right and apparently had the ear of the people who paid his bills. There was absolutely no need to piss her off more than necessary.

She finished her drink in a long gulp and patted Jacobs on the shoulder. "I think I need to head to bed. We have an early start tomorrow. Are you coming?"

MICHAEL TODD & MICHAEL ANDERLE

Sal shook his head. "I think I need to drink a little more to help me sleep. You go ahead, though."

"See you in the room." She winked at Monroe and ignored the other man as she made her way to the hotel elevators.

"I think I should go with her," Monroe said and squeezed past Savage to exit the booth She paused for long enough to leave Jacobs with a light peck on the lips before she jogged to Kennedy and arrived in time to slip into the elevator alongside her.

"Why aren't you going with them?" Savage asked. He toyed with his drink and watched as Sal seemed to calm a little like he had feigned a trace of drunkenness before. "I imagine there are enough drinks in your room to help you to sleep. Among other things."

The other man shrugged. "I don't need that much sleep. I'll join them in a while since I did want to talk to you."

He indicated the booth that was now only shared by the two of them. "Talk away."

"I guess I should preface this with the statement that you are kind of a god to me," he started tentatively and fidgeted with his drink. "Your skills are, as specialists go, impressive on their own. That added to the fact that Molina—who could not be more out of your league, by the way—has obviously pined for some of your particular brand of action all day... Well, I don't know how you do it and would appreciate some pointers."

Savage narrowed his eyes, about to ask the man exactly how old he was, when be remembered from reading the kid's file that despite his many, many accomplishments, he was barely over the legal drinking limit. In the US, not in the Ukraine, which he had surpassed by almost half a decade by this point. He was basically a glorified teenager.

It's maybe best to not go down that road.

"Well, I've heard impressive tales about you too, Mr. 'I'm Having an Affair with Two Women at the Same Time, and by the way, Both Women Know About It.'"

"I'll have you know that it's Dr. 'I'm Having an Affair with Two Women at the Same Time, and by the way, Both Women Know About it,'" Jacobs corrected him quickly and jokingly.

Savage's eyebrows raised. "No kidding? Congrats, Dr. Jacobs."

He chuckled. "No kidding, and thanks, Mr. Savage."

The operative chuckled. "With that said, you can't honestly be impressed by the fact that I seem to only attract psychopaths with daddy issues. It only causes more problems than it solves, believe you me."

"Well, when you put it that way, I guess you do have a point," Jacobs admitted and raised his drink, which looked like a screwdriver.

"Besides," he continued. "I'm not the only bad decision that woman likes to make. There was something that made you suddenly jump onto this mission, and it has to be more than merely your professional curiosity."

The scientist narrowed his eyes. "I thought you were watching the bodyguards."

"I was," he replied. "I was also keeping an eye on you. That's what I'm paid to do."

The man shrugged. "Okay, sure, there was...something that made me decide that we had to be involved in this, one way or another. Making sure Miss Molina doesn't have full rights to a previously untouched area introduced to the alien goop certainly played a part."

"But there was something else," he insisted and tried not to be irritated by what seemed to be prevarication. "Maybe something about those very visible blue veins in her arms?"

"Yeah, I guess," Jacobs admitted and bought himself a little time with his vodka and orange juice. "She's been taking the blue stuff. And not in the way everyone else does in the form of an anti-ageing cream or whatever. Like...ingesting it. The symptoms are all there, and if I were to guess, she's had side effects she's not too happy with."

"And how do you know about these symptoms?" he asked bluntly.

"I...well, some I recognize from a poor sap some Russian scientists ran experiments on," the man replied but sounded deliberately evasive. "The rest...well, I know about them because I've been subjected to them, albeit to a lesser degree. You're a very nosy and paranoid person, you know that, Savage?"

He smirked in response. "Yeah, it's almost like my life depends on it or something."

"Fair enough," he conceded. "Yeah, I've been self-medicating, sure. I guess you could say I'm in something of a similar position, so I'm almost as invested in finding out everything about the Zoo and the alien goop that created it as possible. Are you happy?"

"In general?" Savage asked and smirked a little. "I wouldn't say that I'm...unhappy, but I'm under no impression that my current mental state is anything approaching healthy. So I guess you could say I have my ups and downs."

"It's big of you to admit that," his companion replied with a good dose of sarcasm. "I've taken the stuff personally and categorized the results for posterity. I'm a scientist, and I was curious about what kind of effect it would have on the human body if ingested. I was willing to make myself a test subject."

"And?"

"And what?"

"What were the results so far?"

"Well, they were rather impressive." Jacobs grinned. "There are some things that could simply be based on the causality of my adopting a more active lifestyle by risking my life in the Zoo, like increased muscle mass and durability. There are others I can't really attribute to anything else, like an increase in my liver's ability to process toxins."

"Like alcohol?" It might explain why he'd thought the man had feigned a trace of inebriation.

"Yep," he replied. "There were other changes elsewhere too, like stamina in the...well, no, I guess that's not appropriate to discuss."

"Penis enlargement?" Savage deduced.

"What?" he exclaimed. "Good Lord. No, nothing like that. Merely added...uh, stamina and body control while in the throes of passion. Again, there could be other causality links, but for the life of me, I can't think of any."

"Huh, interesting." He grunted, his mind working while he finished his beer. "It's not the kind of thing you'd think alien goop would be capable of. Given that it seems to be engineered toward changing the biology of virtually anything it touches, volunteering as a test subject for that particular experiment could prove to be one of your bad ideas. If the stuff itself was specifically created to the smallest detail, don't you think the designers had these effects in mind when they made it?"

"You're thinking of little green men in lab coats poking the goop, aren't you?" Jacobs grinned.

"What, did taking it make you psychic too?"

"Don't be ridiculous." The scientist chuckled. "There's no such thing as psychics."

"I heard of this one guy in Afghanistan who was able to accurately predict his death down to the date, time of day, and number and positioning of bullets that killed him," Savage said and leaned forward as the waitress replaced his empty beer mug with a full one. "And that was before we had alien goop that caused a thousand kinds of havoc in the world. There are more things in heaven and earth, Jacobs, than are dreamt of in your philosophy."

"Shakespeare, nice." Jacobs assumed a more serious expression. "Although I suppose that would include your deathly fear of what goes on in the Zoo, right? Or am I wrong about that?"

"Hey, I'm willing to admit how psychologically unhealthy I am," he reminded him. "That means I'm more than willing to admit the fact that going into a jungle filled to the brim with monsters that should be restrained to B-Movies involving once-famous actors who are well past their prime fills me with pants-shitting terror. And it should do the same to everyone else, too, regardless of their mental health."

"So, you think I'm crazy?" the other man demanded.

He smirked. "Think? I thought we established that shit as beyond fact. Death, taxes, and the fact that Dr. Salinger Jacobs is crazy in a hundred different ways. I never said it was a bad thing, though. Lie to anyone you want, Jacobs, but never lie to yourself. Never try to keep yourself away from who you are in your own right."

"That's some serious wisdom right there, Savage." Jacobs chuckled. "You could make a decent living as a life coach. You know, one of those guys who conducts lectures, talks with show hosts, and guest stars in TED talks."

"Are those still a thing?"

"They were before I went into the Zoo. I honestly haven't kept up with them since then. I have better things to do. Seriously, though, you would make good money doing it."

"Which should say something about the amount of money Dr. Monroe and former Colonel Anderson are paying me to risk my life in the effort of killing people," Savage said with a chuckle.

"That or you merely…like to risk your life in the effort of killing people," his companion pointed out.

He opened his mouth with a rebuttal on his tongue but recalled his own words about not lying to himself. He decided to swallow any technicalities he usually used—like saying he didn't like killing people and merely enjoyed being in a situation where it was do or die. Of course, the doing generally tended to include killing large numbers of people with extreme amounts of prejudice.

"Fair enough," was all he said aloud to break the silence that had ensued and took a long sip from his glass of lager. "I imagine it's rather like how you enjoy heading into the

Zoo despite the fact that you know absolutely no amount of armor will be able to keep you alive if shit hits the fan?"

"Something like that, yeah," Jacobs couldn't help but admit with a laugh.

"Seriously." He smirked. "When will people realize that messing around with this alien bullshit can never end well?"

"When they realize money doesn't buy happiness?"

Savage raised his glass, which the other man tapped with his own. "I'll drink to that."

CHAPTER TWENTY-THREE

Kiev: A Private Airstrip

Sal hadn't been on a helicopter that often. Some visits to the various bases around the Zoo had called for haste, which led to them mount up in some of the military helos they weren't using in the base. It could cut the trip between the bases from five or so hours by vehicle to an hour and a half in the air.

That said, the ones he had been allowed to use near the Zoo were the smaller, lighter aircraft with light armor and defenses. These were mostly used to transport high-level officials to and from the various bases without too much trouble and even a modicum of comfort. Those old guys had all kinds of bone problems that wouldn't react well to the shudder and shake of the large helo flights.

This aircraft was definitely not one of those. It had two rotors, for one thing, and it looked like it had been bulked with full armor. Amanda could have probably educated him on what was developed on a larger scale like this. Each plate looked like it had been cut from a beehive and with the green and grey paint, it even looked like beeswax, for fuck's sake.

The helo itself was about the size of most smaller houses and massive guns were mounted strategically to cover every conceivable point of attack—from above, below, or the sides—with a variety of rocket launchers added to bolster the defenses. It appeared to have been designed to carry heavy loads, possibly tanks or APCs or other equipment.

When they entered, the visible existence of bay doors that opened outward from the bottom clearly indicated that the chopper had been specially made for the transport and deployment of soldiers in heavy armor. The suits themselves had parachutes included as well as altimeters that would keep the entire process of jumping from the helo to landing essentially automatic, but Sal had never actually parachuted before.

The whole helicopter shuddered at the takeoff, which made him wonder if they were having an earthquake. The team had been strapped to the sides of the aircraft and were held securely in place when they started to move.

"You look a little green there, Jacobs." Savage contacted him through a private channel. "Have you ever been part of a drop before?"

"Not really, no," he replied as he glanced at the man and wondered why he had kept their conversation private. "You?"

"Most of my training was in what they call Unconventional Warfare," he explained. "One of those parameters includes numerous airborne operations in a variety of situations. Rain, storm-level winds, nighttime jumps, and a combination of all of the above and more. I've jumped before."

"Well, there's no need to rub it in," Sal grumbled. "Do you have any advice for a first-timer?"

"Yeah," Savage replied. "Relax. The way these suits are made, they'll handle most of the minutiae of the jump. They'll keep you upright, settle you into the prime position, deploy the parachute at the right time, and manage the landing. So relax. Let your suit do its thing. Enjoy the ride, unless you have a problem with heights. Or... falling."

"I have no problem with heights or falling," he said and shook his head firmly inside his helmet. "It's the landing with a splat on the ground that's the problem."

"Your suit has inertia dampeners, which means that even if your parachute doesn't deploy, you have a better chance to survive the fall than people who jump with parachutes and without the suit," the operative continued. "So relax. Try to think of a good catchphrase for when you land."

"A good catchphrase?"

"Yeah, everyone has one," he asserted. "It's kind of like a war cry to get you into the mood for a fight."

"Okay, I can do that," Sal declared, relieved to have something to think about rather than plummeting helplessly to a messy death. "I have a couple of good candidates already."

"Awesome." The man sounded approving. "All you need to do is shout the one that gets you fired up the most as loudly as you can."

"Thanks." He sighed. Surprisingly, he felt a little better

and he turned to face the man. "How about you? How do you feel about this mission?"

"Well, aside from the fact that I don't like how we left Anja to fend for herself with only Elena for company?" he asked. "I couldn't be better."

"On a first name basis now, are we?" Madigan interjected with a chuckle, and Sal realized that the other man had included the rest of the team in the conversation now that he perceived the conversation he might not want to share with them was concluded. He could appreciate that.

"Who, me and Jacobs?" Savage wondered.

"No, you and Elena." Courtney laughed. "Did you and her have personal time? We've all seen how much the two of you hate to love each other."

"I won't even bother to dignify that with a response," he retorted and settled into his harness. He still didn't seem terribly comfortable in his suit. Sal couldn't think of a good reason why special forces operatives weren't outfitted with combat suits. Obviously, there was a money situation that might prevent the grunts on the ground from being regularly outfitted with that kind of specialized gear, but those who had literal millions invested into their training and development to shape them into the elite killing machines in the world could—and should—benefit from them.

Maybe they were supposed to rely more on their ability to blend in and stealthy ingress and exit from their operations than having enough firepower to tackle lighter tanks and APCs single-handedly. But if so, why didn't they work on developing suits that could be used for that to capitalize on those skills? It would keep the men safer and give them more firepower for when they needed it the most.

He honestly couldn't think of any justifiable response that didn't involve some kind of budgetary concern by pencil-pushers who cared more about the money that would be spent than the lives that would ultimately be wasted. Idiots like those fixed their eyes on the short-term gains instead of the possibly millions they would save. It was way more costly to train new special forces warriors when those who went into combat without suits were killed due to lack of protection.

"Dropping in five," Kennedy called over the comms and Sal realized that more time than he'd thought had passed while he was lost in thought. He hadn't even considered what he would yell as a catchphrase when he landed.

No, he didn't believe it was something real jumpers did and absolutely knew that Savage was full of shit and pulling his leg for fun. Either way, he didn't mind. It had been enough to take his mind off the upcoming jump. Or, judging by the way the bay doors would actually open from the bottom, fall.

"Weapons and systems check," she instructed. She called up the base schematics of all the suits on the team to double-check that nothing would go wrong once they were out of the helicopter. Interestingly enough, Sal noted that she passed the duties of double-checking her suit to Savage, who took the responsibility without any comment. They were professionals, and between the two of them, had enough combat training to let them know how the other would work even though this could be called the first time they would venture out into the field together.

"Davis, ready," Sam called.

"Mixon, ready," Terry responded.

"Savage, ready."

Sal exchanged a quick look with Courtney before he added, "Jacobs, ready."

"Monroe, ready."

"Kennedy, ready," Madigan finished, satisfied enough with how the suits looked to concentrate on hers for the moment. "The lights will go green to signify ready status and after that, the bay doors will open. The mag clamps on your suits will release. We'll drop from about sixteen hundred feet. The weather is pleasant with negligible wind activity, so keep in formation but don't get close enough to risk a collision with anyone on the way down. Let your suit do the work. You're only in this one for the ride. Got it?"

The speech was apparently more for Sal and Courtney than for the rest of them, but they all responded quickly and firmly a second before the light above their heads came on. It started off red but less than a minute later, turned green.

A siren triggered once the doors began to open beneath them. It was a chilling experience to watch the floor suddenly pull away from you and know that the full weight of your body and a ton and a half suit were held up only by an electromagnetic clamp. Sal swung his feet over the open space beneath him and held his breath as Kennedy was the first to disappear, followed almost immediately by Terry, Sam, and Courtney. He exited next, so Savage would be the last of their team to become airborne.

The software ran through a handful of corrections before he even realized what was happening and the wind whipped him around. His suit worked to keep him steady, first with his feet down, then with the adjustment to bring him to a prone position so he could see the world rocketing up to meet him.

The altimeter read a drop that was much faster than he had expected. With the suit, his terminal velocity would be considerably higher, which meant the descent wouldn't last as long until the parachute deployed. It would have to be strong enough to support a ton and a half of suit, of course. But, like Savage had told him, he was more likely to survive even if the chute failed than someone who jumped without a suit and with a regular parachute.

It occurred to him that the man had neglected to mention where he'd learned that information. Given that he hadn't done any jumping in combat suits before, it suddenly became an all-important question he wished he'd thought to ask before.

The ground rushed a little too close a little too fast and the first stirrings of panic made themselves known a moment before the altimeter went red and the parachute on his back deployed. The tug was rough but far gentler than he had expected. Despite all kinds of fears that had skittered through his mind not even seconds before, he drifted without issues or difficulties. The descent was still fairly rapid but slow enough that their suits would keep them from turning into mush inside.

As they approached the tree line, his confidence grew and since his teammates were already on the ground, with him coming in a few seconds behind them, he thought he would make something of a memorable entrance.

Sal checked the altitude—to make sure it was safe first—and punched the emergency release from the straps on his parachute, fell clear, and allowed the canopy to drift freely away into the nearby forest. He came down quickly and executed a smooth and practiced three-point landing.

"Dammit," Madigan muttered through the comms. "Don't you fucking say it."

He was too high on his own perfect execution to heed her warning. "Superhero landing. Woo!"

"Dammit," she grumbled again. He imagined her rolling her eyes dramatically and wished she could see his trademark cheeky grin. She couldn't stay mad at him and she knew it, and it might even tease one in response, or at least an amused smirk.

The other members of the team seemed to enjoy his antics, anyway. They could be forgiven for reacting with a chuckle since they hadn't been around him much in the past and weren't used to his particular brand of coping with the dangers of what they might face out there. Courtney seemed to enjoy it, too, and she had seen him pull this kind of shit a hundred times before.

Maybe Kennedy was merely a grumpy person in general? All he really wanted to do was get her to crack that rare and awesome smile of hers. He liked to think he'd already succeeded there—well, maybe half-succeeded, anyway.

Sal turned back to the business at hand and noted that the suits' Geiger counters all sang in unison, absolute confirmation that they currently stood in a location that was saturated with enough radiation to kill them. It might not be instant but it would be effective, and sooner rather than later. It was a terrifying thought that only their suits of armor stood between each one of them and a quick and painful death.

Which hopefully explained the awe he felt as he began to inspect their surroundings. Everything he'd read about Chernobyl said that the sheer amount of radiation in the air was supposed to kill literally everything—which included the flora and fauna and all the way to the bacteria that nature designed to break down and decay all living thing when they died.

That had been the case, especially at first, but from where the team stood, he could see Mother Nature's miracle-working hand bringing new life to the desolation. Much of the forest, despite significant levels of radiation, was well on the way to recovery—still somewhat tenuous and shabby in places, but definitely making progress where it seemed all but impossible.

In that moment, he saw the parallel with the way the Zoo changed and adapted to overcome every new threat the humans could invent. Witnessing what amounted to a solidly Earth-grounded miracle suddenly made the jungle and the goop seem a little less alien. The principles that drove both seemed markedly similar.

They had landed in a wide clearing among scattered trees that hadn't yet caught up with the regeneration, although there were signs that they attempted to do so. It took a moment before he recalled that the lab had been deliberately placed in one of the hotspots, which explained the extremely high radiation and the sluggish growth.

He turned and squinted ahead to where their target location loomed a few hundred yards away and walked forward for a better view. Madigan stepped beside him.

"That's it," she confirmed. "It fits the coordinates we were given, and at least we don't have a long walk."

"What's it made of?" Courtney asked when she joined them to peer through the straggling forest. "I've never seen anything like it before."

"I have no idea." He shrugged. "It seems camouflaged, somehow, but super-strong. I'd love to see the specs for it."

"This is no time to geek out, you two," Madigan reminded them and gestured for the team to approach. "From what I can see, we need to circle a little to approach the doors—I assume the front is that way." She gestured to her left and Sal nodded.

They moved cautiously in the direction indicated with her in the lead and Savage bringing up the rear. No one spoke as they approached the enormous structure which seemed out of place but also dominant, like a reminder that man still held a measure of control even in defeat. The team assumed ready positions while Sal entered the code Molina had given him. Madigan swung in the moment the large doors slid open, Sam on her heels. The others entered when they received the all-clear, and Sal paused to close the doors and make sure they sealed.

The brightness of the lighting surprised him. On some level, he had expected the same deep shadows and sunlight-obscured jungle they encountered in the Zoo. He was also somewhat bewildered by the fact that the grass they stood on looked very green and, for lack of a better word, alive. It emerged vibrantly from the soil like it was spring when it was, in fact, the dead of winter and within a dome.

Of course, vibrant growth was a characteristic of the Zoo, but the jungle hadn't had to contend with the incredibly high levels of radiation. He'd expected the goop to have had some effect, but the overwhelmingly lush greenness seemed...alien. Not at all like what Mother Nature worked outside. Aside from that, he hadn't expected the containment area to include a section of the forest.

Thankfully, he wasn't the only one who was confused by what they saw.

"Well...that's unexpected." Courtney stated the obvious in a somewhat disbelieving tone.

"What?" Anja queried through their comms but her voice crackled and was almost inaudible, possibly because of effect of the radiation in the air on the connection. "What are you looking at? Monsters? Deadly Zoo creatures?"

"Not...really," Savage replied as he looked around. He drew both his pistols and spun them idly in his gauntleted hands like a cowboy. "Not at all, actually."

"Another interesting note..." Courtney drew their attention. "The radiation around us is enough to kill us all about fifteen times over, but it's less than half of even the most ambitious predictions in the paperwork the lab sent before it went dark. Not only that, it's unbelievably different than what I saw outside that door."

"What does that mean?" Sam asked as she crouched and poked a weed that sprouted with the barrel of her assault rifle.

"It means that whatever soaked up the radiation has increased its pace," Sal whispered and completed Courtney's thought for her.

"That's good, right?" Terry asked, his attention on the two specialists on their team. "Less radiation is a good thing, isn't it? We could look at this place being habitable again within a decade."

"Well, sure, that part of it is right and dandy," she responded as they moved as a group toward the more heavily wooded area that was apparently where the lab was supposed to be situated. "What has the rest of us worried, though, is the fact that what soaks the radiation up around here is the kind of stuff that tends to spit out the monsters that like munching on our bone marrow."

"Shouldn't we see some of those monsters around us by now?" Savage asked and his tone suggested he wanted anything but that.

"There's not really much we can do to predict what the beasties will do," Sal pointed out. "We have a hard enough time getting a grasp of what they're doing in the Zoo, where we've gone in regularly for the better part of a year now. Out here in Cher-fucking-nobyl? I have not a clue."

"Fantastic." The operative hissed his displeasure. Sam moved closer to him, patted him gently on the shoulder, and talked to him over a private comm channel, probably to check to see how he was doing. A man who relied on people fearing him more than understanding him like Savage couldn't like that his discomfort was so obvious. He was right, though. There was a good, logical reason for people to be terrified of everything the Zoo had to offer. The fact that he was out there despite all his fears told Sal the kind of crazy the man was.

He was crazy too, but he'd put the fears of the Zoo into that healthy place where they helped him react better to the dangers he faced. The other man hadn't reached that point yet.

As they drew closer to the forest within the giant structure, the abundance of green that burgeoned like the first foray of spring could not be described by any word other than creepy. Everything about this place was wrong.

"So why didn't they drop us over the lab building itself? I assume they must have some kind of drop-off hatch given the lack of roads and such." Savage seemed focused now. His gaze scanned the ground and trees around them, and he held his weapons in his hands. "It seems like they made us walk all this way for nothing."

His accent took on an odd, exaggeratedly western quality. When nobody answered, he shrugged and looked around. "Cowboy accent? Nothing? Tough crowd."

Sam patted him on the shoulder again. "As long as you make yourself laugh, that's all that matters."

"Blow me," he grumbled.

"Ask me nicely," she replied snappily.

Sal recalled that the man had asked the same question in Kiev, and they had been sidetracked and no one had replied. He was about to answer the question when he caught sight of movement out of the corner of his eye. Something flickered on his motion sensors too, and he turned to try to get a better view of it.

At the same time, he primed his assault rifle and reached for the sword on his back. Kennedy followed his lead and aimed her weapon to where he pointed. Their teammates moved closer together and readied their weapons in all the other directions to ensure that nothing and no one would be able to sneak up on them from behind while they were distracted.

"What did you see?" Madigan asked. He appreciated the

fact that there wasn't any scorn or doubt in her voice when she followed his lead. They had worked together long enough to warrant them trusting each other's instincts almost as much as they trusted their own.

They both peered through the trees but whatever he had seen was no longer there and nothing could be detected in his motion sensors. If it weren't for the tiny blip he could see on the sensors' history, he might have wondered if he'd seen anything at all.

He was sure, though, that something had definitely moved there, and it wasn't merely something that had been disturbed by an unexpected gust of wind.

"I have no idea," he replied, honestly. "But there is something out there. Probably. Anyway, let's stay sharp. There's no telling what we might run into."

He knew they were all being fairly careful already, so there wasn't any point in reminding them to do their jobs. The only advantage this had was to make him feel a little better.

CHAPTER TWENTY-FOUR

Chernobyl: The Laboratory Containment Dome

Savage had seen pictures of Chernobyl before. Some were more recent than others, of course, but even then, most were damn similar. He'd even seen the place in person. Granted, that had been from a very, very great distance and through the lenses of a scope they had wanted someone with his kind of experience to test.

It had been a high-tech gadget they had developed to combine the low-tech advantages of a scope with satellite imaging that would help to triangulate distances through only the scope without needing to use lasers to judge the same thing. The design had essentially been a bust, as most things that were overly complicated and had too much tech in them tended to be. Either way, the whole area had looked as dead as Jimmy Hoffa, and equally as unappealing.

Since then, of course, the entire area showed every indication that it was coming to life. He'd used a little of the waiting time to research the Red Forest, as they now called it due to the radiation, and so was prepared for the forest out there. Nature had ways of doing things humans could never understand.

He'd been somewhat impressed but not surprised. This, however, was an entirely different nightmare. New buds sprouted literally as he watched from the trunks that were supposed to have been dead for decades already. From the little he understood, the radiation levels were extremely high there. Yet something was bringing these trees back to life after they had been bombarded with enough nuclear shit that no one would have been surprised if they suddenly became really angry superheroes fighting for the protection of the Amazon forest or something. That was some crazy necromancy shit right there.

He joked, but that was only because he felt like something with a million legs crawled up his back. It might have had a little to do with the two or so tons of experimental armor that he wore, but there was also the fact that he strolled into an atrocity of nature. Worse, he did so like it wasn't the kind of thing kids in movie theaters would yell protests at him for since it was literally the dumbest thing he could possibly do.

This was probably what it felt like to be in the Zoo, he decided as he holstered one of the pistols but held the other at the ready. At first, he'd indulged himself by keeping both in his hands and using the trigger guards to spin them like he was in some kind of mega-Western. The motion distracted him enough to keep him away from his very rational fears of what the location had in store for them.

Now that Jacobs had picked up some movement, however, it was time to prepare himself for a possible fight.

That meant stowing the second weapon since it would be virtually useless unless they were in a situation where aiming wasn't a problem, in which case, he could always employ his quick-draw skills.

The operative wasn't ashamed to admit he'd practiced that skill in front of the mirror back in the day when he thought no one was looking.

Jacobs stopped abruptly once again, and his gaze seemed to try to track something that moved on the edge of what their sensors could detect. The fact that it led them deeper into the forest and toward the coordinates that had been marked as where the lab would be situated felt entirely coincidental. He and Monroe were scientists, doctors in their fields, and thus were curious about what they saw and tried to wrap their minds around it.

Honestly, Savage would have possibly felt a similar interest, if less intense, if the premonition that something would pounce on them from a tree and mutilate them in seconds wasn't constantly in the back—and sometimes forefront—of his mind.

He would call it a phobia, but again, this was a very rational fear and had solid reasons to prove it. Phobias were only the irrational fears, right?

Still, everyone else around him appeared to be calm and collected, while he simply felt like he was one tiny misstep from losing his shit completely. Worse, he was afraid his state was only too obvious to the people around him. Sam had come to him to make sure he was okay a couple of times now, and even ever-stoic Terry looked a little concerned about him.

It went against everything he believed in and he didn't

like it. He was the one who was supposed to cover them and make sure they were okay, not the other way around. It was his responsibility.

Jacobs came to a halt again and brought the whole team to a stop. It at least made him feel a little better to know that Dr. Salinger "the Zoo Whisperer" Jacobs had a similar reaction as he did. A small comfort, but still a comfort.

"Do you see anything this time?" Kennedy asked. She looked like she was on her last nerve too, although Savage couldn't tell if her annoyance was directed at Jacobs or if she was merely anxious about being there.

"I've picked up some movement," Sal said softly and gestured in that direction.

The operative couldn't shake the feeling that something was watching him. A trickle of sweat trailed slowly down his spine and seemed to be more pronounced when they stopped. As of right now, he could tell that he wasn't the only one who felt a little paranoid about ther surroundings.

Sam and Terry both held their weapons like they expected something to go wrong soon. He'd been around them long enough to be able to tell the difference between them being on their guard and them tense in anticipation of imminent violence. Kennedy, a military vet herself, looked like she was in the same kind of mental state. Courtney and Jacobs seemed a little jumpier than usual, which meant that while he felt rather out of sorts, they were all in a similar position.

He knew the assurance that the rest of his comrades were on edge shouldn't be what calmed him, but the fact that he felt calmer after that realization was a good thing.

He decided he wouldn't look this particular and metaphorical gift horse in the mouth.

"The movement's still there, and it's coming closer," Jacobs warned, his head turned toward somewhere ahead of the group. Savage realized the kid's sensors must have been far more sensitive than the one he had in his suit since a few minutes passed before he detected the approach of the creatures—if that was what they could be called. There really was no way to tell what they were.

"Should we push forward?" Courtney asked.

"I'd actually suggest we set up some defenses and wait for whatever is out there to come to us," he responded and hoped they'd take him seriously.

"I think I need to have my brain examined, but I agree with the attack dog," Kennedy replied and shook her head.

"You don't need to call him that," Courtney snapped.

"Hey, if the shoe fits, right?" he said aloud and drew his second weapon. He didn't intend to use it for defense, but these pistols had an interesting side use that allowed them to be fitted to use their magnetic launch system with a variety of projectiles. He fitted a flare to the one in his left hand and switched the one in his right to a selection of regular bullets that were stored inside his suit. He had a feeling they would be needed if they wanted to keep any attacking monsters at bay from a distance. It had to be preferable to keep their snapping jaws and claws away from the suits.

"What are you doing?" Kennedy asked, her tone almost accusatory as he took a step forward.

"I simply thought we could use a better view of what's out there," he said, raised the flare, and used the HUD to

MICHAEL TODD & MICHAEL ANDERLE

calculate an acceptable trajectory that would keep it under the tree line and still provide a decent arc to illuminate the forest in front of them. While the bright lighting dispelled most of the gloom, it also cast shadows and created hidden corners between the trees, especially farther ahead. "Clear?"

She sighed but finally nodded. "Yeah, go ahead. Give us some eyes in there."

He made no reply and simply pulled the trigger with his left-hand to launch the flare deeper into the woods.

Something moved in response. He scanned the forest now bathed by the brightness and a whole horde of some-things out there were discernible. They moved together as their eyes watched the flare still floating above them.

"Holy fuck." Savage grunted in disbelief and instinctively took a step back.

Whatever the creatures were, though, it didn't look like they intended to make any deeper investigation into what had fired the flare. As the light faded, the motion sensors showed that whatever was out there still held their position.

"What are those things?" Sam asked.

"Hell if I know," Monroe replied. None of them liked the idea of something they couldn't see, much less some-thing that seemed to ignore them. It felt like a trap to Savage.

"What do we do, boss?" he asked and looked at Jacobs. The kid looked almost surprised that he was the one who was asked.

"Madigan, what do you think?" he asked and turned to the woman.

"Whatever is over there is between us and the lab," she replied in a matter of fact voice. "If we plan to head in that direction, we'll have to at least get a little closer."

"Fair enough." He didn't seem that happy to agree. "Let's push forward, but…be ready to set up those defensive positions if we need them."

"Got it, boss," Savage responded snappily and directed Sam and Terry to flank him at the front as Kennedy brought up the rear of the group. They kept Courtney and Sal between them to form a small, reverse pyramid.

The large gathering of creatures they could see on the borders of their sensors seemed as disinterested in the group of humans who approached them as they had been in the flare. Even when they came within clear view of the animals, a few on the edge looked up from their work to see what all the fuss was about before turning back to… whatever the fuck it was that they were doing.

"What the hell?" Terry muttered through the team's comm, and honestly, the man's question represented what was on everyone's minds at that moment. Thousands of creatures were spread over not only the forest floor but also in the trees and branches to blanket the whole area. From where the team stood, they looked vaguely like insects with wide, compound eyes that turned independently of their heads. This was reinforced by the fact that they looked like they all had more than four limbs, although from this distance, it was difficult to tell exactly how many that they had.

The operative had heard many stories and seen numerous videos on the variety of beasts found in the Zoo and how it seemed they were hybridizations of existing animals with origins on Earth itself. There were countless people, both specialists and non-scientists, who had questioned why the goop that was purported to be alien—although the government was still a little vague on the actual origins of it—would adjust and hybridize animals from Earth.

He made a point to only watch those online videos when he was drunk or high, which would allow him to process all the information but not retain any of it. Or pretend to process the information, anyway.

When they came within a hundred feet of the bizarre spectacle, the team came to an abrupt halt. They hadn't talked about it or even called it. For some reason, it merely seemed like they all knew it was a good place to pause and discuss exactly what they would do next.

"It doesn't look like they...want to attack us," Savage stated, his gaze fixed on the monsters. He had no idea as to whether they were something normally seen in the Zoo or not, even though he did remember something eerily similar when he and Anderson had snuck into one of the labs attached to the Pentagon not too long before.

That said, as they had moved in closer, it was easier to see the details. They definitely looked like insects, but the fact that their backs were covered with fur and they appeared to have very mammalian jaws told him they had to be some kind of hybrid.

Oh, there was also the fact that they were the size of an oversized poodle. It needed to be mentioned as well, if only to remind himself of the impossibility of it all.

"Which begs the question of what they're doing," Kennedy added. She moved to the front of the group and raised one of the rocket launchers on her shoulder. Her entire demeanor suggested she was ready for a fight or to blast a path through the beasts to reach the lab on the other side. If they needed to blow their way through the thousands of creatures between them and their destination, the fighting would definitely be intense.

With that in mind, Savage hoped they would put some distance between themselves and the monsters they needed to go through. They needed to give themselves enough space to kill as many of them as possible before the creatures moved in close enough to try to kill them. Assuming they hadn't found a way to use projectile weapons or something like that, he thought morosely.

"They look like they are humping the trees," Sam pointed out and zoomed her HUD into the mass of creatures in front of them. "Humping the ground too."

"They have stingers on their abdomens," Jacobs said and also took a closer look. "They're...injecting those stingers into the ground and the trees."

"Like I said, humping," Sam reiterated.

"Not really." Monroe shook her head. "They look like they're injecting something into the ground and trees to coax everything back to life somehow."

"Ten bucks says they're using the goop to do that," Sal declared. "Although I've never seen that happen in the Zoo. I always assumed it was transferred through the ground via roots and shit."

"I still don't see how any of this can't be easily explained as the insect monsters humping the ground and trees," Sam insisted and sounded annoyed.

CHAPTER TWENTY-FIVE

Chernobyl: The Laboratory Containment Dome

In all honesty, Sam did have a point. Anyone who saw what they now watched would come to a similar conclusion. It was one of those situations where ignorance was bliss. If it looked like the creatures were doing something humans might interpret as dirty, most would simply assume dirty stuff was going on. In all fairness, they were usually right.

Not in this case, though. Sal had the right of it. They injected the blue goop into the trees to force them back to life. With the same purpose, they released it into the ground too, and he wondered if that didn't have something to do with removing the heavy radiation that had soaked into everything in the area for decades, which would allow the plants to grow.

As he inspected the area further, he realized that some sections of the forest were in worse condition than others. They were still fighting a battle against the radiation, and while the goop sucked all those death rays out, there was still enough of it to kill virtually everything, no matter how alien it was.

There was, of course, the small matter of the stuff bringing trees that had been dead for decades back to life. This was terrifying shit. It was groundbreaking and yet still terrifying.

He realized that the other five members of his team were waiting and looking at him, expecting him to make the call. Obviously, he'd drifted off into thought again and someone had said something and waited for him to reply. Now, if he only knew who had asked and what they'd asked.

"What do we do now, Sal?" Courtney looked like she wasn't sure herself. He knew there were no right answers to that question. They could try to circle, but there was no way to tell if the monsters had surrounded the lab entirely —in which case, they would simply waste time and effort for nothing.

Even if it wasn't so, Savage's flare had revealed a group of monsters that were larger than those humping the ground and trees. Their purpose, obviously, was to defend the lab. He had a feeling that if the team was forced to engage those creatures, the rest would come running. That was how the Zoo worked, and until they were presented with evidence to the contrary, they would have to assume it was how it worked here too.

Still, none of that explained why everyone waited for him—the youngest of the group—to come up with answers.

Once a roundabout route was removed from the table,

they only had two other options. They could sit and wait or power through the mass in front of them.

Neither would be the right answer until they had more data to work from, which meant there really was only one answer.

"We'll move forward," he said softly. "Slowly, though, and press in closer to them to see how they react to us."

"They know we're here already," Savage pointed out. "If they intended to attack, they would have done so and not waited."

"True, but there are some differences," Courtney interjected. "Sometimes, they attack for no reason. At other times, they run away, and now and then, they're simply protecting their own territory or young, or something like that. There's no telling what will happen, no matter what we do."

"There's no predicting the Zoo." Madigan sighed. "I guess that rule applies here too."

"Right," Sal responded and straightened. "Which is why we keep moving…"

He let his voice trail off and drew his weapon closer. Something had triggered his motion sensors from a little too close for comfort—something above them and moving in rapidly.

The other team members reacted too. Savage, Sam, and Terry held their weapons aimed at the mass in front of them but also tried to get a look at what had managed to sneak in so close without being detected by the cutting-edge tech they were supposed to have been fitted with.

"It looks like the same thing we've stared at for the last

however long," Madigan said. "Only one, though—one of those insect creatures."

"Arachnid," Courtney pointed out.

"What?" the other woman asked, her voice laced with confusion.

"She's right," Sal agreed. "Eight legs and only two sections of the body, the cephalothorax and an abdomen. That's an arachnid."

No one disputed the scientific reasoning or that they were qualified to make that call. But the fact that it was some kind of hybrid was fairly obvious. Sal was sure to record everything as the creature descended the tree slowly. Four legs attached to the front of the body and four to the back were a divergence of the usual arachnid physiology. The fact that the legs were different was interesting too.

Those on the outside looked like arachnid legs. They were segmented and gripped the trunk's surface like a spider's would. The four on the inside had no exoskeleton around them and looked more like rat legs. They grasped and held, and the two closer to the head even appeared to have opposable thumbs that could be used for climbing, holding, or a hundred different things.

The skull structure was that of a mammal—specifically a rat—but the eyes were compound and extended from the skull. This enabled the creature to look all around without moving its head.

"That's...fucking disturbing," Savage said.

"I second that statement," Sam said vehemently, and Terry nodded in agreement.

"Make sure not to puke inside those suits of yours,"

Madigan warned them and stepped closer to Sal. "Have you ever seen something like that before?"

"Nope," he replied and calmly collected all the data he could while the arachnid continued its descent. Careful and cautious, it watched the humans who aimed their weapons at it. "Brand, spanking new species."

"Will you shoot it?" Madigan asked. "Or should I?"

"Not yet," he said. "Look at the abdomen—or rather, the stinger at the end of it. It's dripping with something, and that's not silk. That's blue and gooey, wouldn't you say?"

She nodded.

"It means they're infusing the trees and ground with goop from inside the abdomen," he continued.

"I'm still following," she encouraged but with an edge of impatience.

"Either the creatures produce it inside them, or they pick it up from somewhere and bring it here, one way or another. That said, you must remember what happens when a creature with the blue stuff in their body is shot and the goop is spilled, right?"

"Gross, but…yeah," she said and shook her head at the vivid recollection of the Zoo suddenly gone feral. The response was the same when anyone pulled one of the Pita plants from the ground. The entire jungle went berserk and it felt like even the trees thirsted for blood as the pheromone that drove the animals crazy was released into the air. Those weren't memories they would soon forget.

Given the sheer number of creatures they faced here, there was really no point in trying to find out how they would react if one of their own were punched full of holes.

It was best to simply study it, Sal decided and shuffled a

little closer as the beast finally reached the forest floor. Once clear of the tree, it stopped using its outside arachnid legs almost entirely—except for a touch here or there for balance—and walked fully on its rat-like legs and moved toward the group.

"Can we shoot it now?" Savage asked. He turned from where he was supposed to cover their backs and aimed one of his pistols at it. The mutant seemed to approach more out of curiosity than with any noticeable aggression.

"No, hold your fire," Madigan snapped and raised a hand to gesture him back. He did as he was told, but his body language seemed to reflect confusion, annoyance, and even a little fear as the creature stepped nimbly over the ground without any apparent threat.

"I don't think it's attacking," Sal said. He looked at Savage and also indicated for the man to stand the fuck down. "It's only...kind of...investigating us. Trying to see if we're a threat."

"Okay, we're encased in full body suits, so I'd have to say these creatures' view of what humans look like has to be skewed, right?" Courtney asked. "I don't think they've ever seen any humans out of suits before."

"Let's remember we're not the first team of humans to come into this area," Madigan replied.

"Yeah, if you think about it, but if the other human teams were attacked and turned into...crazy-arachnid-slash-rat hybrid food, they would have chewed through the armor and simply assumed it was some kind of natural exoskeleton with a squishy center." She continued to make her point. "Right?"

"All I know is if you are wrong, I'll definitely haunt the

shit out of all of you," the operative declared and swiveled his weapon to aim at the larger number of mutants not a hundred feet away from them. "You especially, Jacobs."

"Wait, why me especially?" Sal demanded.

"Because you're the boss, so anything that goes wrong here is everyone's fault but especially yours," he explained quickly.

"The man has a point," Madigan agreed. She appeared to be warming up to Savage more and more as the mission went on. Sal doubted she would stop calling him the attack dog for a while, though.

"Don't say that the man who will haunt me especially if he dies here has a point," he protested, only half-joking. He didn't believe in ghosts or hauntings, but even though he was a scientist who needed evidence to support the claims, there was no evidence to support a claim that there weren't any ghosts or afterlife. It didn't seem particularly wise to push back on something for which there was no evidence either way.

He decided it was time to try to lighten the mood that had suddenly come over the group. "I've thought about a name while we've been all about the gloom and doom around here. Do you guys have any suggestions?"

"Tell me you won't mash the scientific names of the different creatures that have been hybridized here—will you?" Terry asked.

"Well, we'll obviously have to do that, but that'll be the classification, not the name," he explained. "What do you guys think of...A-Rat-Chnids?"

"I think you've been drinking and still need some time to sleep it off," Madigan said. "That said, sometimes, the

MICHAEL TODD & MICHAEL ANDERLE

best ideas come to people when they're drunk, and the more I think about it, the more it appeals to me."

"We'll seriously let him name them aratchnids?" Savage spluttered and glanced at his teammates.

"It's a working title," he replied defensively.

"Besides, who's going to tell him he can't name the critter that?" Courtney asked and patted him on the back. "I can't really think of a better name for something that ugly."

"Yeah." Sal looked around. "I mean, yeah, it is hideous, but look at it. The fur is thick and full—glossy even. The limbs are lean but powerful-looking, so it seems like whatever it is, it is well fed and honestly, it has the kind of ugliness you come to love. Like a pug."

"Pugs are adorable," Sam replied quickly. "This critter is just...wrong."

"I guess on an alien planet where there are more mammal and arachnid hybrids, they'll probably think this creature is cute," Madigan commented. "But I think we've been distracted for long enough. Do you guys want to talk about how we'll get to the lab now?"

Sal didn't answer and instead, sank onto his haunches as the creature stepped in closer still. Sam was right. It was disturbing how much it had been hybridized, and there was something deep inside him that said it couldn't and wouldn't ever be considered acceptable. But the fact was that whatever had put this thing together had done so with considerable thought and intent. He honestly didn't know the goop could do that.

Well, no, that wasn't true. He'd seen some of the hybrids from the Zoo, although most of them hadn't come this close without needing to be put down lest they chew through his armor and into the squishy scientist under it.

Of course, it did remind him of his first encounter with one of the Zoo monsters. He hadn't thought it was a monster at first. It had been one of the giant blue locusts at a time when they didn't have scorpion tails. The beast had been alone, he remembered, and looked at him and the rest of his team—which had included Madigan—and seemed curious and intrigued by the group it had encountered. It had nothing violent about it and nothing that would make him think to cause it any harm. He couldn't help but think that the first encounter, for lack of a better term, had been what shaped his view of the Zoo.

He knew what had come next had shaped his views too. Lynch, a crazed, violent, and mutinous mercenary from the UK, had shot the creature and laughed as he walked away from it. While he couldn't remember the man's exact words, the intention had been clear. So many people saw the Zoo as something they could profit from, and therefore anything that could possibly come between them and their profit was very easily marked off as the enemy.

As the creature moved in closer and its very mammalian nose pressed against the hard, armored gauntlet, Sal couldn't help but think that maybe, just maybe, there was a chance to put a stop to all the fighting and killing. It was quiet moments like these that allowed him to indulge in his love for animals instead of his enjoyment of killing them. Well, he didn't really enjoy it, but rather the thrill of pushing his body to that kind of extreme and reveling in the fact that he, a skinny scientist-slash-geek, was able to accomplish that kind of shit.

Sal recalled his conversation with Savage from the night before. The man had been considerably more drunk than he was, despite not having been drinking as long, and they had discussed the problems of lying to oneself and trying to find technicalities that let you moralize what you were doing, no matter how horrifying. He was a good egg, despite everything, and he did have a pearl of wisdom or two to share. Sal could appreciate that.

"What the fuck happened here?" Terry asked and walked to one of the trees. He ran his fingers over the leaves and budding branches that began to push through the once dead bark. Truthfully, Sal had noted that it might not bring the dead trees back to life. Instead, it might enable the new trees to grow into the corpses of the old and soak in the nutrients that were still there while provided with some measure of protection. He would need to investigate it further. Another time, though.

CHAPTER TWENTY-SIX

<u>Chernobyl: The Laboratory Containment Dome</u>

Sal watched the group as they began to discuss their plan of attack. They had come to the conclusion that they definitely wouldn't find a way into the lab without going through at least some of the monsters. Also, they realized that once they engaged a few of them, the rest would undoubtedly join the fray quickly and turn it into a few varieties of blood-bath, depending on what kind of blood the monsters had.

But this was a topic for the gunners of their group to discuss while Sal and Courtney were otherwise engaged. It wasn't that they didn't want to join in or that they didn't have any good ideas to share. After all, the two of them had been involved in more than a few people's fair share of fights with creatures similar to the ones they faced now. That said, they were scientists first and foremost and their real interests lay elsewhere.

He assumed Courtney was of a similar mindset. They had the opportunity to study one of the most unique locations on earth, one even more unique now with the added complication of the radiation.

"Do you think all this goop is from what they managed to take from the Zoo and what was left from the probe that they didn't waste in the Zoo?" she asked.

His mind was thoroughly engaged with the creature that remained in their proximity. It appeared to inspect the rest of them now that it had established that he wasn't a threat.

He turned to Courtney, his mind already moving to catch up with hers. "What are you implying?"

"Well, it's assumed that the Pita flowers somehow developed the same goop—created more of it, if you will," she pointed out. "I haven't seen any of the plants out here, and…well, considering the sheer number of the creatures that appear to be injecting this into the trees and the ground, it has to be more than what they brought, either from the original source or from the Zoo, right?"

"So, you're wondering if this is somehow generating its own goop and it has nothing to do with Pita flowers?" He was silent for a moment as he considered this. "It's weird since the flowers are essentially the only thing in the Zoo that hasn't changed since we got there. They are one of the few static circumstances in that fucking place you can count on, I guess is what I'm saying."

"I think you're missing the real problem here," she whispered. "If the goop doesn't come from where it usually comes from, what is the source?"

She definitely had his attention now. "You don't think they managed to recreate it, do you?"

Courtney shrugged. "They've tried it for a while, and if

there was any reason for something to suddenly go wrong in this lab, it would be them finding a way to replicate the goop and for some reason, the goop didn't like it."

"Are you anthropomorphizing it?" he asked. He raised his eyebrows but of course, she couldn't see it.

"Well, do you have any other reasonable explanation for what it does and how it does it?" she demanded. "Whatever the fuck it is, there does appear to be some kind of…master plan for the universe."

"Or the Sahara, anyway," he contested. "Or…where was it the original missile would have landed if all those complicated calculations were correct?"

"I think it was the Arizona desert, wasn't it?" She sounded more like she thought out loud than made an unequivocal statement.

"Well, so it seems there might be some kind of…innate programming that drives it to redo the deserts of the world?" Sal proposed.

"I think there's more to it than that, but there usually is when the Zoo is involved," she replied. "There always is, right? It's always more complicated than it should be and always more dangerous than expected. And I know that to assume that because it always has been like that means it always will be is fallacious, But at this point, there are certain things you can predict, right?"

He shrugged. "If there's any kind of design behind whatever's happening here, I'd put money on it being something we can't even fathom. Besides, the delivery system was obviously flawed. There has to be a better way to do it than dropping it into the middle of the desert to be collected and disseminated by humans."

"I think we can essentially write that off as a technical failure, given that it didn't actually have a chance to land at all," Courtney pointed out. "It was intercepted, brought down, and immediately contained, as I understand it, so it's a moot point. I'd have to have a look at the projectile before coming to any definitive conclusions, but it does seem like it was designed to function optimally in a desert-like setting."

Sal nodded and watched as the creature, seemingly satisfied that the humans present wouldn't pose any kind of threat, returned to the tree it had climbed from. Savage looked curious as he moved closer to them. The group of gunners appeared to be at something of an impasse over what to do and took a break from the discussion.

"You know, I think I've seen something like that critter before," he said tentatively, his head tilted while his hands toyed with the weapons he had holstered. The man was clearly still ill at ease with the whole situation, but all and all, he had shown far more restraint by not killing the mutant immediately than most of the newcomers to the Zoo did. When you were faced with alien monsters and had a gun in your hand, fight or flight instincts came into play, whether you were attacked or not. People like Savage and Kennedy had their fight instincts well-tuned. The man's self-control probably came with his survival instinct too, since Madigan had made it very clear that she would shoot him if he endangered the rest of them.

Still, kudos to the man for resisting his itchy trigger finger.

"What do you mean, you've seen something like that

before?" Courtney asked. She sounded outright skeptical. "I thought you hadn't been in the Zoo."

"I haven't," he confirmed. "And yet, I saw a creature kind of like that while on a mission with Anderson."

"And where was that?" Sal asked.

"It was a lab connected to the Pentagon in Washington DC," the man replied. "It looked like a rat too, but it had wings and six legs like a roach. And it had babies it was protecting. We were in a tight sewer situation where we needed to kill to keep it from killing us."

"Well...that's alarming." She stated the obvious but seemed unaware of it as she looked around at the group that had now gathered closer to the trio. "Do you think that's something you should have brought up with us earlier?"

"I did," he replied defensively. "Well, Anderson did in his report to you about the operation. The fact that you didn't address it when we met to discuss the mission meant —to me, anyway—that it wasn't really a big deal."

"Dammit, I knew I should have read that report," she exclaimed and ground her teeth. "So there are problems growing outside the Zoo. First, here in Chernobyl, and now in Washington."

"Well, I think we ran into the critter in the sewers before everything went sideways around here, actually," the operative clarified.

"Well, sure, but the lab itself has been in operation for months, so it outdates your encounter in our nation's capital by almost as many months," she asserted.

"Good point," he acknowledged with a firm nod. "Anyway, what do you think we should do?"

Sal noted that the man's gaze remained on the creature, which had stopped climbing the tree and now injected the bark with whatever was in its stinger. He wondered how long it would stay there since it would answer the question of whether it produced the goop itself or would go somewhere to gather it. By the looks of it, there was little chance that it would move for a while. It had situated itself on the tree using its outer legs, and the inner legs provided balance as it rocked gently over the bark.

"Sal!" Madigan called and dragged his attention away from his fascination with the bizarre process. She jogged closer to him, followed quickly by Sam and Terry. He was about to ask them what the problem was and why they risked alerting the creatures to the point of violence with their sudden movements and loud noises. No, not loud noises since she had made the call through the comm systems, which wouldn't be audible to the rest of the world thanks to the suits they wore.

Still, though.

He really didn't need to ask her why she had broken protocol like this. The answer was fairly apparent. His gaze was drawn to a handful of the trees around them. They were already populated with a few creatures each and all appeared to do the same thing as the first one they'd noticed without going through the motions of making sure the newcomers were a threat. It seemed they were equally as content to continue their work and ignore the humans as they injected their stingers into the trees, hugged the trunks with their eight legs, and prepared to remain in place for a long time.

Which was when he noted that the remaining monsters

appeared to drift toward them as well. They moved slowly and gradually in groups of tens and twenties but drew steadily closer. Some skittered across the ground while others leapt from tree to tree to reach to the various places on either the trunks around them or the forest floor. It seemed coordinated and yet natural at the same time, almost how zebras and wildebeest in Africa migrated in groups to new grazing grounds.

It was an interesting sight to watch, even with the unnerving knowledge that the creatures appeared to have surrounded them completely and left no room in which to move—neither toward the lab nor away from it. The fact that they hadn't attacked was a small comfort. The reality was that if they were to attack now, the small team of humans would be surrounded on all sides as well as above. He didn't want to find out if those stingers could punch through his armor, nor did he want to discover what they would do to the human body once injected. What was good for the trees might not be so for the people, after all.

That said, they showed no sign of aggression to the interlopers. He would have thought that the creatures ignored them except for the fact that they left a circle about fifteen feet wide around them like something protected them somehow.

"What the fuck?" Savage muttered. He'd already drawn his weapons and this time, Madigan made no attempt to tell him to not fire. Sal still didn't think that was a good idea, but for the life of him, he couldn't understand why.

"Hey," Terry called. "Are any of you guys having any trouble with your Geiger counters?"

"No, why?" Madigan asked. Of course, Sal knew what

the answer was, but in truth, he'd only noticed when the man pointed it out. An understandable oversight, of course. When you were surrounded by a veritable horde of alien creatures, your priorities shifted somewhat away from the thought of the radiation in the air around you.

"The count is dropping," Sal pointed out, stared, and tapped lightly on his HUD to confirm the readings. "Fast, too."

Sam looked around as if in disbelief. "It's like they're soaking up the radiation somehow."

"That's not how radiation works," Courtney interjected but sounded equally confused.

"Okay, you say that, but I'm looking at some fairly compelling evidence to the contrary," Madigan stated. They all had the same readings from their counters, which was confusing enough, but that wasn't what they should focus on at that moment.

More and more of the monsters now moved above and around them, positioned themselves on the trees and the ground, and all appeared to do the same thing. Hundreds, thousands and, from what Sal could tell, potentially millions of them injected whatever was in their stingers into the surfaces. He stood by his assumption that it was the goop, but he still wanted to take samples when the mutants moved away again. If they did.

He inched closer to the tree to see if he could sneak a closer look and, to his surprise, the creatures around him uprooted their stingers and moved away. The movement caused a chain reaction that left him with the same kind of protective bubble.

"Huh." Madigan grunted. Braver than most and

thinking quicker than the rest of the team, she tried to replicate the scene, took a step out of their protective circle, and interestingly enough, saw the creatures pull away from her as well. They simply avoided the humans and even gave them space, then simply went back to work.

"I don't care what you say, that's not normal," Savage declared, his hands still on his weapons. He definitely looked like he was a bad twitch from the creatures away from pulling the trigger.

"True enough," Courtney said. "I've never seen anything like it, not even in the Zoo."

"I'd put good money on this being what the other teams ran into," Sal said. "They saw a horde of alien monsters moving closer, panicked, and started shooting. They didn't realize that if they had merely left them alone, they would probably be left alone too. So…let's take our fingers off our triggers. I think it's safe for us to push on toward the lab."

Madigan nodded in agreement, and so did Courtney. Savage, Sam, and Terry showed no sign of being okay with this arrangement, but they didn't appear to have any reasons to the contrary. They kept their weapons out, though, and the group moved forward with slow, careful steps in the direction of the lab and deeper into the population of aratchnids.

CHAPTER TWENTY-SEVEN

Chernobyl: The Laboratory Containment Dome

For most of the group, it was an entirely stressful and tortuous journey. They proceeded slowly and constantly checked their surroundings, while they kept their weapons drawn in case the creatures launched an unexpected attack. Honestly, at this point, with so many of the creatures around them and their sheer proximity, whatever fight might ensue would be very short and with few casualties. Those would very obviously be the humans plus however many of the creatures they could take with them.

Still, it was never good to plan for failure, and Sal could see Savage load two phosphorus grenades into his left-handed pistol, ready to burn his—and hopefully their—way out of there.

To cause a fire in a location like this was a terrible idea, of course, even with whatever was in progress to reduce the radiation. There was still enough dry wood all around them to generate a massive forest fire in a matter of minutes. That would, in turn, release all the radiation in the dead trees through the smoke and, if it damaged the containment dome, into the cloud cover and might blanket the whole of Europe in a radioactive cloud. The situation, if it went bad, might potentially make the whole continent unlivable for decades to come.

And still, he couldn't bring himself to tell the man to find a different plan. If they wanted to get out of there, they needed to trust each other's instincts, and the operative's instinct was apparently to burn the whole place down in the hopes that they might be able to slip away in the confusion.

Then again, Sal remembered what happened with their attempts to burn the Zoo. He hadn't been there for it, but the video footage had been one of his first real views of the jungle. A few trees burned but the rest refused to do so, and a group of panthers with venomous fangs rushed in to murder the unfortunate bastards who had tried.

Maybe the same would happen there. Then again, they hadn't really tried using the phosphorus grenades to ignite the fire. It was already too expansive a jungle to totally incinerate anyway, but given that the Chernobyl area was still in development, as it were, it might work.

Besides, the deeper they moved into the forest, the lower the radiation levels dropped. It was almost at survivable levels at this point. That would have been a comforting thought except for the knowledge that the levels spiked when the creatures weren't around.

"You know," Savage said and sounded a little calmer despite the fact that they were still moving through the group and deeper inside. "I can't help thinking about how bad an idea this is."

"I happen to think it's a bad idea too," Sal said and twisted to look at the man as they continued their slow march. "But go ahead, share your reasons why this is probably a bad idea."

"Well, before, we allowed ourselves space to retreat if the creatures decided to attack us," he said. His head swiveled constantly to watch the monsters around them. "Now that we're right in the middle of the infestation, we don't have the option to retreat anymore."

"True," Courtney interjected. "And yet we do need to reach the lab and this way, we don't have to fight our way in. In fact, the worst-case scenario we're looking at is having to fight our way out, and I'll take that as a win any day of the week."

"Fair enough," he conceded. "And yet...the problem I see is if we have to fight our way out of this mess, we'll do so from smack in the middle of the population. Those mutants will come from all sides, meaning if a fight starts, we'll...probably not make out of here."

"Agreed." Madigan sounded pissed. "This feels like the beginning of a very gory and low-budget horror flick where the protagonists walk into the very obviously evil guy's house because he invites them in for tea and sandwiches. Like a...puppet maker or something like that."

Sal noted that Savage and Madigan turned to face each other, both made uncomfortable by the fact that they appeared to be in agreement. They had been grinding each other's gears from the beginning, and the fact that they appeared to have found some kind of common ground only showed how bad their current situation was.

MICHAEL TODD & MICHAEL ANDERLE

She shook her head and disengaged before the situation grew more uncomfortable.

Sam and Terry remained silent as the team forged on, but they both seemed tense and alert and their weapons remained at the ready. All of them were still suspicious about the fact that the creatures appeared to always move away from the humans and give them enough space to keep moving. As if by some silent signal, they would close in behind them as they passed, content to ignore them while they continued with their work. No hostility manifested. If anything, they appeared to want nothing to do with the interlopers now that they realized they presented no threat.

After veering slightly off course once or twice—mainly due to their focus on the mutants—they finally found their bearings and very soon, the lab was visible up ahead. They resisted the urge to hurry and maintained the almost agonizing pace, waiting for the monsters to move out of their way first before they could press ahead and repeat the process. None of them wanted to push their luck at this point. The Zoo monsters had never done something like this—not that Sal had ever seen—and he rather enjoyed the opportunity to watch them while he didn't have to fight for his life.

That said, there wasn't much variation in what they did. They were all very intent on pumping the trees and the ground with the goop in their stingers. He was now convinced that they produced it themselves, which was why they were able to stay in place for so long and continue the task.

The closer they got to the lab, the more vibrant everything seemed around them. It began to look less like a dead forest being brought back to life and more like a forest that still needed a little care. This was as close to the finished product that they would see, and it was gorgeous. The Zoo was beautiful in a very exotic kind of way but there, it looked a little more familiar. The European forest structure of pines and oaks and ferns all coordinated with the interesting alien elements—and, of course, the horde of aratchnids humping the life into them.

Sam was right. There was no other way to describe it.

With the daylight type of illumination, they could see the lab a little clearer. It was made up of the prefab materials Sal recognized from his time in the various bases around the Zoo—the same materials they were building the massive wall with too.

Thinking about the Zoo like this helped him calm somewhat as they drew closer to their destination. He had worried that his attachment to the jungle would fade if he spent time away from it, which was why he had been anxious to get back in the saddle again after his kidnap. And yet, there he was, thousands of miles away, and he still thought about the damn place like it would be stuck in his life forever.

Admittedly, their current surroundings were very stark reminders of what he was missing, but still.

As they approached the base itself, the numbers of the aratchnids diminished. They appeared to drift slowly to other areas of the forest, which allowed the team to move a little faster. With the sun well on its way down outside, none of them wanted to get caught out there when night fell. They assumed the lighting would fade to replicate normal cycles of day and night. They were given orders to send a signal up when they were ready to be extracted, and the helos would head in to pick them up.

"We couldn't have known this coming in, but it was a good thing this dome meant we couldn't be dropped off at the building itself," Terry pointed out. Sal eyed the man curiously, but Sam beat him to the punch of asking the question.

"What do you mean?" the woman queried, and her tone sounded unconvinced. "Are you saying you prefer to take this hike through Transylvania's more terrifying cousin?"

"Yes and no," he replied, and his tone suggested a smirk. "We were caught off-guard and almost started a fight when we were approached slowly by the monsters. Can you imagine the kind of shitstorm that would have ensued if we had dropped right on top of them?"

"The man has a point," Savage said with an unhappy laugh. "I can't say I like the walk, but I think we would have had a fight on our hands if we'd landed directly in the area where they were plugging away at the trees."

Sal couldn't help but agree. And yet, he found his gaze and attention drawn to the lab. It still looked to be in fairly good condition, given that he had expected the place to be essentially a crater by now. The walls were all intact and there was still electricity inside, from the look of the lights glowing beyond the windows. He only now registered the oddness of the lighting, both in the building and in the outer part of the dome. The surroundings and the some-what surreal journey through the creatures had distracted him more than he realized.

That said, there were still creatures between them and

it, and these weren't aratchnids either. They looked less like rats and more like wolves, with canid bone and muscle structures. They were four-legged, unlike the other creatures, and despite being about eight feet tall at the shoulder, they resembled wolves or large dogs, with brown, white, and gray fur covering their bodies in a thick coat.

It was interesting to see that they looked fairly normal from a distance, except for the fact that dozens of them stood around the lab like they were protecting it. The pack was entirely focused on the humans and watched them warily as they approached.

Savage and Madigan both looked ready to fire at them if the opportunity arose, but as the group advanced, they appeared to be content to simply study them.

From a distance, they had almost seemed normal, but it soon became obvious that they looked less like regular wolves than the team had first thought. The size was still the biggest giveaway, of course, but once they were close enough to identify the details, Sal could see that the eyes were like their aratchnid comrades—compound and bulbous as well, although seated deep in their skulls and unable to move on their own.

One of them panted and revealed that the tongue was a little longer and a good deal more flexible than a regular canid's. The biggest difference was the fact that the jaws parted down the middle, with fangs between the lower halves. Sal didn't want to think about what would happen if they were actually attacked by those fangs, but he had the sinking feeling the encounter would result in lost limbs.

Exactly as the aratchnids had behaved, though, the wolf creatures appeared to have little interest in the humans after a brief moment in which they appeared to try to decide what they were. The fact that they were tall enough to rival the height of Madigan's suit meant their reticence was a good thing, but he hoped they wouldn't have to fight the literally dozens of them on the way out.

They passed through the line of monsters and reached the lab itself. Sal narrowed his eyes and noticed that while the building had appeared to be intact from afar, small cracks had begun to show in the structure. Faint though they were, they were plainly visible thanks to the plants that had already begun to grow from between them. Vines snaked up the walls too and made it look like it was in a much worse condition than it had appeared from farther away. But it was still standing, and the generators were running.

"Ten bucks says this is where the goop is coming from," Madigan told Sal through the comms.

"No bet," he replied. He couldn't help a sense of excitement that filled him as he filmed and recorded everything he encountered. This was his first in-depth study of the goop's actions outside the Zoo. While the reactions were systemically similar, it appeared to have adapted to its environment and brought about all the changes such an adaptation would require. It was interesting to study, although he could understand the lack of enthusiasm from those who were less academically inclined than he and Courtney were.

"Come on, we have to get inside," he said and gestured for the group to follow him. Courtney was right behind him, but it took the other four a little more coaxing to enter.

CHAPTER TWENTY-EIGHT

Chernobyl: The Laboratory Inside The Containment Dome

"So, I have a question for the scientists of the group," Madigan said as they passed through the building's surprisingly still intact decontamination procedures, which included a nice long wash that thankfully didn't fry any of their suits' electrical components. "That means Sal and Courtney, of course. Why do you think it's combining rats and wolves with ara-whatevers?"

He shrugged as he waited for Sam, who was the last one through decontamination. "It's hard to say, but I guess it's because those were the choices that made the most sense for whatever job the goop wants them to do. Which... Honestly, I still can't believe I'm saying this, but it does seem like they're being directed by a higher power, exactly like they are in the Zoo. I'm still not sure how, though."

"Well, if you think about the way the six of us communicate through a dense and intricate series of radio waves, I'd say any alien kind of anthropologist would be baffled by our communication system as well," Savage pointed out while he checked to make sure his magnetic weapons hadn't been damaged in the decontamination process.

"Good point." Courtney shifted from one foot to the other as if impatient. "And Madigan's question is good too. Why do you think its rats and arachnids? Or arachnids and wolves based the gargantuan monsters we saw outside? We've seen the animals in the Zoo show genetic material from hundreds of different creatures, and while there are probably arachnids galore around here, the natural reclamation has reintroduced numerous different species. Why only choose two of them?"

"Again, I think it's because that's what it needs right now, although I don't pretend to understand the reasons behind it. I don't think it's even necessary for something to be alive," Sal said. "The goop creates and extrapolates from the available DNA, so it won't necessarily create the same mutants here. It would work off the genetic materials it found locally, dead or alive.

"Rats were in the city before it was abandoned, and I assume there were insects, arachnids, and even wolves around here. That's besides whatever animals moved into the area and other creatures that were brought out for the science experiments. If you think about it, that's incredibly ingenious. No animal rights activists will think to come all the way to Chernobyl to protest and break the test subjects out of their cages, right?"

"Right," Courtney agreed. "So, it's worked with what it has. Although, if you take that a little further, it can only be assumed that we'll see monsters similar to those we saw in in the Zoo before too long, right?"

"It might have already done so, which is why I don't

think it's a good idea for us to be caught out here overnight," he said and judging by the nods, it was something the entire team could agree to with a great deal of enthusiasm.

He took a reading of the radiation levels on his suit's Geiger counter before they moved into the facility through the decontamination area and into the actual laboratories.

"So, if the governments all around know about what's happening here," Sam said and stared at the eerily abandoned and yet seemingly functional building they were in. "And assuming they have no intention to allow a situation like the Zoo to happen this close to so many back yards of the folks who have the power to put an end to it, how come they haven't simply bombed this place off the map?"

It was a concerning thought, Sal realized. There were many people in the area with itchy trigger fingers who wouldn't want to have to build a wall around Chernobyl too. If they suddenly decided to carpet bomb the crap out of the area to make sure it didn't happen again, the Heavy Metal team would be caught in the middle of it with no possibility of getting out in time.

"I'd say the other governments around don't know about the data the lab was collecting," Terry suggested as they organized into formation in case they encountered something inside that wanted to pick a fight. "Or at least not all of it. I doubt the scientists here have offered full disclosure with the project still underway. Honestly, the governments out there probably all think the area is still heavily irradiated and have no idea the goop is working on fixing that particular problem.

"With the radiation killing everything in the area,

including the bacteria that would be able to break down the trees and plants and dead stuff and decay it, everything is sitting around here, dead and drying out, and waiting for a spark to ignite the world's biggest forest fire. If they bombed it and couldn't contain the ensuing fires, they would be looking at clouds of irradiated smoke covering the whole of Europe. For all we know, anyway. There's no telling what the reaction would be now."

"I call for a vote saying we don't spill the beans on what's going on here until we are too fucking far away to be affected by that potential catastrophe," Madigan said curtly.

Needless to say, they were all in agreement. The thought of being collateral damage in an effort to cleanse Europe of a potential infestation had been on all their minds, apparently.

"Fun times," Savage said, and sarcasm dripped from his voice as they came to the entrance of a common area of the building. It took a moment, but the automatic doors swung open with a minimum of creaking, and the lights in the common room turned on to reveal a collection of sofas and even a small dining area with stoves, microwaves for food prep, and utensils, crockery, and cutlery. A couple of TVs were positioned around the room too, as well as small outlets where phones and laptops could be charged, plus billiards, foosball, and air hockey tables. Understandably, a light film of dust covered everything, but aside from that, it looked like it was a day's cleaning away from being perfectly usable.

Sal was a little jealous that they didn't have a place like this at the Heavy Metal compound.

"I don't get any signal from the outside," Courtney pointed out as they started to explore the room half-heartedly. "I've tried for a few minutes to get word to Anja that we're at the lab, and there's no sign that she got it. The last contact we had with her was way back at the entrance to the dome, so we might be on our own while we're in here."

"If there's any trouble, we'll blast our way out," Sam said with a grin and patted a pack on her hips to indicate some kind of high-grade explosive inside. "Nothing like getting out of here with a bang to get her attention, right?"

"Right." Savage studied the room. "Hey, science geeks, I have a question. Don't you think we're forgetting another kind of creature that was all over this place when it went dark?"

Sal narrowed his eyes and wracked his brain. The paperwork on the lab had indicated that lab rats, insects, and arachnids had been flown in for testing. No wolves, though, but there were those roaming the safer areas in the outskirts of Chernobyl and the city of Pripyat nearby and even traces of those long dead to account for the DNA. He sifted through everything he could recall and still couldn't think of anything else that might have come up around the same time.

"What are you talking about, Savage?" Courtney asked brusquely, apparently also slightly chilled by his tone of voice.

"Well, I assume there were humans in the vicinity when the lab went dark," he reminded them and gestured at the area around them. "Don't you think there would be some sign of them in the creatures we saw outside?"

Sal shrugged. "The goop doesn't take humans. We've

thought about that for a while, but whenever there have been deaths, there's only been a problem of the bodies being eaten by what kills them with no sign of the DNA being incorporated into the new crop of creatures that show up afterward."

"That we know of," Madigan reminded him. "We don't know what happens to the bodies of the dead inside. We only assume the rest of the fauna eats them."

"We've seen the suits that had people inside," Courtney protested in Sal's defense. "Those the animals couldn't reach—inside armor and the like— all showed the same signs of decay we've seen outside the Zoo."

"Except the Russian team that were attacked and killed were being pulled underground by the vines," Madigan added with a scowl. "That's new. Maybe something has changed in the way it operates with people now too."

"Still, though," Savage insisted, even though he recognized that he was out of his depth in this situation. "Look around. Does this place look like it's the site of a lab that was closed down by an attack by wolf-hybrid monsters? Or that the beasts tore through all the unarmored scientists who were inside and supposedly eaten?"

Sal inspected the room, his attention now entirely focused on the matter. The man had a point, he conceded mentally. The place looked a little worse for wear, even if none of the plants and vines they'd seen growing on the outside were in there. Except for the dust, it looked pristine, and having worked in a lab before, he knew better than to think the room had been abandoned when things went badly.

Where scientists were involved, you would be hard-pressed to find them anywhere else when they needed to get out of the labs and clear their heads—which, as it turned out, was rather often. They didn't stop working while they were there, of course, but they refocused their minds and got some air and walked around to stimulate their blood flow.

The place would not be abandoned, was his point. Which brought on the question Savage had voiced. If there had been researchers there when the proverbial shit hit the proverbial fan, where were they now? If they had been killed, why wasn't there any sign of the violence?

Admittedly, the Zoo had a bad habit of taking the bodies of its creatures when they were killed and assimilating them, which effectively made everything—anything from bone and muscle to the blood that had been spilled—disappear. And Madigan was right—they had seen the corpses being dragged underground. But there should have been other signs that a fight had happened. Furniture turned over, bullet holes if they had been armed, and other indications, at least, that someone had run for their lives.

But the room looked spotless. All the chairs were organized around their tables and the sofas were all in place around the TVs.

"Shit, this place is creepy," Sam grumbled and voiced what was on everyone's mind. She nudged the foosball table to the side using her suit. With the power behind the combat armor, she was able to easily push it around with one hand. "Did the geeks around here have some kind of security personnel to protect them?"

"The paperwork specifies that the security was here to keep them from stealing any of the research they worked on," Courtney said. "That was something of a problem, apparently. They were equipped with combat suits and were supposed to guard the doors and the rooms that contained the suits the geeks...er, scientists, could use to go outside and run their experiments and the like. They were thorough with their work here."

"You'd think the folks in this area of the world would accept that seeing some of their equipment go missing and later appearing on some black market or another was a cost of doing business, right?" Sam abandoned the foosball table and turned her attention to one of the TVs.

They were all connected to a handful of modern gaming consoles, and a few of the nearby shelves were stacked with a variety of games for the staff to pass their leisure time with. "From the experience I have in this part of the world," she continued, "the corruption from the top to the bottom levels of the government bureaucracy would mean they regard minor theft by their employees as so common that it's included in some political bills as spending money."

"That's...interesting," Savage responded. "But I don't think they wanted anything from here getting out, and I can see why. Either way, I can't help the feeling that we've walked into the beginning of one of those horror movies where everyone dies at the end."

His teammates, if they hadn't actually thought that before, definitely did now and they all kept their weapons at the ready as they moved away from the eerily intact common room to continue their exploration.

CHAPTER TWENTY-NINE

Chernobyl: The Laboratory Inside The Containment Dome

When you heard people talk about the technology that was developed and produced in eastern Europe, they usually used the same words to describe whatever they used, despite a large number of different corporations that produced hundreds of different products.

Some would use "durable" as a compliment since things that were designed there were with the need for them to last literally decades in mind. Others talked about how they were a little clunky and difficult to use, with less than optimal and unintuitive operating systems. Most simply called them crap and moved on to the cheaper versions that came out of China, South Korea, or Japan.

That said, whoever had designed and built this lab had their thinking caps on, Sal decided as he studied the facility with real curiosity. There were innumerable signs of genius development and engineering wherever he went, from the actual building design to the technology inside that was still running—which spoke to its durability too, he thought—to the security and the electronics in the building. It was very clear that whoever had put this place together had spared no expense.

Kind of like the old, bearded man with a prehistoric mosquito trapped in amber topping his cane while he talked about bringing dinosaurs back to life. Sal wondered why the places that spared no expense were those that always went down in history as the biggest failures. Maybe it had something to do with how they were expected to do well and due to the sheer weight of expectations behind them, they inevitably blew up in the most colossal ways. Of course, anywhere that had spared expenses went badly too and much more frequently, but the lack of attention on them had avoided greater scrutiny. They were therefore ignored by the general public for the most part.

That said, aside from the lights and the doors, nothing else appeared to be on. Nothing was broken or burnt out the way it should have been if the facility had been violently attacked and left without anyone to care for the electronics. Everything was merely off like someone had taken the time to flip the switches to let the generators continue to run almost indefinitely. He could only assume they had the smaller fusion reactors running—like those they had in their suits but slightly bigger, and maybe three or four of them. They would be able to run the base for decades if all they powered were the lights and the doors.

With the security down, it made navigation much easier. They all had maps of the facility plugged into their HUDs, which meant there was little chance that they would get lost as they delved deeper into the facility and eventually located the stairs.

They would have taken the elevators, but they, like most of the other tech in the lab, were still down and they didn't want to waste the time to find a way to turn them on.

Which brought them all to the next question. They were supposed to look for data. If all the systems were down, they would need to bring some back up so they could find what they were looking for and get the fuck out.

The data on the facility Elena had given them said they would find the main computer servers in the basements, near where the medical bay was supposed to be.

They were on the ground floor, and the basement they needed to find was the second of four. How they'd found the time and equipment to actually dig four levels down and build in an irradiated zone was a testimony to how inventive the people in charge of the project had been.

Savage and Sam led the way down the stairs, their weapons drawn as if they expected and were ready for trouble. Terry and Madigan brought up the rear, with Sal and Courtney sandwiched in the center. They didn't pause on their way down the steps.

Sal wanted to be able to do a thorough check and to investigate and explore, but while they were still dealing with a situation that involved a whole lab with a security team and top-of-the-line security systems in place that had simply dropped out of all communication, they had to assume there were hostiles around. That, in turn, meant they would do what they came for and move their asses out as quickly as possible.

Those were Madigan's orders. Not even the operative

was brave enough to defy the woman when she had keeping her team alive on her mind.

When they reached the second-level basement, Savage and Sam breached it in smooth, practiced motions to make sure no surprises awaited them before they gestured for the team to enter.

This level was altogether different from the ground floor, which was immediately apparent when they stepped through the door. The lights were all on as the others had been, but these revealed a less pristine view. Blood spattered across the walls, instruments were strewn over the floor and drenched in red as well, and overturned furniture and scattered papers completed the scene that greeted them. There had definitely been a fight there, Sal surmised from his position behind Sam and Savage. Madigan and Terry moved into a forward position as well.

"Okay." The operative spoke when no one else seemed inclined to. He grasped his pistols a little more firmly now. "I guess things didn't end very well for the researchers."

"Was there any doubt?" Madigan asked.

"Well, no, but there was always the thought that they might have encouraged the guards to get greedy and between them, stripped this facility of anything they could carry and got the fuck out," he suggested. "No such luck, though. Too bad."

They appeared to have reached the section where animal tests were conducted, as evidenced by the containment units that filled the labs to capacity. All the doors were open, and there was a large amount of blood spread around them. Only blood, though, no body parts and no internal organs or bones that might indicate who or what the blood belonged to.

"It looks like rats were in this section," Courtney said and indicated the smaller cages. "Some containment for larger numbers of insects for testing here in the clear plastic tubs. But…what would they need cages that big for?"

Sal and Madigan both knew what the cages looked like almost before they saw them. The familiar design confirmed what they didn't want to believe. There was no mistaking the way it was made with cutting-edge technology to keep anything from breaking out and with the simplified locking mechanism and the three air holes on the top.

"Holy fuck, they were doing that here too?" Madigan asked and looked at Sal, stiff with outrage. "Who the fuck thought this was a good idea?"

"What are you talking about?" Courtney asked.

"You need to start reading your reports," the other woman retorted and shook her head.

"Human testing." Sal answered the question and stepped closer to the cages. The biggest problem was that they were open and empty, which meant that whatever or whoever they'd run those tests on were gone by now. The question was, where were they? "This is the same type of cage they kept the man they were testing in the Zoo in. It's the same design and everything, which, to my mind, means they were running the same tests. Infusing humans with the goop in there."

"Shit." Sam shook her head, the gesture indicative of a scowl. The rest of the team felt the same sick, cold feeling in the pit of their stomach telling them exactly how wrong everything that happened there was. "I guess we know why they wanted to have this lab in the middle of an irradiated wasteland, huh? There is no better place to break all the Geneva human rights conventions."

They held a quick moment of silence, not really out of respect for the poor bastards who had been sent there to be poked and prodded with alien goop by sick minds but rather because they needed it. The ethical problems aside, the fact remained that someone appeared to be funding these tests on other humans. That or some government or another was paying for this. Evidence pointed toward the Russians, but Sal couldn't shake the feeling that there were other factors in play.

Despite his academic curiosity about what was happening, he suddenly lost all interest in staying any longer. They needed to get their data and get the fuck out. Hopefully, they would be able to get the governments all around the area to bomb the absolute crap out of this facility based on the evidence of what had happened there. His first instinct was to record it all and expose whoever was responsible, no matter what the political fallout was, but common sense told him this fledgling Zoo needed to be destroyed before it gained a real foothold in Europe.

"The server room should be down the corridor to the left," Madigan said, and her brisk, efficient tone dragged them clear of the ethical situation they desperately wanted to walk away from. Sal took the front of the team this time. He needed to get as far away from those damn cages as he could. There were some things scientists simply didn't do

—things he could never see himself doing, even under the most exigent of circumstances.

They headed deeper into the floor, and most of the rooms were in a similar state. All contained cages, although only a few had those made for humans, which demonstrated that there were at least a handful of different tests that were run on those unfortunate enough to be there. He had to hope that the people they sent were the rapists and the murderers, the worst of the worst. Even that wasn't justification enough for this but knowing that bad things were happening to bad people somehow made it a little better, for some reason.

"Okay," Madigan said and raised her hand to bring the group to a halt as she checked the facility map. "The server room should be somewhere around here. The medical ward is there." She indicated the room that had a red circle and a cross painted on the door. "Which means the server room should be directly across from it."

They moved to the unmarked door opposite the medical ward. It was, predictably, locked, but given that it had been put in place to stop scientists in lab coats, the soldiers and researchers in combat armor were able to break through without difficulty.

"Okay," she said and looked around the room. It was filled from wall to wall with a variety of servers, all still on if the blinking lights were any kind of indication. That was something of a comfort. They were deprived of Anja's help without active comms and probably wouldn't know the first thing about turning the devices on and getting them running without burning or shorting something out.

Thankfully, with everything on, they would be able to

plug their suits into the servers, copy the data, and be away from the facility in a few minutes. They would let Anja deal with decrypting and understanding everything later.

"Okay, I think…Sam, Terry, Monroe and I can probably handle transferring the data," Savage said as he scrutinized the room to make sure there weren't any threats inside. "Jacobs, can you and Kennedy keep an eye on the door and make sure nothing tries to attack us while we're in here?"

Sal nodded firmly, hefted his assault rifle, and stepped outside with Madigan. She was silent for a moment, but he could tell by her rigid posture that she was no doubt grinding her teeth and scowling.

"Do you really think we can trust him?" she asked in a hushed tone, even though she had opened a private connection.

"I thought you were starting to warm up to him already," he replied, and she shrugged in response.

"He is cool under fire, I'll give him that," she conceded. "But trust him? I don't think so. I leave that kind of shit to Anderson and Courtney while I watch their backs and wait for him to try to pull something, betray them, and kill us all. Something like that."

"Well, we all know how much you like saying I told you so," he said and closed his eyes for a moment. Something niggled in the back of his mind. A weird feeling crept in, something he couldn't quite shake off and which drew his attention to the medical ward door. "So, here's what we'll do. I'll give him the trust since he's earned it thus far, in my opinion, when he helped to save Courtney's life—and Anderson's and his family's, as well as all the other things he's taken care of. You can go ahead and continue to not trust him and kill him if he ever tries any funny business, deal?"

"Deal." She grunted, clearly still ill at ease, and was about to turn away when she swung fully to face him again. "What the hell are you doing?"

He froze and realized he'd begun to walk across the hallway toward the door, which was weird because he hadn't really meant to do that. While he was vaguely curious about what they might find in the medical ward, he had told himself a second before that there was no point in sticking around to investigate every nook and cranny. They were there for the data, pure and simple. They would get it and get out.

And yet he couldn't shake the need to go into the room.

"I...uh, thought as we had a couple of minutes while the rest of them collect the data we might as well do some exploring, right?" He had thought quickly to come up with a good enough excuse to get past her sharp mind.

She didn't seem convinced, but while she was the gunner of their team, he was the specialist and she was supposed to listen to what he had to say. It was difficult to read what was going through her mind, of course, but she didn't say a word as she crossed the hall to stand beside him.

"I've got your back, Sal," she whispered, and he'd have bet good money that she wore a smirk. She primed her weapon and activated one of the rocket launchers on her shoulder.

He chuckled. "Ready for anything, huh?"

"Of course. I'm reasonably sure I could bring this whole place down if we really needed me to."

"Let's hope it doesn't come to that." He grasped the door handle and turned it slowly. Unlike the one into the server room, it was unlocked and opened smoothly to allow barely enough room for the two of them to step through one at a time.

The view that greeted them was almost more stupefying than anything else they'd seen during the rest of their strange, bizarre trip to the most famous nuclear meltdown in the world.

The lights were on inside, which had to be a huge demand on the electrical system since it was a massive room. There were a handful of medical dispenser units distributed throughout with instructions written in Russian. Even if they were in English, though, he doubted he would have been able to tell what they were for. He wasn't that kind of doctor, after all.

But it didn't take that kind of doctor to know what was happening to the people who were on the cots and beds that filled the room. Sal had to shake his head a few times to make sure he wasn't seeing things, but each time he opened his eyes, nothing had changed. There were still people on the cots, and they were still...alive?

That didn't seem right. He approached one of the nearest beds. There was no medical equipment attached to the woman who lay there, completely nude. Her chest rose and fell rhythmically, though, so there did appear to be some signs of life.

He leaned closer and frowned when he noticed the other telltale symptoms. The veins on her body were highlighted a bright blue against her pale skin and almost looked like they should have throbbed as they pumped blue blood through her body. Her eyes were closed, and she looked unconscious.

"Were they...testing on all these people?" Madigan asked, and he looked up and realized there were about two or three dozen or so who filled the whole room.

"I don't think so," he said and checked the patients one after the other to confirm that they showed the same blue-veined symptoms of overexposure to the alien goop. "There were only five or six of the cages in the labs, and I think the basement would be the only place to store them. If you calculate the weight of those cages and try it against the tensile strength of the prefab slabs—well, I'll let you do the math. Or rather, imagine me doing the math."

"Where have they all come from?" she asked, her tone sharp with disbelief as she moved down row after row of unconscious patients who simply lay motionless in their cots, waiting for...something. He wasn't sure if she could feel it too, but there was a tension in the air that he couldn't shake. She definitely seemed tense as well, but it didn't look right. It wasn't the same thing. He could tell.

"Well, if I were to venture a guess, I'd say the ones closest to the door are the test subjects," he said as something tugged his mind to the other end of the room and the doorway there. It had to be the only place in the building that was in the dark. He desperately wanted to go there, but something within fought back—a survival instinct, maybe, that dragged him away from what he knew would definitely be a bad idea. "The ones after them are the researchers and scientists who were here when the lab went dark, and the rest are members of the teams Molina sent before us."

Madigan looked at him and sensed something was a little off from the distant tone his voice had taken on. "No...we had the numbers of the people who were here and who came after. There aren't enough in these beds."

"I assume some of them resisted or fought back against their conversion or something like that," Sal replied, unsure why he was talking like that. He wasn't even certain where those words came from. Pain bloomed in the back of his head and expanded to the point of distraction.

"Conversion?" she asked, and he could feel her studying him.

Before he could answer, one of the patients on the cots moved. No, not the cots. Despite the fact that there weren't as many people as had been reported, there were still too many for the cots in this medical ward. Behind the cots, others had been placed on the floor or were in wheelchairs. It was one of those in the wheelchairs who suddenly jerked.

"Salinger?" A hauntingly throaty yet familiar voice rasped from the man's lips. "Salinger Jacobs?"

He narrowed his eyes and stepped closer to the man, who looked like he tried to push himself out of the chair. "That's me. Who are you?"

"Don't you recognize me?" the man asked and looked despondent at the questions.

It took him a moment, but there was something familiar about him. Most of his facial features were bathed in blue by this point, and he looked worse off than the others. Something appeared to have paralyzed the right side of his face and dragged it down, but...dammit, there was something familiar about the face and the voice too.

"Holy crap," he gasped and moved closer. "Smythe? Andy Smythe?"

"Wait, the same Smythe who kidnapped you and dragged you into the Zoo against your will, Smythe?" Madigan asked and immediately took a step forward, but Sal waved her back for the moment. He must have been on the team Molina had sent in. None of the reports had included any names.

"Yes," he replied and gasped for breath. "You…you need to leave now, Jacobs. It…wants you. It has you."

"What are you talking about?" Sal wondered.

"Get away from him, Sal," Madigan warned and raised her weapon.

"I don't know what it did to me," Smythe continued and a terrified look of horror spread across the half of his face that he still had control over. "It's…changing me. I can hear a voice in my head, but I don't know what it's saying. It shows me things I don't understand and tells me to do terrible things. I don't know why. I'm trying to resist, to fight back, but…it's doing things to my body to make me follow."

"What the hell are you guys doing here?" Savage asked from the door. He jogged through the room and tried to ignore the unconscious people in the beds as he approached Sal and Madigan. "We have the data and we need to get the fuck out of here. Now."

She looked like she agreed with him again and turned to grab Sal's shoulder as Sam, Terry, and Courtney entered the room as well. They, however, were less focused on getting out than trying to decide exactly what they were looking at.

Sal growled, shook Madigan's hand from his shoulder, and turned to Smythe. "What is it showing you?"

"Come on, Sal!" she snapped. The man didn't answer and simply pointed toward the door he had been drawn to since he entered the room. Hell, since he'd entered the building, even if he hadn't known it at the time. He peered inside where something moved and glowed a soft blue in the darkness, weaving hypnotic patterns to invite him closer and draw him in.

Madigan caught hold of his shoulder and hauled him away, more insistently this time, and he tried to dislodge her again. The weaving lights followed him and drifted into the illuminated ward. He remembered seeing tentacles like those in the Zoo, remembered watching them drop from the branches, snatch people, and drag them away. He didn't know how it was possible in this place.

As they moved closer, the pain in the back of his head turned blinding. He vaguely heard himself scream as he dropped to his knees and grasped his head, his hands stopped by his helmet. The pain only grew worse as he closed his eyes.

CHAPTER THIRTY

<u>*Chernobyl: The Laboratory Inside The Containment Dome*</u>

"Sal!" Kennedy screamed.

The medical unit seemed to erupt into chaos as if her protest had been a signal of some kind. Savage yanked his pistols from their holsters, not sure who or what he was supposed to fire at or why, but something had gone wrong. He had been right when he'd told the folks in the server room that, despite the hiccups they'd faced, everything had gone a little too smoothly. They were due something going sideways, and this was it, apparently.

Now, if he could tell exactly what the hell had gone sideways, he could hopefully fix it.

Kennedy scrambled to where Sal screamed and fell to his knees. His hands clutched his head as if to shake something off. The operative couldn't tell if the kid was merely having a migraine or not, but it seemed worse than that. There wasn't much he could do about it, so he decided the thing he could do was shoot—and in this case, his first targets were the tentacles that slithered insidiously from the room in the back.

That decision was confirmed when one of the appendages attempted to push Kennedy away. Despite the fact that the woman wore the heaviest suit of combat armor of the group, two made a second attempt together and were apparently strong enough to hurtle her into one of the side walls. She actually left a dent from the force of the impact, and the tentacles turned their attention to Sal, who still screamed incoherently and was obviously unable to defend himself.

One of the patients pushed out of a wheelchair. The man was literally blue in the face as he limped to where the scientist knelt helplessly while the mutant limbs snaked toward him.

Well, if there was ever a place to start, that would be it, right?

Savage held a pistol in each hand. Thankfully, he'd replaced the phosphorous grenades with the needles when they'd entered the building. He let the computer in his HUD do the tracking for the left as he focused on the right and pulled the triggers. With a soft whine, more power went into the weapons than the one he was used it, but they each fired a three-round burst of the needles he'd come to know and love.

All six projectiles found their targets. That was a fairly impressive achievement, both for him and the computer, given that the target was about fifteen centimeters wide and moved frantically like a snake.

Unfortunately, that seemed to be the limit of the good news. The wounded appendages retreated instantly but a rumbled roar, powerful enough to shake the basement floor on which they stood, shuddered through the room. As if on cue, the blue people on and off the beds and in the wheelchairs around them woke as one. Their eyes opened and they immediately stood and seemed to prepare themselves for some kind of blank-faced communal advance.

More tentacles snaked from the dark room in the back toward Sal and thankfully, most missed and flailed and whipped as if desperate to locate their target.

"Shoot these motherfuckers!" Savage roared at the team, who appeared to be stunned into total immobility. They simply watched the bizarre scene that unfolded in the room in shocked silence.

Kennedy was the first to react with anything useful. She shoved up from where she had been deposited by the attack, armed two rocket launchers on her shoulders, and primed her assault. One of the missiles rocketed into the appendages that attempted to drag Sal away. The blue man who had approached him first was the only reason why the scientist wasn't already in the dark room. The man displayed almost inhuman strength and somehow held him back. His eyes were closed, and his face twisted into a grimace as he fought against the will behind the would-be abduction with a long, drawn-out scream of pain.

The woman's second rocket was aimed at the humans who were nearest to them, almost obliterated five or six of them, and catapulted them all back with a powerful blast wave.

Sam, Terry, and Courtney were isolated on the other side of the room with dozens of these blue humans between them and the other half of their team. Sam had already come to the same conclusion as Savage had, which was that they were where the team needed to be. The only thing that mattered now was to hold their ground for the moment.

The operative simply maintained his fire with the computer's aim on the tentacles to slow and distract them so they couldn't drag Jacobs away. The one he had manual control over was aimed at the humans who had regrouped and now continued to advance on them. After a few seconds of lethargy, those who had survived the rocket suddenly appeared to gain new purpose. They thrust forward with inhuman speed to where Savage and Kennedy prepared to defend against them and tried to help Jacobs at the same time.

"This is one hell of a time to have a migraine, kid!" the operative muttered. He shook his head in disbelief as the attacking humans simply ignored shots to the head and torso that drilled holes through them and continued their onslaught. "You have the most advanced suit of all of us, and we would sure appreciate the assist."

"It's not a migraine!" Kennedy explained sharply as she bulldozed one of the humans down and stamped on his head. Despite the fact that it exploded like an overripe blue melon, the body continued to move and fumble at her legs. "Something in there is...pulling him in. Mentally and physically."

Savage nodded and launched two of the humans back with a sustained barrage from his pistol. "It sounds like we need to take care of this, posthaste."

"Agreed," she replied and tried to turn to see what was inside that dark fucking room and how to fight it. Three of the blue humans chose that moment to haul her back to face them. They didn't look like they wanted to kill her, though, merely...peel her armor off.

Come to think of it, that was what it looked like they attempted to do with him and the others as well—except for Jacobs, who would be dragged away by the worst depiction of hentai of all time if it weren't for the blue stranger who continued his superhuman efforts to prevent it. It was clear, though, superhuman or not, the man wouldn't hold out indefinitely. They had to do something, and now.

"Fuck this!" He snarled and slipped the concussive rounds Elena had supplied him in the feed line from his suit to the pistols. Two shots forced the characters who attempted to dismantle the woman's suit away. Another volley drove those who advanced toward him back, and with a third, he turned his aim upward at the ceiling. He'd been in prefab buildings like this, and he knew very well exactly how much power it would take to knock a hole in it.

As expected, the answer was not very much.

Savage pulled the triggers on both weapons and delivered the concussive rounds into the ceiling about five yards ahead of him. It wasn't a delicate approach, but given that they were in a room full of blue, zombified humans who simply couldn't take the hint from the headshots and die—not to mention the tentacled monster that attempted to drag his boss away—he was seriously done playing nice with these fuckers. It was time to go big and then go home.

The explosive nature of the rounds was enough to blow a hole not only in the ceiling above him but also in the support structure that held it all up. It wouldn't bring the building down but, exactly as he'd anticipated, it did bring a large section of the ceiling down on the fuckers.

The structure shook as this plummeted and coated the mutants in a hail of prefab chunks before it buried them in the rubble.

They immediately began to struggle and fight to get out from under it. He hadn't expected it to kill them all or even a few of them. He merely needed them off his back so he could deal with the bastard that still seemed determined to drag Jacobs into its lair.

"To hell with this." He connected two incendiary rounds to his pistols and aimed them at the darkness of the room at the end of the ward. "Eat white phosphorus, bitch!"

He pulled the triggers and the chemical fire erupted as soon as it came into contact with oxygen, already about fifteen feet away and in the darkened room. In the bright white light of the explosion, for a single moment, he was given a glimpse of what was inside and what attempted to capture the scientist.

All he could see at first was a mass of tentacles that writhed and roiled inside the room. There were literally hundreds of them, and they appeared to have already spread into other rooms of the building. They climbed vertically and horizontally and slithered through the entire structure to infest the whole facility. He had no idea how something like that had been able to grow so big in such a short period of time, but he didn't understand much about what the Zoo was capable of.

Past the coiling appendages, though, there did appear to

be a body. He thought it was merely another, thicker group of limbs initially, but as the light flared brighter in the small space, he realized it was a thick, fleshy body. The ungainly bulk lurked in the center of the room and might even have been burrowed between the floors and possibly spread across the others. The monster was dark and appeared to have a group of mouths that gnashed and opened in sequence as if waiting for Jacobs.

He'd no sooner had that thought when the fire erupted in earnest and began to spread. The ground-shaking roar thundered over them again as they took a moment to gather their strength. The tentacles wound around Jacobs suddenly released their hold and hissed as they withdrew, while the mutant-humans who tried to fight their way out of the rubble screamed to echo the same pain that afflicted the beast inside the room. Savage set his weapons to the needles and turned quickly to see if any of them were free and might attack.

It was a pleasant surprise to see that the few who had freed themselves had collapsed.

"We need to get the fuck out of here," Kennedy said. She spun to where Jacobs had stopped screaming and appeared to slowly return to his normal self. He blinked and shook his head a few times.

"What happened?" he asked as Kennedy helped him to his feet.

"Nothing much," the operative replied with a smirk. "I simply saved all your asses and opened us a nice little escape route to boot."

"It'll recover," the blue man who had helped the scientist said. He appeared a little more like a normal human being now than he had a few seconds before. "And when it does, it will be pissed off. We need to kill it and do so now."

"How do you suggest we do that?" Savage asked and peered into the room. The tentacles flailed and writhed in the flames in an attempt to put the fire out. *Good luck with that, asshole.* Chemical flames like those used in these incendiary rounds could burn for hours at temperatures exceeding two thousand degrees Celsius. "There isn't exactly a clear way in."

"There is for me," he replied and glanced at Kennedy. "Do you have any grenades? Anything I can use to blow that fucker up?"

There was a short, silent moment in which she looked at Jacobs, then at Savage. She obviously wondered if she could trust this character. He presented with the same blue veins as the rest of them—possibly more—but he had been there to prevent the scientist from being dragged away when no one else could help. She mumbled a curse that was all but inaudible, retrieved a belt of grenades from her pouch, and handed them to the man.

"How will you get the grenades in there, Smythe?" Jacobs asked. He seemed to have fully recovered his faculties again. "It's not like you have a clear shot at the critter."

"I won't need one," Smythe replied. He lowered his head and dragged in a deep breath. "I'm so sorry for what I did to you, Salinger Jacobs. I hope you will forgive me one day."

That sounded like a suicide speech to Savage, who stepped in to try to stop the man. He appeared to still be in some kind of touch with his senses, and with the kind of strength they had seen him demonstrate, he could

make himself very useful, even if he did look a little…
blue.

"Don't do it, Smythe," Kennedy protested and tried to
intercept him as well, but the man had already rushed into
the room where the tentacled monster struggled to extin-
guish the blaze—and apparently, would succeed. The
temperature in the room wasn't enough to cook Smythe
alive as he entered, and he was strong enough to push
through the tentacles, although he roared with pain when
he did so. He pulled the pins on all the grenades in a single
deft movement and lunged toward the creature that
screamed defiance.

They really should have taken cover, Savage thought a
moment before the detonation.

A series of white flashes from inside the small area
flared a fraction of a second before the powerful blast
rocked the whole building to its core. The shockwave
knocked Savage and Jacobs off their feet, and Kennedy was
the only one who managed to remain upright. The operative knew for a fact that if they hadn't worn these suits of
armor, the sudden change in pressure alone would have
been enough to kill them. Thankfully, all they had was a
mule's kick to the whole body, and damned if that wasn't
enough.

"Fuck!" He growled his annoyance and clambered
slowly to his feet again. Jacobs had already recovered and
stood beside him while he brushed his suit clean of the
rubble.

Something was different, Savage thought and squinted
to peer into the room. The fires continued to burn,
although they were dying rapidly. The tentacles scattered

around the room shivered as the last few impulses rippled through their neurons before they ceased. The fleshy mess inside the room was still there too, although a huge, charred chunk of it was missing.

If that didn't kill it, they might have to invest in tactical nukes, he thought belligerently as he looked around the room. The rubble had begun to move again as the humans beneath it recovered.

He knew it was too much to hope that they would be back to their old selves—or that the monsters outside would lose their will and coordination and allow the group of humans to leave the area in peace without any further fighting.

Things had gone too badly by this point for that particular brand of happy ending, and the humans who scrambled free from the rubble shrieked incoherently at the Heavy Metal team. They all seemed determined to wreak revenge with seriously violent intent behind it.

"Let's go!" Jacobs shouted, and the arms of his suit separated into six individual limbs. The two central ones carried a vibro-sword and the others a variety of projectile weapons, ready to protect him.

The operative couldn't afford to be distracted for long since he was suddenly attacked by a group of the enraged humans. They no longer simply attempted to get past his armor this time, he realized when he was thrown across the room like a rag doll. They were very clearly out for blood, and damned if they wouldn't get it too. The armor absorbed most of the impact, but he thought he might have a couple of broken bones inside that were held in place by the suit. It hurt to walk and to breathe too. And he hated that it meant he should consider himself lucky he was alive at all.

Jacobs lunged into the fight, apparently determined to make up for the fact that he'd missed any of it. His sword slid through the blue humans and halved two of them in a single swing. The mechanical arms worked with the impossible coordination only computers could achieve to shoot, push, and hack at any of the attackers who came too close and weren't eliminated by the sword.

Kennedy jogged to where Savage still struggled to his feet and offered him a hand.

"Are you ready to get out of here, soldier?" she asked, her voice crisp but with an undertone of warmth he hadn't heard before.

"You're goddamn right I am." He hissed when he took her hand and she heaved him clear of the wall he'd almost been punched through.

CHAPTER THIRTY-ONE

Chernobyl: The Laboratory Inside The Containment Dome

Goddamn, but it was good to be back in the fight again. Being forced out of it had been hellish for more reasons than one, and there weren't many better ways to push oneself through that kind of trauma than inflicting it on others, right?

It honestly felt like the way to go.

Anja had taken a little time to spruce up the software that controlled the extra arms when they were in combat mode, and it had made one hell of a difference when Sal entered the battle. There were about two dozen of the deranged humans still standing and determined to fight. Madigan looked like she could hold her own and used the melee abilities of a three-and-a-half-ton suit of armor and the shoulder-mounted rocket launchers to annihilate those she couldn't handle on her own.

The other team members had to get creative, somehow. Savage put his pistols to good use and delivered concussive rounds that hurled the attackers back and slowly but surely, those in the front rank were obliterated. He had grenades in his little bag of tricks, of course, but he couldn't use them in a small room where his team was present. His options were limited. Sam, Terry, and Courtney had to work together to hold back the few mutant humans that still remained, but they stayed alive long enough for their adversaries to be decisively cut down by Sal and Madigan.

"Well, who knew giving you six arms instead of two would help with your fighting skills?" Courtney asked with a laugh as the last one fell and they were able to take a breath.

"Are you all right, Sal?" Madigan asked. She apparently still remembered what had happened with the tentacles.

Sal really didn't want to answer that question, which was why Savage proved himself a providential addition to their team.

"No time to check for boo-boos now," he reminded them pointedly and appeared to have a couple of his own. "I can guaran-fucking-tee that all those monsters we saw outside will attack us in the same way these assholes did. We need to get the fuck out of here and put a call in to Anja to send a chopper our way."

"Agreed," Madigan said. They didn't look so surprised at being on the same page anymore. They were in the field and in combat so had no other choice but to trust each other. "How the fuck do we get out of here?"

"I could always blow a hole in the wall," Sam suggested, and Savage pointed at her.

"That sounds like as good a plan as we'll get," he said,

and the others nodded. "If nothing else, it'll open a way to get comms out of here."

"Okay." Madigan snorted. "And how exactly would we blow a hole in the wall? If you've forgotten, we're about two floors underground."

"I have a couple of ideas for that, actually," Sal said with a chuckle and activated the magnetic coils in his boots. He was launched upward high enough that the extra arms were able to grasp the edges and heave him through the hole in the ceiling.

"So you'll simply leave us behind?" Sam blurted, and Courtney immediately punched her on the arm.

"Of course not," he replied and leaned over the perimeter of the hole Savage had created. "You all have the same magnetic coils in your boots that should allow you to jump as high as I did. If you don't make it, I've programmed the robot arms to catch and haul you up. Let's go, people. We don't have much time."

They knew he was right about that, and there was no way they intended to hike all the way to the staircases. If they read the motion sensors right, there was already considerable movement toward them. It seemed logical to assume this had something to do with the monsters outside making their way in, perhaps to try to protect or even revive the tentacle monster. Sal had no idea if they could, but he wouldn't begin to doubt the power of the blue goop now. Maybe later, when he had more time to study it since he definitely would not take any more of it himself without a whole battery of tests first.

Savage and Courtney were the first to make the attempt and cleared the height of the jump easily since their suits were the lightest. Sam and Terry needed more help, and Sal caught them with the robotic hands and dragged them all the way. Madigan would have the most trouble, of course, since hers was the heaviest. She needed help from Savage, Sal, and Courtney to manhandle her up to the next floor.

"If any of you makes a fat joke, I'll stomp you into paste," she warned as they hoisted her the last few feet.

"Don't worry. No one makes fat jokes when tanks need to be hauled individually by helicopter since they know the tank will be able to outshoot all of them," Sam pointed out and patted her lightly on the shoulder.

With Madigan on point, they jogged slowly through the hallways to hopefully find a way to reach the ground floor without having to use the stairs since the motion sensors said that they were completely infested. The hallways themselves didn't look too good, either, with the aratchnids already on the prowl for whatever had attacked their...what was it supposed to be? Their deity? Their hive-mind? A combination of the two? Yes, that sounded about right.

Madigan was the first to engage them when a swarm tried to overtake the group in one of the corridors. Two rocket launchers raised from her shoulders and fired at the monsters, and she used the smaller version of a mini-gun to destroy the remainder one by one.

Once she'd eliminated them all without needing anyone else to help, she was back to feeling like her old self.

"If they didn't already know where we are, they fucking do now," she commented and pushed forward as the sounds of monsters close by and drawing closer became more and more apparent. Sal couldn't think of a time when he was more attracted to her than when she was angry, and this moment seriously took the fucking cake.

Heh. Fucking cake. He felt bad that other people couldn't see inside his head. It was a real riot.

Savage and Madigan took the lead for the team since they were the two with the most firepower. The scientist used his newly acquired limbs to ensure that their flanks were well covered and annihilated any of the aratchnids that slipped past them to try to reach Sam, Terry, and Courtney. The former made their share of the kills in the tight corridors of the building, and Courtney provided support from the back and acted as rear guard to watch that none of the creatures snuck up behind them.

They made a good team, the six of them, Sal thought with a chuckle.

"What the fuck is he laughing about?" Sam shouted over the chatter of gunfire and shrieking monsters around them.

"Who knows?" Terry replied. The sniper sounded much calmer than his teammate did and simply felled his targets in a steady, precise rhythm around Savage, Madigan, and Sal. "The kid is nuts."

Sal couldn't help a grin. He did have a reputation to uphold, even with folks who would probably never go into the Zoo. Let them spread the tale of Dr. Salinger Jacobs, the crazy researcher who laughed in the face of danger while he stabbed that face with his sword.

They powered a path toward the stairs. The few monsters that remained quickly realized that they were outnumbered and outgunned and beat a hasty retreat toward the upper levels.

It was only a temporary respite, Sal knew. The motion sensors told him far more of the mutants tried to find their way inside, and while it looked like the building was still intact, he had very distinct memories of exactly how many of the enemy there were. They were like the hordes of Genghis Khan, and they would eventually find a way in.

He could only hope the team would find their way out of the facility before that happened. It seemed like the only thing that had restrained the denizens of this bizarre landscape was the fact that the tentacle monster was alive and guided them from inside. Since that particular ship had sailed, they were looking for blood and wouldn't hesitate to tear the building apart.

They would find all the blood they wanted if he had a say in it. He used the extra arms on his suit to pull himself up the stairs over Savage and Madigan and came face to face with one of the wolf monsters they'd encountered outside. It was a good deal more active now, of course, although its size made maneuvering through the corridors a little difficult. The massive jaws salivated like a rabid dog, and they snapped at his torso almost before he realized it was there.

Thankfully, the robot arms on his back responded far more rapidly than his brain had and released a volley into the creature's open maw. A loud howl quickly followed as it backed away, most of its face and skull missing. It writhed and continued to howl loudly through its death throes before another of its brethren shredded what was left of it to reach the human.

The crazy scientist was ready for this one, though. A string of bullets peppered the beast's shoulders and slowed it a little. Sal launched into an attack and used his sword to sever the head from its body. The body still moved forward, however, so he raised his leg and activated the magnetic coils on the bottom of his boots in time to launch the corpse of the monster into the others behind it who were as eager to get into the fight as their dead pack mates.

Savage and Madigan reached the top of the landing as he sliced through the middle of a third creature and used its body as a shield to shove the others back. His extra arms extended to maintain a steady stream of fire at the mutants behind him, mostly aratchnids by now.

The operative was quick to see the opportunity they had and called Sam to the top of the landing as the other woman raced ahead to provide Sal with cover fire.

"Terry, Monroe, you cover Sam while she finds a way to blow an exit for us," he commanded in a tone that suggested he was used to shouting orders and having them followed almost immediately. "I'll cover you in turn and keep the way clear for Kennedy and Jacobs to make their way back once we have a way out, got it?"

Sam and Terry snapped quickly to attention and followed their maps to the nearest outside wall. Courtney paused a moment, clearly reluctant to leave her friends behind.

"I said now, Monroe!" he roared as a group of the monsters appeared that had apparently found themselves a way in that wasn't the front door. Sal and Madigan had effectively clogged the direct route, so they could only have come from somewhere else. He opened fire, still using the needles in both his pistols, and unleashed round after round. Thanks to the improved battery functions of the weapons—which was, in turn, thanks to the fact that they were powered by the same reactor that kept his suit running—each shot was accompanied by a soft crack as the slender missiles were propelled forward fast enough to break the sound barrier.

"I'm keeping this suit," he said to himself, although he knew his voice would carry across the comm line.

Sal laughed again as two of his extra arms brandished vibro-knives built with the same tech as his sword. They hacked through any of the monsters that made it past his large blade and the other two arms, which both held assault rifles. The big problem with having as many weapons as you could carry was the fact that a normal two-armed human could only use one of them at a time, and whomever had designed his particular suit clearly had that in mind. He was able to cover most of the corridor and Madigan held the monsters at bay so they merely trickled through the hallway at a pace at which he could easily eliminate them.

It honestly was a whole ton of fun to obliterate wave after wave of the creatures to the point where the bodies began to clog the way in, but they would encounter serious problems if this continued. Ammo issues topped the list and honestly, from the sounds of the building around them, it might collapse at any minute. They definitely didn't want to be inside when it did.

As he stepped in to close the hole those at the rear tried to dig past their dead brethren, he noted that they had already begun to drag the bodies away and outside to allow more of them through. His heart pounded in his chest and he lurched forward, ducked under a rocket launched from

Madigan's shoulder, and circled to avoid the attacks of a group of aratchnids that attempted to penetrate his armor with their stingers. At that moment, one of the wolves powered through and crushed the few unfortunate smaller beasts in its path.

Sal tried to swing his sword at the creature but—whether by accident or by chilling intention—it used the bodies of its fellow monsters as a shield, continued its charge, and bowled him over. It apparently saw the human with larger armor as the bigger threat and left him sprawled awkwardly as it swung to attack Kennedy, followed by a group of the smaller creatures that had scrabbled desperately to get out of its way.

Before he could find his feet, a pack of the aratchnids swarmed over him. They seemed determined to pile on as quickly as possible. Some even sacrificed themselves to the blades and guns in his hands to keep his arms pinned while others scratched and bit to get past the armor. He could feel their stingers trying to puncture the suit around his thighs while they shrieked and screeched. Some assaulted his helmet, obviously to reach his face, and used their elongated, rat-like jaws to gnaw at the metal.

"To hell with this!" He roared in fury and powered the coils on his boots again. While he couldn't see the effect, the assault around his legs suddenly ceased. The few mutants that attempted to pin his arms were flung away when he pushed from the ground and bellowed a challenge as he slashed, fired, and kicked wildly until all the beasts around him had been eliminated.

He continued to swing the blades for a few seconds after that and only stopped when he realized that

Madigan stared at him, her mouth visibly agape inside her helmet. He must had been a bizarre sight, covered as he was in aratchnid blood and viscera. She was rather gory herself, having managed to overpower the wolf that had knocked him over. Its charred and slightly dismembered corpse had been flung to the side of the hallway.

"Are you good, Jacobs?" she asked and reloaded her weapons.

He nodded. "I'm doing great, how about y—"

Before he could finish that somewhat flippant response, the noise and light filters in his suit suddenly went crazy a split second before the entire hallway flashed a bright white. He felt like something kicked him gently in the chest and he retreated a couple of steps.

"What the fuck was that?" Madigan snapped, still on her feet and there to make sure he didn't topple over.

"A solid guess would be that something went wrong with the blow a hole in the wall plan," Sal replied. He scowled and shook his head to rid himself of the ringing in his ears. "I thought Sam was supposed to be an explosives specialist."

"Shut up. Let's see what happened," she snapped and shoved him down the hallway toward where all the smoke still poured out. The floor was covered in rubble, and the first thing he saw was a pile of the aratchnids on the ground.

A large wolf circled as if to find an opening, dragged one of the creatures loose, and lunged forward. An armored boot powered out of the hole and the soft whine of the magnetic coils charging was all the warning they had before the room was splattered with blood, bones, and viscera.

This was immediately followed by what they identified as Savage's pistols firing from beneath the writhing heap and Sal rushed to the man's aid. Madigan did too and heaved the creatures off, crushed them in the robotic gauntlets of her suit, and she tossed them aside.

The operative was at the bottom of the pile and wore the same wide-eyed desperate look the scientist had when he fought the massed assault of the mutants. He looked a little worse for wear, though, and there were gashes all over his armor.

Most of them were superficial, but there were a couple that had penetrated, one on his shoulder and the other on his thigh. That was the only one that seeped blood, and he heaved himself to his feet and brushed at the blood on his suit. It didn't do much to help and merely smeared it even further. That aside, it appeared he would be able to walk with the injury.

"What happened here?" Madigan asked in an accusatory tone.

"I don't know," he responded and looked a little dazed like he might actually have a concussion. He had been close enough to the blast for it to have rattled his brain despite the inertia dampeners in his suit. "Something went wrong, though."

"Thank you, Captain Obvious," Madigan almost snarled in return.

"Just fucking check on the others," he muttered belligerently as he struggled to recover enough to at least be able to participate if a fight erupted and managed to regain a little of his equilibrium. Injured and bruised, he was still in good enough shape to fight, which meant they could leave him be for the moment.

His two teammates read the unspoken message in his demeanor a moment later. Sal rushed to the room where they had tried to blast the hole. The smoke still hadn't dissipated completely, but there was enough fresh air around them to see movement. He moved in close enough to recognize Courtney's armor. It was covered in dust and soot, but she appeared to have been protected from the blast. Terry was up too, although he did look a little like he'd been through the wringer.

"Where's Sam?" Madigan shouted. The volume of her voice was to overcome the ringing in everyone's ears. Whether Terry could hear her or not, he at least understood what she had asked and directed her to a crumpled heap on the floor.

Savage was the first to reach her and dropped to his knees beside her inert form. "Shit...what happened here, Terry?"

"I don't know," the man replied. He seemed dazed and disbelieving. "She said she was priming the blast into the wall and told us to take cover. Some of the critters came in and we were taking cover when it detonated."

Madigan moved to the wall where there was a massive dent from the explosion. It hadn't gone through the wall, unfortunately. "Whoever built this really didn't want stuff getting out. At a guess, I'd say when the force of the explosion didn't penetrate outward, it rebounded back on her. And the rest of us, I guess."

"Do we have any more explosives?" Sal asked and

looked around the room. "I'll bet that if we try again, we could get through."

"Even if we did, Sam is the only one trained to prep them for a controlled detonation," she replied. "How's she doing, Savage?"

The operative connected his suit to hers, presumably to check her vitals. "The inertia dampeners took the brunt of the blast, but she still took one hell of a hit. She's alive and unconscious, but I think we need to get her to a hospital and a doctor."

"Good call." She scowled. "Any ideas? Blowing a hole in the wall is out, and from the looks of things, sprinting out of the main entrance will result in a traffic jam."

"We could always get to the roof," Courtney pointed out as she checked her suit to make sure everything still worked after the explosion. "We'll have to use the stairs, I suppose, but there is a helipad there. There must be a hatch or something in the dome which they used for drops or to bring or collect the people. We'll be able to contact Anja and clear it for her to land and pick us up."

"I don't like it." Savage shook his head. "We'll be exposed up there and too much can go wrong."

"Too much has already gone wrong," Madigan retorted sharply. "And the roof is the best plan we have. We'll go for it. Moving out in thirty seconds. Sal, Courtney, cover the exit. We'll make sure everyone's still alive before we push on. Terry, get over here and let me check on you."

Sal nodded and did as he was told. He made his way to the door, which was mostly a hole in the wall at this point. His additional arms circled to make sure there weren't any nasty surprises waiting for them in the hallway before he stepped out.

"Are you okay there, Savage?" Madigan asked as she connected to Terry's suit. "How's your leg holding up?"

"I'll live," he replied. "The suit's already compensating to keep most of the weight away from my leg and on the hydraulics, and the first aid systems have already applied topical anesthetics. It'll last me until we get the fuck out of here."

"Good man," she approved and helped him to lift Sam, who was still unconscious, and drape her over his shoulder. After a moment to adjust to the added weight, he nodded, and Madigan continued to help Terry run minor repairs on his suit.

They were moving again in thirty seconds.

CHAPTER THIRTY-TWO

<u>*Chernobyl: The Laboratory Inside The Containment Dome*</u>

The blast had apparently scared the creatures off for the moment. On one hand, they were hellbent on avenging their fallen tentacle monster in the same way they did in the Zoo when one of the big dinos was killed. On the other hand, they appeared to lack the coordination that most of the creatures in the Zoo relied on when they conducted their group assaults on the human teams. Instincts kicked in, and when loud and vicious blasts were heard and felt, they needed to retreat for a moment to recover from the fright.

That was what Sal thought, anyway. It wasn't a way to humanize them but rather to give some rationality to their actions. The Zoo—and the goop that caused it—wasn't strong on predictability, but there were flashes when the earthly DNA kicked in stronger than the goop that had used it.

Either way, the pause in the assault was much appreciated and needed, but it didn't last very long. No one really expected it to, and with Savage carrying Sam on his shoulders and Madigan and Courtney helping Terry limp to the staircase, it was on Sal to hold the front of the line, a job he was only too happy to carry out.

The suit more than held its own with the four added arms an impressive display of Anja's coding skills as they smoothly identified what he needed them to do. He would work with her to improve the user interface when they returned but so far, this had been a satisfactory beta test and it was something he hoped to see in the suits Pegasus would roll out in the future. Maybe they would even improve on it. He knew there would be a demand for suits that could protect the users autonomously.

Although the lab was only four stories high, the beasts had already begun their approach when they reached the second landing. They attacked from both above and below and forced the team to fight their way up and to drive the creatures back as they proceeded. It was slow going, but they pushed hard and fought vigorously. Sal held the front while Madigan made sure to send all the firepower she could spare to assist those who kept the monsters from below at bay. Slowly but surely, they made progress.

Sam regained consciousness when they reached the last landing. She looked rather dazed and had definitely been injured but was alive, at least. The team was as grateful for that good news as they were when the comms started to work again once they reached the top of the building. The outline of a massive hatch in the top of the dome was clearly visible but obviously, the engineers or masterminds behind it had seen the necessity to have open comms at arrival and extraction in the event of emergencies.

"Get a call out to Anja," Savage instructed, and Terry nodded, already on it. Sal, Madigan, and the Savage made it their business to clear the roof of any creatures that had found their way there.

A handful of the wolves were quickly dealt with by Madigan, who launched the last of her rockets to effectively decimate them, and Sal and Savage, with their quick-fire abilities, focused on eliminating the smaller creatures. Courtney positioned herself securely and fired constantly to render the stairs impassable and protect them from the mutants that tried to force their way up. When the attempts to launch a concerted assault from the lower floors tapered off for a few short moments, she slammed and secured the door.

Night had already fallen while they'd been inside, and the darkness that draped itself over the forest was a little too eerie. It wasn't quite as dark as it was at night in the Zoo, but it was damn close. No light seeped through from the moon and only the glimmer of the stars gave them some semblance of a view using night vision.

"Hey, guys!" Anja's very welcome voice spoke through their comms. "When I heard nothing and couldn't raise you on the comms, I assumed you might be in trouble. Elena didn't want to risk any of her pilots, so I...uh, might have commandeered one of her helicopters, and it's already on the way. I only need to confirm your exact location, and I'll be there in a few minutes."

"Goddamn, it's good to hear your voice again, Anja."

Savage laughed. "We'll get this hatch thing open and send up a couple of flares to give you what you need. I'll ask you not to dawdle since we are in something of a bind here."

"Yep, I can see that," she replied. "Your suits tell me you guys took some damage but no casualties so far. I'll ask you to let that be the case when the chopper arrives."

"We'll do our best," Sal replied. He and Courtney approached the keypad beside the door and stared at it. "Shit."

"What?" the hacker demanded.

"I don't have the code for this."

"I'm on it," she responded cheerfully. An odd hissing sound drew his gaze upward, and the section of the top of the dome directly above the helipad disengaged and began to slide almost soundlessly toward the rear.

A massive, yawning opening revealed the early evening sky. The operative had already loaded a couple of flares into his pistols. When they were ready, he aimed them upward and pulled the triggers. The bright red lights arced upward against the black backdrop.

The view they were greeted with was nothing short of terrifying. The entire forest and land around them within the dome were covered by the creatures. It seemed they had all abandoned their work of rejuvenating the area and surged into a relentless march toward the lab. When they saw the lights, they immediately deduced that the humans were on the top of the building. The horde lunged and flung themselves at the walls. They scrabbled frantically to climb the prefab structure, to the point where they didn't care if they clambered over their fellow aratchnids and wolf hybrids.

"Oh...shit." Sal grunted his annoyance. "Anja, I have to ask you to pick up the pace. I don't think we'll last a few minutes."

"Roger that," the hacker replied briskly. She'd apparently received video feed from their suits and saw the same thing they did.

"Have you ever watched the *Lord of the Rings* movies, Savage?" Sal asked and glanced at the man, who calmly prepared his weapons for the fight.

"Extended editions, yeah," he replied with a chuckle. "Do you think this looks like the Battle of Helm's deep, except we don't have any tunnels to escape into?"

"I thought more the battle of Minas Tirith, with Anja being the Rohirrim coming to save our asses." Sal's grin seeped a little humor into his tone.

"Right, then. Let's kick some orc ass."

The first mutants appeared over the top of the building and a cacophony of screeches and roars erupted. The team —up to six now, although Terry kept Sam in the back of the group—opened fire on the first scattered ranks of the monsters that pushed forward. They didn't look like they intended to slow, and with Madigan's rockets gone, it forced her to draw the secondary mini-gun from its holster. Basically, they now had considerably less explosive firepower.

Sal knew he could handle himself in this kind of a fight for...well, for a while, but he wouldn't be able to do much in the way of protecting everyone else, which demanded that Savage step up. The operative still had one of his pistols firing those deadly little needles since that was the ammo that needed reloading the least. The other had been

389

quickly adapted for the selection of grenades he had available.

The first one he launched was the last of his incendiary grenades, and he took care to launch it at the edge of the roof to spread the fire as much as possible while it would also spill over the side to cause extra damage to the mutants that scrabbled up.

The scientist thought they might know that the fire was what helped to kill their tentacled friend. While they were driven off the portion of the roof now covered in chemical fire, along other parts of the building that hadn't caught the blaze, they were more riled up than before. Or perhaps it was simply the sight of the flames that got their mutant equivalent of panties in a twist.

He turned his attention from the conflagration and moved across the roof to slash, shoot, and crush any of the creatures that crossed his path. His hope was that it would keep them distracted from where Madigan was forced to fall back to help Terry cover Sam. One of the massive wolf creatures reached the top with a blood-chilling roar and immediately hurled one of its fellows in its way over the side.

"We have trouble!" Savage called. The man still tried to provide covering fire for the team and so was unable to turn away to attack the monster. Sal responded immediately but it saw him and uttered an ear-splitting roar as it launched into the attack. He realized it wasn't like the other wolves barely in time to avoid a potentially lethal gash from front paws that were more like hands with claws. But as his sword severed his enemy's right arm, the left pounded into him and catapulted him violently to land about three feet away.

"Sal!" Courtney screamed and raced to assist him. She was pushed back when the aratchnids reinforced their attack and drove relentlessly toward the group, powered by sheer numbers and combined mass. They pounded on the door from the staircase too, possibly only seconds away from breaking through. Once that last barrier fell, the fight was as good as over. They had survived this far only by using the fortifications of the building.

Not that it would matter, Sal acknowledged. The massive wolf mutant bellowed in pain over its missing limb and barreled into another frenzied assault. Even if he killed it in time, the full weight of the creature would keep him prone and perfectly placed for one of their massed swarm attacks, and there would be no way to escape it this time.

"Did someone call for some cavalry?"

Anja spoke cheerfully over their comms and the monster's body erupted when a stream of bullets delivered instant destruction. The barrage had been fired so quickly that no single shot could be heard, only a loud roar a few seconds before the helicopter's rotors became audible too. In the darkness, they weren't able to see where it was until it was close enough to be illuminated by the chemical fires that continued to burn.

"You're goddamn right we did," Savage shouted and laughed loudly. It wasn't clear if he'd meant it as a joke or merely responded with relief. Sal couldn't tell and it didn't matter. The Russian used the heavy firepower on the helicopter to obliterate wave after wave of the creatures, big and small, until the roof was clear. She banked the craft and positioned it to give them access to the bay doors that had already begun to open.

"They're preparing for another attack, so I'd get on this bird quickly if I were you," she shouted over the comms. The group did not need any more encouragement and they scrambled hastily into the helicopter, assisting those teammates with injuries to make it on board. Anja closed the doors and guided the chopper away from the building.

For a long moment after the doors closed and they set course for their return trip, nothing could be heard except the ongoing fire from the .50 cal cannons and the rocket launchers. Sal guessed that she didn't need to shoot anything and simply wanted to. He could understand that urge. Finally, the hatch slid slowly into place and sealed the dome.

"Anja," Savage finally said, breaking the pregnant silence that ensued once the fusillade ceased. "I don't know what you love most, but as of right now, I'll buy you the best and most expensive version of it."

"Please," she responded. "I'm getting paid ten mil for this job too. I want nothing that I can't buy for myself."

"Still, though." He chuckled and pushed away from the wall, relieved that the sounds of the guns outside no longer drowned out even his thoughts, and made his way to the cockpit. "Or I would, if you bothered to show up in person."

Sal chuckled when he realized that Anja's hijacking of Elena's chopper had been a digital heist.

"Savage, I love you and I love all of you folks," the

hacker replied. "But I don't love any of you that much. Just be thankful that I came to save your asses, okay?"

"Fine," the operative replied and returned to the bay to strap himself in. "But I'll only buy the second most expensive thing you like."

"That seems fair." Madigan laughed and helped Sam to strap herself in before she did the same for herself.

CHAPTER THIRTY-THREE

**Kiev: A Private Airfield Outside The City**

"How's your leg healing?" Sal asked.

It was still immured in a cast and Savage looked at it and shrugged. One of his arms was also immobilized, but that had been more the necessity to keep his shoulder stable. It had been dislocated and put back in place by his suit's first aid functions, but it had been badly done and put pressure on nerves that could have caused problems if they hadn't popped it out and manipulated it into its correct position.

That seemed to be an indicator of how their mission had gone in general. Sam was still in the hospital. The doctors had said her condition was stable and they were hopeful of full recovery, but they still wanted to keep her in for observation.

Terry and Savage had both been treated for concussions, but they had recovered well enough to travel back to Philly.

"The docs said they've never seen a recovery time this

good," Savage replied, patted the cast, and instantly regretted it. He really hoped there wasn't any turbulence on the flight.

"That's great." Sal chuckled and shook his head. "How long before you think you'll be on active duty again?"

"A couple of weeks, hopefully," he said with a shrug. "I'll still be on the roster, though, so you don't need to worry about that. Except I assume I'll technically be reduced to being a consultant instead of boots on the ground."

"Well, when you're ready for it, we'll ship your suit over for you to use in Philly if you need it. And Amanda said she would be willing to make some changes. That would let you use the pistols and some pieces of the exoskeleton if you need them in the field and don't want to go through the trouble of suiting up fully on the fly."

"That sounds perfect." He chuckled, then narrowed his eyes. "Who's Amanda?"

"Gutierrez—a former member of our team who still helps us with technical work," the other man explained. "She said she and her girlfriend need a vacation from the Zoo, so if we're willing to pay all the expenses to provide them with all kinds of creature comforts for a visit to Philly, she'd be willing to work on and improve your suit."

"That sounds like a plan, Jacobs." He chuckled and proffered his left hand for a shake. "It was fantastic working with you, but I hope you understand when I say that I don't want to have a field trip like that again."

"I'll make sure to mention that to Courtney," he replied as Madigan approached.

"So you're headed stateside, Gunnie?" she asked and

definitely seemed far less hostile as she patted him gently on his uninjured shoulder.

"Yes, ma'am," Savage replied with a nod but still flinched at her pat.

"Take care of yourself, Savage," she said. "We need good folks like you, even if you do break a little too easily for my taste."

"Sure thing, Madea." He smirked and turned toward the steps, where he needed help to ascend so he could finally board.

"Yeah, you'd better run," Madigan retorted and shook her head. Her eyes narrowed as she looked over Sal's shoulder at the entrance to the airstrip. "It looks like you have company, Sal."

He turned as a limo drove up beside the plane. Courtney was still at the hotel, helping Anja to move Molina's money through a variety of accounts so as to be able to pay the members of the team their full cuts in a way that didn't make the various tax agencies around the world raise their eyebrows.

With this team accounted for there was only one person it could be.

"Do you need me to tell her you're not taking any visitors?" she asked and scowled when Molina stepped out of the limo and slid on a pair of designer sunglasses on as the plane started warming up for takeoff.

"Nah," he replied. "We might get to kill her later but for now, she came up on her end of the bargain, paid without any red flags, and appears to have pulled her fingers away from the pies that result in attempts on the lives of our friends. We play nice, for now."

She nodded, but while she was willing to trust his judgement, she clearly didn't agree with it. He crossed to where the woman watched the plane that had already begun to taxi toward the runway.

"Savage is on board in case you wanted to say goodbye," Sal quipped with a smirk as he stopped beside.

"Not a problem. I'll simply have to call him next time I'm in Philadelphia," she replied smoothly. "Will you stand by our agreement the way I did?"

Sal sighed. He was tempted to tell her to fuck off and walk away in a 'drop the mic' moment, but as of right now, they were vulnerable with half of their team recovering from that trip to Chernobyl, and she knew it. There was no point in aggravating her into resuming her hostilities against them.

He withdrew a flash drive from his pocket and handed it to her. "That's a copy of everything we pulled from the drives in the facility, delivered right before all hell broke loose in that place. It's the only copy Anja made, so Pegasus will be your only competitor with what can be profited from in their research. There's also a copy of my notes on what we saw and found in there if you're interested."

"I am," she said and inspected the drive for a moment before she tucked it into her own pocket.

"You should know, though, that we intend to lobby to have the test site destroyed. I don't care what it takes. We can't leave a mini-Zoo here to proliferate unattended. God only knows what would happen if those monsters got out of that containment dome."

She shuddered, and he somehow knew it was genuine and not a ploy. "You don't need to worry about that."

"I don't?" He allowed the skepticism to color his tone, a reminder that one mutual operation didn't build a lifetime of trust.

Elena shook her head. "You don't think we would have done all that and not built some kind of failsafe in?" She scoffed. "There was a self-destruct sequence programmed into the entire dome as a last resort. If the staff hadn't been...incapacitated the way they were, they would have initiated it themselves."

"It's a little too late for that, don't you think? Who will initiate it now that the facility is completely overrun?"

She smiled. "It is in progress as we speak. I have a helicopter in the air and on its way. They will open the hatch, activate the sequence remotely, and get the hell out of there. Within only a few moments, it will be, as you Americans like to say, history."

Sal studied her face, looking for signs of deception but found none. It made sense that she would want it erased—the last thing anyone would want was to be linked to the kinds of dark experiments that had taken place.

Elena Molina did not live in the limelight. She operated best in obscurity, so she would do whatever it took to remove any threat. He still couldn't say with any certainty that she knew exactly what went on, but his instincts told him she wanted it destroyed as much as he did.

Finally, he nodded. "I'd rather see it happen for myself,

MICHAEL TODD & MICHAEL ANDERLE

but I'll accept your word on it. You have too much to lose to not do it."

She nodded and he turned away but stopped when she spoke. "Was there...anything else that you might have found? Something regarding their research into humans subjected to the blue goop?"

"That's mostly in my notes, although you'll find data in the lab's notes as well," Sal replied. So she had known. But had she ordered it? He still couldn't be sure.

"You wouldn't happen to want to share your conclusions based on what you found in there as well, would you?" Elena asked. She lowered her sunglasses and looked pointedly at him.

He shrugged. "Sure, why not? I've concluded that you and I are fucked."

She raised her eyebrows. "You and I?"

Sal nodded. "Royally fucked."

AUTHOR NOTES -
MICHAEL ANDERLE

JULY 28, 2019

THANK YOU for not only reading this story but these *Author Notes* **as well.**

(I think I've been good with always opening with "thank you." If not, I need to edit the other *Author Notes*!)

RANDOM (*sometimes***) THOUGHTS?**

So, I was talking with someone WAY smarter than myself here in Edinburgh, Scotland.

(No, not my wife this time, but rather Marc Stiegler - see his website at http://www.skyhunter.com if you want to meander through discussions on healthcare, climate warming and the like. You can find out more about Marc here: https://en.wikipedia.org/wiki/Marc_Stiegler)

Ok, so I've explained that Marc is smarter and more knowledgeable in all things science and I missed an earlier discussion related to crypto-currency and injecting an algorithm into the code to help with inflation. I wanted to talk about that but was embroiled in another conversation.

Or something like that (remember, *smarter.*)

Bummed I missed that conversation when Kevin McLaughlin and I were speaking about the Earth warming and stuff related to snow not staying melted all winter (vs. what he remembered from his youth 40 years ago), I thought I would take the opportunity to chat with the two of them.

That was both interesting and a mistake.

It was interesting because we did delve into interesting theories and concepts (the part of my brain which I use for science fiction was having fun.)

It was a mistake because (1) We couldn't stay on topic to save our lives. We went off into issues related to crypto-currency and the book of Revelations in the Bible (that was my fault.) (2) We went into the stupidity of creating farm-land in the desert when a state is in a drought (that was Marc's fault.)

Then, we discussed something else that had Kevin and Marc discussing something above my head (that was Kevin's fault.)

If you get a chance, talk about something that might happen in the future with your friends, you might just create a science fiction tale when you do.

AROUND THE WORLD IN 80 DAYS

One of the interesting (at least to me) aspects of my life is the ability to work from anywhere and at any time. In the future, I hope to re-read my own *Author Notes* and remember my life as a diary entry.

Edinburgh, Scotland - University of Edinburgh - Salisbury Green (Mansion side)

So, we are in a small room in the hotel on the campus. This part of the hotel was built inside the mansion which (from the outside) looks like an old castle.

Ok, a small castle.

But still, it's really cool.

I've figured out a few things as we go up the very steep stairs to get to our room (3rd floor) and that is:

1) Whoever built this in the 1700s apparently didn't plan for elevators, and I'm out of shape to be lugging two suitcases and a backpack up the steps... the very steep steps.

2) Don't come when it is unnaturally hot - most buildings don't have air conditioning.

3) Did I mention the steep stairs? If not, I should.

However, by the 5th day here, I was getting accustomed to the (now) cool weather and the room. I think my calves are doing better with the forced exercise.

That's my story, and I'm sticking to it.

FAN PRICING

$0.99 Saturdays (new LMBPN stuff) and $0.99 Wednesday (both LMBPN books and friends of LMBPN books.) Get great stuff from us and others at tantalizing prices.

Go ahead, I bet you can't read just one.

Sign up here: http://lmbpn.com/email/.

HOW TO MARKET FOR BOOKS YOU LOVE

Review them so others have your thoughts, tell friends

and the dogs of your enemies (because who wants to talk with enemies?)... *Enough said ;-)*

Ad Aeternitatem,

Michael Anderle

CONNECT WITH MICHAEL TODD

Want more?

Find us On Facebook

https://www.facebook.com/Protected-by-the-Damned-193345908061855/

OTHER MICHAEL TODD BOOKS

PROTECTED BY THE DAMNED UNIVERSE

PROTECTED BY THE DAMNED*
8 Book series

WAR OF THE DAMNED*
8 Book series

DAMIAN'S CHRONICLES*
4 Book series

WAR OF THE ANGELS*
8 Book series

ZOO UNIVERSE

BIRTH OF HEAVY METAL*
10 Book series

APOCALYPSE PAUSED*
12 Book series

SOLDIER OF FAME AND FORTUNE*
12 Book series

TEAM SAVAGE *

3 Book series

Dungeon Core TV*

6 Book series

Dungeon Rails*

3 Book series

Hellspawned Chronicles*

3 Book series

The Sheva Chronicles*

6 Book series

Unlikely Bountyhunters*

6 Book series

House Drakonnen

The Accord

The Anchor's Inheritance Saga

* DENOTES COMPLETED SERIES

www.ingramcontent.com/pod-product-compliance
Lightning Source LLC
Chambersburg PA
CBHW020522110726
47899CB00004B/1209